CITY
of
GHOSTS

BEN CREED

Published in 2020 by Welbeck Fiction Limited, part of Welbeck
Publishing Group
20 Mortimer Street London W1T 3JW

Cover design by: Andrew Smith
Cover images © Marina Pissarova/Alamy Stock Photo; Shutterstock.com

A CIP catalogue record for this book is available from the
British Library

Paperback ISBN: 978-1-78739-494-0
E-book ISBN: 978-1-787-39-503-9

Printed and bound by CPI Group (UK) Ltd, Croydon, CR0 4YY

'If God does not exist, then everything is permitted.'
Fyodor Dostoevsky

'Man is wolf to man.'
Title of gulag memoir by survivor Janusz Bardach

Acknowledgements

Any writers looking for inspiration from the realities of life under the murderous reign of Joseph Stalin would not be short of material. Yet, while we read and researched widely for City of Ghosts, this is not a history book. We have always felt at liberty to **alter** a few dates and places, and to reimagine political rivalries and human relationships, while trying to remain true to the essence of the era. Several people gave us excellent guidance on details ranging from cigarette brands to car models; any deviations and errors are entirely our responsibility.

We would like to thank:

Jon Elek at Welbeck for championing and publishing *City of Ghosts*, and our agent Giles Milburn, for having such faith in this book from the very beginning and – perhaps more importantly – for being the type of agent you can have a pint with.

Rosa Schierenberg at Welbeck, and Liane-Louise Smith, Georgina Simmonds and Sophie Pélissier at Madeleine Milburn for all their help and support.

Niamh Mulvey and Fiona Mitchell for their excellent editorial insights and suggestions, which improved the book immeasurably. Andrew Smith for the atmospheric cover design, and Clare Wallis and Rhian McKay for the meticulous copy editing and proofing.

The forensic pathologist Dr Ben Swift for his expert guidance on issues such as frozen – and defrosting – corpses, starvation, sedation, and other similarly gory matters. And Dr Jana Howlett, emeritus lecturer and fellow, Jesus College, Cambridge University, for spotting the many 'intentional mistakes'.

F

ACT 1

1

Saturday 13 October, 1951

They lay as straight as scaffolding, stark in the glare of the train engine's headlight. A quintet of bodies on the snowy tracks, parallel and neat. Feet together, arms straight, with their heads turned delicately to one side. As though Death had asked them all to form an orderly queue, and each damned soul had politely obliged him.

Revol Rossel, lieutenant in the Leningrad *militsiya*, drew on his cigarette, blew out a ring of grey smoke and observed the crime scene from a distance with studied impassivity. It was a habit now, that face. An expression that so far, even though he was thirty-four years old, had kept him out of the camps. 'Every man must have one face for the world and another for himself, Revol,' his father had once told him, with a stoic wink. At the time, neither his father nor Rossel had properly understood what a sound piece of advice this was, the kind that could help any Soviet citizen live a little longer. Especially one who lived in Leningrad, a city for which Stalin was known to harbour misgivings.

As Rossel watched on from the front passenger seat of the Moskvich, he could hear the car's engine wheezing. Away to the left and across a deep field of snow, a black

3

steam engine wheezed and stood still. Behind the engine and its cargo, the track was flanked by trees for kilometre after kilometre but here, before him, it was crossed by another line of rails, forming a small clearing.

'Come on, then, gentlemen. Time for us to take our bow.'

The car doors beat a tattoo of slams as Rossel and his fellow cops got out. They moved together, lifting their knees high to make progress in the deep drifts. Under their regulation coats, sporting the insignia of their respective ranks in the militia, they wore a variety of pullovers, trousers and thick underwear. Standard uniform alone was no match for a winter's night. A few hours ago, the radio had said it was minus twenty-seven. 'Cold enough to turn good hot Russian piss into icicles,' as Sergeant Grachev had put it the last time he had regaled them all with another story of how he had slaughtered members of the 33rd Waffen SS en route to Berlin.

Next to the steam engine stood two men, frozen and forlorn. Rossel looked to the right at the second track. It met the main line at a forty-five-degree angle, turned and ran parallel for a few dozen metres, merged at a points system and veered off again into the pines.

One of the two men next to the train moved forward to meet them – the train driver, Rossel guessed. He wore a thick, quilted coat over his overalls and a large fur hat that seemed to almost swallow up a shrunken head, and he reeked of burnt coal.

'What kept you?' the driver grumbled.

Rossel ignored the question and looked over him at the other man, from the local militia. This must be the one who had phoned in. He was short and thin and looked like a frightened animal – in his early twenties, practically a boy. The youngster and the driver had sullen faces. They'd been quarrelling, no doubt about it. Rossel guessed the driver had wanted to shunt the corpses out of the way, to hell with it, and get going again; the lad would have been too terrified to touch a thing – a policeman from the sticks refusing to budge until someone else took command.

'What kept you, eh?' repeated the train driver.

Rossel looked at him and returned fire. 'Driving nearly fifty kilometres at four in the morning in a blizzard so thick it would turn a snow fox blind. That may have had something to do with it,' he said.

It had been snowing for three days and it was only mid-October. Nothing like it since the winter of '42, according to survivors of the Siege of Leningrad. Once the militia officers had got outside the city, it had been more like skiing than driving.

Rossel's men drifted off to look closer at the crime scene, peering at the corpses one by one but not touching them.

'What happened?' Rossel asked the driver. They were only a few hundred metres away from the vast shoreline of the already partially frozen Lake Ladoga. Rossel wondered if the bodies were ice fishermen; sometimes they'd sit and drink for hour after hour. Then they had wandered onto the tracks, clinging to each other to stay upright, before freezing to death . . .

'They were on the line, already like that,' said the driver. 'The snowplough went through yesterday but just in case I was going at a crawl. I saw them right enough.'

'The penalty for lying to officers of . . .'

The driver spat and shook his head. 'Go and have a proper look, gundog. You'll see.'

The locomotive's engine hiccupped and shuddered.

'What are you carrying?' asked Rossel.

'Coal. Scrap metal. Twenty wagons.'

A good thing the train had stopped, then. There wouldn't have been much left of the bodies if that lot had thundered over them.

'Is this a main line? Why didn't anyone find the bodies earlier?'

'The last passenger trains stop at eleven, if they haven't iced up – the new diesels can't handle this cold,' the driver replied, rubbing his eyes. 'I was the first of the freights tonight. Some idiot overloaded a wagon at the depot and it tipped. Held me up for more than two hours.'

He muttered something about boilers and valves and made as if to go without wishing to demean himself by asking permission. Rossel shrugged and the driver vanished behind the engine's headlight.

The other one, the youngster from the local cop shop, looked up at him, awaiting orders. He was only a private.

'Where is everyone?' Rossel asked him.

'Arrested.'

'I mean your colleagues. Why are you here alone?'

The lad looked down at the snow.

You're joking.

'All of them?'

A nod.

Well, fuck your mother. The MGB were sweeping through the ranks of the militia like a scythe through a wheat field.

The military, the police, the Chekists' own ranks . . . Where terror reigned, it often reigned most cruelly among men and women unwise enough to have put on a uniform. An entire station, though, even if it was just a provincial outpost? The militia existed to keep some measure of public order but social discipline was mostly enforced elsewhere. The unions, the factory floor, the people's courts, even the criminal underworld – all were in competition for the loyalty of the Soviet citizen. Being a policeman was a simple job that recruited people with a simple attitude to justice, and therefore had a high number of thugs in its ranks. Counter-revolutionary sedition was hardly their forte.

Rossel looked back at the bodies and tried to bring his thoughts into line.

The driver of a standard night-time freight train stops because there is something on the track. He jumps down to have a look. He suspects fallen trees, or cargo spilled from some other train. But it isn't.

He radios to the next station; the station calls the local police. Except there aren't any apart from this pathetic specimen, who – although he's been denying it – calls the first Leningrad militia headquarters whose number he can see on the wall. And Sergeants Grachev and Taneyev, doing their turn on the night shift, call me. And because Sergeant Grachev is a bastard who only plays it by the book when he can cause maximum disruption, he gets Captain Lipukhin out of bed, too, knowing he will have a head like industrial glue.

More than fifty kilometres outside our jurisdiction, in the middle of nowhere. The local militia purged by the MGB.

Rossel knew better than to ask why. Stick to the crime.

He left the wretched private and stomped over to his men, staggering a little where the plough had made fresh peaks of the snow. He reached Captain Ilya Lipukhin first.

'What have we got, boss?'

Captain Lipukhin stared back at him through melancholic, bloodshot eyes. As so often these days, the breath of Rossel's superior stank of cheap vodka.

'Murder,' he said. 'Maniac.'

And vomited.

2

'Number one. Frozen solid – and I mean solid. Right the way through, I reckon. Like the clumps of bread they used to give us in the 8th Guards. Fucking teethbreakers.'

Sergeant Grachev brushed the snow off the body and tapped it with his gloved knuckles to underline the point.

'Face removed, some of the teeth taken out. Or smashed out. Hands cut off.'

At the sight of the corpse's cheerful, toothless grin, Captain Lipukhin turned away, coughed furiously and heaved again. Rossel guessed he'd managed to puke up a fair amount of alcohol already. Lipukhin's little weakness was getting bigger by the day.

'Look at what she's wearing,' Grachev continued. 'She looks like a Snow Queen. But the gown isn't frozen. This bitch has been dressed by somebody after she was killed.'

Too small. Too thin. It wasn't her. Just as always, relief swept through Rossel in an intense but fleeting wave. Every female corpse might be Galya until he knew it wasn't. Until he was certain.

He leaned over and stared at the girl's red velvet dress. Grachev was right. It looked expensive.

'What's that in her throat?' He pointed. 'An icicle?'

A long and thin frosted object stuck out of the corpse's larynx. Grachev took off a glove and tapped it before quickly putting it back on again.

'Glass,' he said.

Grachev bent closer, turned his head sideways. His cap slid off, revealing his scarred and shaven skull.

'Hollow. A glass tube.' He glanced across at the other four bodies. 'Different size tubes but they've all got them, Comrade Lieutenant.'

Rossel straightened himself and clapped his hands together to warm them.

'Pity they aren't icicles, Sergeant. If that was so, all available evidence would be pointing directly at the magic powers of the Snow Queen and our case would be closed. Comrade Taneyev?'

Sergeant Taneyev, their old-timer, only a few weeks from his pension, stepped forward. The flash of his camera flared as he took a portrait or two of the unknown icy aristocrat. Hands by her sides, her body perpendicular to the track, her head exactly in the middle of the rails.

Rossel took out another cigarette – a Belomorkanal *papirosa* – twisted the cardboard tube at one end that served as a crude filter and lit the rank tobacco at the other.

'Number two,' said Grachev, replacing his cap as they shuffled to the next corpse and sweeping the snow off the body. 'A priest. Also frozen solid. I reckon they all are. No face, teeth bashed in, fingers snipped. And – well, look at that.'

Rossel took an extra hard drag.

The priest's throat and chest had been opened and the voicebox pulled out. It lay on the victim's neck, next to a large gold cross, with the robes covering the rest of the body. Above the faceless skull sat a black cylindrical hat. Again, the body was at right angles to the track but in this case the head had been set on the rail. To which it was probably now stuck.

Taneyev stepped forward again and pressed the shutter without warning. The flash went off right in their faces, the flare made worse as it rebounded off the pure white ground. The other three sprang away, temporarily blinded, Sergeant Grachev spewing curses.

'Taneyev, you clumsy prick. Who do you think you are? Sergei fucking Eisenstein?'

Rossel sank to one knee in the deep snow and tried to blink away the imprint of his own blood vessels on his pupils, wondering how Sergeant Taneyev had survived three decades in the militia without someone arranging some sort of accident or denouncing him to the MGB.

He looked back at the train. Its headlight was still shining fiercely and behind it was only darkness. That seemed to be the choice he was facing – searing light or total blackness. Rossel was not normally a religious man – the opposite, in fact. The teachers at the state orphanage in Kostroma had made sure of that. Taught him to worship only Marx and Lenin, after the secret police had come for his parents. In his teenage years he had even been a member of the League of the Militant Godless, and there was nobody more radically atheist than those lunatics. 'The struggle against religion is the struggle for the Five-Year Plan!' – the slogans were etched onto his brain. But there was something about this crime scene, much more than any other he had witnessed – the fastidious arrangement of the figures on the track; the

11

primordial bleakness of the surrounding landscape and the incessant, banshee murmur made by the wind coming off Lake Ladoga. Deep drifts, darkness and dead bodies. It all brought back any number of memories from the siege of Leningrad. And of his sister, Galya, whose face he had last glimpsed fading into a blizzard many years ago. The lieutenant felt the urge to cross himself.

The officers regrouped, drawn together by the next corpse. It was wrinkled all over, like it belonged to an old man.

'Number three,' Grachev resumed. 'As you can see, this one's completely naked. Similar treatment, but with some additional work. I cleared the snow around him a bit and found some delicacies. That's his heart, I reckon.' He pointed to the brown lump next to the body. 'And those other things next to the heart are his balls. His prick's still on, though. Lucky devil!'

All the corpses lay over both sets of tracks where they ran side by side. In three cases the heads lay on the rails; in the other two, they lolled between them.

Rossel stepped away from body number three and took a look around, inwardly berating himself for his carelessness. Bleary with sleep and cold, he'd assumed he was on his way to some sort of stupid accident. Alcohol to blame, nine times out of ten. And if the secret police had been involved, well, the worst it could have been was an execution. In those cases, you made it your job to blunder all over the crime scene and ask all the wrong questions, or none at all. Cart the poor sods off and invent a cause of death.

But there was no blood. The faces were a mess but there did not seem to be any exit wounds, so there had been no shots to the back of the head, secret police-style. No rope binding the hands or feet.

Maniac. Maybe Lipukhin was right.

The cops had all left clear sets of footprints from the car to the railway but none of them had checked to see if there were any other traces of the person, or persons, who had brought the bodies to their resting place. Rossel looked the other way, across the open ground to the forest on the other side of the tracks, along the main line and the secondary line. Where did that lead, anyway? But there were no footprints, no scars in the snow that a dragged corpse might have made, no tyre tracks.

'When did it stop snowing?'

Rossel's voice stopped his men as they were settling down to corpse number four. They looked at one another.

'It was snowing when I went on shift,' said Grachev. 'After that I was head down in paperwork. Seemed to be snowing the whole time, though.'

Paperwork? From eight in the evening until two in the morning? Rossel doubted it. Sergeant Grachev preferred to concentrate on his smoking, and on keeping a weather eye out for any prostitutes brought into the station he could rape.

'It was snowing when I went to bed,' said Lipukhin. 'About . . .' he faltered. 'About ten.'

Rossel saw Grachev and Taneyev smirk. About ten when you slid under the table, comrade?

So, none of them had any idea. Best guess was that the snow had stopped sometime between two and four. But it had been coming down for most of the early winter, coming

13

down like God wanted to bury the world and never see it again. Here it was up to their thighs. You could rake enough powder over your tracks and wait for the weather to do the rest. The five bodies lying on the railway lines near Lake Ladoga might as well have fallen out of the sky.

The fourth corpse was also male. But it looked like the body of a younger man – more muscle definition, no sagging flesh. Perhaps as young as twenty but no more than forty, Rossel thought. It was naked and mutilated like the third except that, as Grachev said with a malevolent grin, 'both prick *and* balls are in place this time. And look at that girth, in this temperature, too. If there's pussy in Heaven those bitches are going to get themselves nice and wet when this fine young gallant turns up.'

Last one. Rossel lit another *papirosa* from the remnants of his previous one and double-pinched the cardboard filter.

'Oh shit,' said Grachev. 'Oh fuck.'

Rossel looked across at the sergeant kneeling over the corpse, saw him brush a clump of snow off its head and point at it.

'This one's a blue-top,' said Grachev. 'This one's MGB.'

Her cap was, indeed, blue-topped with a red band and black visor. The tunic had flashes on the sleeves and throat that Rossel couldn't identify, blue thread at the wrists, and epaulettes without any markings. A corroded badge was clipped to the breast – he could just make out a sword designating the bearer as a member of the Ministry for State Security.

Like the others, most of the face had been removed. Unlike them, her eyelids had been left open though her eyes were only white, milky globes. Grachev inspected the mouth.

'More amateur dental work. Her tongue's gone, too.'

She was naked from the waist down apart from some voluminous knickers. Pink ones, or red ones that had faded. Real passion killers. Whoever she was, she had been short and stout, and the flesh of her thighs had frozen into stubby white lumps that looked nothing like human legs.

'Three men, two women,' said Rossel. 'A Princess, a Priest, Nude without bollocks, Nude with, and now the Secret Police Officer.'

Grachev blew out his cheeks. 'A real fucking jazz band,' he muttered.

'Jazz is bourgeois, comrade,' said Taneyev.

They stared at him. Taneyev cradled his camera, his face as long and solemn as ever. He wasn't trying to crack a joke.

Grachev spat.

'Thank you, as ever, for your close attention to Party doctrine, comrade,' he said, 'and for setting me, all of us, indeed, on the right fucking path, comrade, and for . . .'

Rossel intervened. 'That's enough, Sergeant.' Once Grachev got going, he wouldn't stop.

Grachev, as ever, flirted with disobeying orders but this time fell silent. Probably because Taneyev didn't give a shit how long he ranted for. Mouthing platitudes and scraping through to retirement was the old man's priority now. Or perhaps it was because the sight of the MGB uniform had put them all on edge.

'Comrade Lieutenant, I'm not sure how best to proceed. What do you think we should do?'

This was Lipukhin, sidling up to him. The captain had got the vodka out of his stomach and some colour had returned to his cheeks but he still gave off the petrol scent of cheap alcohol. Tall though he was, Lipukhin still had to raise his head to murmur the question into Rossel's ear.

Rossel knew what they were all thinking. Grachev, crouched once more over the woman, his face set in his habitual mask of rodent insolence. Taneyev, hands twisting over his camera, his eyes round and unblinking, desperate to make it through the last few weeks before the safe harbour of retirement, a pension and anonymity. Lipukhin, with the film star looks that the drink had only just begun to spoil. A captain in name only, these days, waiting for orders.

The thought was: *Might it be possible to forget about the one in the MGB uniform . . .?*

The row of dead was being dusted anew with snow flicked over them by a stiffening breeze. Beyond them was the light that arrowed out of the steam engine. The driver was stamping in the thick drifts and the local copper was still staring at his boots.

Rossel tapped his thumb rhythmically on the ring and little fingers of his left hand – or the little that was left of them – his habit when he needed to think. The twin stubs were a memento from the Chekists, the name still given to the secret police. Rossel was well aware there'd be no hiding anything from them. There never was. In fact, he was mildly surprised MGB officers weren't here already. Dead bodies were, after all, their speciality.

No, there would be no hurried burials, no cover-ups. They had to get the bodies back to Leningrad, get the officers swarming all over the case, smother it in paperwork before the MGB smelt it out and got their hands on four lonely officers of the people's militia.

He could afford no more encounters with the MGB. Not after last time.

Rossel raised his head.

Perhaps they really could pin it on the Snow Queen, he thought. An easy arrest to make, given her legendary temper and fairly obvious royalist sympathies.

His voice assumed an air of command.

'Get that lad to find a truck. And let's get some hot water from the train to unstick that . . .'

But Grachev had already swung a leg back. His boot thudded into the head of the priest.

'Done,' the sergeant said.

3

They had left Grachev and Taneyev behind to comman-
deer an ex-military ZIS-5 truck that the local policeman
had conjured up after an hour's hunt – the only useful thing
he'd done all night. Taneyev had taken another twenty photographs before they loaded the corpses into the back of
the ZIS, wrapping them in tarpaulins. Grachev hadn't been
joking – the bodies were as stiff as tree trunks. The morgue
would probably warm them up. But they were surprisingly
light. Corpses, as all of them had experienced, were usually
a devil to shift, but not these.

Rossel and Lipukhin drove back alone in the Moskvich,
Rossel at the wheel, while his captain hacked at the ice on
the inside of the windscreen that formed when their breath
billowed onto the glass, forming tiny crystals before their
eyes. A broken wooden cooking spoon and old copies of
Pravda and *Soviet Sport* were kept in the glove compart-
ment for exactly that purpose.

They travelled in silence for the first thirty minutes, focused
on staying on the road, Rossel battling with the slipping and
sliding, the car's winter tyres and snow chains grinding and
squeaking under the flimsy floor, Lipukhin scraping.

Once they got closer to Leningrad the road was a little
easier, the snow flatter and more compact.

'Any thoughts, Revol?'

'None worth sharing, Comrade Captain.'

Lipukhin smiled.

'On the case, I mean.'

Rossel shrugged.

'He's neat, our maniac is neat. I mean, lined up like that, as if they were queuing for the Bolshoi? When I think of madness I think of chaos, of utterly irrational acts. This isn't like that.'

'He took out their teeth and cut off their faces,' said Lipukhin. 'That says maniac to me. Drunken headcase.'

'Or he wanted to disguise their identities,' said Rossel. 'He has purpose. He has reason.'

Lipukhin grunted and gave the window a desultory scrape with the spoon.

'He or they?' he said after a moment.

'That I'm not sure about, yet. Are you?'

The captain hesitated before answering.

'No, not really. Although that was a lot of meat, a lot of cold cuts to shift for just one person.'

'Two men, then,' said Rossel. 'They bring them out in a truck and then plonk them on the rails. Piss off well before the train arrives. The fresh snow covering their tracks, as it did most of the bodies before the light from the engine picked them out.'

'Yes, maybe two. But I'm still not sure. Why would they do it? What could be their motive for arranging them like that? It would be a strange pact to make.' The captain took a swig from an imaginary bottle and then put on the slurred and exaggerated voice of a tramp hammered on black-market hooch. 'Care to come out to Ladoga with

19

me, comrade? I have some corpses I wish to place in rather particular poses on the railway lines out by the lake.'

'There could be another, more obvious, explanation.'

'Which is?'

'I didn't want to say anything in front of Grachev and Taneyev. Especially not Grachev. He'd sell his own mother for three kopeks.'

Lipukhin nodded.

'Taneyev, on the other hand, is obviously a man of great integrity,' said the captain. 'Well, he might hold out for four. But your explanation is that the Chekists did this, Revol? Yet why would they murder one of their own?'

On the face of it, this was a fantastically stupid question. The Chekists – as OGPU, as NKVD, as MGB – had spent years liquidating each other as enthusiastically as they had liquidated spies, saboteurs, fascists, writers, priests, *kulaks*, Trotskyites, musicians, generals, doctors, coppers, anyone who spoke a foreign language or who had been abroad, any anti-Soviet elements in general.

Rossel sought a diplomatic answer.

'Most likely, no. But it wouldn't be the first time?' he ventured.

Lipukhin shook his head.

'I can't see it, myself. Not out there, near the lake. Too far for the blue-tops to travel. Especially in this weather. Too much like hard work. I'm told they have a favourite spot for that sort of thing. In the woods near Toksovo. Be careful if you go picking flowers out there, Lieutenant. They say every snowdrop, in every coppice, blooms from a traitorous seed.'

Rossel pressed his foot down on the brake. The Moskvich veered to the right on the icy road as he slowed it down. Then he turned left at a road sign half-buried in a deep flurry: *Leningrad 35 km.* He glanced at his watch. It was well past 4am.

'Maniac it is, then,' he said. 'It seems to me we're looking for a peculiar kind of monster, though. One who first butchers his victims – slices off balls, rips out throats, takes out teeth, cuts off faces – but then arranges their bodies like silk socks in a bourgeois sock drawer, each next to the other. All in a neat little row.'

*

On the outskirts of the city, the snow thinned out and the tyres found it easier to get a grip. The Moskvich had warmed up and Lipukhin settled back into his seat. Rossel was surprised the little car had run out to Lake Ladoga and back without much complaint.

Five thirty, and Leningrad was waking up in the dark. Yesterday had been a typical mid-October day, cold but not unmanageably so. Now, twenty-four hours later, the 'Venice of the North', as the locals called it, with its wide canals and imposing pre-revolutionary palaces and mansions, was caked in ice. Rossel drove back the way they had come, down Piskaryovsky Prospect, skirting the city to its east before cutting in over the Bolsheokhtinsky Bridge. At a depot off Smolny Prospect, tram drivers were lighting fires under the chassis to warm up the fuel – a trick they had probably learned getting T34 tanks going during the war. High above them, lit by spotlights – printed on a huge red poster that was lashed to the stately domes of Smolny Cathedral – three men surveyed the scene. One of them was Stalin. The second, a round-faced lifelong bureaucrat with a disdainful gaze, was Georgy Malenkov, rumoured by some to be Stalin's heir. The third, a middle-aged man with a receding hairline above pince-nez spectacles, was Lavrentiy Beria, deputy prime minister, his name synonymous with state security. The words on the poster read: *VICTORY AND FREEDOM! The Tenth Anniversary Celebrations of the opening of THE ROAD OF LIFE. 19 November.*

As the Moskvich trundled past, Rossel stared upward into the inkblot eyes that lurked behind the giant lenses, wondering if they helped Beria to bring the sins of Leningrad's two million citizens into sharper focus.

Police Department No. 17 was on the corner of Vosstaniya and Nekrasova. The Moskvich drew up outside and Rossel cut the engine. The two policemen sat in silence for a few moments, unwilling to start the day any earlier than necessary now that they had lost a night's sleep, letting Leningraders stumble past them on their way to offices, factories, schools. A gang of construction workers went by, raucous even in the dark morning; eight years since the siege had been lifted and the city was still putting itself back together. Grachev and Taneyev were coming off shift and could go to bed once they had seen the bodies to the morgue.

For the first time since dragging himself out of bed the previous morning, Rossel felt the cold possess him, chilling the lungs and stomach and spine. It could take days to properly warm up from a night like that. He yawned.

'No time for dozing, Lieutenant,' Lipukhin said, now thoroughly sober and trying to lighten the mood. 'I think we need tea. Let's go and warm our hands and our hearts. Lidia will have filled up the samovar.'

The captain got out of the car, slapping its roof in approval. Rossel watched him cross the road and push open the heavy wooden door to the police station. Before he went in, Lipukhin removed his hat and ruffled his blond hair. He could have been a poster boy for the Soviet paradise – until he'd made the mistake of succumbing to the green snake.

Mistakes.

Everyone had made one. Sometimes they were fatal. Sometimes, Rossel wished his own had been. If he'd kept his mouth shut, kept his smart remarks to himself, perhaps he would still be playing the violin – maybe a job at the Kirov Theatre, maybe some solo concerts here and there. Still young at heart, raising smiles, chasing the occasional romantic liaison with singers or dancers – not forced to confront the craggy, chastened face he saw staring back at him out of the shaving mirror each morning. *Prizrak*, he would whisper, pointing back – a ghost, its face as white as the suds plastered all over it.

He took off his gloves and examined his hands.

The ring and little finger of the left were both missing. The middle and index intact but stiff and somewhat twisted. His right hand had fared a little better – no fingers missing. But the ring and little finger were broken and malformed.

Like a scale, Rossel could recall the order with perfect clarity.

Do – the left little finger. Already broken by his interrogator who, when that did not inspire a confession, turned to a chisel.

Re – his mind wandering up and down all the most difficult scales, imagining the tips of his fingers pressing the strings into place just so.

Mi. Severed.

'You can stop this,' murmured the interrogator. 'All it takes is your confession.'

Fa – the ring finger. Down came the chisel.

Sol – the interrogator put the chisel down but started with the hammer on the right. Agony in symmetry.

Scales turned into arpeggios, then the most difficult studies. In the end, he had confessed anyway – confessed to anti-Soviet sentiments, they told him later, though exactly what sentiments he could not quite recall.

Maybe it had been encouraging counter-revolutionary sabotage – that was a favourite during the war. Or enemy propaganda. Plotting to assassinate party cadres. Conspiracy to aid fascism. Profiteering. Wrecking. Diversionary acts. Spreading rumours to undermine morale. Espionage. Hoarding. Choose from an extensive menu, comrades, because in these troubled times, the one thing we've got plenty of is crimes of treason. Choose anything you fancy.

The long, angular nose and scarred face of his torturer. The stench of the cell. The musty straps and iron-cold restraints. The way his back was contorted over the special bench. It was all as clear as a sparkling night sky. But the confession was wrapped in fog.

La.

It hadn't stopped. Not for a long time.

But, when it did, Rossel knew he had become somebody else. It felt as though he had been struck dumb. He had stared for hours at the stumps of his missing fingers. And, then, he had turned to a fellow inmate in that foetid, over-crowded cell and said, *They might as well have cut out my tongue.* He would never be able to play another note.

In the steamed-up confines of the Moskvich, Rossel shivered and decided it was time to search for that tea. *Fuck your mother!* He was cold all over.

Except for his hands, which were already numb. His hands couldn't feel a thing.

4

The blizzard swirling in from the River Neva had turned Leningrad white but everything inside the little station house was shadow. A thick layer of black soot from the logs burning in the fire covered every inch of the walls. Vosstaniya Street was home to Militia Station 17. It was a battered fragment of a lost age left behind by the merchants who once owned it before the October Revolution.

Everyone and everything in it had a nickname. Rossel was the Fiddler, because someone had gone through his file on day one and found his diploma from the Leningrad Conservatory of Music. Sometimes he also got compared to Crazy Borya, a deranged tramp who literally scraped a living in all weathers on the bridges of the Griboyedov Canal with a cracked violin and hairless bow. 'Screeching like a tomcat who's dipped his balls in chilled vodka,' as Grachev had put it.

The violin had marked him out as different. Especially as it was buried in the past of a man who hardly ever took his gloves off.

Lipukhin got 'Comrade Lenfilm' as he bore an uncanny resemblance to Nikolai Cherkasov, Stalin's favourite film star. Grachev was 'Pavel Stalingrad', as he never stopped bragging about his role in the battle, as part of the 8th Guards

Army. And Taneyev was 'Taneyev', on account of being so bland and boring nobody could even be bothered to make a nickname up for him. Even the police station itself had its own moniker: The Black House. Because of the soot and, perhaps, the things Grachev did to those suspects who might be having a little trouble confessing in its dank basement.

'Grachev's in there with some tart from Sennaya,' Junior Sergeant Lidia Gerashvili whispered, intercepting Rossel in the middle of the room amid the chairs and desks of the lowest ranks. Station 17, home to a dozen militia officers, was full. Those supposed to be out on patrol on such a freezing morning had discovered vital paperwork that needed doing without delay, while those who really needed to do their paperwork were concentrating on getting the samovar going. 'He came straight in and dragged her off for interrogation. And you know . . .'

'I know,' said Rossel. 'How long ago?'

'Only a few minutes.'

Rossel headed for the stairs.

Five dead bodies. Five blood-red stains on the soul of Mother Russia. No sleep to speak of. A corpse in the uniform of a state security officer. He needed to think. But first he had to tackle this.

*

Rossel barged into the interrogation room without knocking. Grachev had his hand raised. He had probably knocked the girl about a fair bit already but she had her clothes on and the sergeant's trousers were still buttoned up. It could have been a lot worse.

The girl was probably only in her early twenties but she looked a lot older. Her hair was cut short and dyed a dark red.

Grachev started to say something but closed his mouth again. Rossel outranked him. Just.

Grabbing the girl by the neck, Grachev thrust her back into her chair before taking his own seat. He pulled out a fountain pen and notebook from within his tunic. Rossel closed the door and stood by it. Grachev twisted in his chair but Rossel stared him down.

'Varvara, now you say that's your name?' Grachev said, turning back to the girl.

'Yes.'

She looked uncertain about Rossel's arrival.

The tip of Sergeant Grachev's tongue was now sticking out of his customarily surly mouth and pressing against his top lip. His brown eyes were locked on her face. He was wearing what one of the junior officers had once called his 'pussy-licking face'.

'Not Valentina?' sneered Grachev.

'No, like I told you before, no.'

'It's just that, when they brought you in, they said Valentina.'

'I slurred my words, that's all. I have to take a little vodka to keep out the cold.'

'Keeping out the cold, that's what you were doing, is it? When my officers found you sucking *khui* in an old workmen's hut behind the Hippodrome?'

'No, no, I like to drink, that's all,' said the girl.

She leaned forward and smiled coyly at Rossel.

'Perhaps, would it be possible, officers, to request a little vodka? It's not been a good night for me, after all.'

Grachev opened a table drawer and took out a small bottle of spirit of unknown origin, but probably brewed in a sink in the sergeants' communal apartment. He stood it next to him on the table and half unscrewed the lid. The girl looked at it and smiled. Grachev moved it back a little on the table.

'Ah, ah, princess. First a little information.'

'All right. Yes, it's true, I do offer the odd cuddle for a kopek every now and then. Times are hard. For me they have always been hard.'

Oh, for Lenin's sake – this was a waste of time. They had work to do. Rossel would order Grachev back to his desk and get someone else to charge this girl for hooliganism or offending Soviet morality.

Grachev retightened the cap.

'Not about you, bitch. Sluts aren't worth investigation, since everyone knows exactly what it is that sluts do. About this customer of yours, Comrade Zhevtun?'

Zhevtun? That was different.

Rossel opened up the manila file in front of him and read out the full name of the suspect.

'Zhevtun, Dmitri Viktorovich. Wanted for profiteering, illegal import and various other black-market activities.'

'Never heard of him,' said the girl.

Rossel stepped forward to a position where he could see both their faces.

'That is who she was with, Sergeant?'

Grachev scowled. 'That's why his file is there, isn't it?'

'We didn't have much time for introductions,' the girl said.

'Comrade Zhevtun is someone we've been interested in for a while,' Rossel told her. 'He is a known black-marketeer.'

Zhevtun was being pursued as a part of a recent crackdown on those who 'persistently refused socially useful work and led a parasitical way of life'. Only a few months ago, the Presidium of the Supreme Soviet had issued a decree against them, promising 'five-year sentences of exile to special settlements in remote regions' for anyone arrested for begging, prostitution and racketeering. The decree had thinned out the ranks of the city's beggars – mostly army veterans trying to scrape a few kopeks together for vodka – who made a nuisance of themselves on public transport, in shops, parks and bathhouses. And also dragged in a few prostitutes, like the girl. But the bigger fish, professional criminals like Zhevtun, were harder to pin down.

'Not me. I only met him tonight.'

Grachev sighed and got up from his chair. He walked slowly around the desk and then leaned in close, so the girl could smell his foul breath.

'Stop fucking with us, you little piss hole.'

She moved her cheek slightly to the left, showing the darkening bruise, and raised a disdainful eyebrow.

'All right, I met him a few more times than that, always in the same place, near the Hippodrome. What's he done, anyway? Why are you all so hot for him? It can't just be for flogging a few packs of silk stockings to the wives of the Party nobs coming out of the shops on Nevsky.'

Grachev sat back down. He patted his fat stomach with one hand and with the other rubbed the dirty nail of his index finger over two words of despairing graffiti some long-forgotten prisoner had carved into the desk. '*Pomogite mnye*', it said. Help Me. Rossel noticed the brown stain of the wood varnish was worn a little there. The girl was playing with fire.

Grachev grinned, showing a decaying row of grey teeth.

'Fine,' he said. 'You can think it over in the cell with the Hound.'

'The Hound?'

Rossel rolled his eyes. But perhaps it was the quickest way.

'I think he's downstairs in his favourite cell, the one with the dead rat in it next to the shithouse,' Grachev went on. 'Yes, slut, we have deeper cells than this. For the real crazies.'

The girl's eyes flickered towards Rossel but he kept his face blank. She shifted in her seat. The sergeant's nail began another rhythmic scratching at the graffiti carved into the desk.

'Sad, sad story,' he said. 'Biology professor he was, a brilliant man by all accounts. Some unfortunate views, however, so the authorities wouldn't evacuate him with the rest of those spineless State University intellectuals during the siege. Left him here to eat communal sawdust with the shop girls, street cleaners and cops like us. He managed not so bad for a while. But when his dog died – well, you know what these brainboxes are like when their heads get all fucked up. In my experience the craziest are the ones who suffer from a little too much imagination. I saw a 51st Army captain at Stalingrad, he took out one of his eyeballs with the tip of his own bayonet, told me his eyes had seen more than his soul could bear.'

The girl's bravura was subsiding. Her eyes flicked between the bottle of vodka and the two police officers.

'This professor, his dog died?'

Grachev picked up the vodka bottle and slipped it into his coat pocket.

'A poodle called Pushkin. His pride and joy. The reactionary scum had even managed to get it a separate ration card from some other faggot he knew in the Ministry of Production. Can you believe that? All his fellow citizens are cradling their bloated empty bellies, every other dog in Leningrad has long since been sautéed, along with all the cats, rats and stray fucking children, and this bastard is feeding his precious poodle cold cuts.'

The girl put a hand to her mouth and, just for a second, gnawed absent-mindedly at her palm.

'Bastard,' she agreed. 'My mother died in the siege. And my nephew.'

Grachev thrust his face into hers.

'Someone found out,' he spat. 'Broiled the mutt up. And shared it with him in a pan of broth. That's when it started.'

'It?'

'The barking.'

The girl blinked at them.

'Barking?'

'And the howling,' added Grachev, sitting back. 'And, on occasions when the moon is full, the biting. Do you believe in ghosts, princess? I think the Hound does.'

It was amazing how superstitious people still were, Rossel thought. Thirty-four years since the revolution, thirty-four years of Marxist-Leninist education and atheist indoctrination, and you still found people believing in house elves, forest spirits and magic.

This was Grachev's favourite part. He sat bolt upright, threw back his shoulders and began to howl.

The girl watched him, mesmerised. She pulled her cheap red coat tight across her chest and did up two of the buttons.

Grachev stopped howling and smiled at her.

'Never recovered, did the Hound. Not once the fucking fruitcake realised he'd supped on the bones of his beloved little Pushkin. These days he likes to take a dump in flower beds, piss on trees and howls like the mother of a true martyr of the revolution every time he spots another poodle in the park.'

'The Florist,' said the girl. 'My friend, Natasha, says this Zhevtun sometimes works for a man that he calls the Florist. Some sort of high-up, a Party bigwig. She went to a party with him once at a posh dacha out near Lake Ladoga. He told her this Florist had arranged it.'

'How high up?' asked Rossel.

'Very, is all she said.'

'What sort of work?'

The girl shrugged. 'That's all I know, honest. I won't have to go down there now, with him, will I, the dog man?'

Rossel picked his militia cap up off the table and stared back down at her.

Worked every time, that stupid story.

'I shouldn't think so,' he said.

*

They left the girl to stew.

'Give me ten minutes alone with her and I'll have all the information about this Florist we want,' said Grachev. 'She's holding something back.'

There was a leak in the foundations – no one had attended to the merchant's house for years – and they faced each other on either side of a slowly spreading puddle.

'Thank you for your diligence, comrade, you are an example to us all. But no,' said Rossel.

Ten minutes alone with her? Did Grachev think he was stupid?

Grachev's eyes narrowed.

'What's she to you? She takes cock for a living.'

'Then you can wait until you're off duty and pay her, Sergeant,' said Rossel, leaning forward so that Grachev would have to look up to meet his eye. 'Although in so doing you will be guilty of compelling a woman to engage in prostitution, which as we both know carries a sentence of up to five years' deprivation of freedom, with confiscation of some or all property. So, don't let me catch you.'

The Soviet project of moulding the tsarist-era police into a respected and efficient organ of justice had not yet been completed but Lieutenant Revol Rossel – a man who had been named in honour of the Bolshevik revolution – was damned if he was going to let men like Grachev rule the roost.

Grachev marched off down the corridor and threw open the door to the stairs.

'To hell with you, *comrade*,' he said. 'To hell with you.'

*

After another hour, Dr Volkova rang to say she wouldn't be able to get to Vosstaniya Street until late evening, if at all. Another pathologist had been arrested three days earlier. Now she was one of two left in the whole city and their caseloads were backing up. There had been rumours of another doctors' conspiracy to murder Party officials. Rossel had

seen junior and senior officers stand to attention for no reason and declare, 'These accursed intellectuals must be shown
the full force of Soviet justice, without mercy.' To which he
had bitten back the reply: 'As long as they keep their hands
off our last few pathologists.'

Taneyev and Grachev went home, a few hours beyond
their usual night shift. Grachev handed in a few lines of
scrappy notes from the crime scene, which told Rossel
nothing his own memory could not. Taneyev had clipped
his photos up to dry in the darkroom and left orders downstairs for them to be sent up once they were ready.

It went very dark again, the fire crackled in the grate,
consuming the last scraps of firewood, and the windows
misted up. Nobody disturbed them. First Lipukhin drifted
off. Rossel fought for as long as he could, his pen scratching across the paper, tracing the outlines of five torn bodies
in macabre fancy dress.

*

Desperate to get to the samovar and make some tea, Rossel
pushed through the communal kitchen of his apartment
block – past women in aprons, their sleeves rolled up,
addressing vast tureens of soup and buckwheat *kasha* or
manically chopping piles of vegetables. The smell of cabbage, beetroot and onions, always present to some degree,
was intense and pleasurable. Jars of pickled cucumbers
and tomatoes, grown on dacha plots and preserved for
the winter to guard against the inevitable shortages, lined
the shelves. The swirling clouds of steam lent the scene the
mirage-like atmosphere of a bathhouse.

'Tatyana Borisovna, what is going on?' he asked one of the cooks.

The woman glanced up from the beef bones floating in a seething vat, keeping one eye on a small pan of frying chicken livers.

'The deliveries were late again and everyone had to join the queues after work,' she said, passing a wrist over her brow. 'Long queues, too. We've all only just started. I'll be here till midnight, I shouldn't wonder. Making sure nothing gets wasted.'

Weekends were always busy in the communal kitchen as Soviet womanhood – it was rare to see men labouring in there – attempted to create an entire week's menus in advance. Mikoyan, the great quartermaster of the war and author of the country's most popular recipe book, recommended the preparation of ten days' worth. But now everyone was trying to do so at once. There was tension in the air, blending in with the assorted aromas.

Rossel reached the samovar, found a stray glass and spooned in some tea leaves from a communal jar. He turned, leant against the counter and watched. The radio was on and he caught snatches of Rimsky-Korsakov's *Scheherazade* but the music was mostly drowned out by clanging metal, exchanges of culinary advice, and laughter.

On the side of the room furthest away from him was a woman he didn't recognise. Even before he saw her face, something in the way she carried herself told him she was attractive. Then she did turn, caught him staring, and pointedly turned away again.

'Oy, Kira, your *piroshki* are the best,' one of the women around the table complimented another. Rossel looked over at the mound of perfectly shaped pastries, filled with ersatz cheese or perhaps real vegetables. He needed a second supper all of a sudden. It was amazing what could be fashioned out of extremely limited resources.

He sat down. Across the table was a growing pile of *golubtsy*, cabbage leaves stuffed with rice and a smattering of finely ground mince. Even though he had eaten plain meat patties and kasha at his usual *stolovaya* on the way home, he felt his saliva glands tingle.

He stole another glance across the kitchen. She was wearing a light blue dress patterned with yellow flowers. Her hair was dark as night but in curlers. Like everyone else, she was simultaneously chopping, frying, boiling and tasting. With care, she tasted one of her concoctions and seemed dissatisfied but unsure how to improve it. Rossel wondered if she would welcome an outside opinion.

A poke in the ribs. Rossel looked around into the freckled, grinning face of Lena, a teenager with whom he sometimes shared occasional late-night glasses of tea and – in her case – illegal cigarettes. Lena was seventeen years old, dark-haired, small and boyish with, once she got to know and like you, an engaging gap-toothed smile and the vocabulary of a drunken sailor. She was studying art history at the Repin Institute.

'You've spotted her, then?' Lena said.

'Spotted who?'

'Our new neighbour. She's making a vegetable soup, meatballs and a potato salad. And since you're such a skinny one, I think she'd . . .'

'I've eaten.' Rossel sipped his tea and tried not to stare at the blue dress.

37

'I can find out if she's married, if you like?' said Lena with another poke in his ribs.

'With such investigative instincts, there is definitely a place for you in the People's Militia, Lena.' Rossel tried to poke her back but she wriggled out of reach and shot off, seizing a morsel from the table as she went.

He looked across the room, once more seeking out the stranger, staring through the steam and smoke whirling up from a dozen pots.

But she had disappeared.

5

Sunday October 14

The dead are more trustworthy than the living. They don't inform on you, for a start.

The treasonous nature of the thought unnerved him. What do you have to hide that the MGB needs to know, comrade? Everyone lived with that question burrowing into their minds. Keeping the answer unspoken was the thing that kept you safe. Until the day that Comrade Beria's scientists figured out a way to plant a bug in a man's mind and eavesdrop on his soul.

Rossel sat on a metal chair in the middle of the morgue, waiting for Dr Volkova. The pathologist had not turned up last night and was late again this morning. He sighed and glanced around the room, encircled by a silent quintet of cold corpses.

It had been twelve hours since they discovered the bodies on the railway line. Six since he filed his preliminary report.

And no phone call. No visit. Nothing.

Militia headquarters had reported the unexplained mutilation and murder of five citizens, one possibly an agent of the MGB, Ministry of State Security, up the chain of command

and nothing had happened. They were just being left to get on with this investigation unimpeded.

Which could only mean one thing.

There were many ways to buy a one-way ticket to a gulag: a drunken secret whispered to a lover at a party, an unexpected denouncement for black-market profiteering by a jealous rival at work, poor productivity levels on a tank factory assembly line which an ambitious political kommissar angling for promotion might decide to interpret as deliberate sabotage. Every week, every day, every hour, people disappeared for transgressions such as these.

Rossel turned towards the half-skinned skull, with its badly dyed peroxide hair, which lay to his right. It was staring up at a fly that was crawling around a dead bulb in the metal ceiling lamp.

Perhaps she was meant to be his ticket. Not just him. The whole station's, probably. The blue-top they had discovered on the railway lines at Lake Ladoga felt like a trap. But if she was, he had no idea how the trap had been sprung.

*

Rossel looked up from the faceless body – eyes still resting in the sockets like two delicately poached egg whites – that lay on the mortuary slab and glanced at Dr Volkova.

'Anything to report, Comrade Doctor?' He tried to keep his voice steady to disguise his queasiness.

Rossel had noticed Dr Volkova's gaudy nail varnish before she pulled on her surgical gloves. She had red nails. Very red. She always did them like that. As though the pathologist occasionally came back to the morgue at midnight and dipped her buffed cuticles in fresh blood.

She stood on one side of the slab, Rossel on the other. In between them was Body Number Five, the fifth one in the line of the dead. The blue-top. The other four lay at the far end of the room.

The flesh of the woman's thighs had thawed a little, giving her legs a more recognisable shape. Somehow, she looked a little more human, he thought – a little more feminine. Even though it was hours since they'd found her and her four companions on the railway line, the woman looked slightly better. As if, despite the unfortunate inconvenience of missing a face, being dead suited her.

'Report to you, or to state security?'

'To me first. Then, of course, I will relay your findings to the appropriate authorities.'

Dr Volkova had dark, well-cut hair that framed sharp, curious blue eyes. She liked to joust with Rossel. She had also made a pass at him once. More than once, in fact. But there was none of that in the air today.

'How did she die?' he asked.

'Answering that question will require patience,' said Dr Volkova. 'It takes several days for a body to thaw properly if it has frozen solid, and until then I would only be speculating. Those dark red patches on the knees and elbows are typical of prolonged exposure. She was not shot or stabbed. The removal of the face is crude – not a professional's work – and one hopes she was already dead at that point. A heart attack or stroke is possible, but as there are another four bodies in a similar state to this one, that seems unlikely. Poisoning? Overdose? We will have to wait.'

The doctor looked pale. It took a lot to spook Volkova but five faceless corpses turning up in her mortuary at the same time seemed to have done the trick.

'This is the only place I feel safe these days,' she said in a quiet voice. 'Here, with you, where I work.'

This was flattering and disturbing in equal measure. *Me and these corpses, comforting Dr Volkova.* But if the MGB did come for her as a suspect in the current Doctors' Plot, the five bodies on the slabs would be able to defend her better than he could.

Rossel returned to the matter in hand.

'Captain Lipukhin was of the opinion our murderer was a maniac,' he said.

Dr Volkova's lips quivered but she brought herself under control.

'I would agree,' she said.

'Really? The killer was methodical, not mad.'

'The teeth. I'm assuming they extracted them to prevent identification of the victim,' said the pathologist. 'The face, too, and the fingers or even entire hands. For those acts there might be a pragmatic motivation but the other mutilations – that is malice, pure and simple. Surely you must agree?'

'Malice, yes. But malice allied to method,' said Rossel. He looked again at the face. There was none of the neat musculature he had seen in Volkova's books. Just a mess that looked like . . . He tried hard not to make comparisons.

'Those bodies were placed with care on the railway line,' he continued. He looked away again before speaking further. The light green walls and metal benches that lined them were scrubbed spotless. Like the morgue's guests, everything was sanitised and lifeless. 'We were meant to find them like that. Five bodies loaded into a truck of some sort. Then driven out to the middle of nowhere in a snowstorm. Arranged with care, feet together, heads turned, clothing arranged. It seems to me whoever did this was in complete control of their emotions. I had to visit the Leningrad Psychiatric Hospital once. A big Georgian with a vicious scar on his neck pointed at the sky and told me that the clouds above the golden domes of St Basil's were all oysters and every raindrop was a pearl. No one like that is capable of planning something as considered as this.'

Dr Volkova took off her gloves and headed for the sink.

'Almost all the homicides I see are the result of spontaneous violence. A man walks in on his wife and her lover. Thieves turn on thieves – over status, gambling, money, suspicions that someone is an informer. The killer is almost always a man, and often a man who has been drinking. To have more than one victim is unusual. And so, five frozen and faceless victims are perhaps not the work of a frenzied lunatic. But neither does it look like the work of state . . .'

She stopped herself. Then continued.

'Of higher powers. Nor the habitual drunken thug, nor thieves. Whoever that leaves as the killer may have been in control of their emotions but nonetheless did not enjoy a close working relationship with sanity. Come back in a few days and we'll know more.'

Rossel pointed at the naked body on the slab.

'I'm a layman, of course, but she looks malnourished.'

'She does.'

Volkova walked back across to the slab and dipped her nose towards where the corpse's mouth used to be. She sniffed.

'Nothing yet. Needs to thaw a little.'

'What are you checking for?'

'A faint whiff of pears, a sure sign of starvation. We saw so much of it during the siege we used to call it Eau de Bone.'

Rossel stared at the corpse.

'So, your guess would be?'

Dr Volkova ran a sleeve over her forehead.

'Yes, I suspect so, Lieutenant. Whoever did this, before they cut off her face, they half starved her to death as well.'

6

The tiny rubies bled a twinkling circle of pink light into the surrounding gloom as Junior Sergeant Lidia Gerashvili held up the two earrings a little higher so Rossel could see them better. Even in the dimly lit officers' department, amid the thick curls of wood smoke from the logs in the grate, which could not escape the ancient and partially blocked chimneys, the gems still shimmered.

'They do not match, Comrade Lieutenant,' said Gerashvili.

Rossel held out a hand and Gerashvili dropped them into his glove. He squinted at them.

'They look the same to me,' said Rossel.

'Yes, they are exactly the same,' replied the junior sergeant. 'I expressed myself inadequately. I mean her – our victim. Body Number Five. They do not match her.'

'As she currently has no face, it is my considered view, Junior Sergeant, that it's very difficult to make an accurate judgement on whether the victim suits her earrings or not.'

'Especially, they do not match the cheap red knickers she was wearing. A three-kopek whore would turn her nose up at them. But these earrings are, I think, expensive.'

Rossel's face remained impassive as he considered the junior sergeant's observation.

'I'm just the archive clerk, of course,' said Gerashvili. 'I apologise for my impertinent speculations.'

Her tone undermined the apology. Gerashvili's round, half-Georgian face coloured a little – her sarcasm had gone far too far. It was always a mistake to antagonise your senior officers. Especially when you were right.

Rossel's voice softened. Gerashvili was twenty-five years old, only a year in the militia, and small; just an inch or so above five foot. Her short hair was bottle-blonde with dark roots showing at the centre parting. She had wide round dark eyes that forced an unexpected and immediate playful intimacy on anyone who looked into them. It was not flirtation. No, just simple candour of a kind, Rossel thought, which no longer seemed to exist. An almost pre-revolutionary openness of spirit. And a sharp intelligence and keen eye.

He had missed the significance of the red knickers at which a three-kopek whore would turn up her nose.

'Explain to me exactly what you mean,' Rossel said.

Gerashvili pointed to the earrings in Rossel's hand. He held them up and examined them. They were the kind with clasps fitted to them worn by women who had not had their ears pierced.

'Her ears are pierced. The right one, anyway. I looked at the photographs Taneyev took at the scene when I was preparing the case file this morning. The left earring is correctly attached to the woman's lobe, so I could not see whether it was pierced or not, but the right one was dislodged slightly and so, under a magnifying glass, I could observe that it had been pierced.'

'Why would she be wearing earrings with clasps if her ears were actually pierced?'

The clasp was gold with tiny flowers engraved around its base. They were minute, delicate, exquisite.

'The earrings are small but very expensive,' said Gerashvili. 'I think these rubies are real. There is only one shop in Leningrad that I know of where a citizen might obtain jewellery like this: Djilas, in the Passazh department store. And to access a shop like that, they would either have to be a very important citizen, or a friend of such a person.'

Rossel brought an earring closer to his eyes and examined it in more detail.

'There is no jeweller's mark on the clasp. In an expensive piece I would think that is unusual,' said Gerashvili. She took the other earring from him, opened the clasp and pointed to a tiny, almost imperceptible mark hidden underneath it.

'This one has been soldered, I think. There was a hallmark but it has been removed. The one you are holding has the same kind of indentation, only smaller. I wondered if they could, in fact, not have been bought in Leningrad. If they could be from abroad.'

Her voice trailed off as he stared at her. Gerashvili swallowed and added: 'If someone was trying to hide where they came from . . .'

It was excellent detective work, thought Rossel, and it landed them in a whole pile of trouble. *Not just any MGB agent but one trusted to travel abroad.* Very few people had access to travel passes. So why the hell had no one come for her?

'You have been wondering about a lot of things, it seems,' said Rossel, 'while in fact you are supposed to have been working diligently in our archive department filing reports on stolen bicycles, shipments of black-market cigarettes and other vital areas of criminal administration. I wonder is it possible that the Vosstaniya Street militia station's filing is not, currently, quite as it should be?'

Gerashvili's face gave nothing away at this unjust assessment. Good, he thought – she cares.

Rossel handed the other earring back to her. She placed them both inside a paper evidence bag.

'Good work, Junior Sergeant. I would like you to accompany me to Nevsky Prospect, to Djilas, the jeweller, tomorrow so that we may ask them some questions. Would you like that, Junior Sergeant – time away from your desk?'

He watched as Gerashvili placed the bag inside the correct red folder.

She looked up at him and tried a small smile.

'Yes, sir, I would.'

*

The missing looked back at Rossel as they always did – a little puzzled, even put out, to find themselves incarcerated in a dusty file. A bemused collection of display cabinet butterflies, unable to fully comprehend the strange turn of events that had brought them to reside in such a place. A few mugshots, like those in the standard files of criminals and the condemned, but mostly family images handed to the authorities to help in the search for loved ones. They said nearly a million people had died in the siege. How many more had disappeared? No one knew. But their spirits were here, in hundreds of thin missing persons files, arranged in a cramped room wedged under the staircase of the police station, turning L-shaped at one end to eke out a little more space for filing cabinets and shelves.

No one imagines they will become one of the missing, Rossel thought. *Until, one day, there you are.*

He drew on his Belomorkanal *papirosa*, savouring the acid burn as the smoke reached his lungs, and positioned the battered tin mug of vodka so that it would be within easy reach.

This room was Junior Sergeant Gerashvili's domain.

When he needed to get in, Rossel waited until she had left for the evening, and since Gerashvili was conscientious to a fault, sometimes that could be hours. There were a few hundred files in the station and, every now and then, more arrived.

But Rossel's goal was not to help her keep pace with these lost souls. He was looking for his missing sister, hoping he would open up a file one day and see Galya staring back at him.

It was more out of desperate hope than hard logic, for he had been looking for her file ever since he had joined the militia five years ago, not long after the war had ended, and not found her. On occasions he fed his hope with the thought that she might be using, or have been given, another name, or that her photographs might have got mixed up with someone else's records. Perhaps there would be no photograph, just the written record of the disappearance into the snow of a woman born in 1917, the year of the revolution, on the very same day that Revol Rossel entered the world. And who vanished on 25 November 1935, when she was just eighteen years old.

This ongoing nocturnal quest was also a way of spending time away from the world, of feeling a little closer to the old one he and Galya had left behind. Of recalling life with their mother, a music teacher, and their father, a naval officer and Party stalwart, in a small but comfortable apartment in Kirovsky. Before their parents had been arrested and sent to the camps.

Of pretending to be, even for the briefest of moments, a little more like his old self. A youth once more. Naive and ridiculously hopeful. The abundantly talented violinist who had joked and drunk and sung and once declaimed the poems of Mayakovsky – 'Eat your pineapples, chew your grouse. Your last day is coming, you bourgeois louse' – through a megaphone from the Anichkov Bridge. His sister had laughingly shushed him – 'Let's go home, genius, time to sleep it off.'

After the arrest of their parents, he always felt protected by her. And always returned the favour; coming to blows with any slighted suitor who whispered against her, going into battle against any man who might take her name in vain. Once beating a swaggering brute of a naval officer into a bloody pulp.

As the drink warmed him, Rossel dragged on his cigarette again and kept flipping through the files, stopping at each image to reflect on the life into which he was intruding. Paying his respects and toasting every tenth individual with another slug of vodka. Offering them the momentary respect a godlier soul might pay to a religious icon. The portly midwife from Pskov with the dark hair and steely eyes, the spotty garage mechanic from Kalininsky, the plain-faced Narva teenager, gone missing on her way to a local dance, described by her grandmother as 'Unexceptional, save for her virtue.'

It was foolish, he knew, this ritual, this time he spent with the missing.

Save for the simple fact that his twin sister now lived amongst them too. How could she not do? She had to be somewhere. How could someone just disappear like that, drifting away one night into the snow? At the time, it had felt that a sinister stage magician had broken in while he was sleeping and sawed his soul in two, stealing away the better half of him.

He held the picture of the Narva teenager between the twisted but intact middle and index fingers of his left hand. Then placed it next to his ear – as if the girl was about to impart a secret. He thought of these mute, monochrome faces as Galya's only real friends now, the ones who kept his twin sister company. Until, one day, her brother would find her and rescue her, like a Slavic knight completing his quest. Earning redemption, perhaps forgiveness. The forgiveness he had sought ever since joining the Leningrad militia in an effort to track her down.

7

Monday October 15

All his fingers were present and correct, the missing ones restored, looking supple and elegant. Rossel waggled them, delighted, clicking the new ring finger on his left hand against the thumb.

He looked down again at the victim in the red gown, the Snow Queen. She was lying on the tracks but she had turned face down. That wasn't right – Rossel knelt and reached out to turn the body over but stopped when he saw his miraculous hands.

'Aren't those Stalin's fingers?' sneered Grachev. 'Have you stolen the hands of our great leader? That's ten years in the gulag . . .'

Rossel rolled the body. Her head lolled against her right shoulder. But instead of a mess of muscle and glimpses of skull, he was gazing into the face of his missing sister.

Woken by his own cry, Rossel cursed and clambered out of bed. The nightmare had drenched him in an icy sweat. He pressed a hand to his chest in a futile attempt to steady his heart.

It was too late to go back to sleep, even if sleep had been possible, but too early to do anything useful. He chain-smoked three *papirosy*, laid out his uniform and washed in cold water in the basin that stood in the corner of his room, wiping away the cold sweat of his disturbed sleep. At last, he got dressed, pulled on his boots, took a deep breath and knelt beside his bed.

First, he pulled out a dog-eared poetry book, Baudelaire's *Fleurs du Mal*. He leafed through its pages for a while before pressing the cover to his lips and putting it back where he had found it. The violin case was hidden under two or three bags of old clothes and bedding but he located it without trouble and dragged it out from under the bed. Rossel ran his palms across the cheap, battered leather and sprang the catches.

He picked up the bow and tightened the bow hair. Grasped the dry, crumbling rosin and ran it up and down the bow, exactly six times – a habit from his earliest lessons with his mother. Then he took the chin rest and the violin itself from the case and laid everything on his bed. He stood still, partly in reverence but also to decide on a piece. A Brahms sonata? A Wieniawski showpiece? No, the same piece he always chose – the Prokofiev he used to play in duet with his sister, the first movement, *andante cantabile*.

Rossel reached for the violin, grasping it with the thumb and two crooked fingers of his left hand and bringing it up to his shoulder. The violin settled into place. With his other hand he picked up the bow. His torturer had broken only the ring and little fingers of the right hand before that particular interrogation had ended, leaving them set in a slightly claw-like position that was oddly suited to his bow hold. He pulled away an errant bow hair and brought the bow to rest on the A-string. Allowed himself a bitter smile.

All those nagging teachers who had never stopped talking about the importance of finger placement.

Rossel stood completely still and in total silence. As he always did now – unable to play a single note.

But listening. Remembering.

Rossel replaced his fiddle, bow, chin rest and rosin. Shut the lid and snapped down the catches. Slid the case back under the bed. Then the lieutenant put on his militia cap, picked up his pistol and holster from the bedside table and headed for the door and the city beyond.

*

The snow was relentless and swirling into hallucinatory grey flurries. Rossel tried to pinch a little heat into his cheeks. Gerashvili drew up her greatcoat until her head had sunk into it up to the eyes. A few hardy shoppers, refugees from a nearby butcher's queue for pork and chicken, drifted past them as they stood in front of the imposing sandstone front of Passazh, a pre-revolutionary monolith to everything bourgeois and now a model Soviet department store. It faced Nevsky Prospect, the spine of the city centre, and ran down Sadovaya.

Rossel pushed through the heavy doors. Gerashvili, breathing with a slight wheeze as she drew the freezing air into her lungs, followed him.

They stepped into the entrance of the vast glass-roofed gallery that went back all the way to Italianskaya Street. There were maybe forty stores – doorways guarded by two sandstone columns and a white arched moulding above it – each one alike, on either side of the passage. The stone was dirty and discoloured in places but the repairs after the war were impressive. And how splendid that a relic of the *ancien régime*, when poor, ordinary folk would pay a few kopeks just to be allowed to gaze in awe at the fur coats, fine foods and exotic trinkets displayed in its luxurious stores, was now for the benefit of the Soviet people. Any citizen of old St Petersburg, who had spent a little time with their face pressed to these windows, would have needed little convincing of the need for a workers' revolution by the time Lenin had arrived at the Finland Station.

His mother had talked to him about Passazh once when he was a very young child. An accomplished violin player herself, she had been teaching him and his sister to play when she began to recall a concert she had once seen there as a girl – at the Komissarzhevskaya Theatre. How well the tenor had sung. How beautiful the white taffeta gowns worn by the chorus were. How, as she walked toward the theatre, the emeralds and pearls in the shop windows sparkled under the miraculous new gas lights.

The bourgeois stores were all gone. Replaced by stores for the workers displaying goods from all over the Soviet Union. When they had any in.

But if you knew where to look and you dared to look there, there was a shop about halfway down on the left-hand side with a softly lit window and fresh paint on the sill. A discreet sign in the window said: Djilas.

They walked another few feet and stood directly in front of the entrance.

Rossel looked at Gerashvili and she nodded.

He turned a faded brass handle and heard the tinkle of a welcoming bell.

*

As soon as they stepped in, Comrade Djilas had ushered them away from the shop floor, gleaming counters made from oak and glass, and mannequins wearing sable and mink, and led them into a poky back office.

He removed the magnifying loupe with which he had been studying the tiny ruby from his eye and put the earring back on the table.

Djilas – the name wasn't Russian, Rossel thought. Bulgarian? Serb? A Slav, anyway. The jeweller was tall and broad-shouldered with wide cheekbones and a high forehead. His thick black hair was speckled with grey, his eyes were a deep brown and somewhat elusive. But his nose and chin were weak, a fact he had tried to disguise by adopting a handlebar moustache.

His manner was aloof and untroubled, that of a man whose customers were the wives and girlfriends of the elite. It was calculated to convey, as effortlessly as was possible, the simple fact that two militia officers from Vosstaniya Street couldn't touch him. He tapped an imperious middle finger on top of the glass counter, next to the ruby set in its flowered gold clasp.

'Yes, very good. What the Americans call a "pigeon blood".'

'Pigeon?' asked Gerashvili.

He smiled.

'As rich and red as pigeon's blood. These ones are quite beautiful and of the very highest quality. From Burma, perhaps. Often thought of as being the place where the world's best rubies are mined – although, personally, as a good and loyal citizen of the Union of Soviet Socialist Republics, I, of course, prefer those that are unearthed in Tajikistan. The miners there have a joke. They say the fat capitalist mountains of Rushan wished to yield only diamonds so the ruby hunters read to them nightly from *Das Kapital* and persuaded all those white stones to turn red.'

Comrade Djilas, who, if he was not Russian, had no trace of an accent, began to laugh at his own story.

Rossel's face remained impassive. The joke was a mistake.

'I am surprised that the miners of Tajikistan would put at risk their production targets with the exchange of such inconsequential stories. Make a note of that will you, Junior Sergeant?'

'A note, sir?'

Gerashvili looked a little uncertain but she took out her notepad.

'Yes, a note to send to our esteemed colleagues of the Ministry of State Security in Dushanbe, this note to detail possible anti-Soviet activity amongst miners in the Rushan area. Time wasting, akin to wrecking. Exchanging superfluous stories that may be jeopardising Comrade Stalin's plans for state mineral production whilst filling their lungs with bourgeois laughter. Also, please include in this important message to the Ministry of State Security, Dushanbe, the name of our source: Comrade Djilas of the store of the same name, in the Passazh building, Leningrad. Who I'm certain

BEN CREED

is happy to make himself available, at any time, to undertake the four-thousand-kilometre journey to Dushanbe and testify against these unpatriotic Tajik miners.'

Gerashvili put her pad on the counter and began to scrawl across it with her pen. Djilas watched her filling the paper with black ink.

Rossel reached across and stilled Gerashvili's hand. Then he looked the jeweller straight in the eyes.

'Or perhaps there is no need for my colleague to file her report?'

Djilas licked his thumb and index finger and used the saliva to press down the two ends of his moustache.

'May I ask, is it possible, Lieutenant Rossel,' he said, 'to know where you acquired these earrings?'

Gerashvili opened her mouth but Rossel raised a hand. *We ask the questions. That's how it works.*

'Have you ever sold a pair of earrings like these?'

The jeweller shook his head.

'Have you ever stocked a pair of earrings like these?'

Djilas picked up the earring from the counter and then put it straight back down again.

'These, no. Never. The workmanship is very fine. I think they come from abroad.'

'Where?'

'Somewhere very grand. Other than that, I haven't a clue. Van Cleef and Arpels in Paris, or Tiffany in New York.'

'Junior Sergeant Gerashvili.'

'Yes, Comrade Lieutenant?'

'Have you any questions for Comrade Djilas?'

Gerashvili put her pen down and glanced around the untidy office. It was furnished with only a desk and a chair, a picture of Stalin on the wall and a framed photograph of a family, presumably one belonging to Djilas, stuck on top of a green metal safe near the door. The safe was large, perhaps two metres tall and a metre wide.

She walked across to it and tapped the front with her finger.

'Do you keep your sales ledgers in here?'

Rossel watched Djilas's left hand gently push shut a half-open drawer in his desk before he replied.

'I told you these earrings were not bought here. They are foreign, most certainly,' he said.

Rossel sighed and repeated Gerashvili's question.

'Do you keep your sales ledgers here?'

'No, the company has another office across town. Our daily receipts go there and the records are kept centrally.'

Gerashvili looked to Rossel for a lead.

'Then it is settled,' said Rossel. 'My colleague and I will leave but Junior Sergeant Gerashvili will return tomorrow and receive the sales ledger for the last ten years from you, Mr Djilas, in which case the Ministry of State Security in Dushanbe will not need to be informed of the treacherous counter-revolutionary comedians in their midst. And you will not have to travel four thousand kilometres to testify against them.'

'Settled. Yes, of course.' Djilas's voice was flat. The jeweller half-heartedly licked his thumb and finger again, as if to groom his grandiose moustache. But this time he failed to complete the gesture.

8

Lipukhin had been eating a sweet apple *pastila* to try and disguise the vodka on his breath. Like so many of his other plans, this one wasn't working.

The captain had been waiting in Rossel's office when Rossel got back to the station. He was reading that day's *Pravda*. The lead article was headlined 'Season of Traitors!' and outlined more details of the emerging Doctors' Plot – a conspiracy of 'killer doctors', predominantly Jewish, who had apparently been trying to assassinate the most senior leaders of the Soviet Union.

The captain flicked his eyes across to the framed portrait of Stalin on the wall.

'"From the wall Marx watches and watches, and suddenly, opening his mouth wide, he starts howling." Do you know the poem?'

Rossel nodded.

'Mayakovsky.'

It was hard to read Lipukhin. There was no endless stream of glorious war stories, not least because the dashing captain had been evacuated from Leningrad due to illness. No Stalingrad, no Kursk, no Berlin. But after the war he had shot to the rank of captain in record time – where he had stayed. Such a rapid rise suggested political reliability; such a sudden halt smelt of Stolichnaya.

'My mother read some of his works to me when I was a child,' Rossel continued, adding for safety: 'A great patriot.'

Lipukhin pointed to the black phone on top of the desk between where they both sat.

'Five corpses, found together like that, in one place. One of them a blue-top. It is unheard of. You filed your report yesterday. But only silence. They must be watching and yet no one has howled.'

Lipukhin drew a hand through the full head of blond hair that so suited the role of Soviet golden boy for which he had once seemed destined. But the once chiselled face was now a little softer and flabbier, his fine cheekbones already tinged with pink.

'Perhaps they trust us, Ilya?' said Rossel.

'Trust us?'

Lipukhin held Rossel's gaze as he repeated the question back to him. Then he wiped a last green fleck of the *pastila* from his lips.

Rossel picked up a small pile of photographs that lay on his desk – Taneyev had finished his developing. He spread them out in front of his boss.

'To do our Bolshevik duty?'

Lipukhin picked up one of the photographs. Then turned it around so they could examine it together. A faceless man stared back up at them.

'Of course, of course, our duty to the Party is always paramount,' Lipukhin murmured. 'Which one is this?'

Rossel stared at them and realised they had been taken in the morgue, not at the railway line where they had discovered the bodies. Taneyev must have considered them unusually interesting to leave them on his desk. He was right.

'The priest. The one we found wearing the dog collar. As you instructed, we have concentrated on the blue-top first and so I followed up on the earrings. But the priest is the latest victim the pathologist Dr Volkova has examined. The orderlies only stripped the corpse a few hours ago and discovered this inky treasure trove.'

The tattoos covered every inch of the naked torso. The lines were crudely inked but the drawings themselves were detailed and ornate. Just above his left nipple was an image of the Madonna and child. Above the right a coiled serpent, and above that a series of simple dots. On the back, stretching from one shoulder blade to another, a grinning Reaper, the outline of its cloak not black but blood red, and holding not a scythe but a hammer and sickle.

Only one group of people had tattoos like that: the thieves.

Lipukhin stared down at the photograph for a moment more. Then he pushed back his chair and stood up. The pitch of his voice was considered but also contained a slight undertone of embarrassment.

'Trust, yes. An important Bolshevik virtue, Lieutenant Rossel. And my trust in you is, as always, absolute. I have therefore given you entire jurisdiction in this case. Especially as it is one that may turn out to be of vital importance to the Party. I filed the relevant notifications this morning so as to inform the appropriate authorities of my decision immediately.'

Rossel did not look up. He could hear the fear in Captain Lipukhin's voice and did not feel the need to embarrass him any further by confronting his self-serving pragmatism directly. Something had happened between the conversation they'd had in the car on the way back from Lake Ladoga and now. Presumably, Lipukhin had calculated the odds on their collective survival and wasn't liking them very much. In Leningrad, people made decisions like that every day – to step away from wives, lovers, friends or colleagues as the icy waters began to rise. He was not in any way offended by Lipukhin's desire to save his own skin. He simply accepted it for what it was: a banal, personal case of *realpolitik*.

Rossel heard the glass rattle in its frame as the door to their room slammed shut. Lipukhin's footsteps faded away as he descended the stairs. Then Rossel stacked the photographs into a neat pile and slipped them into the brown case file. In the grate, an ember glowed and died. The fire had been neglected, or maybe they had run out of wood.

An ex-girlfriend at the conservatory had been very keen on Mayakovsky. The poet's father had pricked his finger on a pin when filing some papers, she told him, and subsequently died of blood poisoning. It was now clear to him that, unlike Mayakovsky Senior, Captain Lipukhin had a sound understanding of potentially dangerous paperwork.

*

Rossel undid his zip and emptied his bladder. He had stopped for a glass of vodka at a grubby *ryumochnaya* on the way home – his favourite place when he needed to retreat from the world. For when he needed to think. The first shot hadn't helped so he'd bought another. That hadn't helped, either, but at least it had fortified him for the ordeal of the toilet at his communal flat.

Old man Kostiuk had struck again. Rossel tried to hold his breath while he pissed so as not to breathe in the stench of his elderly neighbour's congealing faeces. Leningrad was built on a swamp and thousands had died toiling in the feverish, foetid air to turn Peter the Great's vision into reality. Rossel knew how they felt.

He shared the apartment with five other families. Sixteen people in all, crammed into six rooms. They all lived together on the fourth floor of a block that overlooked the Griboyedova Canal, and considered themselves lucky to have it. Living with the bitter aroma of Vladislav Kostiuk's repugnant turds was a small price to pay to live in an apartment like this one.

He couldn't hold his breath any longer. But as soon as he breathed out, the toxic odour began to scour the inside of his nostrils.

Mother of Christ!

A sharp drumming sound. Someone standing in the cold passage outside was knocking impatiently on the door.

'Is that you, Vladislav Gerasimovich? It is, isn't it? I can smell your stinking bumhole from out here. Hurry up, can't you? I need to pee like the Volga . . .'

No one else had a mouth like that, and in a *kommunalka* that was saying something. It was Lena, who lived with her younger sister, Irina, in room number three.

'It's me,' he answered. 'Give me a minute, Lenochka. Kostiuk's been here before me and my life is now in grave danger. I have only sixty seconds left before I am asphyxiated.'

Through the door he heard Lena laugh. 'It was borshch last night, Mrs Fyodorovna always cooks him borshch on Sunday nights. I think the beetroot must corrode his bowels.

That's why I generally try to not take a pee all day on a Monday. That tea was a grave tactical error.'

Rossel flushed the toilet and opened the door. He grinned as he stepped out and saw that Lena was now standing as far away from him as possible; next to the hat-rack near the front door of the apartment, piled high with the winter coats and scarves. As a child she'd run messages between infantry lines during the war.

He held the door wide open for her.

'Come, come, Lena, I know you are braver than that.'

'I am fearless, Comrade Rossel, but not suicidal.'

Rossel took a step towards the door of his own room, which was the second one from the right at the end of the main corridor. Behind him, Lena decided she had no option but to risk it and slammed the toilet door after her. If you lived in the same *kommunalka* for long enough, few subjects were taboo.

He stopped and called out through the door.

'Has she played tonight, Lena? Has she been playing *Oy, to nye vyecher*?' he said.

'No,' came the reply. 'Not last night, not for a week.' He heard her giggle. 'Are you in love or something?'

*

Ah, it is not yet evening. 'Oy, to nye vyecher' is a beautiful song.

Rossel's girlfriend, Sofia, would sometimes half whisper, half sing the Cossack folk song to him, on one of those distant days at the conservatory when they lay in bed together. It had been many years now but when he closed his eyes, he could still see her face: the olive-green eyes, so big and wide and questioning; the black, untidy mop of hair, grown long enough to cover the nape of her neck; the lips, far too wide and thin to make her, to the world, truly beautiful and yet to him, from the moment he saw her, she was perfect. She's like Magnus's *Frau*, he had said to himself when they bumped into each other in the corridor, just before their first lesson together. He had not long seen Eduard Magnus's painting of the enigmatic Swedish heiress, which hung in the Hermitage. A portrait of a woman who seemed to have permitted only the tiniest sliver of her true self to be observed by the artist, hiding the rest away from the world in some unreachable place.

And yet, when they were together . . .

'You're my Cossack,' she would tell him before they made love. 'Who comes running, first to rescue . . .' Sofia would roll on her back, put her hands behind her neck and stare into his eyes, '. . . and afterwards to *ravish* me.'

But often, just as he did as she commanded and matched his intensity to hers, she would giggle at his seriousness. Then they would both collapse into laughter.

Afterwards, she would instantly retreat again. Barely acknowledge his whispered questions. Reveal almost nothing of her self to him. Become Magnus's *Frau* once more.

Felix had been in love with her, too, he remembered. As much as it was possible for Felix Sorokin to love anyone other than himself. 'I so dearly want that sultry little dark-haired songstress to whisper me a lullaby,' his friend had told him. 'The way she sings unsettles me; makes me wish to be something better than myself.'

But Sofia hadn't sung for Felix. She had sung for her Cossack.

Oy, to nye vyecher . . .

Oy, it will surely come off, he said, that wild head of yours . . .

Rossel had always loved that line.

He got up from the faded green armchair, walked across his room and, even though it was still snowing, slipped the broken catch on the frame to open the window wider to see if he could hear the music of the guitarist on the floor above better.

Oy, to nye ny vyecher . . .

'*Ah, it will surely come off,*' he whispered to himself. '*Ah, it will surely come off, that wild head of yours.*'

Are you in love or something?

He had been once.

And it had meant everything.

9

Tuesday October 16

Gerashvili pulled on her thick leather gloves and regulation hat.

'Just the ledgers. That is all you need, Comrade Lieutenant?'

Rossel nodded. He picked up a pine log from the meagre pile by the fire grate and threw it into the flames. On the outside, he was calm, playing the part of the thorough, conscientious detective. But Lipukhin had sidestepped the investigation and put Rossel at its centre. It was hard, therefore, to put the threat of the MGB out of his mind – the invisible but merciless threat that haunted every Soviet citizen, dutiful or not. Failure would be unforgiveable. Failure would not merit mere demotion but a much more inventive punishment. And even success might be unwelcome, depending on what he found out.

But there was no point spooking Gerashvili with his fears. 'If Djilas has sold those earrings then there's a good chance they will be listed in there somewhere,' he said. 'Next to a purchaser, perhaps, who may be of interest in our enquiry?'

'He may have doctored them by now.'

'That's the trap I set for him by not removing them yesterday. Let's see if he is a fool. If he doctors the ledgers, under Article 58–14 of the Penal Code that would be classed as counter-revolutionary sabotage – deliberately careless execution of defined duties, aimed at the weakening of the power of the government and of the functioning of the state apparatus. And so he would be subject to at least one year's deprivation of freedom. Obstructing state investigators carries a further automatic sentence of eight years' deprivation of liberty.'

Yet as a man who handled luxurious items of foreign origin without making any attempt to disguise the fact, Djilas was also indubitably a man with political cover.

'Djilas strikes me as a man who likes the finer things in life and moves in circles where he can obtain them. I don't think he will do anything to jeopardise that. If he keeps his ledgers intact and unedited, we may learn something.'

The fireplace in the main room of the station was a grand one, cast in iron. A mixed motif of seabirds and a merchant's ship decorated its mantelpiece. The personal choice, presumably, of the silversmith who once owned the house before it became a police station after the revolution. Rossel watched as a pale blue flame began to lick and flutter around the wood.

Gerashvili walked towards the main door that led to the stairs. Then she turned back towards him.

'I took my niece to the ice rink in Tauride Gardens last night. She's only eleven but a very good skater. In a couple of weeks, she's going to the Soviet championships in Moscow.'

'I'm very happy for your niece.'

'Yes, sorry, Comrade Lieutenant. My point is, my niece wears earrings. They have clasps. Jana, my sister, thinks piercing is only for sluts from Sennaya.'

'So?'

'Those ruby earrings are small. Very small with clasps. I wondered if they might once have belonged to a child? Perhaps our faceless woman has a daughter?'

Grachev, fully dressed in his winter uniform, came through the door and marched to his desk. He glared at Gerashvili.

'You still here doing your make-up? Rossel and me have some proper work to do. We are, apparently, off to interrogate a dangerous subversive who has already served ten years' imprisonment in the hands of the great Soviet state.'

Rossel turned back towards Gerashvili and called after her as she left.

'Thank you, Junior Sergeant, you have made an excellent point.'

Then he picked up his own hat and gloves from the rack in the centre of the room and started to put them on. By the fireplace, Grachev stomped his feet. The flames had gone out.

'So we're off to see a source of yours, Rossel. Who is he?'

'I suppose you could say he is a reader.'

'A reader? Where are we going to meet the bastard, the State Library on Nevsky?'

'Not of books. A reader of bodies.'

Rossel adjusted his right glove and then straightened his hat. One of the seabirds carved into the mantelpiece was a little more tarnished than its companions. Something of an outcast. It reminded him of a Baudelaire poem, *The Albatross*, a favourite of Sofia's. When they were still together, she had read it to him many times. He reached out, as he often did before leaving the station, and touched one of its wings for good luck.

'A bootlegger I know. And occasional informer. Kirill Pugachev is a man who can read gulag tattoos in the same way one of those august university professors can read *Crime and Punishment*,' he continued, 'and then explain to two idiots like me and you, Sergeant, exactly what the artist meant by it.'

*

The reader of bodies sucked on his *papirosa* as he waved his other hand around his head and gestured to the wooden shack's three other customers. They were all nursing tin mugs of vodka around a small brazier in which a blackened log was trying to burn. By the smell of it, petrol had been used to get the thing alight.

'Can you believe that this place, a shitty *ryumochnaya* all the way out in Moskovskaya, has Armenian cognac?' said Pugachev. 'It's been months since I had so much as a dribble of the stuff. Hardly anywhere in Leningrad can a man get himself a glass of Ararat, but the fat babushka who runs this dump apparently has it running from the taps.'

Grachev glared at him.

'Perhaps she sucks cock at the Armenian trade delegation in her spare time?'

The babushka, a whale-like woman who was guarding a crate of dirty bottles in her own foul corner, swore at him.

Pugachev drained his glass and gasped as the fire went down.

'For cognac like this it would be worth it. For cognac like this I'd fucking do it myself.'

'Armenians are a dirty people,' Grachev said, mouth twisting.

'Says who?' said Rossel.

'Your file says you were a teacher?' continued the sergeant, ignoring him.

Pugachev nodded. He had taught art in Moscow before the war. He had even taught the children of some of the Politburo. The sons of Mikoyan. The daughters of Yezhov. He was a big man with a muscular neck and bald head, plus a flat and broken nose. The eyes that stared back at Rossel and Grachev over the little wooden table had been tutored by his time in the camps. They were calculating, secretive and as green as pond lichen.

'I was a good teacher, too, and my pupils loved me for it. Then one day I turned up for a life class and all the students were missing. Only the model had turned up – a red-haired dwarf from the Moscow State Circus. Then the double doors at the back of the class opened and two men in grey coats stepped through. I was taken directly to the Lubyanka and then, after a couple of weeks, sent to Siberia and spent ten years in a gulag. I never got to know why.'

Pugachev took another sip of his cognac. Then fixed Rossel with a stare.

'Does it give a reason?'

Rossel lifted up his own hand and waved away the smoke. The shack stank of cheap tobacco.

'Does what give a reason?'

'My file. Does my file give a reason for my arrest?'

Rossel ignored the question.

'Thank you for meeting us, Comrade Pugachev,' he said. 'I hear you are employed as a kitchen porter in the Hotel Astoria these days, cooking quail for those lucky few who are allowed – thanks to their exceptional service to the Party – to dine there.'

'What?' Grachev was surprised. 'I thought the thieves were barred from work by their code. The Astoria? Do you spread your buttocks for the Party, comrade?'

Pugachev spat into the fire and glared at Grachev.

'You're sure you're a cop? Because you know fuck all about anything, cop.'

Rossel smiled.

'Pugachev has special dispensation,' he said. 'He delivers bootleg vodka to the hotel and swaps it for the good stuff.'

'Our stuff is also good stuff – nobody has complained so far,' interjected Pugachev.

'And takes the good stuff off to be sold in backstreet markets for half the price but still four times the cost of production of the bootleg. In the service of the thieves, Comrade Pugachev is permitted to work, even at the service of the bigwigs who stay at the best hotel in town.'

'Best hotel? Do you know last week they ran out of toilet paper?' said Pugachev. 'Had to cut up a few old copies of *Pravda* and hang them on string same as the rest of us do. There was a Chinese delegation on the fifth floor, some bullshit about military assistance. I like to think of their vice chairman wiping his arse on the latest Ukrainian wheat production statistics.'

He leaned forward and took another puff on his cigarette.

'If *Pravda* is still printing all the sycophantic crap it was last time I bothered to read it then he's probably got a picture of Comrade Beria printed on each of his yellow arse cheeks.'

Grachev whistled.

'And you're looking for a reason they put you in the camps? We've only been here five minutes and you've already said enough to earn yourself another ten years.'

Pugachev stifled a yawn.

'One day they took me. I never knew why. Another day they released me. Ditto. There's a little freedom in that, Sergeant, if a man understands it properly. I can misbehave and be arrested, sure. But I can also behave and be arrested just the same. So why worry? I should be dead by now anyway after sawing pine logs through ten Siberian winters. It's minus fifty in the winter out there. Did you know that? A man can snap off his prick just trying to take a piss. In a place like that, a wise man looks for what protection he can get – and in the camps, that means joining the thieves.'

Pugachev stubbed out the remnants of his cigarette.

'They arrested the model, too – just in case, I assume,' he said. 'As far as I know that hapless dwarf never made it back to the circus.'

He rapped his tin mug on the tabletop. The babushka looked up from behind her counter and nodded.

'These two are paying,' Pugachev told her.

He turned back to the militia officers.

'You say you have some ink to show me?'

*

'Interesting.'

Pugachev tapped the photograph that Grachev was holding up, the one of the priest. His nicotine-stained middle finger pointed to an area just below the shoulder.

'A bunch of dots,' said Rossel. 'What's so interesting?'

'It means he's been in solitary in a punishment block. Not just once. Each dot denotes a confinement. Ten marks, like this guy has got, means ten times.'

'A troublemaker? Someone the guards and other inmates would remember?' said Rossel.

Pugachev nodded.

'A man would have to be a little crazy to put himself in harm's way like that so often. Even I would pass on those odds.'

'A boss, then?' said Grachev. The thieves had their own code and their own hierarchy; in the gulag, bosses had as much power over life and death as the state.

'No. There's no tattoo that marks him out that way. And a boss doesn't often get solitary. They get others to do the dirty work.'

'What about this one? The coiled serpent?' asked Rossel.

Pugachev took the photograph with one hand and peered closer. He prodded a finger of the other against the snake above the man's right nipple.

'It's nicely done. But lots of prisoners have those,' he said. 'It could be drugs. Or it simply expresses polite surprise at being so often ill used by our glorious Soviet state.'

He pointed at the red reaper holding the hammer and sickle.

'This one is unusual, though. I've seen plenty of reapers but not one that is holding a hammer and sickle before.

And not on the shoulder. Or red. Never red. Gulag inkings are rarely coloured as the ink is made in the camps and it's too difficult to get the pigments.'

'How do you make the ink in the camps?' asked Rossel.

'Ashes, burnt tyre, soot, mixed in with a mug of urine. Lasts a lifetime,' said Pugachev.

Grachev yawned.

'This is going nowhere, Rossel. We've been here for half an hour already. I'm going outside – my bladder's about to burst. When I come back, I suggest we take Comrade Pugachev back to Vosstaniya Street and get him to confess to something.'

'Confess to what?' asked Pugachev. The green eyes that stared up at Grachev contained not a single note of apprehension.

Grachev shrugged and pushed his way past a couple of customers towards the shack's front door.

'He's an angry man, your colleague,' said Pugachev. 'I remember you are a little more on the patient side, Lieutenant? Patient enough to send the occasional symbol of your appreciation my way as compensation for violating the thieves' code.'

Rossel was already handing him half a dozen notes. Traditional thieves claimed to shun all contact with the state, scorning anyone who cooperated with the state. Occasionally, however, it was deemed worth bending the rules in order to have a line to a militia officer. As long as he left them largely alone.

'If you have anything else to tell me, I'll listen,' said Rossel.

Pugachev leafed through the photographs, straining to pick out details in the dim orange light. Behind him one of the other drinkers slumped forward off his chair and onto the floor. The babushka tutted.

The rest of the priest's flesh was a confused whorl of cupolas, angels and saints at prayer. Pugachev frowned as he traced them with a finger. 'There's something not right,' he said.

Rossel waited as the thief continued tracing. Grachev reappeared. 'Right. Are we going to arrest this arsehole or what?' he said. 'This is a joke. This prick is wasting our time.'

His voice trailed away. Pugachev had pulled his shirt and sweater off in one movement.

The glow from the light bulb dangling at one end of the shack, barely augmented by the sputtering brazier, was weak but it was enough. Pugachev stood before them, covered in black markings.

'This one,' he said, pointing. 'A tsarist medal. I got it for beating up a guard. It was my first tattoo. It signified my acceptance into the thieves' law. These – the devil's head. Says fuck you to the system. The sword and shield – loyalty to my boss, while the burning book is the life I left behind. All symbols of a thief who lives by the thieves' law. I've got more, but' – he nodded in the direction of the babushka – 'there's a lady present.'

Pugachev replaced his shirt and poked at the photographs the two cops had brought with them.

'Your man, he has cupolas but they could mean anything – faith, or atheism, time in the camps, number of people he has killed, anything. You can only tell from the other tattoos. Is he a killer, a burglar, a rapist, what? He has no cross, and *every* thief has a cross. Everyone's ink tells a story. Except his.'

'So what?' said Grachev. 'He could have been a political.'
Pugachev sneered.

'A political with ink? The thieves would have scoured it off his skin with a fucking cheesegrater. No, your man has got almost the full suit, front and back, and yet he's not a thief. And that makes him a real mystery.'

Rossel leaned forward and pointed to the red reaper.

'What about that one? Can you give me any idea what the rest of that tattoo might look like?'

Pugachev stared down at the photograph.

Then back up at Rossel.

He shook his head.

'No,' he said. 'But I think I know someone who may do. If you're willing to take the risk of meeting him?'

10

Wednesday October 17

The thin glass tube Dr Volkova had extracted from the throat of the corpse they had christened the Snow Queen was glowing. Rossel pushed the head of the desk lamp a little closer. The tube lay in a metal tray on a small table inside the pathologist's lair. It was about 22 centimetres long, 3 centimetres wide at the base, tapering to a point but fluted, so it gradually tapered upwards to become a few centimetres wider at the other end. The end that had been sticking into the Tsarevna's larynx was jagged and tainted with blood.

'Do you think our maniac might be a chemist, Doctor? Or some other kind of scientist?'

Dr Volkova shrugged.

'There is no manufacturer's mark. Besides, although I am clearly not a research scientist, I did study both chemistry and human biology before I specialised in forensic pathology and I have never come across a pipette, burette or graduated cylinder shaped exactly like this one.'

'Burette?'

'Used by analytical chemists to dispense variable amounts of chemical solutions.'

Rossel gestured towards the tube.

'May I?'

Dr Volkova nodded.

He whipped off his leather gloves and picked up a pair of white latex ones that were lying on the table. Out of the corner of his eye he saw the pathologist looking at him as he struggled to get them on; in the end he had to tug at them with his teeth to pull the flaccid tips over his crooked, clumsy fingers. Turning back, he lifted up the tube and examined it more closely.

'Perhaps used to administer a drug?' he asked.

'It would be an unusual vessel. Besides, apart from blood and traces of sputum from the larynx, the tube does not contain any other substances. To me, it looks like it was made by a master craftsman at the Gusevskoi Crystal Factory, not churned out by a laboratory products machine. But your theory about a drug, at least, may have some substance. Our tattooed priest has a series of puncture marks around his left ankle. The same goes for the blue-top.'

Rossel rested the tube back on the metal tray. Then he removed the gloves.

'You have been carrying out autopsies without informing me?'

Dr Volkova shook her head. 'No. It is too soon. I was once present at an autopsy on a frozen body that had not been left to thaw for long enough. It was still solid in the middle. The pathologist persisted out of stubbornness but soon found it was like scraping out the icebox in a refrigerator.'

This was said with relish.

'However, this case is unique so I have been taking a look every so often. There are pressure sores over the shoulder blades, buttocks and heels. Also, over some parts of the spine, and in some cases on one ankle.'

'What does that mean?' asked Rossel.

'Sores develop when a subject is kept immobile for long periods. The irregular pattern suggests confinement in an enclosed space, not necessarily on a flat surface such as a bed or stretcher. That, in turn, could imply sedation.'

'They were drugged?' Rossel's eyebrows shot up. 'What with?'

'I cannot be sure. An obvious candidate from a medical point of view would be phenobarbital, a barbiturate. But an opiate would also do the job.'

'Can they both cause death?'

'Yes.'

'Anything else?' asked Rossel.

'As I say, until I have done a . . .'

'A proper examination, I know. Time is against us, Doctor. I need answers,' snapped Rossel.

Volkova looked hurt.

'Obviously, they all look thin. So, muscle wastage is certain and I expect to see loss of fat layers when I get down to business.'

'Sedation and starvation. That would imply long, slow deaths. With the killer keeping a close eye on the gradual degradation of the victims.'

Dr Volkova flicked a switch and the desk lamp went out. The morgue felt instantly colder in the semi-darkness.

'A murderer who first starves his victims, drugs them, then kills and mutilates them,' she murmured. 'An unusual *modus operandi*, don't you think, Lieutenant? Abnormal, even for a maniac.'

She moved closer in the gloom.

'We live in a city where only eight years ago they lifted a siege that killed close to a million people,' Rossel said. 'Where the cats had to wolf down the rats if they wanted to finish their breakfast before the citizens wolfed down both the cats, the rats and anything else still able to scurry through the bomb craters. Where some husbands ate their wives and some mothers dined on their own children. In those dark years, many people went well beyond normality. It would be no surprise to me if some of them never made it back.'

Dr Volkova turned away from him and stared down at the tube on the tray. She reached out and switched the lamp back on again. And then pointed to the thin curved glass lip at the pipe's larger end.

'My grandfather played in the Admiralty Navy band. Above his mantelpiece at home, next to his navy cap and a chest full of service medals, was a cornet. This looks like that.'

'A cornet? You think our Snow Queen played the cornet in a navy band?'

'No, of course not. It's just the shape of this tube. It being like that makes me wonder if it has been designed to amplify some kind of sound.'

The cynical twinkle in Rossel's steel-grey eyes faded.

'What kind of sound?'

Dr Volkova thought for a moment. Then shrugged.

'You're right. I'm being foolish and seeing similarities that don't exist. You know, Comrade Lieutenant, you are the music man, someone who studied violin at our famous conservatory. Destined for great things, so the rumours go.'

She glanced down at Rossel's gloved hands.

'The rumours, as it turns out, were correct,' he said. 'There can be no greater destiny than to serve the Soviet people, keep order in society and guard against counter-revolutionary tendencies.'

He picked up the glass tube. He held it close to the jagged end so the glass lip of the cylinder occupied the space between them. In the semi-darkness, it looked like a small flower that was about to bloom.

'I don't know about a sound, Dr Volkova. But whoever made this certainly intended it to amplify something.'

Volkova angled the lamp up so the beam shone through the tube, which now became a sinister prism casting a shimmering ripple of light; tiny fluorescent petals began to dapple the ceiling.

She frowned.

'Amplify what, then?'

Rossel took a moment to consider his answer.

'Fear. For the mind that conceived and manufactured this strange instrument, it is possible simple fear was not enough and only absolute terror would do.'

There was a sharp knock at the door. Rossel and Dr Volkova both stepped back from each other.

Junior Sergeant Taneyev's grey face poked around the door. He was sweating at the temples; looking more agitated than usual.

'The captain wants to see you, Comrade Lieutenant.'

'I will be there in five minutes.'

'No, I mean, sorry, but Captain Lipukhin was most insistent. He said now.'

Rossel handed the tube back to the doctor and picked up his cap from the table.

'Trouble?'

Taneyev nodded. 'It's Gerashvili, Comrade Lieutenant.'

'Gerashvili?'

'The captain says she has gone. That she's missing.'

'Missing?'

'Yes, since yesterday. She never returned from that high-class jeweller in Passazh.'

Rossel put on his cap and twisted the rim a half a centimetre to the right so it was perfectly centred.

'I'll take a car and go to her apartment. I'm sure there's a simple explanation. It's unlikely she been abducted by foreign agents, Sergeant.'

Taneyev took a grey handkerchief from his pocket and wiped some of the sweat from his brow.

'No, Comrade Lieutenant. The captain doesn't think she's been abducted, either.'

'Well, then.'

'He thinks she's been arrested.'

ACT 2

11

Thursday October 18

A thin winter sunlight was seeping from behind two bilious clouds. On both sides of Nevsky Prospect, lines of shop girls and office workers bumped and jostled each other in fur coats, scarves and hats as they competed to get home from work before yet more snow fell, as the radio had warned. As their car sped past the Museum of the History of Religion and Atheism, Rossel stared out of the passenger window through the rain towards the brightly lit glass globe on top of the House of Books. His mother had bought him a biography of Rimsky-Korsakov from there for his birthday – his thirteenth? There was a grainy photograph of the composer in its middle pages. Dark eyes stared out through small round glasses. They were the eyes of a detective, he remembered thinking – shrewd and penetrating. Lieutenant Rimsky-Korsakov. Perhaps the good comrade composer could help him solve this case. He certainly did not feel up to it on his own.

And now Gerashvili was missing.

Lipukhin spun the wheel and pulled the car into a side street at the back of Passazh department store. The captain's face was even pinker than usual. He must have upped his vodka ration – he had been reading *Pravda*'s article about the 'Season of Traitors!' just before the news of Gerashvili's disappearance came through.

Both men jumped out of the car and stood side by side in the busy street. Rossel cupped his gloved hands to guard the flame from his match and lit a cigarette, an Elbrus.

'Nothing seemed different when I went to her apartment,' he said. 'She shares it with a couple of nurses from Hospital 40 in Sestroretsk. Except, of course, that she wasn't there.'

'She's been missing since yesterday morning,' said Lipukhin, 'when she went out to pick up the sales ledgers as you had requested. She signed out of the station at 10.35 and never signed back in. It was nearly the weekend so Sergeant Taneyev just assumed that she was as administratively incompetent as him and would arrive back all bright-eyed and bushy-tailed this morning.'

'But Gerashvili is always punctilious.'

'Exactly so.'

'You have had official notification of an arrest, Captain?' asked Rossel.

'No, I have not.'

'Then what makes you so certain?'

Lipukhin turned his head to the right and nodded towards the doorway of a shop. Rossel followed him. Opposite them stood the wire shelves of a newspaper kiosk, each stacked high with copies of *Pravda*, sweets for children and cigarettes. A headline in *Trud*, the union newspaper, caught his eye.

MORE ARRESTS OF TRAITOROUS ELEMENTS. Comrade Beria calls for unrelenting vigilance against counter-revolutionary conspirators.

'I rang our beloved MGB comrades of the Bolshoi Dom first thing this morning to report her disappearance, as you would expect,' said Lipukhin.

'And?'

'Someone took my call and made a note of the incident but otherwise did not react. Even in a week like this one, it's not every day a junior sergeant of the militia goes missing.'

'No.'

'He didn't sound at all surprised. He knew exactly where our girl is. I can feel it in my gut.'

'The cells of the Bolshoi Dom?'

Lipukhin nodded and pointed to the doors of Passazh.

'I think you and Gerashvili must have upset some very important people when you went to see your friend Djilas in there.'

Rossel dropped his cigarette butt onto the slushy pavement and ground it under the heel of his boot.

'Let's go and upset that stuck-up prick a little bit more then, shall we?'

The captain hesitated, but Rossel was determined.

'Or you could leave this entirely to me, Comrade Captain. Like you said yesterday.'

Captain Lipukhin's cheeks went almost rouge.

'Watch yourself, Lieutenant. That was then. I can hardly step back from a case that involves the disappearance of one of my own team. It would be a gross dereliction of duty.' The captain sighed and nodded. 'Anyway, Djilas must be a Serb. Foreign name. I never did like Serbs. Treacherous bastards.'

Lipukhin sounded calm but, as he adjusted his cap, his fingers were quivering.

*

When they arrived in front of the jewellers, the metal shutters were pulled down and the neon sign switched off. Comrade Djilas's oiled moustache and his sparkling trinkets were nowhere to be seen. Rossel and Lipukhin looked around the almost empty arcade. A middle-aged woman with the wrinkled face of an eighty-cigarettes-a-day smoker and erratically dyed red hair peeping out from under her knitted headscarf was closing up a flower shop two doors down.

They walked towards her.

'Djilas, Comrade Djilas, the jeweller, have you seen him today?'

'No, not today,' she said. 'Not since yesterday when they took him.'

'They?'

She looked first at Lipukhin, then at Rossel and sniffed a couple of times, as though she didn't much like what she saw.

'Not your lot. These had blue hats with steel stars on them, and much shinier boots.'

Lipukhin glanced down at his left boot. There was a splattering of mud on it.

'State security, then?' he said.

She pulled down the shutter and twisted a rusty key in a padlock to close it. Then stood up, pushing the dark roots of her hair back under the scarf as she did so.

'Like I say, shinier shoes.'

*

Taneyev was stuffing his face with sauerkraut and sausage, shovelled down with the aid of a clump of black bread that he dropped back onto the plate as soon he saw them walking into the office. He jumped up, looking agitated – looking old.

'Where's Grachev?' Lipukhin demanded.

'Gone, Comrade Captain. He grabbed his coat and just left about two hours ago. He didn't say where.'

'Any sign of Dr Volkova?'

'She is in the morgue, Captain.'

Lipukhin swivelled on his heel and slammed the door behind him. Taneyev turned towards Rossel.

'More trouble, Comrade Lieutenant? I can't stop with the sauerkraut and sausage this week. I get that way when things get tense around here. And then there's all this stuff in the papers about . . .'

Taneyev's voice trailed away. 'And why is the captain so angry?'

Rossel took off his coat and hung it on a hat stand near the fireplace with the carved wrought-iron seabird on it. Then he grabbed the chair from Grachev's desk, turned it around and sat down opposite Taneyev.

'The captain is angry, comrade, because he has decided to take charge of this case and become a proper policeman again. For now, at least.'

'Oh,' said Taneyev. 'And how is the case progressing?'

'The jeweller from Passazh, the one Gerashvili went to see, has gone, just like her. So, now we have five bodies, a missing junior sergeant and a witness who has vanished like a rabbit in a cheap magician's hat. Arrested, most probably. Like Gerashvili.'

Taneyev swallowed.

'Do you think they'll . . .?'

Rossel took another stumpy Elbrus out of his jacket pocket and wondered how many he'd had that day. He lit it anyway.

'I don't think, Junior Sergeant. Not about things like that.'

'It's just – I have a daughter, sir. A son, too. A talented boy. Zenit are looking at him. I want to spend my retirement watching him play football, not . . .'

He tailed off again. There was a tear in his eye.

Rossel got up and walked towards the fireplace.

'Then I suggest you try this.'

'I'm sorry,' said Taneyev. 'I don't understand.'

Rossel beckoned and the sergeant stepped towards him. Rossel tapped the faded metal bird with the tip of the middle finger of his left hand.

'My father told me once that luck was not worth the worship she got from desperate gamblers as she was more of a "reactionary bourgeois slut", distributing her favours to the few and not the many. Both capricious and elitist, which is a tricky combination. On occasions, those days and weeks when I, too, am nervous, I try to placate her nevertheless.'

Taneyev looked at the bird. Then glanced at Rossel's twisted hands.

'Are you sure it works?'

'It has to be worth a try, Comrade Sergeant. I'm still here, at any rate.'

When Taneyev had joined the militia, it had been a revolutionary mob in uniform – brutalised children with no homes to go to, proletarians settling scores with their one-time bosses, peasants with an astounding capacity for violence. Three decades had professionalised it to a very limited degree. Who knew what Taneyev had seen over the years? Who knew what he had already done to survive?

The ageing sergeant stared at the fireplace, mesmerised.

'What sort of bird is it?' he asked

'No idea,' said Rossel.

Taneyev nodded and wiped his eyes, as if that made all the sense he needed it to make, and everything had become clear.

'I have a name for you, Comrade Lieutenant,' he said. 'A name on one of the females – the blue-hat. I've been through all the available missing persons reports and perhaps, I think, maybe, I have a match that might fit her.'

Rossel's smile was a thin one.

'Perhaps, I think . . . maybe. Such confidence. And you wait until now to tell me?'

Taneyev bowed his head.

'Give me the file anyway,' said Rossel. 'I'll take a look.'

He gestured towards the fireplace.

'But first, being capricious and a little bourgeois, the lady demands her payment.'

Taneyev handed Rossel the manila file, before reaching out a hand towards the tarnished seabird.

Rossel opened the file and stared down at the face of a chubby blonde-haired woman.

'Nadya?' he mumbled to himself.

He looked up at Taneyev but it was too late – he had given himself away.

The file slipped from his hand and spilled papers onto the floor. Hurriedly, he bent down to pick them up.

The old sergeant looked like he was going to be sick.

'You know her, Lieutenant? You know our victim?'

'Not know. Knew. She was no more than an acquaintance, really.'

Even to Rossel, it sounded like a lie. As though he was already rehearsing how he might answer the first question of his next Bolshoi Dom interrogation. Aiming for nonchalance. But, just as everyone did, failing.

12

In the photograph in the file, her face was not quite how Rossel remembered it. Nadya was fatter around the cheeks and neck. Her hair was dyed blonde and worn in a bun pinned tight to the scalp. She must have been one of the countless millions of Soviet women who had seen Tamara Markova in *The Stone Flower* and copied the look. 'Majestic Markova. Seen for the very first time in glorious colour!' is what the posters outside the cinemas had said. That's just what Nadya would have done, he thought. She'd always had her heart set on being somebody important.

But the mouth was exactly the same. Small, secretive, unsmiling. 'Like the last smear of sour cream, Revol, squeezed from a baker's pipe,' as Felix Sorokin, his closest friend at the conservatory, had once put it.

Rossel looked up from the black and white shot in the manila file and fixed an expression on his face – half matter-of-fact, half purposeful.

'Yes. I do know her. Knew her.'

Lipukhin's face was granite.

'You knew her. How . . . interesting.'

Rossel glanced up at Taneyev, who was standing next to Captain Lipukhin's desk.

'How did you track the file down, Comrade Junior Sergeant Taneyev?'

With everyone so tense, crushing formality had become the order of the day.

'I just did as you said, Comrade Lieutenant – I mean, I did what Gerashvili was in the middle of doing. I checked all the places where people are allowed lots of foreign travel: the Kirov, trade missions, diplomats. I even tried the football team – FC Zenit went on a tour to China this year. My boy was hoping to go with the juniors but . . .'

Lipukhin slapped the palm of his hand on the desk.

'Your son's level of athletic competence is of no concern to me or Lieutenant Rossel, comrade. *Get on with it.*'

Taneyev jumped.

'Yes, Comrade Captain, I beg your pardon. I was thorough. It took me a while. I had to rule a few people out but then, well, Junior Sergeant Gerashvili had done all the hard work. I just had to make some phone calls.'

'She had?'

'Gerashvili had requested missing persons lists from every police department in Leningrad,' said Taneyev. He paused to blow his cheeks out in admiration. 'Then she had got hold of a list of Leningraders with permission to travel abroad from the central administrative department of the Leningrad Communist Party. How the hell she thought to get that, I have no idea.'

Like the earrings, Rossel thought. A hunch, but a smart one.

'Then she had cross-checked the two and ended up with fifteen names,' finished Taneyev.

Lipukhin mopped his brow. 'You're telling me there are fifteen people with permission from the Party to travel abroad who are all missing?'

'No, Comrade Captain. Almost all of them acquired a permit to live in a new place – Moscow, mainly, though also Pskov, Kuibyshev, Murmansk, others. The paper trail is clear and every permit and registration is official. Only three remain untraced, and only one is a woman. I called the Kirov Opera and they confirmed it. Missing for nearly six months now, since the middle of April.'

'Hold on,' said Lipukhin. He looked over one shoulder and then the other. Both doors leading to the office were closed but that was scarcely enough. 'It's ten to six – they'll give us the weather soon. I have a difficult journey home.' The captain crossed the room and turned on the radio. A crackling Tosca began to sing – it was a great aria, *Vissi d'arte*; anyone listening in, by microphone or with a glass to the door, would find it harder to pick out their words.

'She might not be anyone on that list,' Lipukhin said as the radio began to emit a high-pitched warble. 'She might be a real MGB officer, in which case the usual bureaucratic system won't know anything about her.'

'True,' said Rossel. 'What's worse, even if that is Nadya, she could still be an officer of state security. That would explain her ability to simply disappear. But I doubt it. If she was a real MGB agent, would they not have carted her off five minutes after we brought her in?'

Lipukhin swore. He yanked open a drawer and pulled out a bottle of vodka. More rummaging uncovered three glasses.

'Unless she was very low level, perhaps. An informant of little consequence?'

Rossel stood, leaned over the desk, picked up the bottle and shut it in one of the drawers. The captain let out a cry of protest and extended a finger with the intention of wagging it and demanding his vodka back but realised how that would look and sank back in his chair, deflated.

Taneyev's eyes flitted from one superior to the other. 'There is more, comrades. The last time anyone at the Kirov saw her was shortly after the company had returned from a foreign tour. There had been a dispute of some sort, apparently, between this Nadya and one of the soloists she was meant to look after – she was a dresser.'

'Oh, of course, a dresser,' said Lipukhin, in a tone that said, '*dresser, my arse*'. They all understood. It made sense now – Nadya being MGB. Her role was clear: to spy on the company and keep an eye on them in foreign jurisdictions. And to stop them defecting. A mere informant would never have been so trusted.

'Nadya Bazhanova,' said Rossel. 'Same height as the Nadya I knew, same approximate age, according to Dr Volkova's calculations. A clarinettist. No great talent but always practising. If all it took to be a genius was hard work then little Nadya would rank amongst the greats.'

Lipukhin leaned forward in his chair and picked up the photograph.

'Little Nadya is dead, Revol. Somebody cut your friend's face off and left her out on the railway lines at Lagoda. Genius or not, she won't be playing at the Maly Hall again.'

Rossel shrugged and closed the file.

'She wasn't a friend. She was a hanger-on. Someone on the periphery of people I once knew. That was Nadya, always out on the edge of things, calculating how she could propel herself towards the middle. According to her file she never did play the Maly Hall. She was, as Comrade Taneyev says, a dresser with the Kirov, attached to one of the star sopranos. Back then she always tried to hide it but, as I say, Nadya was ambitious. I can't imagine that being a dresser was something she'd have enjoyed settling for. She had grand plans for herself. I had a friend at the conservatory, Felix Sorokin, who absolutely despised her. Felix used to say she was like Uriah Heep in high heels.'

Taneyev took out his notebook and prepared to make a note.

'Yuri who, sir?'

Lipukhin sighed.

'Uriah Heep, Comrade Taneyev.' He gave the name a great guttural rasp. 'A character in a novel by the English author Dickens.' Dickens, a great chronicler of capitalist injustice, was still safe to read, even if he was a foreigner.

Rossel looked up at Taneyev.

'Nearly six months, you said? That's a long time to be missing. Did they report it straightaway?'

'When they got back, yes, they did.' Taneyev flipped to the last page of the notebook. 'They had been on a tour of Spain and France. Six weeks in all. A big success, that's what the deputy manager of the Kirov told me. They had played Paris for ten nights, the Palais Garnier in the 9th Arrondissement. Everything was going really well but then there was an argument, apparently.'

'An argument?'

'Yes, between this Nadya and Marina Morozova, the opera singer she was assisting as dresser. Immediately on returning to Leningrad, Bazhanova went missing. And they haven't seen her since.'

Rossel got up and pushed his chair back under Lipukhin's desk. Lipukhin got up, too. Tosca serenaded all of them.

Diedi gioielli della Madonna al manto,
E diedi il canto agli astri, al ciel . . .

'What was it about? Did he say?' asked the captain.

The sergeant put his notebook back in his pocket and straightened his shoulders.

'Jewellery, sir. This prima donna, Marina Morozova, reckoned Comrade Lieutenant Rossel's old friend Nadya had stolen some of her jewellery.'

13

Rossel opened his eyes just as the last bars of the music faded away.

He knew the Kirov Theatre intimately – it was directly opposite the conservatory and he and his fellow students had been there countless times to watch rehearsals and performances. Yevgeny Mravinsky had been the maestro there. Now Mravinsky had moved on to the Leningrad Philharmonic and the Kirov's chief conductor was Karl Eliasberg, whose task it was to grapple with *The Blockade*, a new opera commissioned by Stalin himself to honour the tenth anniversary celebrations of the Road of Life. A poster in the foyer proclaimed the premiere was due on November 19. It was to be the culmination of two whole weeks of Party-sponsored trade shows, meetings and events.

Exactly ten years earlier, Captain Mikhail Murov and his transport regiment had carried the first supplies over the ice of Lake Lagoda using a horse-drawn sleigh. The road had initially borne only small amounts of flour into the besieged city, but this was not important. It had given the citizens of Leningrad a different kind of nourishment – hope. A heady moment of optimism that allowed those starving in the bombed cellars, or the wretched souls feverishly twisting and turning in the few remaining hospital beds, to believe that something other than death was to be their fate.

Felix had always been rude about the Kirov – 'The inside is like a Venetian brothel and the outside is like a provincial train station, the kind of thing they built in Kazan or Sverdlovsk to make themselves feel as big and clever as Leningrad.' But then Felix was rude about everything. The theatre itself was, indeed, a riot of velvet and gold leaf. But from the very first moment Rossel had stepped inside it as a student, he had fallen in love with it, and he felt that love rekindling as the music curled around him. It had been too long since he had attended the opera.

The orchestra was having difficulty with the piece, particularly the brass, who bore the brunt of the composer's efforts to depict the frozen lake, the groaning and cracking of the ice beneath the feet of Murov's team, the wind's howling as it swept over the ice, and then, in its last few moments, the distant wail of a lone fighter. It was by turns violent and melancholic, and by the sound of it, technically almost impossible. Yet in the fragments the musicians were conquering, Rossel could hear how the composer had captured the primal essence of the siege, a rhythmic beast hidden deep in the Ladoga pine forests roaring defiance back across the rooftops of the distant city, out towards German Army Group North. Even though the auditorium was almost completely empty, Rossel could sense how tens of thousands of Soviet patriots would soon rise to their feet to applaud it.

The abrupt stilling of the timpani ushered in an unnerving silence. Then a colossal figure, chin on hands, leaned forward from the shadows of an unlit grand balcony just to the left of the main stage.

The giant clambered to his feet. He was almost two metres tall, Rossel reckoned, with a barrel-like chest and shoulders like haunches of venison. His face looked like a bronze bust, at once animated and monumental, as if the cast had only moments earlier been stripped from the sparks of a furnace. His physical presence alone was intimidating; a bear buttoned into a suit from which, at any second, it might tear itself free. Even before he spoke a word, the sheer force of the man's personality filled the auditorium.

Nikolai Nikolayevich Vronsky. 'Second only to Shosta-kovich in the great pantheon of twentieth-century Soviet composers,' as *Izvestia's* music critic had once called him. Vronsky had, it seemed, at last returned to the brilliant form of his precocious youth. Right now, however, he looked far from happy.

Vronsky stood, glaring down into the orchestra pit – a lord surveying his domain. He tapped the backs of two gold-ringed fingers on the brass rail of the box; drumming out a steady beat as he did so. Scratched, momentarily, at his thick black beard. Then he picked up a score from the music stand in front of him and began – very slowly – to rip it to pieces.

'You cockroaches.'

Vronsky threw the torn paper up into the air. The ninety mute faces in the pit stared up as it fluttered down towards them.

'I will have you all shot, do you hear me? No, not shot, hung, no, not hung, too quick, decapitated! No, not decap-itated, too merciful. Drowned, yes, drowned but slowly,

BEN CREED

one at a time. I will call the people I need to call and have them stand you all on your heads on the shores of Lake Ladoga. And then I will kneel down on the banks of that godforsaken pond and pray, yes pray, for the Lake Gods to turn its waters into ten million gallons of beery German piss and then, do you know what I will do? I will *wait*; wait with a big fat smile on my bearded face, for the tide to come in.'

Vronsky pointed directly at a small grey-haired man in the orchestra pit.

'That's what I will do to you, Karlof, the next time you give me a false, farting note on that trombone of yours so abysmally poor that even a deaf mute who has gouged out their own eardrums with a hatpin can tell it is an abomination.'

Karlof's face went a deep crimson. He started to stutter out a reply.

'I'm sorry . . . Maestro . . . I . . . don't . . . I . . . I'm . . .'

'Don't try and tell me what you are, Karlof. I decide what you are. And that is an epic reactionary bourgeois fool who wants to destroy my music. And when a man tries to do that, Karlof, do you know what he is trying to do?'

Karlof looked as though he wanted the sticky red carpet of the orchestra pit to rise up and swallow him. He shook his head.

'He is trying to destroy my *reputation*.'

A woman sat down in the seat next to Rossel. Her perfume was expensive, unfamiliar, heavy with musk. Nothing like that available in the shops of Leningrad. The scent drew him in. He turned away from the confrontation. She smiled.

'The maestro is nervous today, I think. Somewhat at odds with himself. He can be the sweetest of men, I assure you.'

She held out a perfectly manicured hand.

'Marina Morozova. The deputy manager said an officer of the militia had come . . . '

She stopped in mid-sentence.

'Hello, Marina,' Rossel said.

'Revol.'

Rossel nodded.

There was a commotion above them and an anxious murmur from the pit. Rossel and the singer both looked up. In a surprisingly graceful movement for such a big man, Vronsky had stepped onto a stool and then leapt onto the edge of the balcony. He began to slow handclap his musicians, moving sarcastically from one foot to the other. Then suddenly his mood changed. His entire body began to shake with laughter. His voice became softer. Mischievous. Self-mocking. As if, at that precise moment, there was nothing in the world Nikolai Nikolayevich Vronsky found so ridiculous as his own grandiose pomposity.

'Useless,' he cried out. 'Tone-deaf, talentless cretins. I, Vronsky, poet of the Russian soul, heir to Rimsky-Korsakov, to Mussorgsky, to Balakirev, salute you.'

*

The once gleaming crystal chandeliers were covered in dust and the Kirov's café now exuded a decidedly proletarian demeanour. No such thing could be said of Marina Morozova, Honoured Artist of the Soviet Union and leading lady of the Kirov Opera.

BEN CREED

They drank tea either side of a small glass table which had a folded beer mat underneath one leg to keep it balanced correctly.

She was still a great beauty. Her beauty was the first thing everybody, man or woman, noticed about Marina Morozova. When she had stood in front of him and Sorokin on their first day at the conservatory, neither of them could take their eyes off her. She had, of course, become one of Felix's many conquests. 'Don't let that sweet, porcelain face fool you,' his friend had said of her. 'She screws like a navy whore.'

Sat opposite her, Rossel noticed something else. The exquisite, glittering diamond studs in each ear. They reminded him of the earrings on the blue-hat's corpse.

'The conservatory – oh, how I miss it,' Marina said. 'It's where I learned who I was. Who I am! A good Bolshevik, of course, but also myself, too. I'm allowed that, am I not? Certainly, I must be allowed that. Waiter?'

The singer waved an elegant arm at a middle-aged man wearing an ill-fitting black suit, who came straight over to their table. She held up her chipped cup.

'More tea.'

She turned towards Rossel.

'And you, Revol? Can I call you that? I mean Lieutenant Rossel just feels too cold, too impersonal for old friends like us.'

Rossel handed his cup to the waiter and nodded. Then smiled at the soprano.

'I thought it was Felix who was your particular friend, Marina?'

She ran a finger across the top of her brow, just beneath the hairline. Her skin was a dramatic, translucent white

106

and, although, like him, she was now in her mid-thirties, unblemished. It was set off by lustrous dark locks, cut in a page-boy style. Her eyes were sea-blue and guarded.

'Felix, my God. Do you still see him?'

Rossel shook his head.

'Not for years now. At the conservatory, we were very close. But we drifted apart after we left. Like student friends often do. He moved, to Moscow, I think. A teaching job for some high-up member of the Politburo. Or the Defence Ministry. A girl who had some talent, apparently. Felix somehow wangled his way into the family's affections. He will, by now, be either demonstrating Prokofiev's *Romeo and Juliet* to Svetlana Stalin or breaking rocks somewhere east of Perm having been unable to resist ravishing the minister's wife.'

She laughed but the laughter did not come easily. Whether this was because she disliked talk of Felix Sorokin's amorous misadventures or because she had the Soviet allergy to gossip, he could not tell.

'But I may be wrong,' continued Rossel. 'Felix was a wanderer. In every sense. In any case, I have not seen him since the end of the war. He was in the 23rd, I think, fighting the Finns.'

The waiter returned with fresh cups and a silver tray with two pots on it, one for tea, one for hot water. He put them on the table and walked back towards the counter.

'A sweet, red-haired boy, my Felix,' said Marina. 'We were close for a while but I can't say I've really thought of him in nearly fifteen years. You, on the other hand, Revol, well you had exactly what we all wanted. And, so, I have often wondered what happened to you.'

She gestured with her hand to his white cap with its red band, resting on the table.

'I never expected this.'

She lifted the teapot and began to pour. 'Talent, true talent. On a par with Oistrakh, even. I mean everybody said that.'

'Not everybody.'

She smiled.

'That's true, Revol, very true. For you, I remember, did not.'

'Such comparisons are foolish. David Oistrakh is one of the finest musicians ever to grace the stage. I never even had a job in a folk band.'

Marina took a sip of tea. Then reached across the table and touched him on the back of his gloved left hand.

'I heard that you had stopped playing. I'm so sorry.'

Rossel withdrew the hand and shrugged.

'The Kirov's loss is the militia's gain. That's how I try to see it.'

Marina looked blankly at him for a moment before smiling, not without sympathy.

'I'd heard rumours. Why would a brilliant violinist stop playing the violin?' she said.

Rossel put his gloved hands down on the glass tabletop and leaned in. The table wobbled; tea swirled in the two mugs and ran into the cracked saucers. Almost imperceptibly, the tone of his voice changed.

'Little Nadya, Marina. Nadya Bazhanova. Tell me about her.'

She leaned back.

'So that's why you are here. They finally decided to investigate that woman.'

'Yes.'

'Have my jewels turned up?'

'Tell me about Paris and the Palais Garnier, Marina.'

As soon as he asked the question, her mood altered. Marina now assumed the role of prima donna in the Kirov Opera. Rossel leaned forward still further, now a policeman and nothing more.

'Had she been your dresser for a long time?'

'No, not that long really. Six months. Someone recommended her. I didn't even recognise her when she turned up. Or realise we'd been at the conservatory together. I realised later that she had been a little put out about that. But you know how it was there. Circles within circles, all musicians together, all good communists together, everyone equal, of course – but . . .'

'Some more equal than others.'

The soprano nodded.

'"Talent, unlike milk, bread or cheese, is not distributed according to the needs of the proletariat via a five-year economic plan." So says our mercurial maestro.'

She stopped.

'Don't worry, comrade,' Rossel said. 'We are old friends, you and I. I'm simply here to ask questions about Nadya.'

'At first, she was fine, good at her job. I didn't really like her, I can say that, but she was efficient. There was always a feeling with her of endless calculation. That everything she said and did served some strategic purpose. She had a grand design, I think, but I never got to find out what it was. Then, after she'd been with me for a few months, things started going missing.'

'Things?'

'Not jewellery, at first. I had a perfectly divine little Hermès clutch bag that Nikolai had brought me back from Lisbon one time.'

'Nikolai?'

'Vronsky. The maestro.'

'Ah.'

Marina Morozova raised her slender eyebrows. Gently signalling: *Yes, of course, I'm screwing the maestro. This, dearest Revol, is how the world works.*

She smiled.

'It was not particularly expensive, I think, but of great sentimental value to me.'

'How so?'

'It was a symbol.'

'Of, what, exactly?'

She sipped at her tea. 'We took Nikolai's *Inferno*, his opera based on Dante's poem, to the Teatro de São Carlos for a summer season. He told me I was his Beatrice. *Lasciate ogne speranza, voi ch'intrate, Abandon hope all ye who enter here.* Nikolai loves to joke. In that and many other little ways I find him gloriously childlike. He likes to tease me with it sometimes – he quotes the line before we make love; enter what Dante calls: *il secondo cerchio.*'

'Excuse me?'

'The second circle. In the book and also in Nikolai's opera. Those afflicted with sins of lust were kept in the second circle of hell.'

Marina held his gaze for a second and then reached out, picked up her cup and sipped again. Rossel could see she was enjoying herself.

He decided to put a stop to that.

Rossel reached into the pocket of his jacket, then put a picture of the ruby clasp-earrings onto the table.

'Were these amongst what you believe Nadya took from you, Comrade Morozova?'

She looked down at the photograph and instantly shook her head.

'No, I've never seen them before.'

'What, then, beside the Hermès bag, was the jewellery that you believe she stole?'

'A bracelet, a sapphire bracelet. From a jeweller called Tiffany, in New York.'

Rossel picked up the photograph and put down another on the table.

'This is what Nadya looked like when we found her. I don't know what *cerchio* of hell she had visited before she died, only that she must have sinned very greatly to deserve it.'

Marina stared down at it for a moment, but quickly looked away and handed the photograph back to Rossel.

'How horrible,' she said. The singer took out a small yellow silk handkerchief and began to wipe away a tear. 'What happened?'

'It is not clear,' replied Rossel. 'But she was murdered, we know that much. Why, when and by whom? Well, that is why I am asking questions, Marina.'

The soprano leaned out of her chair as if in a semi-swoon.

'No animal could ever be so cruel as man, so artfully, artistically cruel,' she said.

Rossel sighed inwardly. She must think he was an idiot. Was it the uniform? An MGB officer would have had her blabbing away but the militia did not command enough respect. He would have to frighten her.

'I have a recording of Vronsky's *Inferno* at home. In fact, I own many of the maestro's recordings,' Rossel began. This was true. He had always admired the composer's work. Vronsky might, at times, be 'childlike,' as she claimed, but he wrote symphonies like someone who had lived a dozen different lifetimes and, in each of them, fathomed the wisdom of the ages. 'Not the one with you in the lead, the one with Ira Malaniuk. She is superb. Wouldn't you agree? A performance devoid of all superficiality. As I remember there are nine circles in total. Lust, as you say. Limbo, gluttony, greed, anger, heresy, violence, fraud. And treachery. Our glorious MGB would be strongly in agreement with the poet as he reserves the ninth and most terrible circle of perfidy for traitors.'

At the mention of the MGB, Marina put down her cup on the table and straightened her back. Almost as though they had already brought her in for an interview.

'Then you quote Dostoevsky to me,' said Rossel. 'A man who thought and wrote a great deal about murder.'

Marina gazed at him as he stood to leave, all traces of the smile gone.

'This new piece of Nikolai's is influenced by *Crime and Punishment*,' the singer replied. 'Themes of thwarted ambition, destiny, sacrifice. He says Dostoevsky is the Dante of the Russian soul.'

Rossel picked up and put on his cap. He gave her a small salute and spoke formerly.

'Thank you, Marinochka. It will, I'm sure, be of little interest to him but please pass on my own admiration of this sublime new work to the maestro.'

She nodded.

'Of course. And what of Sofia, Revol? Are you and she still in touch? For a time, you were the conservatory's very own Tristan and Isolde.'

He coloured slightly. Then shook his head. Why, even after all these years, was it still so difficult for him to hear her name dropped into a conversation?

'Ah, I see,' said Marina. 'Perhaps, in the end, she grew tired of you?'

*

'*You!*'

Rossel spun on his heels.

'Yes, you. Come here.'

The maestro was sitting on one side of the Kirov's foyer on a gold chaise longue, almost filling it with his bulk. Before him stood a small grey-haired man. The hapless Karlof.

Rossel walked towards them and then stood next to the trombone player.

Vronsky was, it seemed, still in a playful mood.

'So here you are, our mysterious visitor from the militia. How perfect.'

'In what way, Comrade Vronsky?' said Rossel.

'I saw you from the balcony. Listening – actually listening. I like the way you listen, attentively, with your eyes closed, paying all proper respects.' He glanced up at Rossel's epaulettes with their thin red band and two gold stars. 'Bravo, Lieutenant.' Then he gestured to Karlof.

'Despite all aural evidence to the contrary, Vitaly here believes that he is good enough to play in the brass section of Vronsky's orchestra at the Kirov Theatre. Don't you, Karlof?'

Karlof took off his glasses and wiped them with a grubby handkerchief before putting them back on again.

'I have a family, maestro. I have responsibilities. Please, another chance, I beg you.'

Vronsky sat back in the chaise longue and rested his arms on its gold-lacquered back. Like one of the great marble Romanov eagles that decorated the foyer, brought suddenly to life.

'Vitaly has a family, Lieutenant, and so has been begging me not to sack him. What do you think of that? Some heroic daughter of the Soviet Union has allowed herself to be impregnated by Vitaly's apologetic appendage. They should give her the Order of Lenin.'

Karlof's face reddened. He looked as though, family or not, he was about to turn on his heel and leave the theatre. That would be a mistake. One word from the maestro and Karlof would be lucky if his next job was playing in a folk band in a Siberian village. Rossel decided to change the subject.

'I am a huge admirer of your work, Comrade Vronsky. Symphony number 3, in particular. You broke new ground – I dare to suggest it was the work that marked you out as a pioneer in Russian composition.'

In a crowded field of Russian musical geniuses, either as Soviet artists or exiled ones, Vronsky had somehow found a distinctive voice between the unabashed Romanticism of Rachmaninov, the exhilarating modernism of Stravinsky and the gut-wrenching emotion of Shostakovich. Vronsky took Russia's suffering and made it sound beautiful.

Vronsky grinned.

'The Third? Really, you like that? No one plays it now. "Too experimental for the common man, exhibiting an un-Soviet sense of unfettered individuality," is what that imbecile Denikin wrote in *Pravda*.'

He tapped the back of two gold-ringed fingers against the chair and began to beat out a few notes of his suppressed symphony.

'And quite right, too, of course. We do, after all, live in a country where the will of the people and therefore the tastes of the proletariat, be they, on occasions, ever so slightly tedious, are paramount. The Third, eh? You know your music, for a *militsioner*.'

'We have met once before, maestro.'

Vronsky's fingers stopped tapping.

'We have?'

'I was honoured to perform for you once, during the war. An ensemble piece, a rehearsal of something you were developing to honour the courage and nobility of Soviet sacrifice. I'm not sure you ever completed it.'

'And was I impressed?'

Rossel smiled. Then shook his head.

'No, maestro, you were not. You told us that it was a first-rate composition but our playing had done something impossible and rendered it fifth-rate.'

Vronsky threw back his head and laughed. He stood up to his full height, dwarfing Rossel and Karlof, and then slapped the trombonist on the back, whose short legs almost buckled.

The maestro took a step closer to Rossel. Brown eyes, whites tinged a smoky yellow, held Rossel's gaze. The detective felt oddly queasy – claustrophobic, even cowed by their power. As if the composer possessed the ability to take an X-ray of his soul.

'You are a listener, Lieutenant, as I said. So, I ask you, you heard our own rehearsal today. Do I persevere with Karlof here? That is my question. Is he deserving of a place at my table for my opera's last act?'

Rossel thought for a moment. He didn't want the trombonist to lose his job.

'How could he meet your standards? He lacks your empathy, your genius for understanding the infinite capacity for suffering that marks out the Russian people from all others. No one could feel and encompass their triumph in the great siege of Hero City, like you have done, except Shostakovich himself. But give Comrade Karlof time, and the continued honour of your masterful tutelage, and then, perhaps, he may do.'

Vronsky glanced at Karlof's expectant face. Then sighed as if he was disappointed with himself. Before breaking into a broad grin.

'Perhaps the lieutenant is right, Karlof? Very well. On this occasion, I relent. But don't make me regret it.'

Karlof looked relieved. Vronsky turned back to Rossel.

'Sometimes, I wonder if I have the rigour of mind, the discipline required, to make the harsh decisions truly great art demands of its creators, Lieutenant Rossel. But good answer. Very good, in fact. You are indeed the listener I have been looking for.'

The composer took a small piece of card from his pocket and handed it to the policeman.

'With my compliments, comrade.'

Then he stretched out his arms and slapped Rossel and Karlof hard on the back before bursting into booming laughter.

'Yes, very good. Except for the part about that pompous arse, Shostakovich!'

14

In the hall outside his bedroom, he could hear one of the Sazonov children playing hide and seek. There was a small storage cupboard in the alcove opposite and it was a favourite hiding place.

On a glass ashtray by the windowsill was a pile of cigarette butts. Next to that, propped up against an empty glass, was the golden card Vronsky had given him. Black letters on it read:

The Blockade – N. N. Vronsky. *A new opera to celebrate the glorious opening of The Road of Life and the victory of the Soviet people in the Great Patriotic War. 19 November 1951. Honoured guest.*

If the music he had heard at the rehearsal was anything to go by, it would be a privilege to attend the premiere. A talent like Vronsky's was given to few men.

Rossel lay on his bed staring up at a long thin crack in the plaster, a cigarette stuck to his lips. Two hours spent turning over the facts of the case in his head and he still had nothing of substance. Only a list of unanswered questions.

Why five bodies? Not three? Or six? There was something about the way they had been arranged so neatly on the tracks out at Ladoga, which made him feel that the actual number of corpses, in itself, had peculiar significance to the murderer, or murderers. As though he, or they, were leaving a message.

But why go to such lengths to conceal their identities and then dump them on a railway line where they were bound to be discovered?

And why had they all been starved before being slaughtered? If Dr Volkova's theory was right, each of the victims had lost a catastrophic amount of weight before being killed. Who would do something like that? Why would they inflict such a slow and deliberate ratcheting up of pain and terror?

And the blue-hat? What kind of person was supremely confident enough to do something like that? To kill an officer of the Ministry for State Security was to risk everything. Admittedly, she was, as Lipukhin had pointed out, low level – using her role as a dresser to spy on the company abroad. But that act alone should have ensured a relentlessly thorough investigation. It was spitting in the face of the Chekists, and that never went unanswered. The fact that the Vosstaniya Street militia department had been given any time at all to investigate such a crime on their own, was, to Rossel's mind, still the biggest mystery of all.

And now the ruby earrings had led him to Little Nadya. Led back to the conservatory.

*

He awoke with a start. The butt of his cigarette had burnt a black hole into the blanket. He was not sure how long he had slept. The music was starting up once again. The mystery guitarist was tuning up. And this time it sounded like *Oy, to ne vyecher* was going to feature again.

A minute later there was a knock at the door.

Rossel got up and answered it.

Lena smiled, revealing the gap between her two front teeth.

'Mama says she can't take any more, Revol. Not tonight, she's on early shift at the factory in the morning. It could be anyone playing that guitar on the fifth floor, she says.'

Lena dropped into an impression of her mother's country-bumpkin Urals' accent.

'And so she is wondering if the handsome militia lieutenant in room four, the one with the dark eyes and the beautiful smile, would go and do something about it?'

*

The singer's voice did not sound as though it was coming from inside one of the main apartments on the fifth floor. It must, he reasoned, be from one of what were called the janitor flats. Each floor had a cupboard-like apartment that, at one time, when the block was first built, had been used for a live-in cleaner. Now they were greatly prized because being allocated one meant that an unmarried and childless citizen could enjoy the luxury of living alone.

The janitor flat doors were painted brown, not green like all the other doors on the floor, and positioned nearest the stairs. Rossel stopped outside the only brown door on the corridor and listened. This was it, all right. The guitarist was not singing any more but they were still strumming gently at the strings. He knocked sharply – his policeman's knock.

The strumming stopped.

He heard footsteps. *Ah, it is not yet evening, Oy, to ny vyecher*, the song was the same. Even though the voice was completely different, for the briefest of moments, he allowed himself to entertain the ridiculous notion that it might actually be Sofia.

The sound of a bolt being turned. The door swung open.

It was the woman in the light blue dress Lena had teased him about in the communal kitchen.

She was in her mid-thirties and short. The singer was wearing black workman's boots and a blue towelling dressing gown, pulled tight at the waist with a cord. Her hair was dark brown and held tight by a battery of plastic red curlers and hairclips. Her eyes were blue, he noticed, and radiated determination.

'Yes?'

Rossel caught himself eyeing her. Trying to cover his embarrassment, he stared directly into her eyes. She pulled at the neck of her dressing gown, drawing it across the exposed flesh. He saw a vicious red scar, about two inches long and wide, between the nape of her neck and her left breast. She pulled the dressing gown even tighter and hid it.

Rossel risked a grin.

'It is a beautiful song and you play it delightfully, comrade. But there are children trying to sleep on the fourth floor. May I respectfully request that this is your last rendition of the evening?'

The singer reached up and began to take out some of the clips in her hair.

'If it disturbs the little ones, sure.'

She began to push at the door to close it, but he put the tips of his fingers on the handle.

121

'Have you got a name, comrade?' he asked, wondering why on earth he was asking.

She glanced down at his hand, which, his cheeks colouring slightly, he immediately removed. Then back up at him; her face softened. Relaxing, he took a step backward into the corridor.

The door slammed shut.

15

Friday October 19

The blue hat with the red band and polished steel star was lying on Captain Lipukhin's desk when Rossel entered the room. Taneyev, Grachev and Lipukhin himself could not take their eyes off it.

The owner of the cap was an MGB colonel who was occupying Lipukhin's usual seat. He was middle-aged and portly with a florid complexion. His dark but greying hair was a little too long for regulations and swept down over his brow.

Rossel was holding a tin mug of tea. He parked it on a nearby filing cabinet, stood to attention and saluted.

'Now, at last, we are all here,' said the colonel.

His tone was clipped and officious, and he looked at them as if they were merely paperwork that he needed to sort, process and file before sitting down to lunch. He nodded at Rossel.

'I am Colonel Sarkisov, Fifth Main Directorate of the MGB.' The Fifth was the department tasked with monitoring internal dissent and counter-revolutionary activity. 'I have been sent here from Comrade Beria's office to ask about this current case of yours. The bodies on the line.'

BEN CREED

'Comrade Beria?' Taneyev whispered, looking as though he was about to swallow his tongue.

'Indeed. I trust you have no objection?'

'None at all,' replied Lipukhin hastily. 'It is a great honour.'

Colonel Sarkisov sat up straight. 'Not, perhaps, for me. We shall see.' He picked up a brown leather briefcase from next to his feet on the floor and opened it. Taking out a file, he flicked through its pages, making the occasional note. He was in no hurry whatsoever to resume the conversation.

'Five bodies,' he said after a long while. 'Unusual, is it not?'

The question was not specifically directed at any of the four militia officers. As a result, no one said anything. Everybody understood speech, of any kind, was a high-risk activity in front of a member of the MGB. Sarkisov turned to Grachev.

'What about you, Sergeant? Do you think this case is unusual?'

Grachev shifted from one foot to the other.

'In what way do you mean, Comrade Colonel?'

'The number of bodies, of course. And also, in the way it is being investigated. Or, should I say, *not* being investigated quickly enough.'

Lipukhin glanced sideways at Rossel but when Rossel looked back, he tried to avoid his gaze. Rossel realised the captain was sensing an opportunity.

'I . . . if there are issues the MGB have with the way the militia has handled this particular case, Colonel Sarkisov,' said Lipukhin, 'then I can only apologise. Station 17 is a small local station; we would not normally have become involved in a case like this. There were, as you must know from my report in the file, unusual circumstances around our call-out, but we will do everything we can to apprehend the murderer. Or, if you would prefer, I will of course be happy to hand over the case and everything we have on it to higher authorities. To be frank, I had assumed someone from MGB would be assigned to the case from the very beginning, given its somewhat extraordinary circumstances and the death of one of your own.'

'How do you know it was "one of our own," as you put it?' asked Sarkisov.

'A female victim was in the uniform of an officer of state security, comrade, as you will see from the file.'

'It could be an imposter. A trick?'

'But comrade,' said Lipukhin, 'Who would dare to? Moreover, how would anyone get hold of an MGB uniform, unless . . .'

Lipukhin stopped.

'Unless?' asked Sarkisov. He worked his jaw, as if chewing an errant piece of breakfast.

Unless the killer – or killers – were from the MGB itself, was the unspoken line.

'Someone could have made it,' Sarkisov added. 'A skilled tailor, employed by a member of the criminal class. Perhaps you should have investigated this possibility? Perhaps you should have interrogated some clothes factories, some tailors, some theatrical costume designers? Perhaps you should have requested information from the Ministry for State Security itself? In short, comrades, there has been a distinct lack of progress, of legwork, of a revolutionary spirit of duty towards Soviet justice.'

And it is this lack of revolutionary spirit inside an insignificant police station in a district of Leningrad looking into five murders that has brought Colonel Sarkisov of the Fifth Directorate of the MGB, a man who begins his day with briefings to Beria and Stalin, all the way here to bawl us out, thought Rossel.

'We are working under difficult circumstances, Comrade Colonel,' Lipukhin began.

'Difficult circumstances?' Sarkisov sneered. 'I am glad you were not one of our military commanders during the war, Captain.'

Perhaps Comrade Sarkisov could be persuaded to give some more indications as to the reasons for his presence here, thought Rossel.

He stepped forward, treading on a squeaky floorboard as he did so. The noise echoed around the room.

'I believe the circumstances to which Captain Lipukhin refers are a shortage of personnel, given the arrest of the entire local militia department in the district where the crime was committed and the further difficulty in procuring the services of one of Leningrad's pathologists for more than five minutes,' Rossel said. 'Which in turn may be to do with the nefarious conspiracy of doctors, apparently including pathologists, we read about in our newspapers. It is not easy for mere militia officers to determine a person's identity when they have no face, teeth and fingers. Or perhaps I missed that part of training?'

Sarkisov's thin blue lips turned upwards at the corners. The smile looked exactly like what it was: a strategic expression that he needed to practise a lot more if he were to come close to making it in any way convincing. He closed the file and put it back into the briefcase.

'You have a tendency to insolence, Lieutenant. The NKVD officer who interrogated you, after your arrest in May of 1942, made the same observation. It took Major Nikitin some time, I believe, to properly convince you of the need to pay proper respect to the essential role played in Soviet justice by the organs of state security.'

Major Nikitin. For the first time, Rossel heard the name of his torturer, the man who had ended his musical career. The Chekist bastard who had taken his fingers. *Major Nikitin.* He bit his lip and stored the name away in his brain just as neatly as Sarkisov had tucked the file away in his briefcase.

That was his first thought. His second was that Comrade Sarkisov had not come to Leningrad without doing his homework.

'But you were fortunate, is that not so?' Sarkisov's smile widened. 'A month later, the chance of rehabilitation presented itself. For thousands, Lieutenant Rossel, the Sinyavino Offensive was a meat grinder. For you, your time with the 2nd Shock Army was an opportunity for redemption.'

Rossel felt everyone's eyes on him.

'You fought in the Sinyavino Offensive?' Grachev said with a look of disbelief.

'Many people did,' Rossel answered.

'But very few of them lived to tell the tale,' Sarkisov broke in. 'Although it seems you have not been telling your comrades much about your past – both distinctions and indiscretions. Understandable, if regrettable. Comrades, before you is a man who in the early stages of the siege was denounced by a concerned citizen – concerned, according to the record, over his disdain for, even hostility towards, the Soviet state – and yet who was given the chance to rehabilitate himself on the battlefield in Leningrad's hour of need. In other circumstances, had his status not decreed otherwise, he might have been awarded a medal. Or two. Instead, he was grateful to seize with, if I may put it like this, *both* hands, the opportunity to wipe the slate clean.'

Rossel felt his face colouring. Over six years he had worked his way from private to lieutenant while managing to reveal almost nothing about his past to his colleagues. Pointed comments about his gloved hands had been deflected early on with vague references to the war. Grachev was a braggart but most survivors were guarded about their experiences and Rossel had managed to brush off any enquiries with the habitual reticence of the veteran. As a young violinist, the spotlight had been nothing to fear. As the ghost of Vosstaniya Street, it was toxic.

'The sacrifice of the officer that stands before you,' continued the colonel, 'earned him the right to be accepted for further service to the Motherland in the Workers' and Peasants' Militia – though we might not call it that any longer, I am not sure – enrolling in, it says here, late 1946. And he is already a lieutenant. Promotion comes fast to those who fulfil their responsibilities and whose loyalty, though sorely tested, is no longer in doubt. Probably. But back to the matter in hand. Your erstwhile colleague, Junior Sergeant Gerashvili, is helping us with our enquiries on a related matter at the moment.'

So she had been arrested.

'A related matter?' said Rossel.

'An instance of fraud. We believe she may have fabricated some entries into the sales ledgers of a noted jewel merchant in Passazh.'

'But why would Lidia – why would she do that? She is an exemplary junior officer. She wouldn't make up evidence.' Rossel's voice was too loud. 'Many would, but not Gerashvili, comrade. It is barely credible.'

'What you can, or cannot, bring yourself to believe is of no consequence here, Comrade Lieutenant,' answered Sarkisov. 'All that matters is revolutionary justice. And it is clear to me that, in an attempt to further her career, Gerashvili created evidence which she hoped would facilitate a prestigious arrest. One of the nurses she shared a room with at her apartment is a reliable informant who has confirmed to us that Gerashvili was dissatisfied with her role as the archive clerk here at Vosstaniya Street and felt she could, I gather, "better herself". A very bourgeois sentiment. Many important Party members have purchased items from that shop. She sought to blackmail them with fabricated information. The jeweller, Djilas, had agreed to be her accomplice in exchange for her overlooking some of his less official business activities. The man was a blackmarketeer. It took a little time but, eventually, he confessed as much. We suspect others were involved. We will soon discover just how far this plot spreads.'

Rossel was about to protest Gerashvili's innocence again but before he could, Lipukhin leaned forward.

'In your phone call, you said this was a matter related to the murders, Comrade Colonel. How so?'

Sarkisov picked up his briefcase and stood.

'Treachery, of course. If Lieutenant Rossel's vigilance is anything to go by, you have all been keeping a close eye on the newspapers. Both these murders and Gerashvili's jewellery scheme are the work of agitators and fifth columnists. How else could it be that acts of such depravity have taken place in the USSR? How could *you* have permitted it? This is not America, gentlemen, where due to the iniquitous exploitative social structures of capitalism people starve on the streets of New York, Chicago and Washington and, as a result, homicide is commonplace.'

He picked up his cap and put it back on. There was a plastic paperweight on Lipukhin's desk. A present his sister had bought him from a seaside holiday in Khosta on the Black Sea. It had a white sailing ship sealed inside it and *Sailing Club of Khosta* was written on its base.

Sarkisov pointed at the paperweight.

'Complete dump, Khosta – I went there once for a military conference. Not a decent plate of food to be had in the whole town. Nothing to eat but *ukha* all week – they'd had a delivery of pike, and I hate pike. I couldn't wait to get back to Leningrad.'

He picked up the paperweight with his left hand and then tossed it into the air, catching it with his right.

'The coming celebrations in honour of the opening of the Road of Life are only a few weeks away. Leningrad will be welcoming many of the very highest-ranking members of the Party as honoured guests. Stalin himself, I am told by Comrade Beria, is anxious that all troublesome matters of law enforcement, state security and Soviet justice are cleared up long before then. I will give you a few more days, no more, to make some progress on this case, comrades. These spies and traitors – whoever you think may have committed these terrible crimes . . . Consult your own records and you may find, I'm sure, that some of your usual suspects may well be implicated. Well then, round them up, have them confess. A simple honest confession is, as you know, the key component of our unsurpassable Soviet justice system, so extract one. Solve the case and let us all move on. That is the message I have brought for you.'

Colonel Sarkisov tucked a small strand of his long hair under the rim of his bright blue cap. Then dropped the paperweight onto the desk.

'Like I say, comrades, Khosta is a dump. But I can think of worse places. And so, I reckon, can you.'

*

As soon as Colonel Sarkisov left the building, it started.

'You bastard,' Grachev hissed at him. 'I always knew you were suspect. Denounced, interrogated, sent to die, and you would have done us a favour if you'd blown your fucking brains out. And now this. You stuck-up, *kulak* scum.'

The words were out – Grachev knew words, said loud enough, were all it took to daub you from head to foot in treachery. It was another name Grachev had for Rossel – 'our *kulak* lieutenant'. A landowner, oppressor, exploiter. A whispered insult. But not whispered today. A class enemy because he could walk upright, read books and deal with prostitutes without raping them, which in Grachev's world was beyond comprehension.

The sergeant wasn't finished.

BEN CREED

'First, you send Gerashvili to do a man's job and bring the blue-hats down on our heads and then, when they turn up – an MGB major from Beria's office, fuck your mother – you give them some lip, when we – *all of us* – are the ones who will pay. It turns out you knew one of the victims, which is a nice detail, and one I'm sure the MGB will make hay with once we're all nailed to the floor of the Bolshoi Dom. Just who do you think you are?'

Lipukhin, standing next to his desk, watched, crouched, ready to step between them. Taneyev just watched. It was the most prudent thing to do.

Grachev and Rossel were eyeball to eyeball now. Rossel took a fractional step backward. Grachev leered, sensing surrender, and followed, pushing his face into Rossel's. Nothing, he believed, could stop Senior Sergeant Grachev, who had fought a path from the burning craters of Stalingrad right the way to the Reichstag and would have had the skulls of dead Germans dangling from his backpack if there had been room to buckle them all on. The keeper of his own legend, Grachev had spun enough tales of wartime heroism for every junior in the station to hold his combat skills in awe. Some of the rougher ones over the years had worshipped him, emulating with enthusiasm his ways of extracting compliance from men and women in the cells. He'd had his factions, had Grachev. At times they'd bordered on insurgency. Nothing could topple him.

Especially not this musical cripple with his missing fingers and poncey manners.

Grachev pushed his face into Rossel's. Swung his fist. The lieutenant stepped nimbly to one side, dodged the blow, and hit him.

132

Now the sergeant rasped in earnest, his grey teeth bared and his eyes wide, but his left knee had buckled for a split second.

Then the right fist followed up.

Grachev staggered but kept to his feet.

Say it again, thought Rossel, staring him down. Say it, he whispered inside his head, enraged by Grachev's contempt.

'Say it again,' he shouted.

The sergeant's fat, sneering lips framed the word but nothing came out. Then the hero of Stalingrad grimaced and shook his head.

He straightened up and stalked over to the door.

'Stay where you are, Sergeant,' shouted Lipukhin. 'You haven't been dismissed.'

Grachev muscled his squat frame through the door.

Then slammed it behind him.

*

Lipukhin put the radio on. It wheezed and crackled before finding a rousing march to blare out.

Taneyev had immediately sought permission to follow the sergeant. Lipukhin waved a hand at him and he was gone.

'He'll denounce you, Revol. If he didn't fight, that means he's plotting something.'

Lipukhin reached for a matchbox and shook it.

'We are safe for only a few more days,' said Rossel. 'Beria's henchman has just ordered us to solve this case. Our orders now come directly from the Politburo.'

'Shit,' said Lipukhin, lighting a cigarette and shaking his head as he blew out the match. 'Is that a good thing?'

The captain sank into his chair.

'Were you really in the Sinyavino Offensive?' Lipukhin asked.

'For a time.'

'I didn't think many had survived that.'

Rossel shrugged. 'There weren't many left when it ended. That is undeniable.'

'Fuck your mother.' Lipukhin struggled to strike a match. 'What did Sarkisov mean by a "chance at redemption"?'

'The comrade major may have become confused by the passage of time,' said Rossel. 'In May 1942, as his records indicate, I was indeed brought in for questioning. Although some of that questioning was fairly robust, it ended without warning when the Red Army emptied the jails and sent us into battle. Some of us were even given weapons. A few of those who survived were rehabilitated. Unusually, the Chekists didn't have much say in the matter. If I recall rightly, my interrogator was disappointed to see me go. But those were desperate times.'

Lipukhin stared into the fire.

'I wish I could have fought the fascists,' he said in a soft voice.

'Those of us who did are very glad that the next generation will not have to do the same,' said Rossel.

'But how do you know if . . .'

Lipukhin tailed off. Rossel would have liked to give him a drink but he knew where that would end.

The captain threw his cigarette into the flames.

'I don't know how to make sense of any of this,' he said.

'There are many aspects of this crime that make no sense, Comrade Captain,' Rossel replied, 'and that's not including our interview with the good Colonel Sarkisov. Five mutilated corpses. This is no drunken argument that ended with the killer waking up with a hangover and only the vaguest memory of knifing his best friend across the kitchen table. It's not, to my mind, MGB either – the MGB would herd a hundred people into the Bolshoi Dom and we'd never see any of them again. State security does not deal in groups of five, comrade. Criminals might, but a turf war would have ended in the bodies being buried under a thousand tonnes of concrete or dumped in the river, not splayed out on a railway line dressed like characters from a baroque fairy tale retold by Mayakovsky.'

He began to pace as his reasoning unfolded in his mind. Saboteurs and wreckers? Nonsense – what were they wrecking? Anti-Soviet agents didn't draw attention to themselves by dressing up corpses and leaving them in plain sight. This was the key to the crime, he thought – being *noticed*.

'The whole thing is un-Soviet, yes. But why that merits a personal visit from Colonel Sarkisov presently eludes me.' Rossel picked up his greatcoat and his cap. 'Nonetheless, I am going to take his advice.'

'Which part?' asked Lipukhin, looking nervous.

'The bit about legwork.'

16

Saturday October 20

Hospital 40 at Sestroretsk, a satellite district to Leningrad's west, was only half the size it had been before the blockade. It had been heavily bombed by the Luftwaffe in the depths of the siege. When the war ended, there were more bomb craters in its formerly leafy grounds than beds, wards and operating theatres.

As Rossel walked down the corridor leading to the maternity ward, the sound of drills and hammers came from a nearby corridor. Seven years since the siege was lifted, Hospital 40 was still being rebuilt. He sat in a little room next to the ward, listening to the mewling of babies and the shushing of their mothers, for about ten minutes, waiting for the nursing shifts to change.

Finally, a bell rang. Moments later, two young nurses, chatting and giggling about their exploits at a dance night, shot past him, buttoning up their coats.

Then – he checked the small black and white photograph in his wallet, *yes, definitely her* – Nurse Durova appeared.

Now is the time I find out whether that stupid seabird really is lucky, he thought. He'd made a special journey to the fireplace before he left the station. One of Gerashvili's flatmates had to be an informer. Perhaps both were?

'Nurse Durova?'

The girl – she was little more than that, maybe only eighteen years old, with dark hair and a pretty face – turned towards him.

She looked at his uniform.

'Yes.'

'I have a question for you. Is there somewhere we can talk?'

The girl looked around the empty corridor.

'I've already told the others everything I know.'

'A minute of your time is all I need. It could help Lidia Gerashvili.'

'I don't know anything.'

She was very nervous. That was good. He had picked the right girl, he figured. The informer would have been expecting him – would even have been pleased to see him. Another opportunity to prove her worth to the MGB with a full report of his visit. Their vicious internal politics were legendary. Just because Rossel was under orders from the Fifth Directorate, in a manner of speaking, that wouldn't prevent him being arrested by the Second. Ratting out two militia officers in the same week might even get her some privileges.

No, this one was not on the payroll.

*

Tears trickled down both of Nurse Durova's cheeks. She and Rossel sat side by side on two green chairs about halfway down the hospital corridor.

'Dominika, the other nurse who shared with me, said we couldn't trust Lidia, you know, with her being a . . .'

She stopped herself.

'In the militia,' said Rossel.

'Yes.'

'Tell me, again, exactly what happened on the night she was arrested.'

'I liked Lidia. She was kind, *is kind*, she let me borrow her best dress to go on a date a couple of weeks ago – not every girl would do that. It's green with a beautiful pattern around the collar. She said I looked like Lyubov Orlova in it. I know I don't look like any film star but she does, sometimes. Dominika says she's a little fat, but I think she's really pretty. Dominika's too thin. Thin enough to slip through a crack in the floorboards. Men don't like that. I think she's just jealous.'

'Please, the night she was arrested. It would help me.'

'We sometimes eat together, the three of us. We did that night. Lidia was late in, about seven thirty. When she arrived, she was carrying a package with her – it was books, books covered in brown paper.'

'How many books?'

'I told them already,' Nurse Durova said.

'Tell me again.'

'Three, there were three of them.'

'And what did she do with the books?'

'Put them in a small cupboard next to her bed. Then we all sat around the table in the middle of the room talking, smoking and eating *piroshki* that I made.'

'Did any of you leave the room before the security officers came?' he asked.

'Only Dominika for about ten minutes. She went to use the telephone.'

'Did Lidia say anything to either of you about the books?'

Nurse Durova shook her head.

'No, Dominika asked her what was in the package, but she said it was nothing important, just work stuff.'

'And what happened when the MGB came?'

'We all were laughing about this old man, Volodya, on the second floor who has his eye on Lidia and sometimes leaves posies outside our door. There was a knock and we all cried out, "It's him, Volodya has come courting." And then . . .'

The nurse took a hanky out of her bag and dabbed at her eyes.

'Yes?'

'Dominika opened it, and the officers came in. MGB, we all could tell. It was terrifying. But one of them read out Lidia's name from his notebook. They said they needed to talk to her about a matter of state security. Lidia got up from the table and went with them. She didn't say anything at all, either to us, or them. Not a word. It was like she knew they were coming. She didn't act surprised in any way.'

'And the books?'

'That was the really odd thing. They never mentioned the books. Never asked Lidia about them. But one of the officers went straight to where they were, straight to the little cupboard next to her bed, and took them.'

'Nothing else? They didn't search your room?'

Nurse Durova shrugged.

'No. And I, well.' She looked away. 'I was glad they hadn't come for me.'

Rossel thought for a moment.

'Was there anything else out of the ordinary that happened while the three of you were together before the officers came? Anything she did? Anything else she said?'

The girl started to shake her head. Then stopped.

'You know there *was* one thing. I didn't think much of it at the time but . . .'

'Go on.'

'Pskov, she asked about the town of Pskov. Dominika's grandma is from somewhere near there. When I first put out the plates of blinis, she asked Dominika if she had visited any of the famous churches there. I mean, Lidia wasn't religious in any way, not at all.'

'And what did Dominika say?'

'Nothing. Just that she thought most of them had been turned into storehouses, libraries and museums, same as everywhere else. "No priests left in Pskov, then?" Lidia asked her. Dominika just laughed and said: "Not many. Once God left, so did most of the priests."'

He stood up.

'That's it, no more questions?' She sounded confused.

Rossel smiled and pointed in the direction of the maternity ward.

'You watch the babies in there, am I right?'

Nurse Durova's expression softened.

'Sometimes on the incubation ward with the ones who are premature, on a night shift, it's just me and them. It's so quiet in the darkness, all you can hear is their soft breathing, coughing and crying,' she said. 'After a while, you can tell just from the way they breathe if something's not quite right.'

Rossel began to walk away but then stopped himself.

'Your friend, Dominika. Is she a good friend?'

'Yes, I think so.'

He nodded.

'Yes, I'm sure she is. Just as you watch over those little ones. So attentively. I'm certain that, in exactly the same way, your friend, Dominika, watches over you.'

*

Rossel sat in the filing room in Gerashvili's chair. There were seventeen files in front of him. They constituted every file he had found on Gerashvili's desk – the exact paperwork she had been examining just before her arrest. He had sorted through them and piled fifteen on one side of the desk, two on the other. All were of priests and clergy who had gone missing over the past five years in the administrative regions around Leningrad.

As he settled down to examining the files, he reached for the radio switch, an on-off button that activated a speaker on the wall. It was All-Union Radio or nothing. It took him a moment to recognise the music – the second movement of Shostakovich's Symphony No. 7, about halfway through. With the celebrations of the Road of Life coming up, they were playing it a lot, he'd noticed. The composer had dedicated his mammoth work to his home city of Leningrad, which at the time had been in the grip of the German and Finnish blockade. Nine hundred days of hell. Rossel stopped for a moment to listen. By the time of the premiere in Leningrad itself, in August 1942, the symphony had been played around the world, hailed as the sound of Soviet defiance. But for those who had endured and survived the siege, it also evoked a great many terrible memories.

Rossel flicked the radio off.

He turned back to the files. The pile of fifteen were cases he had already discounted. The other two were the ones who had a connection to the monasteries around Pskov. According to Nurse Durova, the city seemed to have piqued Gerashvili's interest.

The first of the Pskov files was that of a former archbishop who had been patriarch of the Cathedral of St John before the revolution. He had taken to drink in his declining years and been reported missing by one of his old parishioners about fourteen months ago. The parishioner wondered if he had been kidnapped. According to the file, the local militia suspected he'd got blind drunk on moonshine, wandered into the forest near Lake Peipus and frozen to death.

The second one was much more interesting.

17

Sunday October 21

In the twilight, the great stone walls of the Pskov-Pechersky Dormition Monastery rose and plunged like a giant white serpent in some twisted Slavic fairy tale. Driven into sloping ground, over the centuries the walls had been built and attacked and rebuilt; now they were going through the same process and, as Rossel did a circuit, he could make out rickety scaffolding clinging to the thick fortifications. The weather was still but cold – minus twenty, he had heard someone say on the bus from Pskov – and thick clouds kept the day dark. The city was nearly three hundred kilometres from Leningrad. A long drive at the best of times but in this freakish winter, a true odyssey. The train journey had helped him to think before the rattling bus had set him on edge again.

Every now and then, at even intervals, a large wooden gatehouse jutted out of the shadows, their pointed roofs looking like the hut, minus the fat chicken legs, of Baba Yaga, the old witch with iron teeth and an appetite for a human supper. His mother had read the stories to him when he was small. '*Do you know what it means to allow a wicked thought to enter one's heart? The wicked thought grows all the time like a poisonous plant and slowly kills the good thoughts.'* Rossel's mother had often read him that line from the folk tale. Lifting her head up from the book and staring, so he understood its meaning and importance. She needn't have bothered. Stalin and Beria made the same point daily, in the papers, on the radio and in the propaganda posters. And besides, a few years spent mingling with the blackmailers, spivs, prostitutes and corrupt cops of Sennaya Square had convinced him of its truthfulness.

He dropped the cigarette he had been smoking under the glare of a flickering street light and started to walk through dots of snow across the cobbled path that led towards the monastery's St Nicholas Gate and, he hoped, information on Father Tikhon, the troubled priest who had attracted Gerashvili's attention.

*

Archimandrite Pimen was sitting at a large zinc desk whittling a piece of pinewood with a small, pearl-handled penknife. The head of the monastery had long and yellowing nails; his fingers were curled and gnarled. The image of what looked like a tiny bird was emerging from the pine.

There were not many places left in Stalin's empire where a man could believe the revolution had never taken place but the caves of the Pskov-Pechersky monastery was most definitely one of them. Built fifty kilometres away from Pskov itself, it was on the edge of the Russian Socialist Republic, a stone's throw from Estonia. Its blue and gold domes stood proud above the walls and the grounds; under the churches was a network of caves in which the holy men who had established the community had once lived. The caves were freezing and the damp air penetrated everything Rossel had put on as a defence. How the archimandrite could stand it for more than an hour or two was beyond him. But Pimen preferred to work here, he had been told.

There were icons everywhere, lit by candles hung in the alcoves; each stony nook and cranny housed a golden image of Christ, the Trinity, St Catherine or some other saint. Pungent, cloying incense filled the air. From somewhere impossible to trace, Rossel could hear monks chanting plainsong.

'My predecessors generally preferred to live and work in the monastery proper, but I like the solitude of the caves. I have been an archimandrite, here at Pskov, since 1915 and a humble monk for twenty years before that. This working into the wood is a habit I have affected to quiet my sometimes-troubled soul, Lieutenant Rossel.'

'You have lived through turbulent times, Father.'

Rossel sat opposite the monk on a low stool, the table between them.

The archimandrite, himself seated on an ornate, cushioned chair with his arms dangling off high rests, nodded. He rested the incomplete bird, if that was what it was, on the bench and then pulled at a loop in his long grey beard. Twisting it with his fingers so it slowly began to smooth and straighten. Well into his eighties, he looked younger, no more than sixty-five. But his face was gaunt, his cheeks hollowed.

'Before the war, our troubles were many. All the churches and monasteries were dissolved and our buildings absorbed by the state but, in its darkest hour of need, the Great Leader, guided by God, called the faithful back to into his own fold, so we could help fortify the Russian soul against the Nazi aggressors. I recently carved a figure of St Catherine. Do you know her story?'

Rossel shook his head.

'At school, I was taught only to genuflect before statues of Marx or Lenin,' he said.

Pimen let go of his beard.

'A stunning beauty, St Catherine, as the story goes, desired by the Roman emperor Maxentius. He had the greatest philosophers of his day converse with the young girl in an attempt to break her faith by force of their reason but they could not. She broke them, can you believe it? She converted some of those wise minds to the one true path and Maxentius had them all put to death on the spot. Then, finally, unable to convert her to his own way of thinking, he had Catherine broken on the wheel.'

The archimandrite's grey pupils appeared unnaturally large in the candlelight.

'When earthly power is denied, when it is not allowed complete conquest, it shows no mercy.'

'Is that the moral of your tale?' said Rossel. 'I expected something a little more uplifting.'

'I simply make an observation, Lieutenant.'

'About our great and noble Soviet Union?'

'About human nature.'

The monk picked up his knife again and began to whittle at the stick once again.

'You were asking about Father Tikhon,' he said. 'Yes, I remember him. We all do. As you say, he had many tattoos about his person – from time spent in the camps, we all

assumed, where all manner of vice and depravity is practised – but I cannot be certain if they were exactly the same
as the ones on the picture you showed me. What I can say,
with some accuracy, is that he was a troubled man.'

'With drink, with women?'

The archimandrite shrugged.

'With everything, I think. Eventually, I expect, he gave
way to all the vices. I sensed a darkness within him – a
secret of some sort – but even within the binding sacrament
of confession, he refused to share it with me.'

'Apart from the missing person's report that brought me
here, I could find no other file for a priest named Tikhon,'
said Rossel. 'My assumption is that it is not his real name.'

'It is the one he gave when he arrived here at the monastery.'

'And you did not think to check it?'

'God is not interested in names, only souls.'

'How long did he stay here with you?'

'About three years in all. Initially, he was very much a
perfect novice. Always first to appear for prayer. Always
obviously fervent in his devotions. But then, after a while,
the incidents began.'

'Incidents?'

The archimandrite closed his eyes for a moment. In the
flickering light and relentless cold Rossel could see the old
man's breath forming streams of vapour from his nose.
Pimen opened his eyes again and looked straight at Rossel.

'It became obvious that he no longer took communion.'

'Obvious, how?'

Pimen picked up his carving knife. Two sharp stabs of
the little knife cut ridges deep into the table.

'Our day is well described by a line from Psalm 119: "Seven times a day do I praise Thee because of Thy righteous judgments." Tikhon began to pray incessantly, even when alone. He was constantly muttering the Troparia and prayers for intercession by Angelic Hosts. And one night one of our novices heard him muttering something else. An unholy prayer.'

'And what did this prayer say?'

The priest rose and bent towards a tiny desk next to the wall. He reached into the drawer in his desk and took out a file.

'We kept his records,' said Pimon.

'You keep records of your monks? I thought they were supposed to leave their old lives behind and start anew,' said Rossel. 'I thought God was not interested in names.'

'God is not interested in names but the Kremlin is very interested in paperwork, and everyone who starts a new life here starts a new file. Especially if they encounter disciplinary issues. When they told me a *militsioner* was coming, I had them dig this out. There is little information in it – we do, indeed, start the file from scratch, but we see no need to be too assiduous. But there is one piece of paper you should see.'

He pushed the file across the bench towards Rossel, who picked it up. Opening it, he saw there were only two pieces of paper, both small. A barebones personal history listed the exact date of Father Tikhon's arrival and the exact date of his departure from the monastery.

The other piece of paper was yellowing and slightly crumpled, with scrawling and erratic writing on it – small dots of black ink dripped between the words.

My appetite was sin, and of that sin I made a feast.
   And through that feast I came to know you.
   You are the Master of the Shadows
   And now, for all eternity, I must sit at the foot of your
bountiful table.

Rossel picked it up and placed it on the bench top. The old
monk stared at it.

'We searched his cell and found a large number of pieces
of the communion bread. They were black with mould. He
had been taking the host into his mouth but then refusing to swallow it. Secreting them into a handkerchief and
hiding them in his room. A terrible sin. That prayer was
exactly what the novice had heard him chanting in the
Greek. I had this piece of paper he had written it down on
confiscated but it made no difference. He became relentless
in his incantations. Other strange rhymes, too. In the end I
had to consult Patriarch Nikon in Moscow and he recommended expulsion from the monastery.'

'On what grounds?'

'Why, blasphemy, of course. The Master of the Shadows
is not a name that would sit lightly on the shoulders of any
member of the church. Amongst the novices, gossip is commonplace and it had already become a testament of faith
with them that Father Tikhon was making obsessive pleas
to some kind of devil of his own invention.'

The monk stopped whittling and turned the little
wooden piece face up on the table. It wasn't a bird at all. It
was a winged angel holding a tiny harp. The archimandrite
tapped a curling, yellow fingernail on the harp.

'My sense is that it was his love of our chanting that brought Father Tikhon to us and held him here. Music was the only thing I saw that made him smile. And yet weep, too – sometimes when I observed him during vespers, I saw tears rolling down his face as he mouthed the words of the plainchant. He had an all-consuming passion for religious music.'

'You have no idea, then, what happened to make such a devout man turn away from his God?'

The old priest shook his head. As he did so, the straggly piece of beard he had tried to smooth earlier popped out from his head and became crooked again.

'No, but we came to believe that Father Tikhon had purposefully cultivated the mould we found on the consecrated Eucharist.'

'Why would he do that?'

'Why?' The archimandrite's eyes grew misty but what they saw was hidden by the flames of the candles.

'I do not know why. But for some reason known only to himself, he began to first corrupt the body of our blessed Lord and then consume it alone, in secret, as he declaimed his perverse prayer. May God have mercy upon his soul.'

*

Rossel's guide, a novice, was barely out of his teens. Apart from the wispy, apologetic beard that all young priests and monks had to endure, he had pale skin, blond hair, light blue eyes and a sprinkling of pockmarking across his brow and cheeks. Archimandrite Pimen had given Rossel permission to see where Father Tikhon had lived and worked and, beyond that, any part of the monastery he cared to examine.

They had no secrets, said the archimandrite. Rossel rather doubted it.

There was nothing out of the ordinary about Tikhon's cell. Bleak, spartan and cold, like every other cell in the brothers' living quarters. As for where he had worked, that was apparently in the field beyond the monastery walls, growing vegetables and herbs for the refectory. And all the fields were deep under snow.

The novice reached down into the pocket of his black cassock and took out a heavy bunch of iron keys. Then selected the biggest and fitted it into the large and ancient lock that opened the gatehouse door that led back outside the monastery walls.

Rossel fished into his own pocket as he waited and pulled out his cigarettes. He was trying a new type, *Jubilee*. He took one out and pushed it between his lips.

'Not while you are on the monastery grounds,' said the novice. 'It is forbidden.'

Rossel put the cigarette back into the cardboard pack, wondering if the power of prayer and some religious observance might lead to divine inspiration. He still knew almost nothing. This Father Tikhon might well be the tattooed body on the slabs back at Vosstaniya Street, but either the archimandrite, who was clearly a practised politician, was not being truthful about checking the past lives of those who were accepted into the brotherhood, or for some reason he did not understand, no one really had bothered to find out Tikhon's true identity. The monastic life was not for everyone and perhaps they took who they could get. Either way, time was passing quickly and the trip to Pechory had barely taken him forward. If only

Father Tikhon had confessed his secret. Sanctity of the sacrament or not, he was sure the archimandrite would have revealed it to him. The Orthodox Church had been almost entirely destroyed after the revolution but Stalin had seen its potential – history, nationalism and religious fervour. Just what the troops needed. He offered an ultra-pragmatic reprieve during the war to lift morale. After that, well, the MGB had its fingers everywhere. He sensed the old monk was a practical man who knew who to call if he needed his own guidance. And what it took to keep the MGB off the monastery's back.

The boy's key was sticking in the lock.

'I'm sorry, Lieutenant, sometimes it won't turn. I will only be a moment.'

'Did you know Father Tikhon, when he was here?' Rossel asked.

The novice's hands fumbled at the lock. There was a click as the key turned. He stood back, turned the iron handle, pushed at the door and it opened.

'Yes.'

'You knew him well?'

The novice sighed. Then nodded.

'We even shared a cell at one point.'

Rossel was startled. Then he realised the shrewd old archimandrite had not chosen his guide at random.

'Did you notice the tattoos on his body?' he asked.

The boy shook his head. 'He never undressed in front of me. He was careful about that. He usually slept fully clothed in his black cassock. The other monks thought him eccentric and would comment on his crumpled robes but, at least for a while, the archimandrite seemed to put up with it. People just thought he was a little odd but I wasn't so sure. I think he was hiding something.'

'Hiding what?'

'I never found out.'

'Did you and Father Tikhon get on?'

'Fine, at first. He was quiet, devout, kept himself to himself.'

'At first?'

Even in the late afternoon, even under the lowering clouds, it was lighter once they were out of the shadow of the monastery walls. The novice did not head down the road into the town of Pechory but instead followed the line of the fortifications, into a ravine. The darkness returned. He stepped behind some trees and stopped.

'May I have a cigarette?' he asked Rossel. 'It is forbidden but I am still getting used to life here and, well, I pray God will forgive me in exchange for helping the militia with uncovering the truth about a truly diabolical man.' He crossed himself three times.

'Here.' Rossel lit a cigarette and handed it over. The novice placed it to his lips with reverence and exhaled with bliss. Rossel wondered what else he was finding difficult to give up.

'How long have you been a novice?' he asked.

'Two years.'

'And it's the life for you?'

The novice shook his head.

'It's hard,' he said. 'I admit it. I was studying literature at university. But I got kicked out for . . . well, never mind. So I came here. There is food, peace and the occasional drink. I keep my head down.'

'You were going to tell me about Father Tikhon.'

The boy took another puff and nodded.

'After he left the monastery there were stories put about that he had set up his own parish out in the forest, on the shores of Lake Chudskoye, north of here. There's a big flat granite outcrop near the lakeshore. The locals call it Nevsky's Pillow because, some say, Alexander Nevsky slept on it when he came to Pskov. But I don't think Father Tikhon was using it to sleep on.'

'What then?'

The boy was shivering. Rossel wasn't sure if it was from nerves or from the cold.

'The archimandrite has tried to hush everything up. He's worried that the Patriarch in Moscow will get to know. The Church has to keep the Party happy. A scandal like this, they're already shutting some monasteries down again.'

'A scandal?'

'There's a cave near Nevsky's Pillow. Tikhon took up residence there when he left here. Then he got some followers – a few at first. Some foolish girls, a boy, a teenage simpleton from one of the farms near Pechory. But the rumours started almost straightaway.'

'Tell me about those rumours.'

'People said Tikhon was using the place as some kind of altar. The boy, the simpleton, was found dead by the lake shore. He had eaten some wolfsbane in the forest. It was terrible, the things the other novices said after his body was discovered.'

Rossel dropped his cigarette onto the snowy ground and stamped on it.

'Go on.'

The novice sucked on his own cigarette and then blew out a sharp puff of smoke.

'I wasn't there, Lieutenant, so all I can tell you is what people said.'

'Which was?'

'When they found the body, he'd been dead for at least week. He had some small cuts on his belly. Missing pieces of skin and muscle. The talk was that Father Tikhon had blessed these trophies on his altar and then offered his remaining followers a perverse Eucharist made from human flesh.'

Rossel thought for a moment.

'A dead body lying for a week like that in a wood would be disturbed by animals – wolves, foxes,' he said. 'The novices like to gossip, as you say. The archimandrite told me that. Your tale is a gory one, the kind people like to believe might be true. It appeals to their darker instincts. What makes you so certain there's something in it?'

The novice took one last draw on his cigarette. Then dropped it onto the ground between their feet. The hot tip glowed in the dark and began to melt a little of the snow around it. He looked straight into Rossel's eyes. His pupils were dilated with fear.

'We shared a cell, he and I, like I said. One night I awoke with a start. There was an atmosphere in the room. A pulse of strange electricity. I turned around and Tikhon was sitting bolt upright on his bed, staring at me. His robe was pulled down and I could see some of his tattoos. One of them was of Death. His eyes were like two dark moons and filled with desire.'

'So, he was a queer?'

The novice shook his head.

'No, he wasn't looking at me like that.'

'What then?'

The boy pulled up the collar of his cassock around his neck.

'As if I was a side of pork hanging in a butcher's window.'

18

Monday October 22

The dark rings under Captain Lipukhin's eyes put Rossel in mind of the giant panda that had arrived in Moscow a few weeks previously, a gift from the Maoists in China. There the similarity ended. The captain's breath stank of stale tobacco and cheap vodka. Lipukhin sat on one side of his desk. Rossel, Grachev and Taneyev all sat on the other. Grachev and Taneyev had drawn their chairs together so there was a gap between them and Rossel. They were avoiding eye contact with him.

The thin official militia file on Father Tikhon, which included his missing person's report, lay on the desk. A thicker file on Nadya, the MGB agent, was underneath it.

'I assume you went out to this rock, Nevsky's Pillow?' the captain asked Rossel.

'Of course.'

'And?'

'I contacted the local militia at Pskov and went out with them. We found little. The cave was empty, although there were signs of a campfire with some broken vodka bottles and empty tins of food around it. But nothing unusual, really, around the rock itself. All the members of this dark congregation of Tikhon's – and no one seemed to have any idea how many there had been – had vanished. Probably several months ago.'

Taneyev leaned forward in his chair and addressed Lipukhin.

'You think it could be them, then, Captain? Our five bodies, all members of this cult that this Father Tikhon had started. He persuades the others to travel to the forest outside Pechory, kills them, and dumps them on the tracks a few hundred kilometres away as some kind of crazy sacrifice.'

Grachev gave Taneyev a withering look.

'Unlikely, don't you think? Not unless he chopped his own face off afterwards and then lay down on the railway lines beside them.'

Lipukhin dropped a couple of aspirin into a glass of water and sighed.

'What do you think, Revol? You are the one who went out to Pskov.'

Rossel pushed his chair back and stood up. 'A death cult?' he said. 'I'm not sure. Tikhon had certainly scared the novice I talked to half to death. He looked like he would believe anything anyone told him about the things that were going on out at the cave. And then there was the case of the young lad who had died and been, so he said, partially eaten. I talked to the local militia about that, though, and they thought it more likely there were animal bites on his body. As for the wolfsbane, he wouldn't be the first to eat the wrong root or plant in the forest and suffer the consequences. People talk. And from the foolish things they say, others make giant leaps of imagination which often turn out to be nonsense. That, at least, was my first thought.'

Lipukhin drank down the glass of water with the aspirin in one gulp. Then slammed it down on the desk.

'But?'

Rossel's tone was considered.

'No one knows what happened to Father Tikhon after he left the area. He sets up by the lake in early 1949, starts attracting followers that summer – although the local police say they drifted away when the weather turned cold. But he himself stays all the way through the winter. Who knows who visits him or how he survives? But he is there in the spring. Then the body turns up. More acolytes arrive and then – gone. Father Tikhon disappears in June this year, just when the days are long and the opportunities for deluded souls to enjoy themselves in the countryside are at their peak. Why should he have disappeared then?'

Rossel took up position, right behind Grachev's chair. The sergeant didn't move a muscle.

'Assuming the archimandrite was telling the truth, Father Tikhon had an obsession with the consumption of flesh. He starts fantasising at the monastery about perverting the communion process and does so, initially, by allowing the blessed host to moulder and then consuming it. But that is not enough for him. The incident with the novice shows a progression of his thinking – he now wishes to consume a Eucharist made of human flesh. So, when he is expelled from the monastery, he goes out to Nevsky's Pillow and puts his plans into action. The simpleton is, perhaps, the first of his victims. Then finally, like a dark Moses, he leads his followers out to the railway line and disposes of them in some way.'

Spoken aloud, the theory sounded even more far-fetched than it had in his mind. But he remembered the novice who shared a cell with Tikhon. The young monk's fear had been genuine.

Grachev snorted.

'Now you are thinking like Taneyev. Unless this Tikhon was a real devil, there's no way he killed himself. Not with those injuries.'

Lipukhin sighed again.

'Grachev is right, Revol. A man cannot cut off his own face somewhere else and then travel to the railway lines and lie down next to his victims.'

'Then he gets a loyal acolyte to kill him, carve him up, and disappear,' said Rossel, taking his hands off Grachev's chair. 'But it's not that which bothers me.' He leaned across the desk and picked up Nadya's file.

'I knew her. She wasn't the kind to get involved in an occult death cult. Little Nadya was all about the real world and how to make her way in it. There is one link. The archimandrite said that Father Tikhon had a passion for religious music. That he actually cried during vespers. Music connects Father Tikhon and little Nadya, perhaps. But what else?'

'Connects them how?' said Grachev. 'She was a clarinet player who packed it in after the Chekists recruited her as an informer at the Kirov Theatre, posing as an assistant to one of the Soviet Union's leading opera singers. All we know about the monk and his music is that his eyes got a little wet when the choir sang hallelujah. That's not much to hang a case on. How are we going to get our confession for Sarkisov and the MGB? By rounding up all the monks in the choir at Pskov and getting them to say they were all screwing the fat clarinettist? That she sucked Father Tikhon's cock so hard he was smiling so wide his face split in two? I don't think so. A death cult, on the other hand, the MGB might buy that. But first, we're going to need to find someone to give us a confession.'

Rossel dropped the file back on the middle of the desk.

'Someone like who? Confessing to what?'

Grachev could not hold back a smirk. 'I've got someone in mind.'

Rossel sat back down on his seat and moved it a little to the left so as to close the gap between him and the chairs that Grachev and Taneyev were sitting on. He reached out and gently patted Taneyev on the back. Then he leaned in towards Grachev. His voice became soft and cajoling.

'Who is it – Pavel Konstantinovich? Aren't you going to share the mysterious name with me?'

Taneyev's cheeks flushed. Grachev, refusing to take the bait, turned his face away from Rossel's, and addressed Lipukhin.

'Can I have a word, boss?'

Lipukhin shrugged.

'About what?'

Grachev stood up and picked his cap off the table. He glanced contemptuously down at Rossel. Then turned back towards the captain.

'In private.'

19

Lipukhin's communal apartment was in Pulkovo, near the city's Shosseynaya Airport. He had moved there when his marriage broke up. His parents and two of his three sisters died in the siege – a direct hit from a German bomb. The other sister, a doctor, had survived and lived here with him. Rossel had been to the place once before when he and the captain had gone to a football match together about five years ago. Zenit had beaten Traktor Stalingrad 1–0. Lipukhin celebrated a little too much afterwards, ended up puking in the gutter and Rossel had had to help him back to his apartment. Zenit had been playing today, as it happened, away to Daugava Riga. Rossel had heard on the radio that they lost 2–0.

It was dark by the time he arrived. He knocked on the captain's door. There was no answer. Another rap. Still nothing. Then he heard the shuffle of feet and the clank of several locks. The door opened an inch or so and a child's face appeared in the crack. A little girl with blonde hair. It was Darya, Lipukhin's seven-year-old niece.

'My name's Revol, Darya. Do you remember me? I work with your uncle. Is he here?'

She nodded.

'Mama's at the hospital,' she said. 'Uncle Ilya is looking after me but he fell asleep.'

'Can I come in?'

The girl opened the door to let him pass.

'Uncle Ilya threw a bottle at the mantelpiece and it smashed into a lot of pieces. He's done it before. Mama won't be happy when she gets back.'

*

Shaken awake, Lipukhin sat on a small couch in the shared room, looking even more puffy-faced than usual. His hair was out of place and his clothes were dishevelled. His niece was playing with a doll behind the curtain that separated the sleeping area she shared with her mother from the space where her uncle slept.

Rossel swept the last pieces of the glass into a dustpan and walked towards a bin in the little kitchen area that was part of the apartment.

'No, don't put it in there, Revol.'

Rossel looked around.

'Where then?'

Lipukhin lit a cigarette.

'You'll need to take it with you.'

'Take it with me?'

The captain nodded.

'There's a copy of *Pravda* next to the sink. Wrap it up in that.'

Rossel walked towards the small kitchen area, folded out the newspaper and then slid the broken glass from the dustpan inside it.

Lipukhin suppressed a belch.

'Raisa will get back from the hospital at ten. Tongue like a rusty saw, my sister. I don't want her to know I've been on the sauce again when I'm supposed to be keeping an eye on Darya.'

'Losing family is hard for anybody,' said Rossel. 'Just because it happened to so many people during the war doesn't make it any easier for you.'

'Sometimes I wish the bomb that took our parents had seen to one extra Lipukhin. Raisa is stronger than me, in that way. She copes better.'

Rossel folded the newspaper with the glass inside it. A shard sneaked through both the paper and one of his gloves' thin fingertips. He muttered a curse.

'Shall we have some music?' he asked.

On the wall was a wooden radio. Lipukhin reached up and pressed a button. The radio only had one channel, which at that moment was playing a stirring march. He adjusted the volume to the precise level to which all Soviet households had become accustomed – to the point where a private conversation could not be overheard.

Rossel sat down on the couch.

'Grachev wants you to tell Sarkisov it's me, doesn't he?' he said. 'That I'm the connection to the bodies on the line – on the flimsy basis that I knew one of the victims so I must have killed them all. That if you give me up, everyone else at Vosstaniya Street will be saved.'

'Well, you did study at the conservatory with her,' said Lipukhin.

'That's not enough for you to condemn me,' said Rossel. 'For Grachev, yes – but you?'

Darya had come out of the bedroom holding her doll, which was now in two parts. She held them out.

'It's broken again, Uncle.'

'Give it to me, my sweet.'

'I'm asking you to get me some more time to investigate the case and keep the MGB off my back, that's all,' said Rossel. 'Will you do that for me, Ilya?'

Lipukhin ran a hand through his ragged hair. 'That's all, he says. As if it's that easy. We're all in danger, Revol. All of us.'

'This would have put the fire in your belly once, Ilya. This case would have obsessed you.'

Lipukhin sat up straighter, grabbed Darya by one arm and wrapped her in an embrace. The child submitted without enthusiasm. He let her go and she retreated to a corner, still clutching the broken toy that her uncle had already forgotten about.

'Why did you never tell me that you were in the 2nd Shock Army?' Lipukhin asked. He sounded almost angry.

Rossel shrugged. 'We live in a world where many things are best left unsaid.'

'It makes you a bloody miracle. The 2nd, well, that's a legend. I know you don't like talking about the past. But you're asking me to trust you. So, I need to know a little more.'

'Mine was a short and undistinguished military career,' Rossel said. He stopped but could see that was not going to be enough. 'When the war started, I was in civil defence – digging trenches, hauling tank traps into place, putting out fires. Then, in May '42, I was arrested. That's when my hands were . . . But, in June of the same year, when they needed every last man who could hold a rifle and run a hundred metres without falling over – that, quite literally, was our training – they bandaged me up and sent me forward.'

He held up his right hand.

'I was left with a functioning trigger finger. As you gathered, my call-up got me out of a spot. They needed every last man for the Sinyavino Offensive and, at that point, they didn't give a damn about your fidelity to Marxist–Leninist orthodoxy. The idea was to make sure the Germans used up all their bullets on the first few waves so that later attacks might have a chance of breaking through. It didn't work. Nothing did.'

'Stupid doll!' Darya threw the doll on the floor in frustration.

'Quiet, Dashenka,' said Lipukhin. 'Let Uncle Revol speak.'

'I spent the next few weeks sucking filthy water out of a ditch and watching my comrades get blown to pieces,' continued Rossel. 'I was one of a few dozen men in our battalion who walked out of that shithole alive and there was not a shred of heroism involved. If it's a test of courage you want, this case – pursuing the killer, not whitewashing it all away – takes far more of it.'

Lipukhin stared at his feet. The military march ended and for a moment the radio emitted nothing but a quiet hiss. Darya hummed a tune in a voice that set Rossel's teeth on edge.

'And there is Grachev, bragging about his scalps for all this time,' said the captain in a low voice. 'Now you – fuck your mother, the 2nd Shock. And after that?'

The little girl's eyes widened in delight at her uncle's bad language but before she could imitate him the radio started up again.

Dear comrades, now for our evening concert of songs and symphonic works dedicated to our beloved collective farms . . .

'In '43, fighting near Shlisselburg, I got shrapnel in my lower back,' said Rossel. 'Once I recovered, I spent most of the rest of the war with an anti-aircraft battery. Then joined the militia in '46. And that's it.'

Lipukhin cleared his throat.

'Now, thanks to Sarkisov, you know his name,' he said.

Rossel, confused by the interruption, followed the captain's gaze until he realised it was fixed on his gloved hands.

'Yes, Nikitin. Major Nikitin,' he said.

Rossel's voice gave nothing away. But he shoved his hands deep down inside his coat pockets.

Their eyes met for a second. Lipukhin broke off first and looked over at his niece. He gave a loud sniff.

'Dashenka, my little one, bring that dolly over here,' he said. He took the two pieces from the girl's outstretched hands and began to twist them back together.

'It's not broken, it just clips together like the others, but I will fix it for you as long as you don't tell your mama about the broken bottle and the glass. Is that a deal?'

There was a click as the two halves became one again.

'You know what a deal is, don't you, Dashenka?' he said.

The little girl held out her hands and nodded.

'You do what I want as long as I do what you want. That's what you told me about deals, Uncle Ilya.'

Lipukhin patted his niece's head.

'That's right, Dasha, that's right. Good girl. We have a deal, you and me.' He glanced across at Rossel. 'As do Uncle Ilya and Uncle Revol.'

Rossel nodded back. The exchange had drained him and he wanted to go home and collapse into bed.

He stood up, holding the newspaper and broken glass in both hands.

'One last thing,' said Rossel. 'Pugachev has been in touch.'

'Pugachev?'

'The reader of bodies – the thief who looked at the priest's tattoos.'

'And?'

'He has a rather unusual request.'

20

Tuesday October 23

The priest's body was wrapped from head to toe in a black tarpaulin. Lipukhin opened the back of the van. Rossel was holding one end of the corpse, where the head was, Pugachev the dead man's feet.

'*Raz, dva, tri* . . .'

Lipukhin gave them the count. They both lifted their arms up together and then let go. There was a metallic clunk as Father Tikhon's body dropped into the back of the van.

The three men stared down at it.

'He won't start decomposing or anything, will he?' said Lipukhin.

Pugachev slapped his gloved hands together to warm them and blew out a misty cloud of frozen breath.

'I shouldn't think so, Captain. Not in this weather. It's seventeen below. Colder in the back of this van, in fact, than in one of those dead men's filing cabinets we stole him from. Let's hope those rusting snow chains you've got will hold up until we get there.'

Lipukhin slammed the boot shut.

'I'd prefer to come.'

'Sorry, comrade. Like I told you, Gubaz said only one officer from our noble militia. Only one. And he's not a man to cross.'

'How long will it take?' asked Lipukhin. They had been kicking their heels all day, waiting for the call from Pugachev. The captain had failed to master his impatience.

'Half an hour there, half an hour back, and in between depends on how chatty Gubaz is feeling. I'll try and get the good lieutenant home by midnight. Like Cinderella,' said Pugachev.

The three men walked around to the front of the truck. Rossel and Pugachev clambered inside. Rossel turned the key in the ignition.

'Why did Kerselidze say he needed to see the monk's body?' asked Lipukhin.

Pugachev shrugged.

Lipukhin pulled the collar of his greatcoat up around his ears.

'And you didn't think to ask him?'

Pugachev leaned forward and started to scrape at some of the ice on the windscreen.

'Of course not. There have been many people, down the years, who thought it would be a good idea to ask Gubaz Kerselidze silly questions,' he said, 'and, today, most of them are almost certainly feeling a damn sight less optimistic about life than the human ice cube we just dumped in the back of this van.'

'I'll see you in the morning with my report,' Rossel addressed Lipukhin. The captain nodded and turned away.

Pugachev gave a snort.

'There's a comrade with a little too much on his mind. Come on, Lieutenant, let's you and I go and do some detecting.'

*

The hat-rack was an ingenious touch. Two of Kerselidze's henchmen had made use of it to keep Father Tikhon fixed in position, lashing him to it using a couple of old rubber engineering cables. The naked body of the dead priest stood bolt upright next to a red leather barber's chair. Beside the chair was a man Rossel presumed to be the shop's owner, a small, swarthy, middle-aged man wearing a stained purple fez who might have been Georgian, Turkish or a combination of those two plus more thrown in. And next to him, in another barber's chair, sat Gubaz Kerselidze himself, huge and brooding with thinning grey hair. The gangster was eating a pie that dripped hot fat and grease onto the fading yellow linoleum.

Thick white scars cut across Kerselidze's brow and cheekbones. His nose was so broken that it no longer resembled a proboscis, more a collection of bone fragments held together in a thin skin bag. The gangster's neck was a fat Kamaz truck tyre made flesh. There were words inked on it in Gothic lettering. But it was the rest of his tattoos that really held your attention. Almost every inch of available skin on his body was covered in the spidery, hand-drawn inkings – reapers, satyrs and Christs crucified – that were used to project status and fear in the gulags. In the very centre of his brow was an unblinking third eye. It created a strangely beguiling impression: a human Cyclops, all-seeing and monstrous.

Rossel stood in the centre of the room, opposite Kerselidze, the barber and the hat-rack. The little shop had two doors, both guarded by thieves – ethnic Russians, Rossel guessed, not from the Caucasus. Kerselidze stuffed the last of the pie into his mouth and licked the grease off his fingers. Then he stood up and took a step towards the dead monk.

'The last militia man who got this close to me was an unlucky soul they rounded up in the Terror, before the war, and sent to north Urals camp, 34th Kilometre, where I was generally agreed to be King Wolf. Pretty boy he was, so I had him trussed up like a tutu-wearing ballerina and fed him to the camp faggots. First they fucked his arsehole into a mush, then slit his throat. Nasty business. You are very pretty too, cop.'

Kerselidze lifted the little barber's fez, planted a big sloppy kiss on his bald skull and then popped the hat back down again.

'Loma, here, used to be a *kozyol* back in the days of his youth. Isn't that right, Loma? Until Gubaz found him.'

A *kozyol* was a prisoner who got singled out as a weakling and passed around for general sexual gratification. Loma reached up and straightened his fez. He looked as though he'd spent a long time learning how to tiptoe on eggshells when in the vicinity of Gubaz Kerselidze.

Loma the barber grinned sheepishly.

'Things is just as you say Papa Gubaz, things is always exactly as you say. Loma is happy to please, as always, he is, of course, your *kozyol*.'

He took off his fez and performed a sweeping bow.

Kerselidze's cheeks reddened as he burst into laughter. Then, almost in the same moment, standing next to the dead priest, he became serious again. He stabbed a meaty middle finger against the third eye in the middle of his own brow.

'A lieutenant, eh? Let's hope you have brought me a man who can solve my problem, Pugachev, or I'll slit your fucking throat and turn your ugly Ukrainian ass into a mitre for this dead priest, you understand me?'

Rossel stepped forward.

'A problem, Mr Kerselidze? How can we help you?'

'I have a friend, Major Timoshenko, he runs the militia station here at Frunzensky District.'

'And this friend has a problem?'

Kerselidze shook his head.

'No, I have a problem with my friend.'

'Which is?' said Rossel.

'He's not my friend any more. This piece of shit, Timoshenko, he's nobody without me, you understand? Nobody. But now he tells my men he can't help Mr Gubaz no more. I give this shitbag everything, you understand? Kickbacks, pussy, caviar. A nice little cut of the heroin I'm running out of . . . not your business. I even build him fucking *dacha* in the woods near Ladoga, now he don't want to know. Normally, an arse-wipe like this I cut out his heart and serve it up with some *kapusta*. But I kill one of your boys and there's a chance shit might rain down on old Gubaz's head.'

The thief boss stubbed his finger against his third eye again.

'Gubaz not stupid – he sees the future before the future sees itself. So, when friend Pugachev here tells me some

BEN CREED

Leningrad militia men need someone to read a ten-day-old corpse like it was *War and Peace*, that got me thinking.'

Kerselidze smiled. 'Who better to rat out the militia than other militia? I can only kill him. The state can make him disappear. File a report on this shit. I can give you all the information you need, send him to a gulag, my friends give him friendly time.'

Rossel cursed Pugachev. He hadn't known this was the deal and t

'No,' he said.

The thief stared at him. 'Where is the harm? The major is a crook. Soviet justice will catch up with him, who cares how?'

'You overestimate my influence, Mr Kerselidze.'

'I know you are just a flunky, a *kozyol* in a stupid uniform. But you find out his rivals, you leave a file on a desk. In fact, now you *know* Major Timoshenko is crook, you breaking the law by not informing on him.'

'I have no evidence.'

'Fuck you, *kozyol* – no one in this country has evidence!' Kerselidze lumbered towards him. 'No one needs it, and if they need it they make it up.' The gangster pushed his battered face up to Rossel's own. 'You think you are on side of justice? You are on side of liars and murderers.'

Rossel clenched his fingers.

'I'll tell you why I won't do it,' he said. The whole room was silent. Kerselidze's men were still. But ready for action.

'An informer. An informer did this.'

He held up his left hand, glove removed, and waggled the two remaining and crooked fingers to draw attention to the missing ones.

174

'So, comrade, you can use that fish knife if you want to.'

Kerselidze's eyes flickered down to the weapon he was holding three inches from Rossel's gut. Then they came back up to linger on Rossel's hand.

'You can have these idiots perform their tricks on me and give me a bath at the bottom of the Neva,' said Rossel. 'But the answer is still no.'

The gangster drew back his lips, exposing a row of broken tombstones embedded in his fleshy pink gums.

'I like you,' he said. 'But you are on the wrong side.'

'I am on the side of working out who killed that poor bastard over there,' said Rossel, putting his glove back on. 'So, if you aren't going to kill me or help me, I'd like my priest back, please.'

The head thief swivelled on his heel, marched over to Loma and slapped him so hard on the back that the barber's fez slipped over his left eye.

'You got your scissors, little Loma?'

Loma frowned.

'You want me cut the cop's hair, boss?'

Kerselidze clapped his hands together in childlike glee.

'Not his.'

He pointed at the faceless body held up by the hat-rack.

'His.'

The gangster scratched himself.

'Like I say, Gubaz Kerselidze sees the future before the future sees itself. You're a skilled man, Loma. A trim from you, a little parma-violet pomade, and I reckon you can make this fucker look just like a Yankee movie star.'

Loma picked up his barber's scissors from a silver tray on a table.

'No one knows pretty boys like Loma knows pretty boys, Papa Gubaz. One movie star bitch coming up!'

*

Strands of hair were floating through the air and landing on the linoleum. As Loma stood on a pair of metal step-ladders and clipped away at the mane of the corpse, the gangster walked around the naked body and pointed to particular markings on the dead priest's torso. Kerselidze knew his subject.

'He's not so fresh. The ink is a little blurred where his skin's beginning to bloat. OK. The snake around his neck denotes a drug addict. This one here,' he pointed to Father Tikhon's left side, 'the ring with the little round eye in the middle, means he was an orphan, alone in the camp when he arrived, with no protector. Not a good place to be. You say the other priests said he was fucked up? Then good for him. In the world of the gulag, being fucked up is best. It makes the other bitches careful. Make them think twice. If you can make them think three times, even better.'

Rossel stepped forward and pointed at the red reaper with the hammer and sickle etched into the priest's right shoulder.

'What about this one, Comrade Kerselidze?'

As soon as he heard the word comrade, the gangster's face coloured. Then he spat on the floor next to Rossel's feet.

'I'm not your comrade, militia. I am King Wolf, here and in camp, and no thief in Leningrad or Kolyma knows any power greater than Gubaz Kerselidze. Not even Generalissmo fucking Stalin.'

Kerselidze's hand closed around the white handle of the knife that was attached to his leather belt. Rossel glanced over at the thugs near the door who, on hearing their boss's raised voice, had turned to face them. Rossel reached up and took off his cap, doffed it and bowed.

'King Wolf, as you say.'

Kerselidze's sneering mouth relaxed. 'You got balls as big as Abkhazia watermelons to walk in here and only pretend to kiss my ass, gundog.'

Rossel tried again.

'The red reaper on the right-hand shoulder.'

The gangster raised his eyes heavenward and pretended to think. Finally, he shook his head.

'Most prison ink has no colour. Ink is made from blood, piss, ash from burnt tyre, boot, whatever a man can get his hands on. That's how when friend, Pugachev, here,' Kerselidze patted Pugachev on the shoulder, 'told me about a distinctive red reaper tattoo, well, straightaway, it made me think of someone. A coloured tattoo is not unknown but is unusual. Especially if he was not a thief. Who knows where he had it done? But I remember a man with a red Death on his shoulder, yes.'

Rossel tried to keep calm.

'You remember a name?'

Kerselidze spat on the floor.

'I rule not just in one camp, militia officer. I have men in six, seven, eight camps. And friends in twenty. These past years, since the war, some bitches help Stalin, help Chekists, still call themselves thieves.' He spat again with added venom. 'Bitches. Fuck your mother. But look, I hear stuff. And I hear about crazy man with red tattoo and God in his head who slashed two thieves. So, I'm almost sure. But one more thing and I will know. Loma,' he commanded, 'do as Papa Gubaz asked.'

The barber had already managed to cut away enough of the tangled black hair with his scissors to now use his clippers. He flicked a switch in the wall and the blades began to buzz. Kerselidze pointed to a spot at the very centre of the back of the dead man's head.

'Just there, Loma, just there,' he said.

Rossel, Pugachev and the head thief stared as Loma's clippers moved, up and then sideways, across the back of the priest's scalp; cutting a perfect cross into the middle of it. Rossel heard the shuffle of feet and with a lurch in his stomach realised that the other thieves were crowding around them to get a look. The skin of the revealed scalp, although still discoloured from the slight decomposition, was whiter than that of the rest of his body. Except, that was, in the exact centre of the cross, where, clearly visible, was a mark about six inches long. Rossel stepped closer to the body and started upward. The black tattooed letters were in Latin.

Capital letters, large enough to be eligible, and very neat. Three words only:

HOMO HOMINI LUPUS

Pugachev let out a low whistle.

'The schoolboy Latin I learned in my former life was never up to much but I think that says: Man is wolf to man. What's that all about?'

Kerselidze slapped his hands together in glee.

'That's him, all right, I knew it. The red tat on his shoulder and some gibberish on his head. No hair in gulag – too many fleas. Not a thief's tattoo. A man like that, his name gets around.'

'And his name is?' Rossel said.

Kerselidze pointed at the body. It lolled in its straps, its grey flesh softening.

'Avdeyev, Maxim Avdeyev. That was the name he answered to at roll call. Avdeyev – always first name on the list. Then he got religion and called himself something else. Like he was a real priest . . .'

'Maxim.'

Something in the tone of Rossel's voice made all the other men turn towards him. Kerselidze looked him up and down.

'Something wrong, gundog?'

Rossel took a moment to reply.

'An acquaintance?' the gangster persisted.

Rossel nodded. The priest's face, bone and gristle, leered at him. He felt sick.

Kerselidze roared with laughter and slapped him on the back.

'You in big trouble, now, gundog? Yes, I know you are. I can tell.'

The gangster's men were all chattering now, some in Georgian, some in Russian but laced with slang he only half knew.

'No one survives twenty years in camps without being able to see shit coming from a million miles away.'

The thieves began to cackle. Kerselidze carried on laughing too, delighting in the show.

'Like I always say, Gubaz see the future before the future sees itself!'

*

Pugachev drove the truck back towards Leningrad, talking incessantly. Rossel sat next to him in silence.

'So this has been a reunion of sorts?' said Pugachev. 'Well, that's a turn-up, Lieutenant. Wait until your superiors hear about this.' He gestured to the body of the priest behind them. 'That you and this painted popsicle are old friends.'

Pugachev swung the wheel as the truck slid around a bend. 'If you don't mind me saying so, you look like a man who swan dives into a bucket of shit and then discovers it's an ocean.'

Rossel turned away and stared out of the window into the darkness.

'I mean, bunch of corpses in the middle of a field and you actually know one of them? Turns out to be a lunatic who fancies himself as a saviour of souls. Any of the other corpses friends of yours too? Maybe one's your mother? Maybe one's Tchaikovsky? Maybe one's an old girlfriend, eh? An old flame?'

Rossel grabbed Pugachev by the collar and bellowed an instruction.

'Stop the fucking truck.'

'All right, all right. You need to take a piss? Then why not just say?'

'Just stop!'

Pugachev pressed his foot down on the brake. They rolled to a halt at the side of the road.

Rossel yanked the handle, flung open the door and jumped down into deep snow. His heart was thundering and he was gasping for air. Waves of panic and dread rolled over him, making him drop to one knee. He grabbed handfuls of snow and thrust them into his face, crying out with the shock, trying to freeze his thoughts and stop his mind exploding out of control. The snow clung to his skin and slid under his collar. A bout of furious coughing took hold but when it passed, he was back in control.

Without a word, the lieutenant clambered back into the truck and slammed the door. He pointed forward. Pugachev, knowing better than to open his mouth, rammed the truck into gear.

ACT 3

21

Wednesday October 24

'*Oy, to nye vyecher . . .*'

The song – Sofia's song – swirled discordantly around his mind; fast, too fast. A perverse lullaby. It mocked his now-brittle sanity.

By the time he got back to Vosstaniya Street, he had convinced himself that his worst fears would be confirmed.

'I have narrowed it down to six,' said Taneyev, handing Rossel a collection of crisp files. 'These are the six missing women who approximately fit the description of the one you and the captain call the Snow Queen.'

Rossel took them.

'What about her gown?'

'I have been calling around all the city's theatres to see if they have any costumes missing, just as Sergeant Gerashvili said she was going to do.'

'Anything?'

'As the junior sergeant said, the gown is very good quality – difficult to find something like that in the usual shops. And it is, of course, not an item for a worker. A school or kindergarten might have something like that for a New Year show but a theatre *would* seem more likely,' he said.

185

'I agree. I think you should try the opera houses, too.'

Rossel's voice was flat, lifeless.

'Aren't you going to look at the files, Lieutenant?' asked Taneyev. He was after at least a little acknowledgement of his detective work. Even though Rossel was dreading the thought of seeing her name – Sofia's name – drummed onto a flat, unfeeling page by the keys of a clerk's typewriter, he nodded.

'Six women of about the same height – one hundred and seventy centimetres – and aged between thirty and forty. All recently reported missing in this region and far beyond. I even had to send to Moscow for some of them,' said the sergeant.

Rossel opened the files one by one, pulling out the first sheet with the photograph clipped to it. Then stopped at the fourth page.

'Are you all right, Comrade Lieutenant?'

Number four gazed up at him through enigmatic, olive-green eyes set above cheekbones as white and strong as stone. He read the name again and again to himself.

Sofia Fedotova . . .

As if it was a charm. As if it was his sacred mantra. As it once had been.

Rossel took a deep breath. Then handed the other five files back. 'Thank you, Comrade Taneyev,' he said.

Taneyev took them back.

'Don't you need all of them, Lieutenant?' he asked as Rossel headed for the door. 'Why only that one? Is she the one? Sofia Fedotova? But she was a hospital cleaner from Ivangorod. Surely she can't be your Snow Queen?'

*

Dance with me, Sofia.

She had looked at him, surprised.

You, of all people?

Every man in the conservatory was a little in love with Sofia – in some cases, more than a little – and because she smiled at them, many thought they had a chance. She had one long-term boyfriend, a tall, habitually off-key Estonian trombonist who was either very tolerant or oblivious to her occasional one-night stands. She was available but choosy. It alarmed and irritated Felix in equal measure that he had never seen the inside of Miss Fedotova's chemise.

Dance with me, Sofia.

It was another drunken party and he could no longer contain himself. It had been his policy to wait until she had tired of her admirers and her supposed relationship with the trombonist had blown itself out, so to speak. Then their friendship would blossom into something else – love, of course! – and she would see him anew. But tonight, he could not resist, so he took his courage in both hands, waited for that split second when she was alone – dark, frowning, voluptuous, perfect – and approached.

Sofia took his hand and stood up as somebody struck up a tragic waltz on the piano and somebody else called for more vodka. More couples joined them in the middle of the room – a dusty student room in the hostel, smelling of smoke, of good proletarian food and bad proletarian drink. The beds and tables had been shunted to one side and the dance floor was full. A tenor began to wail as Sofia rested her head on Revol's shoulder. She was a singer, too, a mezzo.

'It's Revol's night tonight, the lucky devil,' he thought he heard a voice say in the darkness, but he couldn't be sure. Her breasts pressed against his thumping heart.

They danced amid the flickering candles and the clinging couples and emptying glasses and bottles, and Rossel held Sofia as if she were a bisque doll. Only as the song drew to a close did he draw his lips closer to hers.

After that ... glorious nights of cheap vodka and cheaper tobacco, concerts at the Kirov, picnics in Primorsky Park, and passion. Such passion. She bought him a copy of Baudelaire's Fleurs du Mal *and read* The Albatross *to him, again and again – 'Poets are like these lords of sky and cloud, Who ride the storm and mock the bow's taut strings.' Musicians, too, she said. Once he had awoken to find her softly singing her Cossack folk song to him.*

But then.

'No, Revol, not anymore,' she had whispered one evening as she lay beside him. Informing him with inexplicable detachment that it was over.

'Not with you, because . . .'

'Why not?'

She had always refused to tell him.

*

Dr Volkova looked at him with an expression that conveyed she expected him not to be able to stomach what was coming next.

'Proceed, Doctor,' he said. But his voice was wavering.

Rossel patted his pockets for the reassuring shape of his cigarettes. Trying to drown out the melody that was still echoing around his brain. Matches – *fuck your mother, where are my matches?*

The Snow Queen's ribs – *Sofia's ribs* – stuck out like a xylophone. Her long, dark hair spilled behind her head, in sharp and still elegant contrast to the purple and black pudding of what had been her face.

'Because of the investigations into the Doctors' Plot, I am one of only two working forensic pathologists left in the whole of Leningrad, Lieutenant, so my time is precious. But now that her internal organs have thawed, I have been able to examine the body and gather evidence,' said Dr Volkova. She went through the official checklist.

'Dental records and fingerprints were not possible, as with the other bodies. Our murderer had already eliminated that line of inquiry.'

The doctor had sliced the corpse open from the bottom of the rib cage to below the abdomen and removed the internal organs.

'As with the other female, this victim had little blood and no urine left. There was practically no fatty tissue on her.'

Rossel was still fumbling for his matches. He felt the burn of acid rising in his throat and felt like throwing up, but he was determined to resist the compulsion.

'What are those marks?'

Dark green tendrils were spreading over Sofia's corpse, and her skin was starting to blister and peel.

'When bodies defrost, decomposition is rapid,' said Dr Volkova. 'That discolouration spreads through the veins. I had better finish examining her quickly, before unpleasant fluids start to exit the orifices.' She caught his expression. 'Sorry.'

'Is the killer's method of starvation and sedation supported in this case, too?' said Rossel.

'Indeed,' the pathologist replied. 'Pressure sores, lack of fat, nothing in the gastrointestinal tract, muscles showing signs of wasting – all that is the case here. My tests reveal the presence of an opiate rather than a barbiturate but confirm sedation. Also, can you smell?'

He took a sniff in spite of himself. Yes, a faint whiff.

'Pear, just like you said.'

Dr Volkova nodded. 'Eau de Bone. The aroma of pear would be clearer if you came closer but perhaps that is inadvisable. The smell was particularly clear when I depressed her lungs. It is the smell of acetone – a ketone, which is produced when your body runs out of glucose and burns fat. It is found in higher concentrations in people who have been starved. Anyone who worked in a morgue during the siege would be very familiar with it.'

Rossel swallowed hard. In an effort to distract himself from the body, he found himself staring fixedly at the doctor's full, red and slightly quivering lips.

At last!

His fingers closed around the box of matches in his pocket. He took them out and went through the complicated, two-handed process of extracting a lone match from the box that he could manoeuvre into position to strike. Two went on the floor before match, matchbox and cigarette were all where they needed to be.

His eyes pleaded. 'She wasn't conscious then? An opiate, you say.'

'I'm afraid I cannot be certain. There is certainly evidence of haemorrhaging when the face was removed.'

'Could that not have been done later?'

Dr Volkova lowered her eyes. 'No. Doing all that to a frozen corpse is not possible. All the mutilations must have taken place shortly after death. Or . . . shortly before.'

The pathologist went over to her desk and returned with a piece of paper.

'These are the basic details. Height, hundred and seventy centimetres. Hair colour, black. Age, early to mid-thirties. Unfortunately, with a frozen body it is very difficult to estimate time of death.'

Rossel took the paper and thanked her.

Dr Volkova reached out and took Rossel's cigarette from his lips. Then took two quick nerve-steadying puffs and returned it to him.

'I heard Captain Lipukhin call this one the Snow Queen,' she said, reaching down to smooth a crinkle in the lapel of her uniform.

'A joke. Of a sort.'

'Do you know the fairy tale?'

Rossel nodded. 'A little. Something about a magic mirror?'

'Yes, a devil and his magic mirror,' said Dr Volkova. 'A mirror that distorted the reflection of everyone who looked into it, magnifying all that was ugly and hiding everything beautiful.' She began working at the crinkle in her blouse now, he noticed. Hardly looking up at him.

'It shattered, the mirror shattered, and its tiny shards were blown all over the world and into the eyes and the hearts and the minds of men and women, boys and girls, everywhere. "Freezing the fragile hearts of all Mother Russia's children," is the phrase my babushka used when she would recite the tale to us little ones.'

Dr Volkova dropped her hand and glanced up at him.

'They froze their hearts,' she said, 'those poisonous shards, freezing them – just like our Snow Queen's, here, has been – and making all around see only ugliness.'

She sighed.

'I think she was pretty, this one. Not a head-turner, perhaps. But beautiful of soul. Sometimes, I have noticed, they are the ones men obsess about more than any other. A certain type of man, anyway.'

Rossel tried to make his voice sound unconcerned but failed.

'She doesn't look so good right now, Doctor. I fail to see how you can reach such a conclusion,' he said.

Dr Volkova studied him.

'Not by looking at her, comrade. By looking at you. Your hands are trembling and I've never seen you so pale.'

22

Thursday October 25

Time ticked away with every clack of the train's wheels.

After a couple of stops, a little girl of about ten got on with her mother. They sat opposite Rossel. One of the girl's legs was missing and her face was scarred. The mother, without being prompted, blamed the girl's misfortunes on a German incendiary bomb. Soon she was in full flow about her wartime misfortunes and the punishments that should be visited for all eternity on the German people, the way it was a disgrace that half the country had got away with it. The girl kept silent, glum and embarrassed, so Rossel took off his left glove and showed her the two stumps, with their smooth white tips, where fingers should be. She stared at them without any sign of being impressed until he mimed playing the piano and pulled the stupidest face he could, which elicited a giggle, though the mother did not join in. By the time the train reached his stop, he and the girl had bonded, if not healed, and he had decided to feel a little less sorry for himself.

The journey was brought to a halt by the river, which barred the way to the Soviet Socialist Republic of Estonia. On the Russian side was Ivangorod; on the other lay its twin town, Narva. Both had their fortresses, medieval struc-tures that glowered at each other over the dark water. A rusty bridge yoked the two scruffy settlements together. If Sofia really had been a fairy-tale queen, he thought, then this seemed the perfect place for some ogre to imprison her.

It was easy to find Ivangorod's police station, a squat, red-brick building in the shadow of the town's castle. Rossel walked up the stone steps and went in.

Lieutenant Yuri Shumilov was amicable enough towards an equal from the big city but gave the impression of a man who had other things to do, though in an outpost this sleepy it was hard to imagine what that might be.

'Here is her regional file, Lieutenant. Sofia Semyonovna Fedotova. We collected some items from the room she was staying in when she was first reported missing – letters, drawings, bills, her work permit.'

Rossel wondered if it was possible to get a transfer to somewhere like this – somewhere well out of the way, where no one got to bother you with corpses on railway lines.

'There are also some volumes of poetry, a sketchbook and a couple of photographs, all in this bag,' continued Shumilov. 'There is no next of kin we have been able to find. Do you know of any? The clothes are in a package and will be donated to factory workers. The papers I thought you might want to look at. Feel free to take them, I don't want them anymore.'

Rossel looked around the station at the three other mili-tia officers leafing through meaningless paperwork and realised that a transfer would be a mistake. The biggest killer out here was boredom.

The radio was on. A staccato, patriotic march, indistinguishable from all the others, crashed to a close and a voice brimming with enthusiasm announced the broadcasting of a speech by 'our dearest, greatest leader, the great architect of Communism, General-Secretary of the Central Committee of the Communist Party of the Soviet Union. Our beloved Stalin.'

Over the radio came a soft but unmistakable voice, a pleasant tenor with a light Georgian accent, greeting delegates from the republics of the Soviet Union and from communist parties around the world to the forthcoming celebrations.

Shumilov and his colleagues froze.

'Comrades,' crackled the general-secretary's voice. 'The entire country is celebrating this meeting, the first Congress since our victory over Nazi Germany, Japan, and other fascistic powers in the Great Patriotic War. Since 1945, new fronts have opened against new enemies who wish to see our achievements in culture, science, society and other peaceful endeavours crushed. Yet we have prevailed thanks to the unity of the communist fraternity, at home and abroad. We have . . .'

Shumilov glanced at Rossel. Both men got hurriedly to their feet and stood to attention; the other three militia officers did the same.

'. . . imperialist ambitions to undermine us, to sabotage us, to provoke us into disunity and strife, emerging with glory into a new age of prosperity and happiness. Yet we must remain as vigilant as ever against the snakes and devils of the capitalist exploiters and fifth columnists. They, and

195

all traitors who offer them help, must be annihilated *without pity* for the good of the state.'

Stalin rarely spoke with anger in his voice. Since the war, indeed, he had made fewer and fewer speeches, and when he did, he sounded pragmatic and downbeat, as if he were announcing that month's agricultural production figures.

There was no mistaking the venom behind his words now.

'We must cut out the infected parts of the Party to save it from illness. We will march onwards, under the flag of Lenin, with the guidance of Marx, trampling underfoot those who dare to stand in our way. Traitors, wreckers and fifth columnists – we must be ever vigilant. Do not hesitate to strike in the forthcoming campaign to root out our enemies, wherever they may be lurking. Do not fear to give your assistance to the guardians of Bolshevism. Find the Trotskyites. Unearth the counter-revolutionary doctors plotting against our government. Isolate and destroy the conspirators. For, as you learned during the war against the fascist Hitlerite aggressor – and as we see again with the imperialist ambitions of the United States and her lackeys in Europe – nothing can be taken for granted, and no perfidious so-called ally can be trusted.'

Rossel stared at the wooden walls of the police station, not daring even a sideways look. Better to die in the line of duty than of boredom. But better still not to die at all.

When the speech ended, Lieutenant Shumilov cried out, '*Three cheers for our beloved Stalin!*' and everyone in the station clapped furiously, bellowing their hurrahs, smiling in rapture. Their applause rang on and on for three, four, five minutes – with a stranger in their ranks no one dared to be the first to cease. Only when Shumilov at last cried out, 'Comrades, a toast to the great and mighty Stalin!' and pulled out a bottle of vodka from somewhere under his desk did they rest their stinging hands.

You had to admire the lieutenant's thinking – the only way to safely stop applauding Stalin was to start toasting him.

*

Rossel opened the file and stared at her photograph once again. Sofia Fedotova. Age thirty-four. Born down the road in Kingissyepp, educated at school number twenty-two and then at the special music college, before winning a place at the opera faculty of the Leningrad Conservatory. Spent most of 1942 working as an ambulance nurse in the city before being evacuated to Kazakhstan.

But he knew all that. What he didn't know was what had happened to her after the war.

She had returned to Leningrad but by August 1946 she had moved here, to Ivangorod, mopping floors and empty-ing bedpans, apparently having made no attempt to con-tinue as a singer.

'She went missing in late July of this year, according to her co-workers at the polyclinic,' said Shumilov. He had a faint Baltic edge to his speech and, despite the Russian name, Rossel thought he was probably an ethnic Estonian. 'She said she was going to Leningrad to meet a friend and never returned.'

'Where is the polyclinic?' asked Rossel.

'Over the river. Here and in Narva, many of us work in one town and live in the other. This Sofia woman of yours lived in a *kommunalka* on the Ivangorod side – the address is in the file. Go if you want but they have already found someone else to live in her old apartment.'

Rossel looked up.

'So soon?'

His opposite number shrugged. 'Small town, too many people. Living space is not easy to come by. Word gets around fast. Besides, she hadn't been there for months – people were getting impatient, there's always a queue.'

There were three unfinished letters to friends – a few small moans about her work, mocking remarks about doctors trying to get her into bed, an account of a week's holiday in Tallinn. All three were less than a page long and who knew why she had kept but not finished them. Her work record was almost completely blank – no commendations, no complaints.

Rossel turned to the books, lifting them in twos and threes out of the bag. Pushkin, Lermontov and Baratynsky. Nothing controversial – nobody had yet outlawed Pushkin. 'Better the illusions that exalt us than ten thousand truths.' She had always loved the poet's line from *The Hero*, declaiming it one night as they walked back from a concert just as an air-raid siren started up. There was not a trace of fear in her voice, he remembered.

Last of all was a green, leather-bound sketchbook. Rossel leafed through, past trees, cats, street scenes, drawings of the meandering River Narva. A grand, domed building he did not recognise, like a nineteenth-century country estate belonging to an aristocrat. She had sketched this three times from different angles.

Now came an interior drawing. Behind a bed was a table and a vase. Scattered around were a few playing cards, not a complete deck, not even a complete suit. At the foot of the bed was something else: a musical score with a couple of notes drawn on it. There was writing on the score where the title should be – *Thanatos and H* . . . something. The second word was unfinished.

And then a drawing unlike all the others. A shadowy presence lying on the side of the bed, sheets tangled about it. Rossel stared down at the hatching on the page but could make out no discernible features. He could only just be certain the prone figure was human.

Sofia had been an accomplished rather than a brilliant artist but somehow this drawing had an intensity, a meaning that the others lacked, as if it was rooted in personal experience, not mere observation or imagination.

There was something else too.

A second erratic scribbling. A crude attempt to deface the first image. The pen pressing so deep it had torn a small hole into the paper.

Whoever this shadow was, she was petrified of them. The certainty of this drove a cold blade through him from his throat to his guts.

*

Rossel crossed the bridge into Narva to looks of indifference from the guards and one lazy, semi-insolent salute. Shumilov had written him a pass to get over the bridge and the nominal border separating Russia from the Estonian Soviet Socialist

Republic. The town might have been in a different country but there was no need to learn the language: everybody here was either Russian or spoke Russian.

When he got to the polyclinic, he stopped any nurse he could find of about Sofia's age. The third one he asked, a careworn thirty-year-old with short dark hair and boyish features, knew her. Yes, she said, we were friends but Sofia was elusive. She didn't like to talk about herself too much.

'What did she do out of work hours?' asked Rossel.

'Oh, I don't really know,' said the nurse. 'She lived on the other side. But she sang at workers' canteens sometimes, she got some extra money that way. She had a beautiful voice – she was classically trained, you know. But she gave that all up.'

'Did she ever say why?'

'Yes, once, she did,' said the nurse. 'She was in Leningrad, during the blockade. All of that horror' – and here the woman paused to flick the fingers of one hand as if warding off flies from a plate of jam, a gesture apparently intended to convey the months of slaughter and misery – 'left a scar. Inside, I mean. We got drunk together, once – the only time. And she blurted it out. "You cannot sing all *that*, you cannot express that. A genius could, perhaps, but why would they want to?" She was crying. Which was unlike her. So, she had run away from Leningrad. It must have been bad for her in the war to come here of all places. Do you know where she is now, Lieutenant?'

'Yes,' said Rossel. 'Did she ever talk about any family or any relationships?'

'Her mother and father were killed in the Great Patriotic War. All the doctors,' added the nurse in lower tones, 'all the doctors wanted to be with her. But they are all either too married or too old. Not suitable. She never found anyone, I believe – not anyone that she talked of, anyway. She still looked after herself though, you know, spent money on her lovely long dark hair. Too much, in my opinion.'

'No one else?' asked Rossel. 'Are you sure?'

The nurse thought. 'Before she finally went away, she mentioned meeting up with an old friend in Leningrad. That was odd, you know? She never went back there, never said much about the rest of her time there. But one day someone had got in touch and she seemed very happy about it at first. I could tell when she was happy because she got a little more talkative. When she was upset, she went very, very quiet. She ended up going to see whoever it was a few times, I think. But it didn't end well.'

'Why do you say that?'

'I bumped into her one day. Asked her how it was going. She just looked sullen. Wouldn't say a thing . . . Is she in trouble? I hope not. Girls like that, ones who men lust after in that *particular* way, romantically. Pretending they are all poets, right up to the moment they first unbuckle their pants. Well, it's my experience that they don't have to go searching for heartache. It just comes to them. Poor Sofia, she would never have gone looking for trouble, herself. I'm sure of it.'

23

It was past six o'clock before the train from Ivangorod chugged to a halt back in Leningrad's Baltic Station. Rossel leapt from his carriage and hurried to catch a tram that would take him to Theatre Square.

As he looked through the tram window, he saw the first flakes of a renewed snowfall tumble through the light of the street lamps. He began to hear Stalin's voice again – his tired mind was playing tricks on him, he thought. He listened carefully. No, it was real – the great leader was still exhorting him to be vigilant against spies, wreckers, counter-revolutionary rightists and capitalist vampires. Just as he had been on the radio in Ivangorod.

Rossel pressed his nose against the glass and looked up. On lampposts and buildings, he could see loudhailers that hadn't been there yesterday, nestled among the flags and banners, hailing the forthcoming celebrations. Not long ago, more loudhailers on the lampposts had signified national crisis; now they prepared the populace for a national triumph. Though sometimes the two went hand in hand, as the populace knew well.

The tram halted in Theatre Square and Rossel jumped down. The huge doors of the Kirov were locked so he strode round to the artists' entrance, swatting aside the guard, demanding to know where Marina Morozova was. To be taken to her immediately. A young man dressed as a troubadour pointed him in the direction of her dressing room and he hammered on the door, wishing that the terrified guard who had accompanied him all the way but who seemed to know nothing useful would push off.

She wasn't there so, with an increasing entourage of stage hands and chorus members pressed into the cause of finding her, Rossel blundered about the warren of corridors until he found himself at the edge of the great stage of the Kirov Opera itself. All was confusion, a harsh blur of lights, crashing chords and frantic movement.

'It's the rehearsal,' said the guard, reproach in his small voice.

It was, in fact, a break in rehearsal – stage managers were yelling, men and women in filthy rags or wearing uniforms of the Red Army were talking and laughing while men in overalls hoisted shattered walls, bullet-pocked vehicles and heavy machine guns onto their shoulders and wandered off into the darkness.

Vronsky's opera *The Blockade*, rumoured to be his most accomplished work, was almost ready – with a cast of thousands, by the looks of it. It was intended to be a masterpiece to rival that cry of defiance and tribute to the city's unconquerable spirit, the Leningrad Symphony, by the only Soviet composer thought able to surpass Vronsky, Dmitri Shostakovich.

Just as Rossel was wondering how he would ever find her in the chaos, Marina Morosova ran straight into him.

BEN CREED

In the rough shirt and trousers of a hero of socialist labour and anti-fascist defence, she looked a far cry from the elegant figure he had spoken to a few days ago.

Marina drew back and berated him for his clumsiness but cut it short as she espied the uniform.

'That is not a costume for the opera,' she said. 'Ah, Revol. It is you.'

'Marina,' Rossel said, taking her to one side. The crowd was thinning out. A stage hand shouted out, 'Fifteen minutes, only fifteen minutes!'

'Marina,' Rossel repeated. 'Marina, I believe that . . .'

He stopped. What did he believe? That her life was in danger? That the leader of a rogue Orthodox death cult had been murdering musicians? That this crazed priest was still capable of killing from beyond the grave? Of course not – it was ridiculous. So, then what?

'When we last met, we spoke of Felix, did we not?'

'Yes. Yes, we did,' she said.

'Has he been in contact? Has he been here, or to your home?'

She coloured.

'What are you insinuating?' she said. 'I have not seen Felix Sorokin for a long time. For many years.'

'How many years, exactly?'

She paused. 'Three or four, perhaps longer,' she said. 'He just dropped out of sight. Must have got tired of me.'

'What about Maxim?' asked Rossel. 'Maxim Avdeyev?'

'Max? Not since the conservatory. He was not in my circle.'

Indeed not, thought Rossel.

204

'Do you ever see a priest?'

Marina glared. 'For my many sins, you mean?'

Rossel looked her back in the eye. 'For whatever reason.'

'I see them at Easter and I see them when I go to lay flowers in the cemetery,' she said, jaw tight. 'Otherwise, no.'

'Where is your apartment?' he asked her.

Marina laughed, but without merriment. 'You get ever more personal, Lieutenant.'

'My interest is your safety, Marina. You must forgive the intrusion. Where?'

'Near the Nikolsky Cathedral,' the singer said, looking bemused, 'a stone's throw. Why?'

'And what is the security there? What protection do you have?'

'Comrade Lieutenant, this is a melodrama worthy of grand opera. What is going on?'

Rossel rubbed his eyes. It was dangerous to tell her too much . . . *On what authority did you divulge crucial information in a murder investigation potentially involving members of state security to the prima donna of the Kirov Opera before you gave it to the MGB, comrade?*

Particularly if she was an informer.

He would have to go step by step, listening for the ice cracking under his feet.

'Sofia Fedotova,' Rossel said. 'Last time we spoke you mentioned her.'

Marina removed her flat cloth cap and unbundled her hair. 'Sofia? Yes – of course. Such a sweet soul. Never quite had what it takes. Perhaps she could have been a junior chorus member . . .'

'But not Maxim Avdeyev?'

'Are you planning a reunion, Revol? Is that what this is all about?'

'When did you last see Maxim?' Rossel pressed her.

She thought for a moment. 'Not since the war. You were friends with him much more than I was; you played in the conservatory's orchestra together, if I am right. Wait – didn't you both play in the *Leningrad* symphony? The performance here, I mean?'

Rossel shook his head.

'Max, perhaps, but not me. I was at the front.'

He pulled out Sofia's green leather-bound sketchbook and found the drawings of the house and the room. 'Look at this,' he said. 'Sofia drew it. Does it mean anything to you? Do you recognise anything?'

Marina took the book from his hands and held it up so that some of the stage light would illuminate it.

'All I can make out is badly hatched shadow. A bedroom scene that she has subsequently scribbled over. But, as I remember, she had the good sense to have many lovers.'

'Do you know what the writing might mean?'

'Thanatos and something? No idea. Greek? For opera, I have to know Italian, German and some French, Lieutenant, but there are no Greek masterpieces that I know of.'

Rossel turned the page. 'How about the domed building?'

Marina looked down again. The lights were behind her and Rossel could not see her face properly, but he heard the sharp inhalation. The soprano turned the pages and stared at the other sketches of the same house.

'When did she draw this?' Marina's voice was tight.

'Do you recognise it, Marina?'

She bent her head again over the pages, flicking through the rest of the sketchbook.

Rossel asked her again if she knew the place. Marina snapped the covers together and handed it back to him. She opened her mouth just as a huge figure stepped directly behind her and almost blotted out the light. Marina whirled round, straight into the hulk of Vronsky.

The composer was enveloped in an enormous wolfskin coat, like a Red Army general surveying the frozen wastelands after a battle with the Wehrmacht. He looked at once eccentric and terrifying. There was not a trace left of his previous affable charm. In his presence Marina wilted, bowed her head and walked off into the wings without another word.

Vronsky towered over Rossel for half a minute – relishing the silence, as if daring the militia man to speak – before swaggering past him.

In the Kirov, the composer was the law.

*

Rossel was escorted to the foyer of the theatre and then to the exit. But he did not feel like going.

He stopped at the heavy swinging door, turned, and headed back in the direction of the auditorium.

'Comrade Officer, you can't go in there,' bleated the stage manager sent to ensure his departure. 'We are nearing our conclusion. *The Blockade* is almost complete. Maestro Vronsky says he is not comfortable with observers at today's rehearsal.'

Rossel pushed past and yanked open the door that led into the opulent interior of the Kirov Theatre. He marched without pausing down to the very front of the stalls. *Fuck Vronsky. Fuck Colonel Sarkisov. And the MGB.*

Nothing mattered to him now. Sofia was gone. Someone had to pay for it.

Rossel glanced into the orchestra pit where the musicians were gathering after their break. It was a huge ensemble: he counted thirty violins, twelve each of violas and cellos, as many double basses as they could pack in, four each of all the woodwind including contrabassoon, bass clarinet and cor anglais, six horns, five trumpets, four trombones, tuba, and enough percussion to lead an army to Berlin and win the Great Patriotic War all over again – timpani, xylophone, bass drums, side drums, tam-tam, cymbals, bells. The players were cheek by jowl, barking at each other to take care as they high-stepped a route to their chairs, flapping their music as they made their own markings or scrawled reminders to themselves to make the correct changes of tempo or dynamic. It was probably double the size of the usual pit orchestra that hacked its way through *Nutcracker* once or twice a month. It was both a raucous, anarchic assembly and an elite club. Rossel felt like a pauper watching the princes at play. Compared to this, every other existence seemed drab. How he had missed it.

Suddenly a man in his fifties, the conductor, Eliasberg, a stalwart of the Kirov company, elegant, with swept-back, nicotine-stained hair, pale bullfrog-like cheeks and a pinched mouth, came threading his way through the second violins to reach the rostrum. He paused halfway up the steps, catching Rossel's eye for a split second, giving him a curt nod.

This was the man who had conducted Shostakovich's Leningrad Symphony in the depths of the siege, with the worst not over by a long way. He had taken a band of starving musicians, forced them to defy their privations, master Shostakovich's gigantic work and hurl it into the face of the surrounding Germans. Vronsky had spoken of the toughness of mind necessary to 'make the harsh decisions truly great art demands of its creators'. Eliasberg was notorious for it – denying his players half of their meagre bread rations until they did his bidding, hauling them from their beds and demanding they put bow to string, mouth to reed, forcing them to play on.

Eliasberg turned to the orchestra and quelled it into silence with a glare.

For the second half of that evening's rehearsal, the conductor declared, they were to receive a huge honour: the opera would be conducted by the great composer himself, Nikolai Nikolayevich Vronsky, 'People's Artist of the Soviet Union, winner of the Stalin Prize, winner of . . .'

Whatever else the maestro was winner of was drowned out by tremendous applause as the mighty frame of Vronsky, now shorn of his wolfskin and in a dark three-piece suit, trudged through the pit to take his place on the rostrum. Eliasberg, keen either to learn or to pay calculated homage, found a space at the bottom of the steps that led up to the rostrum and sat down.

Vronsky pointed at the oboe for an A and the orchestra began tuning up. On stage, a chorus of no fewer than one hundred singers gathered in the ruins of Leningrad to bury their dead and shake their fists at the Fuhrer.

Vronsky looked slightly behind him, along the front row of seats towards Rossel. If he was displeased, he didn't let it show. His gaze fell instead upon the lieutenant's still-gloved hands. Rossel had rested them on the brass rail along the first row; he drew them back, not knowing where to place them, before thrusting them in his pockets. Vronsky smiled.

'Let us begin,' he murmured.

The lights in the auditorium began to dim – as if, it seemed to Rossel, the great man controlled even the heavens – and a hush blanketed the stage and pit as he raised his arms.

It began with an undulating pulse in the violas and violins, a motion suggesting quiet bleakness, a troubled peace. The key was E flat – the hero's key. An abrupt crescendo and a sudden return to pianissimo was the only change for perhaps sixteen bars, before a clarinet sounded a note of slight dissonance, an F, like a drop of paint in clear water.

More strings joined in, the pulse beating a little harder. A bassoon stabbed a hard A – *sforzato, subito diminuendo*. Vronsky's hands were barely moving; he cued in one of the French horns with his eyes – an E flat, the core note. The sound was rising now, the cellos and basses adding more dissonance but gradually, in layers, as the major key became minor with a muscular clench of Vronsky's fist.

On stage, the members of the chorus rose from the rubble of the flattened city. Rossel looked for Marina but the survivors of the blockade, the tank makers, the armaments workers, the firefighters, trench diggers and soldiers, the lorry drivers who risked the Road of Life across the frozen

Lake Ladoga to bring supplies to the city that bore Lenin's name, they were all one. The people.

The oboe played a B flat, this time sustained, with a sweet, shallow vibrato, and the chorus began a soft chant.

Here men work without ceasing, rest and sleep forgotten – burdened and labouring with dread . . .

Was that Marina? A slim and feminine figure stepped forward to the sound of a repeated staccato G from the principal trumpet. Now Vronsky turned towards the mass of his first violins and now the music became sublime, epic; inside his coat Rossel felt himself curling his already twisted and broken left hand into a protective fist.

Let our gruel be no more than mere water, our bread worth more to us than gold. Like men of steel, we will endure . . .

He stared at Vronsky, who was exhorting both orchestra and singers to ever greater heights, and sensed the maestro could somehow feel his eyes upon him. At that exact moment, the composer began to conduct the piece even more intensely, more passionately, forcing the violinists towards new peaks of excellence, forcing them to play at a level Rossel could once reach but was now far, far beyond him. The musicians were being pushed to the limits of their technique, some clinging to the soaring melody, others tackling a furious *moto perpetuo* that underpinned this section. Playing as if their lives depended on it.

As the volume subsided, Marina's not quite crystal-clear soprano – his ear detected an imperfect but almost indiscernible emotional tension – floated through, a wordless line following the notes of E flat major before ending on

an ethereal A natural at the top. Rossel closed his eyes and let the rest of the section wash over him until, at last, the music subsided and only a regular rhythm in the double basses and timpani remained – the sound of a cortège.

The lieutenant opened his eyes again and saw Vronsky conduct the final bars with only the faintest gestures from one enormous paw.

Rossel himself was the thing that connected them all. Nadya, Max and now Sofia – they had all gone to the conservatory with him. Lipukhin and Taneyev were still working busily on identifying the other two corpses but he had no doubt now – whoever they were – that they, too, would lead back to his past. *Lieutenant Revol Rossel.* He was the biggest clue in his own case.

As he looked back down into the pit, he noticed Eliasberg, still sitting at Vronsky's feet, staring up at him. An insouciant half-smile momentarily flickered on the conductor's lips. Then he glanced back down at his score.

How could have Rossel been so foolish?

The arrest of all members of the local militia department out at Lake Ladoga had deceived him into believing that his involvement was a coincidence. Those arrests were more than plausible – one person's slip of the tongue could condemn a hundred friends and colleagues. So, it had seemed credible – just another evening of misfortune – that the Vosstaniya Street station, far away from the scene of the crime, should merely have drawn the short straw on a filthy winter's night to journey into the wilds of Karelia. Now, that plaintive telephone call direct to Rossel's station was as tell-tale as a spot of blood in the snow. The killer had arranged it. He was certain of it.

Inside his coat he tried to flex his broken fingers, to get them to resist the tone, resist the rhythm, resist his own sickening conclusions. But they would not obey.

*

Vronsky's right arm was fully extended, jutting out from the spotlight into the shadow that surrounded him. As the music stopped, he let it fall for a final time.

'No orchestra other than a Soviet orchestra could reach such heights,' he told them. 'I am honoured to have you perform my music.'

The composer smiled at the excited turmoil as the Kirov's orchestra – lighting cigarettes, exchanging compliments, pulling on fur coats and hats – struggled out of the pit and the chorus cleared the stage.

Before long only two men remained in the great hall.

Rossel had waited. Marina had recognised the building in the sketch. He was sure of it. It seemed significant to her. And she was, after all, sleeping with the maestro. So Vronsky might recognise it too.

The composer pulled on his wolfskin coat and then picked up a green manila file, bursting with manuscript papers, from his stand. His voice boomed from the stage. The silent auditorium emphasising its aggressive autocratic sibilance.

'This time you didn't listen, Listener. I sent word that you had to go.'

Rossel was sitting on one of the red velvet seats in the middle of the stalls. He got up and began to walk towards the stage. Talking as he moved down the aisle.

'Marina's top A, maestro. A little flat, didn't you think?'

Vronsky's eyes twinkled. For a moment, as last time, Rossel half expected the composer to break into laughter, changing his mood in an instant. But it passed.

'Your hands may be twisted and contorted but there's nothing wrong with your ears. People here remember you. They saw us talking and thought they recognised your face. And Marina cannot stop talking about "young Rossel". How your professor had told her you were the best student she'd ever had. That when you first turned up at the conservatory you could already play the Tchaikovsky concerto well enough to make people fall at your feet. Raw talent, talent of the kind that turns up once in a generation. And so handsome, too.'

The composer gestured with his huge right hand back towards the set of *The Blockade*. 'A tiny fragment of this piece is, in part, inspired by an earlier work of mine, based on *Crime and Punishment*. And you are every inch a young Raskolnikov, like Dostoevsky describes him. "Slim, well built, with beautiful dark eyes and dark brown hair." That's what Marina said. But you know what women are like? They do tend to wax a little overlyrical about any exotic fruit they feel nature has forbidden them.'

Rossel was standing next to that stage now; staring up at the great man.

'There was a certain tension in her voice, don't you think so, maestro? Marina sounded distracted, perhaps?'

Vronsky ran his fingers through his thick black beard and then nodded.

'Yes, there was some imperfection of tone, Lieutenant, a barely perceptible trace of it. I, too, I like to believe,' his voice was mocking, 'have something of an ear. We'd squabbled a little earlier, she and I. It's Marina's way of getting her revenge, refusing to deliver of her very best. Keeping something back to torment her admirers. She does the same thing when she's flat on her back – a cheap courtesan's trick to elicit further payment. A tawdry negotiation around the level of attention she believes her beauty demands. Trouble is, I've had her so many times now it's beginning to grate a little. Especially in the White Nights, when the sun slips through the drapes and picks out the ragged lines around her eyes. Such is life, eh, Lieutenant? Once a man is allowed to dine on *foie gras* every evening, he soon begins to dream of a simple breakfast of *kasha* and black bread.'

Rossel climbed the steps to the stage and stood a few feet away from the composer. This close, in his all-enveloping fur and still singled out by the stage lights, Vronsky's presence was as intimidating as ever.

Rossel opened Sofia's book and proffered it. Letting the composer get a good look at her sketches. 'Do you recognise anything in here, maestro? I think Marina might have.'

Vronsky took the book and glanced through it, as if uninterested. Then sighed deeply.

'Ah, you disappoint me, Lieutenant, you really do. I, just now, cast you in the role of Dostoevsky's greatest creation, Raskolnikov, an exceptional individual who was daring enough to take all the steps that are necessary for his will to triumph in this world and you reveal yourself, with this persistent plodding inquiry, to be nothing more than his sanctimonious, foolish detective, Porfiry Petrovich.'

'So, you don't recognise anything there, in the notebook?' Rossel persisted.

Vronsky shook his head. 'No, plodding Porfiry, I do not.'

BEN CREED

'You are sure about that, maestro? There's nothing in there that stirs even the most distant memory?'

The composer slapped the notepad shut and handed it to him. 'Have you ever seen a moth near a candle?' said Vronsky. '"He'll keep circling around me, circling around me, as around a candle; freedom will no longer be dear to him, he'll fall to thinking, get entangled, he'll tangle himself all up as in a net."'

The maestro held Rossel's eye for a second.

'The words of plodding Porfiry. So certain that his man would trip up. But then, you knew that.'

Vronsky leant forward and reached out to the detective's neck. The lieutenant did not move, letting the composer touch a raised brown mark on the left side, under his ear. Many violinists had them, caused by years of holding the instrument between the shoulder and the chin. Even after all this time, his had not faded. Which was why he took care to keep his uniform buttoned up and the mark out of sight. Sometimes, though, the collar slipped a little. The composer was tender, as if stroking a kitten.

Rossel took a step back and hitched up his collar as high as it would go. As he did so there was a click off-stage, as a stage hand cut the lights, and they were both plunged into darkness. Amongst the shadows, Rossel heard Vronsky's voice become softer again, teasing.

'You like to hide your fiddler's mark, Lieutenant, am I right? Need to. Not from others, no, *not* from others, but from yourself. Is that because you no longer play the Tchaikovsky concerto as you could, and are condemned instead to spend your life playing poor, lost Porfiry Petrovich instead?'

*

216

Rossel took off his gun and holster and dropped them on his bedside table. He picked up his copy of *Fleurs du Mal*, which was lying open upon it. Turned to *The Albatross*. Baudelaire used the bird in the poem as a symbol for an artist, poet or musician. Someone whose talent lets them 'soar' above the crowd but, also, separates them from it; making them sometimes mocked, forever awkward, ill at ease amongst their fellow men. There was a handwritten note in the margin: *This is who I am. Always. Remember that, whatever happens. Love S x.*

Rossel closed the book and placed it back down on the table. Then he knelt down and dragged his old violin case from underneath his bed. He needed to feel the change, to prove to himself he wasn't hiding anything.

He sprang the catches and pulled out bow, instrument and chin rest. Tightening the bow, he worked the rosin into the hair, hard. Then he picked up the violin with his broken left hand and whirled it into position, tucking it under his chin, feeling the edge of the body run into the remnants of the mark on his neck.

His head was pounding.

'You like to hide your fiddler's mark, Lieutenant, am I right? Need to. Not from others, no, *not* from others. But from yourself.'

Fuck you, Vronsky, he thought.

But, in his heart, he knew the maestro was right.

24

Friday October 26

And so, at last, they came.

A dozen of them or more, yelling orders and waving automatic rifles, pushing and kicking militia officers to the floor. Rossel and Taneyev were on the ground floor with two of the most junior ranks, sorting through missing persons reports. Trying to identify the two remaining victims – the older man who had been castrated and the younger one who had, at least, avoided that fate. Winnowing out the impossibles – 'too young, too old, too tall, too, no . . .' They saw the doors burst open. A dozen MGB crack troops, followed by an officer holding a Nagant pistol.

The officer stood in the middle of the station and waited for his men to finish subduing the cops. It did not take long. Rossel stared at him. The man's face was a sea of scar tissue that flowed over his left eye and up to the temple. The nose a mess, as if it had been held to a fire on one side. His one remaining eye was as grey as Magnitogorsk steel and swept over everything.

Rossel had seen the face before.

It had been a long time – almost a decade – but this was a face he had not forgotten, and never would.

You had to keep still. Motionless. Beside him, he heard Taneyev's breathing quicken. Rossel put out an arm. It was too late. The older man was leaving the safety of the desk. He approached the leader of the MGB detachment.

'No,' said Taneyev. 'No, please. I have a . . .'

A shot roared and flashed in the dark confines of Station 17 and Taneyev staggered. A hole had opened in his back as the bullet punched its way through his torso. He fell to the floor and lay there, wheezing and alone.

'Sergeant Pavel Grachev,' the officer shouted.

No one answered.

'Find this counter-revolutionary scum Grachev. Get the others into the trucks.'

Amid the sudden movement, Rossel stepped towards Taneyev and dragged him into a chair. He slumped in it like a sandbag, head back, a small bubble of blood and air stuck to his bottom lip. Buoyed by his rasping breath, the bubble rose and fell almost imperceptibly, looking like a tiny but macabre Christmas bauble, of the kind his grandmother hid in a box under the stairs of her old dacha. The Nagan swung towards him and Rossel froze. Taneyev was trying to whisper something. A name – *Artyom*. That of his boy who played for Zenit.

He said it twice. Then the bubble popped.

Above their heads came a yell and a series of thuds – Lipukhin was prudent enough to submit but Grachev was crazy enough not to.

They, then, might be the next to die.

The MGB officer spoke again. 'I am notifying all members, without exception, of this department of the People's Militia, Vosstaniya Street, Station 17, that they are under arrest for harbouring and possibly collaborating with a reactionary fifth-columnist traitor to the Bolshevik cause. Anyone else who resists will be shot. I advise you to prepare your confessions now as they will be required in full and in writing. Outside with you.'

More sounds of protest and resistance resounded above their heads. Someone, most probably one of the most senior ranks, prised out of his office for the first time in weeks, was threatening to write to Stalin. Stalin's in-tray must be overflowing with complaints from outraged citizens certain he would help them, if only he knew of the injustices being perpetrated in his name.

Had this been the army, whose officers hated state security and where the average captain believed he outranked anyone except Beria himself, there might have been a battle. But the militia was no match for the MGB. In meek silence a dozen cops shuffled towards the double doors and to the waiting vans and trucks. Rossel stopped and looked at the scarred face, wondering if it recognised him in turn. Or if it had tortured and broken so many people that one more old victim strapped to a chair and having its fingers crushed with pliers or severed with a cold chisel was very much like another.

'What is Sergeant Grachev accused of?' Rossel asked the MGB officer.

One of the security troops drove the butt of his rifle at Rossel's stomach but he had been ready for such an attack. He sidestepped and parried the blow with his forearm. The trooper swore and pointed the barrel straight at Rossel's face, cocking the weapon – but at that moment Sergeant Grachev came crashing down the stairs head first, closely followed by the MGB soldiers who had ejected him from the upper floor.

The sergeant had the same question as Rossel.

'What the fuck have I done?' Grachev shouted as the soldiers dragged him to his feet. 'Fuck your mothers, what have I said that was so wrong?'

His hands were cuffed and he held the chain before him as if it was an affront to Lenin himself.

The MGB officer regarded him and sniffed. 'We do not only look at a man's words or his deeds as he lives today. Also his class, his ideology, his past,' he said. 'And your class is that of a treacherous imperialist. You have been unmasked as a former soldier for the imperialist cause in the Civil War. As a youth living in Kharkov province, you joined Kornilov's vipers and fought against the Bolsheviks. Your past has just caught up with you, Comrade Grachev.'

'I am a Soviet worker and only ever a Soviet worker, comrade.' Still Grachev fought, earning him a punch in the kidneys. He barely winced. 'And when you check my deeds,' he snarled, 'you will see I – I fought at Stalingrad, at Kursk. I fought in Prussia, I fought in Berlin. I have done nothing wrong.'

The MGB major looked at him with a dulled eye before he gave a response.

'They all say that.'

Grachev's face fell. For he knew, better than anyone, that they did all say that.

They were led outside, Captain Lipukhin the last to be brought out. He looked up into the grey sky and sighed. As if his main regret was to have not opened a second bottle of vodka that morning.

BEN CREED

Rossel clambered into the back of the squat truck
and took his place on the bench between Lipukhin and
a spotty, trembling private who had only been with them
for five weeks. How meekly they all accepted their fate.
But then most of them, unlike Rossel, had no idea what
an MGB torturer was capable of, what agonies he could
inflict and the relentlessness and relish with which he
would inflict them. For sure, everyone had heard tales of
the filthy, freezing and brutal prison that was The Crosses.
They knew how fast the camps of the north and east could
annihilate body and soul. But they would trudge to the
crowded cells, to the courts to stand before the ranting
prosecutors, to the place where they dug their own graves,
and there they would stand without a murmur. Because
they had not yet experienced for themselves what an MGB
interrogator could do to human flesh.

Fear rose in him like bile – better to die in a hail of
Chekist bullets than endure for a second time what he had
endured then. Even after a decade, the terror of it haunted
him. But it was too late; the vehicles were all moving now
and Lipukhin and the young militia private were both
clutching Rossel's arms against the truck's swaying.

He yearned for a believer's faith – it might comfort him
in the cells or in the interrogation room or as they were
about to execute him. Around him, men and women were
murmuring prayers and shedding tears. But faith had never
come easily to him. Even in the 2nd Shock Army.

He fought to suppress the memory and focused on
Grachev instead. A former White? Possibly – Grachev had
been born belligerent and would pick any side if it meant
the chance to kill people. Rossel knew nothing about the

222

sergeant's life before the Great Patriotic War but Grachev was committed to Grachev, not to the cause of Bolshevism, and if he had done a spell after the 1917 revolution in the service of the monarchist White army fighting for the Tsar's cause, it would come as no surprise.

Or was the raid linked to their investigation? It seemed excessive when you could just dream up a charge against Rossel himself. But there were always things you didn't know, enemies you had no clue existed, plots that you discovered only when you were implicated in them.

The column of vehicles rumbled through the arched, red-brick entrance of The Crosses and they were all ushered from the trucks, led under the white dome of the prison's huge church and formed into an orderly line of the condemned.

Rossel already knew the name of the man with the scarred face. It was the man who had – all those years ago – sung scales as he worked on his fingers. Nikitin.

The face chilled him more than a Leningrad winter ever could.

Acting on instinct, Rossel glanced over to his left, at a clutch of his fellow militia officers from Station 17. Grachev was looking right at him, face twisted with hatred, and Rossel realised the sergeant thought he was responsible for this disaster, that Rossel had denounced him. Rossel held his gaze and shook his head but Grachev only spat at him.

But on the other side of the fear in Rossel's gut was another thought. The thought that he might get close to his torturer again. A chance to sing a song of his own. A chance to get even.

*

He would not scream. He refused to give them that.

After the first one, when he realised he would never play the Mendelssohn or the Tchaikovsky or any of the Beethoven sonatas or the Paganini caprices again, the pain didn't really matter anymore.

Pick a concerto, he thought. Pick that bloody Brahms. Start from the second subject, put some passion into it. He heard the admonitions of his professor . . . Revol, my goodness, what's the rush? Fill every note, Revol, treat everyone like your own precious child. Technically this is one of the easier sections yet everyone is in such a hurry to finish it. Then they moan about how hard the rest of the piece is. What did Brahms write at the beginning?

Allegro non troppo, professor.

Allegro non troppo. Non. Troppo. Again, please.

Allegro non . . .

In his mind he tried to pick up his violin but his arms would not respond.

More, said the one-eyed major, as he carefully placed the chisel at the knuckle of Rossel's left ring finger. We've sung do, and re. What is next? Mi? Do, re, mi . . .

From far away, there was a screeching sound. God, was that him? No, another hapless victim. Someone hopelessly out of tune. If he could only get to the pegs and do some tuning . . .

Do, re, mi, fa . . .

No, he would not scream.

But later, when he awoke with a start and found himself staring down at the splattered crimson of the cell floor, he stared down at his two severed fingers, clutching at the others that gave him nothing but unrelenting pain.

Now he cursed. Now he sobbed. Until there seemed to be nothing left of him, save for one singular animalistic sound.

Not because of the blood. Or the pain.

For the music.

Without that, Rossel knew, he would never be himself – his true self – ever again.

25

Monday October 29

Major Nikitin sat with his pen an inch from the paper. As if he were a factory book-keeper applying himself to a particularly stimulating chess puzzle in the few minutes he had left to relax before starting his proper work.

Stripped of his shirt – another MGB thug was preparing to continue the beating with a rubber truncheon and coils of wire – Rossel shivered in the cold and damp of the interrogation room. He dangled by his wrists from a beam that ran the length of the cell, only just able to touch the floor with the balls of his feet.

Pick another concerto. Something easier. The Bruch. All about beauty of tone.

Nikitin put the cap on his blue fountain pen with two slow twists and tucked it inside his breast pocket. He raised his head, displaying in the cell's dim light the smear of burns and skin grafts that ran from his temple to his neck, and fixed Rossel with his lone eye.

'I do remember you now,' he said. 'Yesterday you caught me by surprise – in truth, I have no memory of our previous encounter. Thanks to an incendiary bomb in the very first days of the Great Patriotic War, of course' – he reached up and touched his own scarred cheek – 'my own face is much more difficult to forget. But something in your manner, your stubbornness during these interrogations. Why, it's beginning to ring a bell. I apologise, Lieutenant Rossel, if in any way I came across as being impolite. But you know how it is – at this age, the years roll by, and the people we meet at work, well, after a while, their faces just blur one into the other.'

'I am sure you have my file, Major, so you must have known,' replied Rossel.

Nikitin sighed. 'No. Your prison file from The Crosses is, it seems, regrettably missing. We lost a lot of paperwork in the last days of the siege. A 7.5mm from a Kraut *Leichtgeschütz* hit the admin block. It does not matter. I need a list of your own crimes and a list compiled by you of the crimes of each and every officer in Station 17. Are you ready today to confess?'

'Only to doing my job,' said Rossel.

The major nodded at the guard, standing to attention in a corner of the cell. The truncheon hit him on his right side, just below the rib cage. He groaned and spat a little fresh blood onto the stone floor.

'We can spend several more days like this, Lieutenant, weeks even, if that's what it takes,' said Nikitin, watching his victim's face contort. 'The boy, one of the privates, has implicated you all in Grachev's crimes already, anyway. All I had to do was lean forward and gently squeeze one of those nasty pimples on his lily-white cheeks and he crapped his pants. Most unsavoury. Your most prudent course of action would be to back up his story and save yourself any more unpleasantness.'

Rossel fought to master the agony.

'As a member of the People's Militia, I am ready to discuss any criminal case with our glorious MGB,' he said, fighting for breath. 'I shall recount the investigation to date for you. First identified corpse. Nadya Bazhanova. A former student of the Leningrad Conservatory. She studied clarinet but became a dresser at the Kirov. One of yours – an MGB officer of lowly rank, whose job it was to keep an eye on the leading singers on foreign tours. Too many defections of late, I am assuming.'

'I can find all this in the militia files we have brought in from Vosstaniya Street,' interrupted Nikitin. 'It is not relevant to your confession.'

'Small, round dumpling of a girl,' said Rossel. 'Problem with dandruff. She used to gossip like a drunken babushka. At the conservatory she was everyone's friend but nobody's friend. I wasn't surprised she found a way to go abroad; she had a problem with inferiority – she was one of those average players who talk big and suck up to the right people to compensate.'

Nikitin nodded. The guard hit Rossel across the shoulder blades. *A good place to whack them*, Grachev had once told a small audience of junior officers before Rossel had broken up the tutorial. *Stings like a fucking bastard*. He was, as it turned out, quite right.

Rossel writhed but kept going, blurting out the first memories that came to mind. It helped him to forget where he was to try and keep ruminating.

'Corpse number two. Maxim Avdeyev. French horn player, from Pskov, always wore black, hid his pale mystical face behind his floppy hair. I never saw him drunk, not once. Older than us because he'd had to take two years out to go and look after his mother. Could beat anyone in the conservatory at chess. Even the professors. You'll have masses on him – he spent ages in the gulag, more ink than skin by the time he left. Went crazy for religion, prophesying the Apocalypse, said the Jews were just the start and we were all going that way, may have been cannibalising human flesh, blessing it and then swallowing it down as if it was some sort of black Eucharist.'

What was coming next?

Not his fingers?

Not for a second time, please . . .

'You knew three of the victims, three!' said Nikitin. 'Do you know what that makes me think?'

'Number three. Sofia Fedotova. Singer. Wanted to join the Kirov – always dreamed of going abroad. Of sailing away. Of lakes, of the sea. She *loved* the sea. And French poetry. She hated her parents; I think her father beat her sometimes but she never ever said so.'

'If you know them so well, Lieutenant, why do you not know who killed them?' Nikitin pointed at him. 'Unless it was you. Of course – and this *is* your confession?'

'I thought it was Maxim for a while,' said Rossel, slowly rotating like a carcass on a butcher's hook. He had to twist his head to look at Nikitin. 'He was obsessed with death. I believed he had old grudges against the others, or had gone mad, or both. I believed he got his followers to kidnap four people and slaughter them, and then him, in penitence, or revenge, or whatever. But now I do not think that, at all. There is something else. Someone else. Whose motivation is stranger still. So perverse somehow that it is impossible for me to imagine.'

The guard raised his truncheon again but this time Nikitin stayed his hand.

'Spare me the incoherent, irrelevant details of your non-existent investigation, Lieutenant. Do not waste my time or yours. Confess to sedition and harbouring a traitor. In the end, you will anyway.'

'Just before you arrested us, Dr Volkova was able to examine one of the remaining two bodies,' said Rossel. 'The older male. He was the only one of the five not to have starved so Dr Volkova extracted traces of alcohol from his blood and caviar – beluga – from his mouth.'

Nikitin took the truncheon out of the guard's hand and tried out a couple of practice swings.

'You will confess. Colonel Sarkisov says it must be so, and so it will be. For the colonel has Comrade Beria's ear. Station 17 is a traitorous counter-revolutionary unit corrupted by the imperialist and fifth-columnist Grachev. Admit it.'

Nikitin drew back the truncheon for a third time and aimed it at Rossel's already livid belly.

'Confess,' he said as he set to work. 'Confess.'

A banging at the cell door. A junior female officer stepped inside and saluted.

'Not now,' said Nikitin. 'Can't you see I'm . . .'

'A phone call, sir. It's Colonel Sarkisov from Moscow. He says it's urgent.'

*

How much we all want to live, thought Rossel. *We should all rise up, we should damn them to hell and spit in their*

*faces, and yet we will clutch at any tiny scrap of hope they
toss our way.*

Uncounted hours later. Time spent in oblivion. Time
spent conscious but reluctantly so – time spent longing for
death, less to ease the agony, though that would be welcome,
and more to remove the need for further interrogation. Time
spent licking moisture off the floor of the cell with a swollen
tongue. Time spent trying to give up and fade away – and,
failing that, time spent mildly surprised at one's own indifference in survival.

Doors in passages opening, words spoken. More time
spent alone. Then the dread sound of the rusty bolt in the
cell door turning . . .

*

'Your uniform, Comrade Lieutenant.'

Rossel sat on one side of a small wooden table. Nikitin
sat on the other. With his eyes the major indicated a small
bench to Rossel's right. This interrogation room was smaller,
darker. His militia uniform was folded on the bench, his
boots parked next to it.

'Your papers.'

Nikitin pushed them over the desk. Rossel looked at
them through swollen eyes.

'What?' he began. But could go no further.

Nikitin placed two fists on his desk, as if preparing to
rise. 'Colonel Sarkisov called. He says there is now talk in
Moscow of the murders by the lake. Of how the city of
Leningrad, always seen since the days of that reactionary

231

BEN CREED

scum Trotsky as a hotbed of dissidents and reactionaries, is running out of control. Those protectors of our city in the highest circles, the very highest, want this case solved. And, despite what I would see as your abject failure to date, someone believes you are, as the leading *sober* officer on the case, still best placed to perform that task. As you will be aware, the Party Congress begins in Leningrad very soon, the beginning of two weeks of events running up to the tenth anniversary celebrations of the opening Road of Life. There will be parades and concerts. I hear you have been making a nuisance of yourself at the Kirov. Maestro Vronsky's grand opera *The Blockade* will open the festivities. Stalin himself may attend. Minister Beria wants everything just so. Neither the Leningrad Party nor its protectors, it seems, need any distractions at this time. And certainly no repeats.'

So that was it. No unpleasantness to mar the Party Congress – no whispers of crime out of control. Soviet justice and the forces of law and order must prevail.

'I will need some assistance,' said Rossel.

Nikitin shook his head. 'Comrade Lieutenant, I am amazed that you make any requests of me at this particular moment,' he said.

'Minister Beria, you say, "wants everything just so". Ask yourself this, Major: are you the kind of man who wishes to prevent the minister getting his way?'

A look came over Nikitin's face. That of someone who had been unexpectedly cuffed in a fight with a lesser opponent but who was enjoying the sting of the blow. The major smiled a crooked smile, his razor-thin lips blending with the ragged scars on his face.

'You can take only two people,' he said. 'I will not put my name to any more than that. Do you have someone in mind?'

Rossel could still taste blood in his mouth. As he changed position in the seat, a sharp jolt of pain shot up from his right side and centred itself just behind his brow. Feeling exhausted and a little faint, he sighed.

'Yes, I do.'

*

Snow clung to his face as he followed the River Neva west – it was a driving blizzard and Rossel relied on the embankment wall to guide him. Two MGB guards had marched him to the gates of the prison and shoved him out into the street – clothed and shod but with no coat to shield him from the rising wind. Disbelief at his change in fortunes mingled with jolts of agony from his battered torso. One eye was almost shut.

As one of the ethereal white dots turned to meltwater on his tongue he felt for a moment as close as any veteran of the League of Militant Godless could get to sipping from a chalice of holy water. The temperature was falling again – they were in for another bitter spell. If this was the weather in October then they were in for one of the worst winters since the war. And yet every step was intoxicating; any taste of freedom was to those few changelings – he, miraculously, being among them for a second time – who had clambered out, reborn and blinking, into the weak morning sunlight, from the black womb of The Crosses.

Sofia. He could smell the spirit on her breath. He could see her lower her eyes, feel the hand she placed on his chest.

No, Revol, because . . .

'Because of what, Sofia?'

As he cried out for her to tell him, an old woman in front of him turned around, then drew up her collar and hurried away – but nothing came in answer. Only after a moment, and he did not understand why, Vronsky's otherworldly music, an eerie melody from the scene he had watched at the Kirov, skulked around inside his brain. And Eliasberg's dark, sneering face stared down at him from the stage. The snow drifts were piling up higher and higher, pushed by the east wind against every obstruction. His senses were dulled a little more with every step and yet with each one, he still savoured the feeling of simply *being*, of being allowed his own thoughts, of tramping, childlike, through the powder.

He stopped. He should have reached Liteiny Bridge by now. From there, if he went south, he could get to Station 17 on Vosstaniya and try to light a fire. He needed to do that quickly. The shock of all he'd uncovered and the beatings he had suffered had almost undone him. If he went north, he could reach his apartment in another twenty minutes – to the sanctuary of the kitchen, of little Lena's jokes and a delicious plate of her mother's greasy, unctuous borsch. But where was the bridge?

Ahead of him, on the very edge of his vision before the blizzard closed over the world, he could just make out the dulled lights of a car going over it. Trying to move too fast, he stumbled and fell, jamming the remaining fingers of his left hand into the snow. It was the first time for months, even years, that he had felt snow on the dull, scarred skin there. Nikitin's lackeys had forgotten to return his gloves – or, more likely, not forgotten. He dug deeper into the powder, clutching at it, willing it to heal him. The cold was there, somewhere, on the edge of his feeling. But not anything like close enough. An image of the five bodies on the railway tracks came into his mind. Only this time he saw them anew, as if, like the albatross in the Baudelaire poem Sofia had given him and loved so much, he now soared above them. Becoming the bird itself, a lord of 'sky and cloud'. Feeling truly alive – as he once did only when he played his violin. Beneath him, the tracks stretching out into the distance, black as coal and twinkling in the moonlight against the impossible whiteness of the snow. Parallel lines etched into the earth, studded with five torn corpses.

Now he felt as those abandoned souls must have done in the moments before their last breath.

Rossel realised he had to get to his room and his bed as soon as possible or, his spirit and body broken, lie down here, next to Liteiny Bridge, and let the flakes cover him, too. He veered north, the snow whipping at his face, with Vronsky's haunting music and memories of Sofia swirling around him.

His skull still in a blizzard all of its own.

26

Tuesday October 30

His eyes grainy, encrusted with sleep, blinked open in the grey morning light. He felt as though he'd slept for a thousand years. His ribs ached but someone seemed to have dressed and padded them, so he managed to turn himself in the bed. There she was, a soft, warm body next to his. He kissed the nape of her neck.

'*Sofia*,' he whispered. '*Sofia*.'

The woman sat up in her bed, the white sheet slipping down and revealing a figure trussed up in a blanket over a thick dressing gown, all over layers of undergarments.

'No, I'm not your precious Sofia,' said Tatiana Vasiliyeva, his upstairs neighbour with the guitar and the beguiling voice.

Rossel's eyes widened. Under the sheets he patted himself down, absurdly concerned for his modesty. But he, too, was trussed in a dressing gown and on top of that swaddled in blankets.

'You have been mumbling her name half the night. I like you, comrade policeman, because from our short acquaintance so far, I have formed the view that you're relatively honest. And so, with you, right from the start a girl gets to know where she is in the pecking order.'

Rossel sat up.

'How did I . . .?'

Everything hurt. It was the sharpness of the pain in his ribs that took his breath away, but he had been beaten so thoroughly that as he subsided back into the mattress, every other part of his anatomy began registering its own agony.

She got out of bed and took off the blanket, her dressing gown and most of the undergarments. Then picked up her clothes from a small green armchair and began to dress. Even though it was so cold in the room that her breath froze in the air, she dressed unhurriedly, holding his gaze as she spoke.

'I found you last night, lying in the street in front of the apartment block. A stray dog was licking at your heels. Everyone in the building knows you have been in The Crosses so I figured at least five or six of our friends and neighbours had stepped over you before I came. Another hour, I think, and it would have been too late. If you had leprosy or bubonic plague, they might have taken you in, propped you up in front of the fire and nursed you back to health, but a trip to prison can be just as contagious and is something they fear more.'

'Not you, though?'

She did up the last button on her plain white shirt.

'It's cold,' she said. 'I'll brew some tea.'

Rossel tried to lever himself back into a sitting position and half succeeded. He glanced around him at the ruffled sheets and his uniform, discarded on the floor.

He looked at her. It was hardly possible, given the state he was in, but . . .

She shook her head.

'No such luck, for you, comrade. You were shivering and barely conscious. I got in beside you to warm you through. You were in the war?'

He nodded.

'So you know it's the only thing that works. Besides, as a rule, I like to do the deed with people who can at least get my name right.'

*

She fried him some eggs, all she had, and served them on a chipped blue plate with two slices of black bread. He wolfed them down.

Although she had the luxury of a secluded room, she was forced to share the kitchen on his floor. Back on familiar territory, Rossel felt his appetite return. Vassya – she preferred to be called Vassya, a play on her surname – got up and went over to the window. She rested half her backside on the sill and blew hard on her tea. Rossel leant back, at last finding himself a little at ease with her. Enjoying watching her be herself. An errant pink curler – she had set them in her hair – sprang free and rolled away under the table.

'Talking of names,' Vassya said, 'your parents must have been dedicated Bolsheviks to name their son after the revolution.'

'It was my father's choice,' he replied. 'I was born a few weeks after the storming of the Winter Palace. Babies were being given all manner of revolutionary names, in my case literally. It could have been worse. Vladlen, or Barrikad, or Spartak. Elektrofikatsiya or Oktyabrina for the girls. I've met a few of those.'

'That is impressive devotion to the Communist cause on your father's part.'

'It cooled.'

After a while, Vassya began to talk.

She had been a pilot in the war. 'We cut our engines as we approached our targets,' she said. 'Biplanes, the slowest thing in the air, slower than big Mongolian geese, so we cut the engines to fly in as quiet as we could. But you can't stop the wind whistling around those heavy wings and the bracing wires. The Krauts said it sounded like witches zooming around the night sky. Except that we were dropping bombs instead of casting spells.'

Rossel had heard the story of the *Nachthexen*, the Night Witches, many times before – it was a staple of wartime propaganda – but he let her talk on as he sipped his tea.

The women of the Night Bomber Regiment had flown hundreds of sorties each, bombing arsenals, supply lines, depots, enemy airfields. 'The Nazi planes were too quick for their own good. If they saw us, we just had to bank hard and they would fly right past. But the flak and the ground fire – we weren't too slow for that. Get caught in the searchlights and they would turn you into mincemeat if you didn't know what you were doing.'

She looked sad.

'What were you doing before the war?' he asked.

'A student. Engineering. I was only in my second year when I flew a plane for the first time.'

'Difficult to go from engineering studies to dropping bombs from biplanes.'

'Difficult?' Vassya shook her head. 'It was beautiful. I was alive, truly alive. You understand that?'

239

She looked at him as if he didn't. But he had fought a very different war.

'That's why, unlike our neighbours, I'm not bothered about you and the Bolshoi Dom, militiaman. Up there you learned to take your chance. You needed luck to get you home. At first, I was scared every time I took off. But then I taught myself a trick – to pretend I was already dead. That way, I told myself, it doesn't matter if a bullet or a piece of shrapnel hits me. The dead are braver than the living. They have already lost everything there is to lose. We weren't witches. We were ghosts.'

'So, why didn't you stay on after the war?' he asked.

'In the air force? When the war was over, the men took over again and they threw us out. "You have a womb, comrade, go and fill it." That's what a staff officer told me. He very kindly offered to help with that, too, but I declined. I'm choosy about who I allow in my bed.'

'Not last night,' said Rossel.

Vassya tried not to smile. 'It was cold,' she said.

'So then what?'

'Now I work as an engineer for Comrade Samodurov, who is building the underground system.' The window bubbled with condensation. She traced it with a knuckle.

Rossel got up from the table. Right now, more than anything else in the world, he wanted to stay.

But he had to go.

27

A light was glowing through the grimy windows of the militia station. The snow before the main doors had been recently disturbed. Rossel went inside.

He had asked Nikitin for two officers. Not really expected to get them, but he had. And Junior Sergeant Gerashvili and Captain Lipukhin had been joined by Dr Volkova – not present at the time of the raid, but who had found the courage to visit the morgue – to form a small, scared welcoming party.

In just two weeks Gerashvili had become a ghost. Her head was shaved, she was as thin as a wire and one of her front teeth was chipped and broken so she whistled slightly as she spoke. Which she did infrequently, in slow, faltering sentences that trailed away before she was able to finish them. All three of them embraced him, even Lipukhin. However this miracle had been engineered, in their eyes Rossel had arranged it – whatever the reasons for their freedom, Rossel was the source. It seemed that the MGB had relented, had a change of heart. Or simply given them more rope, enabling them to further condemn themselves with their own failure. Who knew which?

'What did they tell you?' he asked them.

'Nothing,' said Lipukhin. 'They came and took me from the cells, brought us here and told us nothing more than we are to give you every assistance. So the investigation continues? It must be very important to somebody.'

It was disconcerting, actual leadership. Responsibility, duty, authority – with these he was familiar. Previously, the captain had been in charge, at least in name. Rossel had led not from the front but from the wings, guiding as subtly as he could, stepping in only when he felt it absolutely necessary. It was different to have all eyes on you, expecting you to make all the decisions, with people unable to act without your say-so.

The MGB had gone but, in case they had planted microphones, he chose his words carefully.

'Let us proceed, comrades, according to the guidance of Lenin,' he told his new charges. "To delay action is the same as death." He may not have been referring to murder investigations but we must do our Bolshevik duty.'

Lipukhin sighed. 'We are only four.' He reached up and touched a yellowing bruise on his left cheek. Then glanced at Gerashvili. 'And none of us exactly in the best of shape.'

Rossel raised his index finger and pointed around the room, ending at the grubby ceiling light. The captain nodded. They all understood.

'Lenin also said that a Marxist must proceed not from what is possible, but from what is real,' Rossel continued. 'Following his advice, we shall now descend to the morgue.'

*

Three down, two to go. If they could uncover the remaining two identities, enough of the puzzle might become clear for Rossel to understand the intent behind the murders. The militia officer in him was hungry for progress.

But the more primal parts of his brain were making him as tense and wary as a hare that had heard a twig snap in the undergrowth. He was prepared for those two remaining bodies to point to him but that would hardly lessen the dread if and when everyone's suspicions were confirmed.

He had no choice but to find out. The only way was forward.

Lipukhin looked a touch green around the gills but seemed ready to put life, or rather death, in perspective. He had, after all, just had a taste of MGB hospitality and now, by some miracle, he was out of jail and able to witness an autopsy other than his own.

'Are you all right, Junior Sergeant?' Dr Volkova took care in her tone to establish Gerashvili's lowly rank. The question was redundant. It was obvious, simply from her appearance, that Gerashvili was in no way her former self.

'I shall sit here and tell jokes to keep myself light of heart, while you dissect the corpse,' Gerashvili replied. But the flatness of her voice robbed the words of all meaning. As if lightness of heart was a concept she could not fathom.

Vassya is right, Rossel thought, we are all ghosts. Just look at Gerashvili. A shade in human form. Why does any of this caution really matter now?

Dr Volkova bent over the mottled body and resumed her usual external examination, recording height, weight and other external characteristics. When she inspected what was left of the genitals, she clicked her tongue. 'I hope our friend was not alive when they cut his balls off because whoever did this was no surgeon,' she said.

'Thank you, Doctor,' said Rossel loudly, hoping to discourage further commentary. In a quieter voice he added: 'Are you all right, Comrade Captain?'

Even in the cold, Lipukhin's temples were flecked with sweat.

'Comrade Lipukhin, please take notes,' said Dr Volkova. 'I have completed the external examination and will begin the autopsy. I am beginning with the incision from the shoulders to the sternum, and then down to the pubic area.'

Lipukhin seized a pad and paper, panicking a little at the onset of his new emergency duties. The noises were terrible. If you looked at the wall you could prevent yourself from seeing the doctor at work but you needed ear plugs to blot out the ripping and cutting. It was no use. The imagination cut bloodier incisions than the pathologist did, using sound alone.

'No abnormalities in the chest cavity,' said Dr Volkova. 'Comrade Captain, pass me that elongated bowl.' *Clunk*. 'Let's have a look inside the abdomen. Captain, this can take time so please take a seat and smoke as many cigarettes as you are able.'

Lipukhin slumped down in an old green leather chair in the corner of the room. Freedom, it seemed, was not all he had hoped it would be.

*

A person can mask joy or suppress hatred. But fear, an intense and unrelenting fear experienced over a few short weeks, marks a face as much as death. Gerashvili – cheeks pinched, eyes haunted – seemed since her return from The

Crosses incapable of formulating a sentence. But she could listen, and they were all listening to Rossel. Their lives depended on him now. This would be an added burden for his soul to bear, he realised, if they all ended up mining uranium in Kolyma. *What are we going to do now?* The question hung in the air.

They had adjourned to the stairwell at the back of the station for Dr Volkova to take a short break from her grisly work. The rest of the building was silent, paperwork left unkempt and unattended, crimes left unrecorded. But the possibility of microphones had not disappeared and so Rossel spoke in an undertone. They all leaned in to hear him.

'I cannot explain why Major Nikitin has let us go to continue with the investigation,' he began. 'But he has, and he would not have done so unless he had good reason. The identification of each body brings us closer to it. Dr Volkova, I require all the information you can elicit from the last two corpses.'

'Comrade Lieutenant,' said Dr Volkova. 'The fourth body has revealed very similar results. My work is becoming more difficult as the bodies are now rapidly decomposing and emitting noxious fluids.'

'I am, as ever, grateful for your professionalism, Doctor, but sometimes it would be enough to just say "same as last time,"' Rossel said.

'My apologies,' said the pathologist, her face solemn. 'I will examine the fifth body in a moment. There is one obvious difference: he was about twenty years older than the rest of them.'

'What do you remember of those others, Revol?' asked Lipukhin.

'Not a great deal.' Rossel tried to calm his mind, to steady himself so that he could talk about them merely as professional cases. 'The first three victims all attended the Leningrad State Conservatory before the war, as I did. And they were all student acquaintances of mine. So, I would place a large wager on the corpse Dr Volkova has been inspecting just now being someone else I knew back then, since I see in her report that Dr Volkova has recorded his age as between thirty and thirty-five – like them and like me.'

'But, if they were all your student friends, surely you must now have some idea who it is already? Who were you close with back then?' said Dr Volkova.

Rossel shook his head.

'I didn't say friends, I said acquaintances. And there were over a hundred and fifty students in my year alone – students from all over the Union. You might know people by sight but not really know much about them. Nadya, Max, Sofia – yes, I knew them, to varying degrees.' For now, he would play it safe and withhold the true nature of his relationship with Sofia. 'That they all knew me, and I them, still has to be, of course, significant. So, much depends on you, Dr Volkova. Is there nothing else you can tell me about our fourth victim?'

Dr Volkova straightened her back. 'There is one thing,' she said. 'His head was shaved. I thought it was odd and I should have guessed before, but I took out a tiny fragment of an existing follicle, one of the few that had escaped the razor. I then examined it under the microscope.'

She paused.

'What?' There was a tiredness in Lipukhin's voice. 'Out with it. No matter how trivial, if it's better than what we have.'

'Our corpse was a redhead,' said Dr Volkova.

Rossel's face gave nothing away. But he took a prolonged draw on his *papirosa* before exhaling deeply.

They looked at him.

'Lidia, look for a file marked with the name Sorokin,' he said. 'Felix Sorokin.'

'A file?' The way Gerashvili said the word made it sound as though a file was a mysterious artefact from another world.

'Oh God. Not another one,' said Lipukhin.

'Was he an acquaintance of yours too, Revol?' asked Dr Volkova.

Rossel shook his head. His voice was leaden.

'No, he was my best friend.'

*

'Gambling is idle and bourgeois. You are very much in danger of becoming a counter-revolutionary, Felix.'

'Nonsense, Revol. Lady Luck just likes to lift her skirts for me. All the ladies do.'

'Are you still bringing your girls to the Yusupov Palace?'

'Of course. It's a question of keeping up feminine morale in a time of national crisis.'

A blast resounded through the earth and jolted the park bench they had been lounging on, soaking in the sun. Too late, the air-raid siren began its wail.

'Let's run.'
Another blast, and then another.
'Come on, Felix, only you could saunter to the shelter like that, as if you were marked by the Fuhrer so his bombs knew to let you live . . .'

*

Dr Volkova emerged at intervals throughout the afternoon to feed them information about body number five, the man with beluga in his stomach.

'He shows signs of strangulation. The eyes had an extremely high level of abnormally blood-filled cells, though skin impressions in the region of the neck were very light.'

'What does that indicate, Doctor?' asked Rossel.

'Someone who is enjoying the kill. It takes a lot less force than your average murderer realises to finish someone off. Most victims end up with massive bruising around the neck, whether strangulation is manual or by ligature. But this suggests repeated asphyxiation of a pliant victim, with the minimum force required, and probably therefore a prisoner who was made to lose consciousness whenever the strangler wanted. He was really playing with this one.'

The rest of the day continued in similar fashion, making phone calls in order to book more phone calls, while Dr Volkova continued to dissect, weigh and analyse the cadavers as Lipukhin stayed with her taking notes.

At around eight o'clock in the evening, Lipukhin dropped two neat reports onto Rossel's desk and sat down opposite them.

'I sent Gerashvili home. She needs more time. But I have followed up on the file you asked her about. I have looked everywhere. Missing persons files are circulated to all departments in the city but there is no Sorokin.'

Rossel sighed.

'Felix was at the heart of every rumour, every party. Always flirting, always laughing.'

'I'm sorry about your friend. About all of this,' said Lipukhin.

'Don't be. Just because there is no file doesn't mean that nobody knew he was missing,' he said. 'Only that, if he was, nobody reported it. And the reason for that, I suspect, was that he was either still registered in the army or the Ministry of Defence. If he went missing, it would be the army on the lookout for him, even the MGB, but not the militia.' He thought back to his conversation with Marina in the opera house. *A sweet boy – we were close for a while but . . .*

'Call the ministry in Moscow first,' said Rossel. 'Don't just establish if he was working there. Find out as much as you can about his movements – where he lived, where he went on holiday, where his family is, if anyone is still alive.'

The captain nodded, both accepting his task and acknowledging that their roles were now reversed. He pointed to the map Rossel had splayed out over his desk.

'What's that?'

Rossel stood and pointed his finger at the place on the map where the bodies had been found.

'Why there? Have we thought enough about that?' he said. 'We know who three of them are and now have a good candidate for number four. We will have the fifth soon, I hope. But perhaps I have been asking the wrong question all this time. Concentrating on *who*, too much, at the expense of *where*. Normal passenger lines run side by side but anything you left on them would get run over within an hour or two. I've scoured this map and there are only two places in that area, along the length of Lake Ladoga's western shore and for thirty miles inland, where two single railway lines, along different routes, meet and run directly parallel, side by side like that, for a few metres before diverging. These are old freight routes. One is near Sosnovo, next to a brick factory. The other is where we found the bodies, further north.'

'You think the place itself is, perhaps, personally significant? To the murderer, I mean?'

Rossel looked up from the map, exhaled a cloud of smoke.

'There's nothing there except those lines, and a turn-off in the road. But after another 55 kilometres, that turning leads to some large dachas, which in turn indicates the presence, at least occasionally, of some very important people.'

'Party officials. Do you think that's why Nikitin let us out?'

Rossel sighed.

'I'm not sure. It's just possible he genuinely doesn't know who murdered those poor bastards and he actually wants someone to find out. But he doesn't want to be standing anywhere near them when they do.'

28

Asking Vassya to join him for a cognac in the communal kitchen was the closest Rossel had got to asking anyone on a date for a good while. Now, despite his dire situation, he still felt a little foolish.

The potential significance of the stranger in their kitchen did not go unnoticed by the other residents of the fourth floor. Most confined themselves to sticking their heads around the door. Either because they were ashamed, since some of them had walked past him when he was lying in the street outside, or because he had recently been in prison, which could be contagious. Only Lena, the art history student, scornful of her neighbours' behaviour, attempted to wait on them hand and foot. Conversation with a grinning, gurning teenage girl present was difficult, however, so in the end he sent her away.

'This won't work,' said Vassya, once she was gone.

'What won't?'

'You using me like this to make everything seem normal. To make it seem like it can all go back to the way it was before you discovered those bodies out by the lake. That you could hear my music through the floorboards, and then, somehow, we could meet and take a liking to each other, and drink tea, like this, and go to the Maly Hall to listen to a concert or two and then go back to my room and complete the evening's entertainment. Like you used to do with her – Sofia, I suppose.'

Rossel reached across the table and touched her hand. She looked down, curious at the stiffness of his touch and the bumps and strange angles of his fingers.

Then the front door to the *kommunalka* shook as someone began to batter it from the outside.

Vassya withdrew her hand. The two of them stared at each other. The background chatter and commotion of half a dozen families fell silent.

The visitor or visitors resumed the assault on the door. Failing to open it would achieve nothing. Besides, almost everyone had a bag packed under the bed, ready for an impromptu journey to the camps. Almost everyone was prepared. Though Rossel had never got around to it.

He walked down the corridor.

'Who is there?' he said through the door.

'State security,' came the reply. 'Open up.'

*

Major Nikitin was in full uniform.

Rossel's stomach lurched. There had been a change of heart, he thought.

But the major was alone – no squad of MGB officers, lists in hand, burst in behind him.

'Should I pack some possessions, Major?' he asked.

Nikitin's mouth twisted. 'You misunderstand. I want an update on your progress, that is all. May I come in?'

It was not the MGB's style to toy with its prey. Or to ask permission. They didn't have the time. Nikitin's politeness threw him a little.

Rossel stood to one side. 'Please.'

The major stepped over the threshold and removed his boots and cap. Rossel felt his hands curl into fists. *They won't just take me. They'll take Vassya, the whole kommunalka.* Would anyone notice if Major Nikitin failed to report for duty in the morning? If Rossel surrendered to his rage and started beating Nikitin to a pulp, the way the major had done to so many others?

Crouched down, the back of his neck bulging over his collar, the MGB man tucked the boots into the long line of footwear along the hallway and perched his blue and red MGB cap on top of the small hill of fur and woollen hats piled on the hat stand. These niceties came as a shock. His torturer must do this every evening, Rossel realised – wipe his feet, hang up his hat and then wash his hands before supper, as if he were just a normal person.

Of course they would notice. And then the entire apartment block would be rounded up and disappeared. Rossel's hands uncurled. For the time being. *One day*, he thought. *One day.*

Nikitin strode on and nearly collided with Lena, who had emerged into the hall to see who the new guest was. Dwarfed by Nikitin's bulk and looking straight into his scarred face, the teenager turned pale and stood rooted to the spot.

'Good evening,' said Nikitin.

Lena mumbled a greeting before turning tail and vanishing down the corridor. Rossel could hear a great deal of whispering and slamming of doors. Before he could think of a way to divert him and get Vassya out of the flat, the major was already entering the kitchen. Rossel hurried after him.

'A nervous child, that one. Nevertheless, it's good to be around young people. I have a son myself.'

'Would you like some tea, Comrade Major?' Rossel asked.

Tea? What the hell was he thinking?

'That would be wonderful. On a night like this the cold is unrelenting. Ah, forgive me – your file makes no mention of a Mrs Rossel. Good evening.'

'Major Nikitin,' Rossel said, flustered. 'Allow me to introduce Comrade Tatiana Vasiliyeva. A neighbour.'

Vassya got to her feet. 'Comrade Major,' she said.

'It is very nice to meet you,' Nikitin said.

'It is very nice to meet you,' Vassya echoed, failing to convince any of them. As Nikitin found a seat, she shot Rossel a look. 'I must go, excuse me,' she muttered.

But the MGB man had smelt them out. He looked from one to the other and smiled, his eye blinking above that mass of scar tissue.

'Please stay, I insist. I have come only to encourage Lieutenant Rossel to proceed with all haste with his latest investigation.'

'I thought you said you had come to ask for a progress report?' said Rossel.

Nikitin's good eye was like a searchlight. 'There has been progress?'

Rossel nodded.

'Yes, I think so. But I need to go back to the crime scene. I want to take another look at how the killer arranged the bodies.'

'Then what are you waiting for? Why are you still here?' The major's voice was filled with impatience.

'I am waiting for the weather to clear, Major. All the roads towards the crime scene are blocked by thick drifts. I reckon a day at least before I can get out to Lake Lagoda.'

Nikitin scowled.

'I can buy you more time, Lieutenant. But only a little. Any more than that may prove impossible. The powers that be are becoming increasingly impatient for an arrest.'

Vassya stepped forward and stood by Rossel's side.

'I think I may know a way,' she said.

29

'Is it much further, Comrade Vasiliyeva?'

Nikitin had to shout to make himself heard over the biting headwind and the sound of the engines. They dropped fifty metres, leaving Rossel's stomach fighting to leave his body through his nostrils. Then the little Polikarpov Po-2 rose again.

Some Russians called it the best plane ever built, though fewer praised its levels of comfort. In this model – modified to take non-military personnel, so with an extra seat behind the pilot and a covered cockpit – Rossel had had to cram himself into position. Behind him, Nikitin, shorter but stockier, was having an even worse time.

Vassya, piloting the Po-2, yelled over her shoulder. 'I'm doing close to top speed, hundred and thirty kilometres per hour. So not far to Lagoda, another ten minutes, maybe fifteen . . .'

'What did she say?' bellowed Nikitin in his ear.

'I didn't hear,' Rossel yelled back at him.

'Fuck your mother!'

Both men were wearing thick flying jackets and hats that someone had unearthed at the aerodrome. It was barely good enough.

Vassya raised her gloved left hand, five fingers splayed. Then did it a second time.

'Thank fuck for that,' shouted Nikitin. 'Rossel, why have you pulled back the screen? My bollocks are beginning to freeze to this tiny metal circle of a seat. I'd have less chance of getting piles if I had shoved an ice cube up my arse. And every time she touches the joystick I want to puke. This idea of yours had better be good.'

These days the Po-2 was used as a trainer at a small airfield at Pavlovsk, just outside Leningrad. Nikitin's presence was all the authority they had needed to be allowed to borrow it.

Above Rossel's head, in the almost pitch darkness set by the thick cloud cover, he was sure he could hear the rivets rattling in the biplane's upper wing. The noise had beaten its way into his skull ever since take-off and now felt as though it would be a relief if the little plane plunged into the white fields of the Leningrad Region. He leaned forward with his torch and crouched down to look at his map but the tears in his eyes from the intense cold made it almost impossible to make anything out. He had marked the place where they had found the corpses but the map was not sufficiently exact to be sure. But there were the railway lines, vaguely drawn, there was the main road they had driven along, and there was the turn-off – a stubby line that came to an end in the middle of some white space.

*

So far, he had concentrated on who the victims were: identification, history, links to each other, links to him. But not enough, he was now sure, on *where* the bodies were found. And definitely not enough on the manner of their arrangement.

In the car en route to the aerodrome, Nikitin had still needed convincing. The photographs Taneyev had taken were close-ups – not one shot was from a general point of view.

'At the station today I inspected an old military map,' said Rossel to the back of Nikitin's head. 'There are only two places in the entire region where two tracks run together, as they do out here.'

Nikitin, at the wheel, gave an exaggerated shrug.

'And?'

'I'm not sure yet.'

'Too much of your investigation has been based on hunches, Comrade Lieutenant.'

This was fair enough, Rossel had to admit.

As they were clambering into the plane, Nikitin had slipped, stumbled to the ground. He cursed, lay prone, hands splayed out. The left had been touching the tip of Rossel's right boot. Neither man moved. Nikitin looked up, waiting for Rossel's heel to grind down in vengeance.

But it had not been done. They had an unarticulated armistice based on mutual need.

*

Rossel jammed the map onto his knee to keep it from disappearing into the night sky. Tucked inside his coat were five dark prints – images of the victims in exactly the same order they had been found. Vassya pushed the joystick forward and the Polikarpov pitched downward and broke through the icy cloud that had blanketed them for the entire journey. Almost immediately, Rossel heard a guttural sound and was grateful for the direction and ferocity of the wind, as the major bent over the side and vomited. He was no aviator, but he was certain the constant upward and downward pitching of the Po-2 had become more exaggerated once its pilot had realised one of her passengers was a little airsick.

As the cloud broke, moonlight bathed the fields below. Rossel reckoned their altitude at about five or six hundred metres. He leaned forward slightly in his seat and tapped Vassya on the shoulder. She turned her face toward his.

'I can see Shlisselburg over there. Those pointed tower roofs are built on top of the fortress walls.' The engine was on lower revs but Rossel still had to shout above the sputtering cacophony. 'We're not far away from the place where the bodies were found. Can you get lower?'

Vassya nodded and pushed forward on the stick. The plane nosed downward again and Nikitin groaned. Rossel leaned out of the right-hand side of the cockpit as it descended. In the distance he could see the vast shore of Lake Lagoda and, beyond it, the ethereal, glittering whiteness of the frozen waters, looming as large as the ocean.

As the plane glided over the snow-swaddled pines, Rossel could see black smoke rising up from one of the old U-class locomotives that still worked these lines – old passenger trains dating back to before the revolution, now reduced to pulling freight. This one was hauling about forty carriages of coal from, most probably, the mines at Slantsy to the power station in Narva.

As the snaking line passed underneath and then began to disappear eastward, Rossel could see the twin tracks – temporarily cleared of snow by the passage of the locomotives – standing out dark against the frozen earth.

Five notes.

The image had first come to him as Nikitin had thrashed at his body and he strove to set his mind free. It had returned to him as he was walking, trance-like, towards Liteiny Bridge after his own unexpected delivery from The Crosses.

Notes. *Five notes.* A simple refrain.

One railway line came from the northwest before it straightened and travelled east. The other, along which the coal train had just travelled, rose from the southeast, met the first line and then bent westward.

This was it. For a few metres only, two tracks, four lines.

He felt inside for the photographs but there was no need to take them out – he knew them by heart. Five bodies, stick figures, curled like a stillborn in a newly barren womb. The earth of Mother Russia herself was the musical score. And, by some as yet unknown hand, five black notes had been etched upon it.

ACT 4

30

Wednesday October 31

A five-note sequence.

Five bodies arranged between Leningrad and Ladoga. The snow-clad countryside of the *oblast* was the pure white score, the black railway lines that ran parallel to each other on that short stretch near the lake were the stave upon which the melody had been composed, and then, in a final flourish, each body had been set, head laid to one side, as a cadaverous note.

Fa, la, mi-bemol, si-bemol, sol.

F, A, E-flat, B-flat, G.

As he tried to start a meagre fire in the grate next to his desk in Station 17, Nikitin pacing up and down behind him and cursing with impatience, Rossel hummed the notes under his breath.

The refrain had dissonance at its heart, like a folk song from the Caucasus. Three of the notes formed the triad of E-flat major – a key associated with heroes. The F was the second note of that scale. The A natural was the odd one out – not part of the scale at all. From E-flat to A was a tritone, what composers three hundred years previously had termed a *diabolus in musica*. The devil's interval.

The five bodies on the line had been composed into their own funeral dirge. One which Rossel increasingly believed had also been composed for him.

*

'Two train lines running in parallel form a stave – the name for the lines on a piece of sheet music. The top line is missing but the killer didn't need that.'

Rossel held the pencil in a dagger grip and drew four jagged lines on a blank piece of paper. Next to him, splayed on the table and reflecting the lamp light, were the photographs taken from the biplane as well as the images Taneyev had taken when the bodies were first discovered.

'The way the bodies were arranged looked stylised in every way but one. They were dressed up, mutilated, and laid out at equal distances. But the positioning of the heads was different. Some were resting in between the lines, some on the rails. There had to be a pattern; it's just that standing on the ground we didn't see it. But from above . . .'

He tried to get a better hold on the pencil but writing was always an ordeal. After adjusting one hand with the other, he was able to draw stick figures onto the stave – oval blobs for heads and nothing but a brusque line to show the direction of the body.

'Sofia. First in the row, though the fourth body to be identified. Her note is F – F in the German naming convention, *fa* in the solfege system that we use in Russia.'

Nikitin looked annoyed at this. A code he did not recognise.

'How do you know you're not reading this upside down?' the MGB officer demanded.

'I don't know,' admitted Rossel. 'It's just a theory. Her head rested between the tracks of the lower railway line, her feet pointing south, like everyone else's feet.'

'Go on.'

Nikitin had grumbled at coming to Station 17 and his mood was not being improved by Rossel's unhurried presentation. Vassya, who sat muffled from head to toe in Sergeant Grachev's chair, seemed unperturbed.

Rossel returned to his diagram. 'Maxim. Second in line. His head was here,' he made two more marks. 'That would make him a *lya* in Russian but an A in German.'

'What's with the German? Is our killer a German?'

Rossel shook his head. 'Not necessarily. But someone familiar with musical notation. More familiar than most. Composers, conductors, musicologists. Bach used the letters of his name to make a motif. Schumann, too.'

'Germans,' said Nikitin.

'Comrade, it is quite difficult to escape the presence of Germans in classical music. German scores are played up and down the Soviet Union every week. In any case, our very own Dmitri, Dimitri Shostakovich, does it. The motif D-S-C-H appears . . .'

'Get on with it.'

'. . . in many of his works.'

Rossel leant over the paper and waved his pencil again.

'Felix.' He drew an E.

'What is it in Russian?'

'In Russian it is a *mi*. But look.' He arranged two of the original photographs next to each other. 'These three bodies have hats placed next to their heads, instead of on them. Positioned with care on the left-hand side. If that is intended as a musical sign, it would mean the killer wanted to alter the note, making it slightly higher or lower. So instead of *mi* it might be *mi-bemol*.'

'More complicated,' said Nikitin. 'What's this *bemol*?'

'It flattens the note, comrade. Makes it a semitone lower.'

'That's not a Russian word, either.'

'It is French, I believe,' said Rossel.

Nikitin grunted. 'Too many foreign influences in this musical language of yours,' he said.

Rossel could think of a dozen Russian words off the top of his head that were borrowed directly from other languages, including French and German, but chose not to comment.

'Corpse number four. Little Nadya, the first to be identified but the fourth in line.' He dotted a B on his crude musical stave. 'The head is in the correct place, lying on the third rail up.' He showed Nikitin the photographs, from the ground and the air. 'It could be a *si*, but the hat could make it a *si-bemol*.' He added a flat sign.

Rossel made a final couple of strokes.

'The last note. The fifth body had its head lying on the second rail. The means a G. *Sol*. This is assuming that the killer was writing in the treble clef, of course.'

Nikitin looked at Vassya.

'Does any of this make sense to you?' he demanded.

Vassya nodded. 'Now I've seen it, it does.'

Rossel put down his pencil.

'Those are our five notes.'

*

This case had always been a trap. Right from the very start of the investigation, he had felt it. Yes, he had moved forward, placing one foot in front of the other but always suspecting the trap would be sprung.

And now, it seemed, he had his own personal musical score. A murderer who must have known from the outset that only a musician would have been able to decipher his refrain. And how many musicians could be found in the Leningrad militia?

Nikitin sat down at the table opposite him with a thick glass of tea in his hands.

'So, I passed word of your crazy theory up the line.'

'And?'

The MGB major took a sip, then sighed and slumped back in the wooden chair.

'Congratulations. We are invited to Moscow tomorrow, you and me. They are, it seems, more convinced of the possibility of a musical murderer than I am. A special someone wants to get a personal update on the progress of *your* investigation.'

Keep on moving forward, Revol, placing one foot in front of the other. Now, perhaps, the only way to escape death will be to court it.

Rossel sat back in his own chair.

'A special someone?'

Nikitin took out a cigarette, a foul Bulgarian import, and lit it. Then he blew out a ring of smoke that floated towards the soot-covered ceiling before curling into nothingness.

'They didn't give a name. They never do. But I think I can guess.'

31

Rimsky-Korsakov, Tchaikovsky, Sergei Prokofiev, Dmitri Shostakovich and Nikolai Vronsky. Either as a student or a professor, they had all walked this walk, across Leningrad's Theatre Square towards the classical façade of the conservatory. Rossel had passed by many times since he left, in the summer of 1941, just before he had been called up to protect the city with the civil defence. But this was the first time he had ever attempted to go back inside.

The grey and white painted stone was looking a little shabby, but the imposing frontage with its oblong and arched windows still made his heart miss a beat as he stood in front of it, remembering the first day he had arrived here as an awkward teenager, believing he might, in some small way, follow in the footsteps of his heroes.

He turned and stared back across the square at the Kirov Theatre, with its green and white stuccoed walls. The two buildings were separated by only a few hundred feet, but the musical journey between them – that of starting out as a student at the conservatory and ending up on stage or in the pit of the Kirov – was a chasm. Nevertheless, it was one his old violin teachers had expected him to make.

Until he had been diverted to make his confession to Major
Nikitin.

*

Inside the conservatory, everything was just as he remembered. Branching out from a central staircase were long,
airy corridors of rooms for practising, teaching and lectures.
As a student, he loved to linger here in the evenings, when
lessons were over but the rooms still full. Better to practise
here than in the hostel, where other students were always
crashing around, shouting and singing.

If you walked slowly enough along these corridors you
could wander into a Beethoven sonata and pass through
into a Chopin étude, like slipping through an aural curtain –
passing from one reality to the next, from C minor to A-flat
major, from darkness into light. You could stop and moor
yourself in one world for a while or move on to the edge
of another; something comforting and familiar yet, at the
same time, hard to discern until you took only two more
steps and passed into the storms of a Rachmaninov prel-
ude. And all the time, out on the edge of hearing, out on the
edge of your very self, was the siren call of a Tchaikovsky
violin concerto, or the sarabande from a Bach cello suite,
or an aria from *The Tsar's Bride*.

It was, Sofia had once said, a little like being in Heaven's
aviary.

The halls were busy with chattering students moving
between the classrooms and the rehearsal halls but he spotted Professor Lebedeva immediately. She walked directly

towards him. She looked older, of course, he tried to calculate her age – mid-sixties now, at least. Her hair, once garishly red, was now almost completely white. She was still trim and behind some small wire-framed glasses – a new addition – her green eyes flashed the intelligence that he had always found, even as her student, a little beguiling.

'Revol, it really is you!'

'Yes, Professor, it really is.'

He took a step forward and kissed her formally on the cheeks, three times.

*

Rossel brought out his notebook and opened it at a place where he had written down all four names and, then, a question mark to signify the still unidentified fifth victim.

Sofia Fedotova
Maxim Avdeyev
Felix Sorokin
Nadya Bazhanova
?

They were sitting before the stage of the conservatory's concert hall, beneath an ornate ceiling on which were painted clouds, cherubs and a muse in a Grecian robe playing a golden harp. The walls of the room were pure white and crystal chandeliers glittered in the October sunlight that shone through a row of large, arched windows.

Rossel had performed here countless times but all those memories eluded him. Instead, it was Sofia whose presence filled him, just as it filled the concert hall – the pang of jealousy he had felt seeing her laughing with another student after a rehearsal, jealousy he could still taste. The longing as he watched her prepare for a solo in one of the Mahler lieder, eyeing her from his seat in the orchestra.

His sense of Sofia, of everything he had lost, was tangible here, in this grand room, amongst the ghosts of their shared past and, for a moment, he was lost.

He tapped on the notebook with a finger, using this small motion to pull himself back together.

'Do you remember them, Professor?'

Professor Lebedeva glanced down at the notebook and then back up at him.

'Felix, yes, naturally, how could I forget Felix? So mischievous. And of course, I taught him, as I did you. I used to wonder why he bothered, frankly, given the amazing amount of practice he didn't do. I nearly kicked him out of my class but he was entertaining so we would talk instead of playing. He was the only lazy student I have ever tolerated. A real charmer.'

Lebedeva glanced down at the four names again and sighed.

'Memories. Sofia, so charming and sweet. Beautiful of heart. Her voice had a magical purity about it, though she had yet to learn control. The other two, I have some recollection of the names, but that's all really. I have been teaching violin here for twenty years now. That's a lot of students. And not all of them as talented as you, such a shame. What happened?'

'The war happened, Professor.'

'Do you miss playing?'

Rossel shook his head.

'No. Not anymore.'

He put the notebook away.

'What else connects them?' asked the professor. 'Sofia, I knew through you, but those two, Maxim and Nadya, well, so many students pass through this conservatory.' She tapped her cigarette into a metal ashtray. Beneath her calm demeanour she could be an absolute tyrant. It was considered all but impossible to get into her class, and certainly impossible to please her once you got there. 'We lost so many students, past and present, during the war and since. From the German bombs, the siege and the starvation. I used to dream of food. One night I dreamt it was New Year's Eve and instead of making dumplings I had married one.' Lebedeva smiled but the smile did not last.

'It is bad to be on a list. They must be in danger,' she added.

'Not anymore,' said Rossel. 'They are all dead.'

She recoiled and crossed herself, then caught herself doing it and stopped.

'Why are you here?' she said, looking him in the eye – no longer reminiscing with a favourite old student but confronting a man in uniform who was talking of the dead.

'I am asking people who knew the victims.'

'But why me?' Professor Lebedeva spread her hands. 'I told you, I barely knew those two, this Max and this Nadya.'

'But you knew the others well.'

'Not well,' she protested.

'Felix,' said Rossel. 'Him you knew very well.'

'My student, yes, but how well do a student and teacher ever know each other? Passionate when he played, so I knew there was more to Felix than the prancing peacock he let us all see.'

'Passionate in other ways, too, Professor?'

She held his gaze for a moment as if to convey she was making a mental note of his impertinence. As if she wasn't scared.

'He told you that?'

Rossel nodded.

'Felix told me about all his conquests. That's why I came to see you.'

'Yes, he would mention it to you. The pleasure for boys like Felix is always less in the act itself and more in the telling of the tale. We were lovers, I admit it. I did not know the war had claimed him. Do you know how he died? Was it terrible? I hope not.'

Rossel saw no need to tell her the truth. The professor took a last drag at her cigarette and stubbed it out.

'I loved him a little, Revol. Foolish I know. He was twenty. I was twice his age – more. But the heart cannot be tamed.'

'Did Felix talk about any of them, back then? If they were all connected by something other than the murders themselves, my investigation shows it has to be by something that happened when they were here at the conservatory, when they were all students. I've checked the files and after that they all go very different ways.'

The professor stared down at the four names for a moment. Then she pointed to one of them.

'The one called Nadya. Describe her to me.'

'Short and round. A clarinettist. Chatty.'

She nodded. 'Well, there is one thing then,' she said.

'Go on.'

Professor Lebedeva took off her glasses for a moment and gave them an unnecessary polish.

'Felix liked to gamble, you remember that?' she said.

'He would bet on anything.'

'One wager sticks in my mind. He told me he might be able to get us some food, horsemeat from a conservatory graduate who was in the army. That he'd put a bet on with this soldier about who would win what Felix – and others by then – were calling The Great Symphonic Contest. And he said a girl, who I think was the clarinettist you describe, would help him win because she had the inside track on what the outcome would be.'

'The Great Symphonic Contest? Vronsky versus Shostakovich?'

Professor Lebedeva nodded.

'Why not?' she said. 'It was the perfect game for someone who was being classically trained. The race between the two leading composers of the day to see which one of them would have their work become the anthem of the war. "Nadya has the inside track." That's what he said.'

Rossel closed his notebook. Then slipped it into his pocket.

'I played at that contest, Professor. The great symphonic battle, the great audition. But so did many others.'

She stood. 'Revol, may I be allowed to continue with my teaching duties?'

'Of course, my apologies.'

She walked down the side aisle towards the double doors at the rear of the hall. She stopped halfway and turned, starting to say something. But she thought better of it and scuttled off.

*

On a whim, he called in at the library on the ground floor – a dusty maze guarded, as it always had been, by a couple of fearsome women. But they had no idea how to find a score written during the years of the siege.

'Madame Shishani would know,' said one, 'she knows every piece of music that ever went in and out of this building. But, she's away today, comrade, nursing her mother. Can you come back tomorrow?'

Rossel shook his head. Then sighed.

'Not tomorrow. Later this week, yes. I have a prior appointment in Moscow.'

32

Thursday November 1

The round clock in the stone tower of Moscow's Leningrad Station read 7.15 as Rossel and Nikitin walked down the granite steps that led to the city's busy streets. A black limousine was parked up on the south side of Komsomolskaya Square. The morning crowds milling past it tried not to stare or get too close. They didn't want to be noticed taking notice. But everyone knew a car like that must belong to someone important.

As they walked towards the black American Packard limousine, an MGB officer got out from the passenger side and came over to greet them.

Nikitin held out his hand.

'Colonel Sarkisov.'

The officer shook it.

'Comrade Nikitin.'

Rossel stood to attention and saluted.

'This is the lieutenant I told you about,' said Nikitin. 'The musician.'

Sarkisov gave Rossel a quick appraisal.

'We've met,' he said. 'Comrade Beria has read your file with interest, Lieutenant. I even heard him laugh at one of your many ill-advised student jokes.' Sarkisov turned away again. 'The chief used to play something – did you know that?' he said to Nikitin.

Nikitin shook his head.

'I didn't. He's full of surprises, I have to say. Play what?'

Colonel Sarkisov smiled and opened the door of the limousine. He held out a hand to usher Rossel and Nikitin inside it.

'When he was in Baku, so I'm told, Minister Beria did, on occasion, like to perform Mingrelian peasant songs on the balalaika.'

He looked at Rossel again.

'You already have a love of music in common. Perhaps that's why he so very much wants to see you, Comrade Lieutenant.'

*

The journey through the busy Moscow traffic was considerably quicker for black limousines than for other vehicles. During it Nikitin and Sarkisov exchanged small talk about Vsevolod Bobrov; the CSKA winger also played ice hockey for the same Red Army club. Sarkisov thought he should stick to football. Nikitin thought not.

After about ten minutes they turned off Sadovaya Kudrinskaya Street into Malaya Nikitskaya and, moments later, swept through black metal gates into an impressive courtyard. Rossel's knowledge of Moscow was poor and he was uncertain what district they were in but they had come from the station around the ring road so this must be on the city's western side. Two junior officers were piling up snow on either side of the yard with a brush and shovel.

As the three men got out of the limo the junior officers stood to attention and saluted. The house was a large blue and white one with painted alabaster pillars and fresco work; some kind of scene from Greek mythology. Originally a merchant's or a banker's, Rossel surmised, before the repercussions of the revolution had led to it becoming the home of Lavrentiy Pavlovich Beria.

*

The wall was painted a reptilian shade of jade. The large door was a very dark oak and Rossel was having great difficulty taking his eyes off its faded brass handle. Next to the door was a small table on which stood a white vase filled with pale yellow irises. He checked his watch for the tenth time. They had been waiting for over an hour and a half now. His mouth had dried up completely. His stomach was churning. No one had uttered a word since they had been shown to the leather chairs in the corridor outside the minister's office by a junior officer. Sarkisov and Nikitin presumably knew the building well but their mood was not one of relaxed familiarity. They had become noticeably less jocular ever since the Packard had pulled into the courtyard.

Now the brass doorknob rattled. In the silence, the noise was as alarming as a shot – all three men jumped to attention. A sharp twist to the left. The junior officer who had shown them to their seats earlier stuck his head around the door.

'He will see you now.'

*

Music was coming from an old Victrola gramophone that sat on a piano stool in the corner of the room, next to a bay window through which the winter sunlight streamed. Rossel recognised the music immediately – a piece the student orchestra at the conservatory had played, albeit rarely: Rachmaninov's symphonic poem *The Isle of the Dead*. It was supposed to evoke Charon's oars cutting through the water of the Styx as he rowed lost souls towards the island. And there, behind a small desk covered in neatly stacked manila files, sat the great Soviet Charon himself.

The deputy prime minister of the Soviet Union was smaller than Rossel had been expecting. Apart from propaganda posters like the one attached to Smolny Cathedral, he had only ever seen Beria in pictures on the front of *Pravda* or standing directly behind Stalin reviewing the May Day parade in cinema newsreel footage, his balding and wrinkled head and darting black eyes reacting with a calculated condescension towards the adoring masses. The press portrayed him as a Bolshevik colossus, a towering defender of Marxist-Leninist purity against reactionary capitalism and traitorous fifth columnists. He would actually be, in his stocking feet, Rossel guessed, a little less than 165 centimetres tall.

Beria stood as the two men entered – Sarkisov had not joined them in the inner sanctum. Somewhat unexpectedly, considering his rank, the minister shook hands with both Rossel and Nikitin, holding onto Rossel's just a little longer than was necessary. His palms were soft, Rossel thought. It was rumoured that Beria had personally strangled

Nikolai Yezhov, his predecessor in charge of the NKVD, the People's Commissariat for Internal Affairs, the forerunner of the MGB. If so, thought Rossel, it must at first have felt like a gentle embrace.

Beria gestured towards two scarlet leather armchairs in front of his desk and resumed his own seat. He wore small pince-nez spectacles which he slipped off and, using a tiny piece of red cloth he took from a green leather case, began to clean them. No one spoke. All they could hear was the music playing on the Victrola and the steady rhythmic squeak of the cloth moving back and forth across the lenses. Beria buffed and polished in his quest for perfection, in tempo with the music.

After a minute, he put the cloth back into the case and repositioned his pince-nez. He blinked a couple of times and then stared at Rossel and Nikitin as though he had only just noticed them.

'You like Rachmaninov?'

It was not clear to which of them the question had been asked. Nikitin, a forced jauntiness in his tone, got in first with a pre-emptive tactical denial.

'Rach who, Comrade Deputy Premier?'

Beria used the middle finger of his left hand to set the glasses more firmly upon his head. He fixed his gaze upon Rossel.

'And you?'

'His music, yes, Comrade Deputy Premier.'

Beria raised a hand. 'Comrade will do, Lieutenant.'

'Yes, comrade – his music, that is. I despised the man. A reactionary bourgeois recidivist and enemy of the people.'

Rossel felt his heart pound as he negotiated the trap. The dead were, he thought, fair game for denunciation.

Beria sat back. He looked pleased with the answer. In the same way a man who has spent the morning laying out a minefield might take pleasure in watching his quarry avoid the first detonation.

'I share your contempt. His traitorous sojourn in America was discussed many times at the highest levels. Before his death from a fortuitous melanoma, plans had been made to return him from his deckchair in Palm Springs and grind his soul into dust in a corrective labour facility. I had placed myself personally in charge of the operation. It is my experience that creative talent and the greatest treachery often go hand in hand.'

Once in full flow, Beria spoke with machine-gun rapidity. He glanced across at a portrait of Stalin above the fireplace, then back at Rossel.

'Comrade Stalin also places particular importance on the arts, especially music and literature. There was an incident, you may remember, with Shostakovich. Before the war, when his music became – and I quote the words used by Pravda at the time – "Too formalist, too bourgeois". To all intents and purposes, Comrade Stalin was the music critic of *Pravda* that day; the words he used in private, however, were of a more colourful and peasant vernacular. These days the Party has trained musical ears everywhere, Comrade Rossel. It is Comrade Stalin's view that a traitorous mind reveals itself in every conceivable place, yes, even in the spaces left between one note and the next. Nikitin tells me you think these bodies found out on the line near

Lake Ladoga were deliberately arranged to allude to some devilish melody.'

'That is what I now believe, comrade, yes.'

'And who do you think is the culprit?'

'In all honesty, I have no idea.'

Beria picked up a file from the top of the stack.

'Leningrad has always been a troublesome city. There were the regrettable incidents around the trade fair in '49 where my MGB officers uncovered a nest of capitalist vipers; many bohemian artists, writers and musicians amongst them. Minister Malenkov made the initial accusation but, in my humble opinion, failed to pursue the traitors with the required amount of Bolshevik vigour.'

It was widely known that Beria found it hard to resist criticising Malenkov – the man thought to be his main rival in the race to be Stalin's successor.

He handed the file to Rossel.

'I have circled a name in there that may be of interest to your investigation.'

Rossel started to open it. Beria waved a discouraging hand in the air.

'No, not yet. Later, when you are alone, I think. Once you have perused the information, Lieutenant Rossel, I have every confidence that you will know exactly how to proceed.'

Now I understand, thought Rossel. Stalin puts pressure on Beria to clear up the crime. Beria decides on a culprit. But, then, as added insurance, he calls in an expendable militia officer to do his dirty work. Just in case there are any further issues. Allowing the deputy premier, should that happen, to distance himself from the outcome and blame the bumbling militia.

There was a burst of static as the needle on the Victrola reached the end of the record. Rossel nodded.

'Of course, comrade.'

*

The Packard sped back through the black gates out into the grey Moscow evening. Colonel Sarkisov was driving. Rossel and Nikitin sat in the back. The lieutenant lit up a *papirosa* and then opened the file on his lap. Both he and Nikitin stared down at the name – ringed in blue pen – on the bottom left-hand corner of the second page: *Karl Ilyich Eliasberg*.

After a moment, Nikitin spoke.

'It makes sense, don't you think? Bears out your crazy theory, Rossel?'

Nikitin sounded calm but his cheeks were waxy and white. Rossel was not the only man in the car who was happy to get out of Beria's office in one piece.

He took a couple of seconds before answering.

'I suppose so.'

'You suppose so?' Sarkisov broke in.

Rossel looked up to find the MGB man staring at him via the driver's mirror.

Sarkisov resumed looking at the road ahead but kept talking.

'Show me the man and I'll find you the crime. I've heard the boss say that many times, Comrade Rossel,' said the

283

major. 'He's shown us our man. Maestro Eliasberg. I strongly advise you to first find him, and then a nice crime to hang him by. Beria wants this all tied up before the Party Congress, and we shall damn well give him exactly what he wants.'

33

Friday November 2

Often the chase has an uncertain beginning until a shout –
or a shot – rings out. So it was this time.

To Rossel's left was a ragged expanse of snow that somewhere became salt water. In front of him, a whole street of
poorly constructed apartment blocks extended towards the
distant, blue-grey smudge of the Gulf of Finland.

It was hard to believe that Maestro Eliasberg had been
reduced to living here.

Rossel's pulse was racing as the thin line of MGB troops
spread out. Two men advanced to the target building, two
more took up positions to their right, tucking their AK-47s
into their shoulders, while three others tramped out into
the wasteland to encircle their quarry, untroubled by the
formless terrain.

Only now did Rossel notice the sky, and in the same
instant wondered how he could not have noticed it. It was
livid, tiger-striped in red and purple. Someone kicked the
door in and the first two MGB troops dashed inside. Nikitin
stood still, attentive, one hand resting on the roof of the ZIS.
Yet after a minute the men had not re-emerged. The major

strode forward and disappeared inside the building, which groaned and cowered in the teeth of the surging wind.

Rossel braced himself. Expecting the sound of a shot.

But none came.

The foetid wretch who was propelled through the door, pursued by Nikitin, was drunk, drunk beyond the power of thought and speech. And was not Eliasberg – more of a stairwell-dwelling tramp.

Now Rossel heard the shout.

Then the shot.

Who had spotted the furtive brown figure struggling through the snow would never be clear. The lieutenant leapt forward as if he, himself, were running from enemy fire and followed the two MGB men who had seen the conductor, perhaps a hundred metres ahead. His boots crunched on snow and, under the snow, grasses and clumps of dirty sand. It was energy-sapping and soon he was breathing hard, sweating even in the cold. This world was like a painting, he thought – blurred whiteness punctuated by muddy brown trees as thin as single pencil marks; ugliness thinly veiled.

Rossel looked over his shoulder. As well as the two MGB officers in front of him, the others were also in pursuit. With them would be Nikitin. But Nikitin would shoot Eliasberg. Almost certainly, yes. That would be case closed. He was already roaring at his men to bring the fugitive down. The MGB soldiers, muffled in coats and boots, stumbled where the snow covered the boundary between road and pavement, pavement and shore, even shore and the half-frozen fringe of the water. No one fired yet – the first shot had been a warning and the warning had been ignored. The next bullets would be for strictly practical purposes.

Eliasberg was silhouetted against the white as he tried to climb one of the walls of stone and wood that jutted out towards the water – breakers to stop the port channels from silting up. Eliasberg dropped over the other side and kept on running. But it was clear now. He had no hope. The chasing packs had already halved the distance and would vault the breaker far faster than him.

Rossel was gaining on the two leading men. His heart was bulging against his lungs and his legs were leaden. When was the last time he had slept? Properly?

Eliasberg scaled another of the wooden breakers. An MGB officer stopped, raised his weapon and bent his head to one side, but hesitated. Rossel charged past him, putting himself in between the weapon and the musician's silhouette. Eliasberg's face was now discernible – he was running in a heavy coat but no hat, or most likely his hat had fallen off somewhere. Rossel scaled the breaker himself but fell heavily down the other side and his knees sank into the deep snow. Eliasberg was yelling something now. Rossel raised his head and saw the conductor also on his knees, his hands waving frantically in the icy roaring wind.

'I confess,' the conductor screamed. 'I confess, I confess.'

34

Saturday November 3

A pair of manacles dangled from the ceiling. The metal was rusty but it was possible to distinguish between the brown of patient corrosion and the darker, fresher stains of blood. There were streaks of russet on the concrete walls, too, about three metres from where any interrogation victim would be suspended. As well as splashes on the floor, spots on the ceiling. And the first thing that would enter anyone's head, no matter how brave, no matter how innocent, as they entered this room would be: *what could they have done to the person who was here before me to extract so much blood?*

Eliasberg's file lay before Nikitin but the MGB major was not looking at it. Rossel could not see his face but from the angle of his head, the tapping of his fingers, he thought Nikitin must be preparing his attack.

Two loud clunks snapped the major out of his trance and the iron door to the chamber scraped open. Eliasberg was escorted only a metre or two inside before the guard let go of his elbow, turned smartly and locked them in again. The conductor took a half step towards Nikitin's desk before his eyes flickered to the dark traces all around – *a spoor of horrors*, Rossel thought, *like stumbling upon the jungle trail of some, as yet unidentified, man-eating beast.* The musician espied Rossel, took him in, tried to fit him into the overall scene. An empty chair, bent with wooden slats nailed to a cheap metal frame, beckoned.

Rossel simply gazed back. That was his duty. He was once again in the place where the road of his life had forked and he had ceased to be the carefree, scruffy young musician who everyone at the conservatory expected to forge a successful solo career, or, even, lead the great Philharmonic Orchestra. Instead, he had become another, harsher version of himself, a poker-faced militia cop who wouldn't take no for an answer.

There were no clues as to how this would unfold, if it did not follow a typical course of out-and-out torture, signed confession and death. And so the conductor advanced to his seat and sat. Eliasberg, always thin, now looked skeletal. He was pale, unshaven, and unrecognisable as the haughty principal conductor of the Leningrad Radio Orchestra and guest maestro of a dozen other ensembles and opera houses. There was bruising around both of his eyes and his bottom lip was bloodied.

At first, Nikitin seemed to stare past the conductor. Or through him. Finally, after an icy pause, he spoke.

'Karl Ilyich Eliasberg, you have said that you confess to your crime.'

Eliasberg nodded. 'That is correct. Yes, I took it.'

Nikitin's brow crinkled.

'Took it? Took what?'

'The score. Shostakovich's score, of course.'

'There's no use in prevaricating, Karl Ilyich. We have not brought you here to talk about the stolen score. Although, of course, when they searched your apartment last night, my men found it. The score of the Leningrad Symphony that you used to conduct the premier in this city is a historic document, not your personal possession. But enough of that. You are here to confess to murder.'

Eliasberg's eyes widened. 'Murder?'

'You murdered and mutilated five people. All members at one time or another, we are beginning to suspect, of your own orchestra.'

The conductor shook his head. 'No, no, no,' he said, 'you are mistaken. All I did was steal an orchestral score, Shostakovich's score. That I will admit to. But I never murdered anyone – the idea is preposterous!'

The major stood. He grasped the manacles with his right hand. Yanked at them so they began to swing, pendulum-like, backward and forward.

Eliasberg's eyes followed them.

The conductor began to speak. The words and syllables falling, rushing, leaping from his bruised lips.

'I was a great conductor with a wonderful reputation,' he said. 'I was given the honour of performing the Shostakovich symphony, his seventh, the symbol of the siege in Leningrad. The symbol of Soviet defiance. But after the war, Mravinsky, the great maestro, returned. Disdainful, bitter and jealous. He found me celebrated. Decorated – an Honoured Artist of the Soviet Union. So he used his influence and blocked me from ever again conducting in this city. And then, yes, I stole that score of the Leningrad Symphony – one of a bare handful of originals – because although Mravinsky conducted the premiere of Shostakovich's fifth and sixth symphonies, the seventh is mine, the Leningrad belongs to *me*, to Karl Ilyich Eliasberg. Because while Mravinsky was cowering thousands of miles from the front, I was here, *here*, rounding up an ensemble of half-dead violinists and clarinettists and percussionists, nurturing them back to life, bullying the famished horns into perfection, driving on my band of skeletons and ghosts. Murder? After all the trouble I had in finding them? Don't be ridiculous.'

Nikitin thumped the table and half stood, leaning over and glaring at Eliasberg.

'When they searched your house, my men discovered a list of fifty names inside the score,' he said. 'Six of them are underlined. Underlined by you. Four of them are dead, that we know for sure. And when we are certain that another dead body lying in the morgue is the other musician you marked out for murder, you will be further condemned. Besides, Minister Beria himself gave me your name, comrade. You say you are not a murderer but, in my eyes and in the eyes of the Soviet state in that moment – the moment of the minister's intervention – you became one.'

At the mention of Beria's name, Eliasberg's head dropped. A small tear rolled down his nose and he emitted a soft, low mewling. The pathetic whimper of a tiny trapped insect.

Nikitin reached out and patted him on the shoulder.

'I can save your family,' he said. 'You have a sister in Gatchina and your father is in a sanatorium in Novgorod. I know this. Let them be. Let them enjoy life. Confess. Why did you select those victims? Why did you place the bodies on the tracks in that way?'

With one finger he pushed the list of fifty names towards Eliasberg. Six were underlined. 'Look at these names. Just point to your victims and confirm their identities,' he said, with a voice of molten honey. 'Artists are famous for their petty jealousies, are they not? We are now assuming you were motivated by some sort of twisted professional rivalry. You have already talked of your resentment of Mravinsky. It boiled over. Poisoned your soul. Presented itself in unspeakable acts.'

Eliasberg was sobbing in great gulps now but raised his head.

'I wanted the seventh to be mine. To capture it for myself. That's all. I knew I was a fool to take the score but I couldn't help myself,' he whimpered. 'Mravinsky, the bastard – yes, I hated him in the way you describe. But nobody else.'

Nikitin looked pleased. Rossel watched the conductor destroy himself. It was never comfortable to see someone fall apart like this. Even the maniacs whose nerves dissolved in the considerably less menacing environment of ordinary police cells. No, it was never good to see such a creature as a man collapse into a formless pile of emotions and instincts, like a sail whose spar had snapped in a storm.

'Confirm the identities, Comrade Eliasberg. Confess to your crimes,' said Nikitin.

The major pushed once again at the chain.

Eliasberg sighed as he watched it swing. Then fumbled for the paper and peered at it, sniffling. His finger slid up the list and stopped.

'This one,' he said.

He paused and looked closer, the tears dripping off his nose. The finger moved again.

'This one . . .'

When the conductor pointed to the sixth underlined name, the one who had not yet turned up dead in any frozen field, Rossel knew he was lying.

*

Nikitin led Rossel out of the interrogation cell and down a narrow, whitewashed corridor with grey-green metal doors lining each side, closer together even than in a *kommunalka*. They climbed two flights of stairs – Rossel wondered if they were back above ground level, out of the dungeon, but there were no windows in the room the major took him into so it was impossible to tell.

'Let us be seated and drink,' said Nikitin, stomping over to a corner cabinet full of files and yanking open a cupboard. Out came a bottle of Stolichnaya and two tin mugs. He slammed them on a crate and lowered himself onto one of two stools either side.

'Let us drink, gundog, to the speed and certainty of Soviet justice as exacted by our great MGB. Little victories like this pathetic arsehole's confession. In this short, weary life I find it pays to celebrate them.'

*

Nikitin threw some more of the vodka down and grabbed a slice of some black bread he had placed on the table. As he chewed, he regarded the back of one hand and licked a crumb off his forefinger. The major's voice was a little slurred now. He and Rossel had been drinking for almost an hour.

'A simple man does not make life complicated. He does what he has to do to survive,' said Nikitin. 'For me, survival and talent were one and the same. When they recruited me, I had no idea why – I had never been good at anything before. But they train you, try you out, and together we found that I was good at something: the clashing together of heads, the breaking of noses.'

He sploshed more vodka into their mugs.

'In the end, I got so good that I could get people to confess just by walking into the room. Before the war, Rossel, before the war there were so many. So many: like you, like this stuck-up shit Eliasberg. We had no time for anything but our work, and as we worked, we improved. I became like one of your conductors myself, my friend. Sometimes there was no need to even pick up my baton, or take the slightest preparatory bow before they crapped their pants in appreciation. Now that's a symphony of sorts, is it not?'

'Do you ever allow them to confess without interrogation?' asked Rossel, knowing the answer.

Nikitin belched before answering.

'Never. We always ask questions. Sometimes they confess to the wrong crime or omit important details.' He raised his chipped blue mug. 'Anyway, enough of that. Your turn to propose a toast.'

Rossel raised his own mug. 'To the efficiency of Soviet justice.'

Nikitin, the tip of his nose beginning to redden a little, blinked. 'Very good,' he murmured. They drank a little more.

'What about you, Rossel?' said Nikitin. 'Why the militia?'

There was a pat response to that, too. But there was another, a truer one. If the vodka was intended to make him reckless, he would let it happen – he was already at the major's mercy. Rossel stared into Nikitin's eyes.

'Until I came to Leningrad before the war, I lived with my parents. They were – well, you have my file. They were transported to the gulag. And died there. My sister and I were put in the care of a state orphanage in Kostroma, a small town on the Volga, near Yaroslavl. Galya and I played in the town orchestra. The orchestra gave its big concert every spring and it was one of the most important days in Kostroma's life. In the winter of 1935, we were rehearsing something very ambitious – a Mozart symphony, number 40 in G minor. Everyone knows it, everyone can hum it.'

Rossel broke off and whistled the notes.

Nikitin recognised the piece and banged his tin mug on the table in crude accompaniment.

'It was a hard winter,' Rossel continued. 'You could walk onto the river and skate, and jump up and down, play hockey with sticks and a can, and it was like playing on concrete, no chance of going through. Cars and trucks wouldn't start, trains wouldn't start, roads were cut off. It came in waves, spells of minus thirty, minus thirty-five, lasting for weeks. Minus fifteen felt like a tropical respite.'

Nikitin's face was very flushed now. But he poured more for them both.

'When I had you hanging from the ceiling,' the major said. 'When you were dancing in the air. You whispered a woman's name. Was that her?'

Rossel ran the remaining two fingers of his left hand over his stubble to cover the twist in his mouth. He wondered how quick the bastard was – if he would be able to stop a glass being driven into his eyes or the bottle smashed over his head.

'*Everyone must have one face for the world and another for himself, Revol.*'

His father's advice filled his mind and stayed his hand. He sought his refuge, the place Nikitin had never been able to get to him. That eyrie, beyond the predator's reach – cold and in solitude.

Patience, Revol. There will be a time for the settling of old scores.

'After the concert we played together, I went drinking with my bandmates,' said Rossel. 'Galya and I had a row about it. She didn't like me drinking so much. About midnight, I staggered drunk to the front of the concert hall and saw Galya, alone in the twilight as the snow was coming down, cheeks like pink roses under the street lamp. She began walking, drifting down the middle of the road in her long coat, and there was no one else around. Just her, and me, meandering, half blind, fifty paces behind. Galya was heading back to the orphanage. I don't know if she saw me or heard me – the snow muffled everything. She never looked round and I thought, I'll just follow her home and everything will be all right.'

Nikitin laughed. A drunken guffaw. A crude attempt to mask emotion. But it fell away.

'I have a daughter, Rossel,' he mumbled almost to himself. 'A beautiful daughter. Did I tell you that?'

'I got home,' continued Rossel. 'I went to bed and passed out. Then awakening in the night, I looked through the window and thought I could see her, still in her coat, her head wrapped in her shawl, standing and looking at the house.

She never moved. Just watched and waited. Soon I lay back and fell asleep – perhaps I had never actually awoken – and in the morning Galya wasn't there. She wasn't there and she never ever came back. I have been looking for her ever since. That's why I joined the militia. It gave me an excuse to go looking.'

Rossel held his torturer's gaze.

'Now there are three of us,' said Rossel.

'Three of us?'

'I know this story. Sofia, the girl I once loved, knew it – I told it to her. And now you do.'

'Was she good of heart, your Galya?' asked Nikitin. He did not ask gently but with the quick, clipped voice of an interrogator.

'Always,' said Rossel.

'How old?'

'When she disappeared, she was eighteen.'

'Hm.' Nikitin stared back at him but his eyes were rolling and the moment of acuity had been blown away. He rocked forward and poured again. The bottle was almost empty. Vodka splashed into Rossel's mug. Nikitin filled his own to the brim again.

'Your sister is a mystery and so you became a cop. I like that story, gundog. I'm not sure I believe it but I like it very much. To the good of heart.' He jerked his head back and the liquid gushed down his throat. 'Here, let me show you.'

Nikitin fumbled inside his tunic and pulled out a black wallet.

'My daughter,' he said. With his fingers getting in each other's way, he nonetheless managed to tease out a creased photograph of a very serious, very pretty young woman.

'Svetlana. After Stalin's daughter. In this picture, nineteen. *Sveta, Svetochka, Svetulya.* My little light, my little flower.'

Nikitin pressed the picture to his lips, as if he was kissing an icon for its blessing. Through the fug in his brain one thought jumped out at Rossel. In the kitchen of his *kommunalka*, Nikitin had only mentioned one child, a son.

The major was maudlin now. Two tiny droplets pooled in the corners of his eyes and sought a convenient wrinkle down which to trickle.

'I can't imagine how it would be for me,' he said, 'if little Sveta went missing.'

He kissed his photograph again, a long, reverent fatherly kiss. And then, slumping forward, began to snore.

35

'Major Nikitin has requested me to interrogate the murderer Eliasberg,' Rossel said, tapping the conductor's personal file. 'Cell fourteen.'

The guard stared at him. 'Where is the major?'

Rossel's head was reeling with the vodka but was counting on adrenalin to carry him through. As long as Nikitin didn't wake up too soon.

'The major is studying the file of the accused to prepare his case,' he said. 'You could, of course, ask him yourself.'

For a second Rossel thought the man would call his bluff. But it took a fool to challenge the orders of an MGB major. The guard pulled aside the viewing hatch and glanced in before opening up.

Eliasberg jumped to his feet and stood next to his chair. He was pale and shaking.

In five paces Rossel was face to face with the conductor.

'Karl Ilyich,' he said. 'You are lying about the list we found in that score of the Leningrad Symphony. I know none of those people was killed by you.'

Eliasberg's long, soulful face and dark, expressive eyes now looked into Rossel's own, hunting for what he must believe was impossible: mercy. Rossel gave him a policeman's wooden stare in return. He walked round to the other side of the desk. Eliasberg's knees gave way and he fell into the chair.

'Stand up,' said Rossel. 'I did not say you could sit.' The maestro struggled to his feet once more, hands on the front of the desk for support.

Rossel picked up the list of fifty names. 'Who are these people?' he demanded.

Eliasberg's eyes blurred with tears. 'I confessed. I willingly confessed.'

Rossel shook his head. 'In the camps – Major Nikitin says, at best, you will be going there – your life will be in the hands of people who will despise everything about you: the quickness of your mind, the softness of your hands, those academic, bourgeois tones. In Vorkuta recently, I heard they actually chopped a man's head off with an axe in front of the inmates simply for the purposes of entertainment. They stood around and applauded like it was an afternoon recital. Why are these people on this list?'

The conductor was silent. Rossel knew he was trying to guess the answer his interrogator wanted. For the MGB, that was the ideal state of their prey. For his purposes, it was useless. Galya, his parents, his music. And now Sofia. All mysteries to him. All ripped from him. He needed the truth. It was all that mattered. And though Rossel felt his heart almost still as he acknowledged the thought and all its implications, he was prepared to ignore even Beria's orders to get to it.

'Maestro,' he said. 'This is my militia identification. Read my name. I don't care if Major Nikitin or Comrade Beria himself thinks you are guilty. I want to know the truth. You know who is on this list and why, and it has nothing to do with your relationship with Mravinsky. But I think it relates to an event that is very important in my investigation.'

Eliasberg reached out and took the ID in his long fingers. He peered at it for a moment and handed it back.

'Read the list again,' said Rossel. 'And read my ID again.'

The conductor held the paper close to his face. After a moment, he put it back on the desk, very slowly.

'The first performance of Shostakovich's seventh symphony in this city was conducted by you and the Leningrad Radio Symphony Orchestra – your orchestra,' said Rossel. 'My name is on this list but I was not in your orchestra because by that time I'd first had my fingers broken a few cells down the corridor from where we are now, and then been sent to the front. Other names here were also not members of that ensemble. So, it is not a list of the radio orchestra.'

Eliasberg's eyes widened.

'Yes, that's right,' said Rossel. 'I really am not one of *them*. To continue. Sofia Fedotova was not in your orchestra. She was a singer. She turned her back on music after the siege and became a nurse. Nadya Bazhanova, a clarinettist. Not good enough to make it and joined the MGB. Maxim Avdeyev, French horn. Went to the gulag, came back a priest. An insane one, but a priest all the same. Felix Sorokin. Joined the Red Army. They, plus myself and someone by the name of Gusts Landau, comprise the six underlined names in the list of fifty. The question is why.'

Rossel held Eliasberg's gaze.

'Nadya, Maxim, Felix and Sofia were indeed murdered – the MGB is not lying about that,' he continued. 'There is

301

another victim who we have yet to identify but Comrade Landau, whoever he was, is a prime candidate. And then there is me. The fact that we are all on this list may be a giant coincidence but I am inclined to doubt it. So, I need to know, maestro, the true nature of this particular list. What was it for?'

Rossel took out a pack of cigarettes and offered one to Eliasberg. The conductor, his hands shaking, accepted. Rossel lit it and the maestro blew smoke out into the air where it hung between them like a bilious fog.

'Early in 1942 there was a contest to decide whether Shostakovich or another composer would be chosen to write the Soviet Union's war anthem,' said Eliasberg. 'I was handed that list by the political officer who oversaw the Philharmonic Hall. I was told to round them up – I would get help, but mostly it was left to me to find enough musicians to stage this contest. Those six names were already underlined – I swear to you, it was nothing to do with me. Some apparatchik had arranged everything for the contest. I just did what I was told.'

From the bowels of the Bolshoi Dom came a muffled scream. Eliasberg flinched.

'Many of the names I recognised – some were old comrades from the Leningrad Radio Orchestra. Others were new to me, including those ones you are most interested in. Yet amid the dreadful carnage of the siege, it became the most important mission of my life – to find these musicians, to save their lives, to keep Soviet culture itself alive in a city that was otherwise dying. So I kept the list. At some point I must have tucked it into the score of the Shostakovich symphony, my other treasured souvenir from the war. But I do not remember.'

And in that instant, in that momentary contortion of the maestro's face, the clues began to fall into line like a parade. If he could just transform the cascade of deductions and connections into one moment of clarity to make it all work, everything would make sense. He was sure of it.

But he had to go step by step. *One thing at a time, Lieutenant.*

'Tell me about the great contest, maestro. You conducted the two submitted compositions. What do you remember about that?'

Rossel's voice was steady. Another *papirosa* gave him further comfort.

'The contest pitted Shostakovich against Vronsky – you are familiar with Vronsky?' said Eliasberg. 'It was a vicious rivalry for years before the war. There was a competition, an audition of sorts. A contest to find the composition that would be the musical accompaniment to the war effort. A foolish idea.'

'Why so?'

'You cannot make music by competition, Lieutenant. Music flows, or it does not. Inspiration strikes and a composer's ability turns it into something divine or something banal, depending on the talent available. Music by competition results only in bombast.'

'Are you saying the Leningrad Symphony is nothing but bombast?'

'Of course not,' said Eliasberg. 'Shostakovich had instinctively realised what was required to win. He had already sensed the mood of the people – and the Party. Vronsky was the up-and-coming man at that point, but only his political connections could have won him the contest. I know – I was there. I conducted both submissions for the audition.'

'And do you remember those compositions?'

'One of them I know from memory,' said Eliasberg. 'The Shostakovich. At the contest it was still embryonic but it was clear how it could blossom into a true masterpiece – the work that became the seventh symphony, the Leningrad. Vronsky's piece was bizarre – a *sinfonia concertante*. Six soloists and orchestra, though a much smaller group than the one Shostakovich demanded. Neither one thing nor the other. Insipid stuff – in musical terms, Vronsky never had a chance.'

'That must have infuriated him,' said Rossel.

'Yes, his public mask of indulgent affability, the genial artist everybody knew, slipped. He was furious. Exploded and stormed out after his piece had been played, I remember. But his time has come again with this new opera, *The Blockade*. While Shostakovich's reputation has, of late, fallen once again in the eyes of the Party. And in the mind of Vronsky, victory is everything, you see. It does not stop. I have never, in all my life, met a man with such a hunger for personal glory. Even when we were at school together, he was . . .'

Rossel leaned forward.

'You went to school with Vronsky?'

Eliasberg nodded.

'Where was this?'

'On Krestovsky Island, out on Lake Ladoga. Before the revolution.' A wistful look crossed his grey eyes. 'At first, for me, it was a very happy place.'

'At first?'

The conductor shifted in his seat.

'There were twelve of us in Professor Loban's class. Only ever twelve – it was the most elite of elite upbringings. Loban's Apostles, we were called by the servants and ground staff. The tsar owned the palace itself but the royal family were seldom seen there. They allowed respected courtiers and politicians to live in it during the summer months. Stolypin, the prime minister, was the most regular tenant.'

'Stolypin himself?'

Eliasberg nodded.

'The very same. His daughter was badly wounded by a bomb – one of the many attempts to kill him. Because of that, I think, he was kindness itself to us children on the odd occasions we saw him.'

Stolypin sent so many suspected Reds to the gallows they rechristened the noose 'Stolypin's neck-tie'. The kindness of such a man was always limited, thought Rossel, and highly selective.

'And Professor Loban? Tell me about him.'

'Fyodor Loban, a great man, a great educator. He created the school himself from scratch, selecting gifted boys from across the empire, those supremely talented in different areas: science, languages, mathematics and music. Stolypin, when he was chairman of the tsar's Council of Ministers, funded the scholarships and the school itself. He had an ulterior motive – he wanted to attract the tsarevich Alexei to the school and use this to exert even greater influence on the royal family but the tsarina refused to let him attend. Such a delicate child.'

'You were one of the chosen? That must have felt like a great honour?'

Eliasberg gave a small smile.

'As I said, it was a happy place.'

'Until?'

'Until the arrival of an unexpected thirteenth apostle. Back then he had a pretentious nickname for himself. Something Greek, now what was it again? Thanatos, yes, that was it.'

Rossel felt an itch prickling across the mark on his neck.

He leaned further across the table.

'Vronsky?'

Eliasberg flopped back in his chair as if he had been punctured. He breathed in through his nose, more and more, seeming to give himself new energy with the foetid air. At last, he pulled himself upright and stared at Rossel.

'Comrade Lieutenant, you are dealing in both music and murder, am I correct? Then let me tell you a tale. Professor Loban never wanted him in the school but Vronsky's mother was a schemer, a great beauty, a lady of society and blessed with some powerful friends. Ever met her?' Eliasberg twisted his lips. 'The kind of woman who bites into a lemon and makes the lemon recoil. Close to the court then. Close to the Kremlin now. Loban had no choice. He had to accept the boy.'

'And did Vronsky receive special treatment?'

Eliasberg shook his head.

'No, not really. That was not the professor's way. Loban was indulgent of all his prodigies. If he was annoyed at having Vronsky forced upon him, he did not show it. For a while, things remained as they had been. But then there was a recital – a musical competition.'

Nikitin might burst in at any moment. But Rossel's instincts told him if he pushed the conductor too hard, he would clam up. He needed to be patient.

'What kind of recital?'

'Stolypin arranged for the tsarina to visit the island and observe Loban's charges in person. It was decided that she would view each group in turn. Mathematicians first, then scientists, then those boys particularly proficient in language would read out some poems they had written and finally we musicians would perform something. Something one of us had written.'

'And Vronsky was the chosen one,' said Rossel.

'No. No, Comrade Lieutenant, that was just it. He wasn't. A boy named Suvorin, Andrei Suvorin, was the chosen one. A remarkable prodigy, a talent some compared to Mozart. Alas, the world never got to hear a Suvorin symphony. I have carried a tiny fragment of his composition lodged in my head for almost half a century. Even then it had a haunting quality. As if, though a child like the rest of us, the boy already knew too much of the bestial undercurrents, the darkness of this world.'

They both looked at the door. Footsteps sounded in the corridor outside but drifted away.

'Continue, maestro.'

'In the weeks before the recital, that's when the atmosphere began to change. Petty acts of abuse and bullying. Suvorin, victimised by Vronsky. We were all encouraged to gang up on him. A few did, a few kept their distance. Suvorin kept on trying to compose, but Vronsky would steal his manuscript paper and sing it out loud, taunting him.'

Eliasberg held Rossel's eye for a moment. Then he started to hum – a simple, five-note musical phrase.

F. A. E-flat. G. B-flat.

Fa. La. Mi-bemol. Sol. Si-bemol.

Rossel felt a twist of recognition.

Eliasberg opened his lips and then repeated the refrain, louder and more clearly.

Rossel pounded the table to silence him. 'How did you know?' he shouted.

'Know what, detective?'

'Those notes. That they were the notes we found on the tracks?'

Eliasberg looked at him. He was calm now, his face marked only by serenity and acceptance.

'I do not know what you are talking about, comrade,' the conductor murmured. 'I only know these as the notes Suvorin wrote, that Vronsky sang out in a mocking falsetto to us in the grounds of our school. And which formed the *leitmotif* of the piece that was performed to the tsarina in a simple but elegant string trio written by Vronsky.'

'But I thought you said Suvorin was the chosen one.'

'He was. But a week before royal inspection, Suvorin disappeared. His parents came for the recital and had to be told he had vanished.'

Rossel's mind was racing. 'Why tell me this?' he said. 'It is ancient history.'

'Because you asked me about the great musical competition. And because you should know what Vronsky is capable of. Incidentally, if you have heard that refrain before, that is because it appears in every Vronsky composition.'

'What?'

'Yes, every one. Sometimes it is hidden. Almost impercept-ible. Sometimes it is inverted. Every time it is harmonised dif-ferently. But it is always there. I have always found it. Even though it is not his, but Suvorin's.'

Rossel got to his feet and pounded at the door. The outside bolt slid back and a sliver of light thrust into the interrogation room.

He paused at the threshold.

'I will do my best for you, maestro,' he said. 'I will tell them you are innocent.'

'Will that help me?'

The maestro looked more curious than concerned, save for the two tears dampening the whiskers of his cheeks.

Rossel shrugged.

'The six people whose names are underlined were stu-dents from the Leningrad Conservatory who were called upon to play the solo parts in the Vronsky. But having that list found in your possession has been unfortunate. People have been condemned for far less.'

He turned and opened the door wider. Over his shoul-der, Rossel added: 'It was an honour to play under your baton, maestro, even if for only one rehearsal.'

36

Sunday November 4

The dark skin on Madame Shishani's cheeks looked just as it had when he was a student – drier than the leaves of the oldest scores she kept on the library shelves that surrounded them.

Sixty years old, half Chechen and proud of it, Madame Shishani seemed to have lived her life in the conservatory library. There were whispers she was a Muslim and kept a tattered copy of the Koran hidden among the symphonies and sonatas, but they were very quiet whispers; it didn't pay to be a Chechen Muslim in Soviet Russia and the students liked Madame Shishani. In any case, her thin blue lips and contemptuous dark eyes were straight out of the savage, northern world of Russian folklore.

The library was on the bottom floor of the conservatory. You filled out a request for a score and Madame Shishani would take it and disappear behind countless shelves, sometimes for several minutes, before materialising with the work you needed. As she had done so many times when he was a student, so she did now, handing Rossel a thick green tome. On the front of it was a neatly typed title:

310

Raskolnikov's Feast. N. Vronsky.

'Professor Lebedeva told me about your enquiry so I put this to one side, Lieutenant Rossel.'

Rossel opened the score and leafed through the sheets of white paper. Six solo parts, all jumbled up, nothing sticking the disparate pages and parts together, and in a separate box folder, the full orchestral parts. On the back of the last page was Vronsky's flourish of a signature.

This was the composition Vronsky had submitted to the All-Soviet Contest to find the greatest patriotic music for the Great Patriotic War – a work for an orchestra and six soloists. Where Shostakovich had gone for scale, grandiosity and sheer volume, Vronsky had tried intensity, intimacy, a foray into the Russian soul, darkness laced with light. Shostakovich had scored his work for a vast ensemble, an orchestra you could hear in Berlin. In total, close to a hundred musicians. The advantage was size and noise – the kind of fist-waving defiance the authorities would love. The disadvantage was that it had been almost impossible to find enough musicians of the right calibre who were alive and had the energy to blow, scrape or bash their instruments. That had been Eliasberg's task. Every able-bodied adult was either at the front, in armaments factories, fighting fires from incendiaries or digging ditches. But he had found enough to form a ragged orchestra – and turned them into something worth listening to.

The soloists for *Raskolnikov's Feast* were a soprano, two violins, cello, clarinet and trumpet. The accompanying orchestra was of roughly the size needed for a classical symphony. To be sure, compositions for smaller forces could have extraordinary power – but as a piece to rouse the masses in the name of war? It was a gamble. And it hadn't paid off.

'Did you ever receive a complete copy of *Raskolnikov's Feast*, Madame Shishani?'

'A copy? No – these are the only parts ever printed,' she said. 'These are the originals.'

Rossel reached into his coat pocket and pulled out the list of everyone who had played in both pieces on the day of the contest. He thought back to that day. Most of the time he had been gazing at Sofia when not struggling to play his violin or thinking about food. The rest of the day was wrapped in fog.

He showed the list to Madame Shishani. 'Forgive me, I know you are the librarian, not the administration. But do you remember this name? Gusts Landau – it is an unusual one.'

She took the paper from him and held it right up to her face, her lips moving as she read.

'Oh!' She jabbed a finger at the paper. 'Oh yes – that was a bad business. I could never forget that one.' She beckoned him to look with her.

'Gusts,' said Madame Shishani. 'The poor man . . .'

'What do you mean?' asked Rossel, his heart racing.

Madame Shishani looked around for hidden Chekists and spoke in a whisper.

'Not one of ours,' she said. 'A Latvian. They said he was a big band trumpeter really. And a Jew . . . we thought someone had murdered him because he was a Jew.'

The memory hit Rossel between the eyes. The trumpeter in the rehearsal – '*Normally I play for dinner dances so forgive me all the wrong notes.*' A refugee from Riga after the Latvian capital had fallen to the Wehrmacht in the earliest days of the war. But Gusts Landau had ended up surrounded by the Germans anyway a few months later in Leningrad. A rotund, cheerful soul, bemused at finding himself preparing Leningrad's anti-tank defences one minute and having to sight-read Shostakovich and Vronsky the next.

Madame Shishani nodded with vigour. 'He had played in some sort of rehearsal of *Raskolnikov's Feast* but forgotten to hand back his part. I should have reported it at the time, I know, but there was so much death, so much suffering, it hardly seemed worth it.'

'Reported what?'

'Isn't that why you're here, asking about this piece? What the girl saw in that flat on the Griboyedova Canal? It's a very long time ago now, but I thought that must be why you were interested in this particular composition.'

Rossel raised an eyebrow.

'A girl?'

'Alla, she was an assistant here during the war. She, well, it was all very strange, really. Or, in those terrible times, perhaps, not so.'

'Describe it to me.'

'It was in the second summer of the blockade, so 1943, maybe July – the last days of the White Nights. I missed the last evacuation train out and in any case I refused to go. I would fight and die with my home city, I told them. Alla was only fourteen. Her parents had died so she had gone to live with her aunt and uncle, out near the St Peter and Paul Fortress. Then the aunt and uncle went, too, in the winter of that year. I let her stay with me, shared what little food

I could find with her. We came to work here each day, just to try and do something, anything to take our minds off the monsters our bellies had become. Not very much was happening. By then the only time anyone ever picked up an instrument was to burn it or turn the strings into soup. Then one day a messenger came from the Deputy Kommissar for Culture, Nikolai Shevchuk himself, with a special executive order.'

'An order to do what?'

'It seemed crazy. I could hardly walk, neither could Alla,' continued Madame Shishani. 'But we were told to go to the homes of everyone who had any music by Vronsky in their possession and return them all to the library. This Landau character had played in his rehearsal and wandered off with his part instead of returning it, do you see? He was a stranger. His Russian was only so-so. He didn't know the way things were done. And there were all sorts of other bits of music missing, as you can imagine. Library candy, do you remember that? People boiling the glue out of books and manuscripts to make soup. And also, we presumed, because some of those who had borrowed them in the first place were already dead. I objected – what a waste of time, when everyone was fighting just to survive. But the messenger made it clear that we would be failing in our duty to the Party if we did not comply.

'We split up the list between us, I took the ones furthest away – the Vasilieostrovsky and Petrogradsky Districts, and as far north as I dared go before it was too dangerous. I gave Alla the ones in the centre of town, around the Moscow Station, the Smolny Institute, places like that. We agreed to just do a few each day; by then the bread ration was down to a hundred and twenty-five grams and most of that was sawdust. Walking anywhere was difficult.'

Rossel broke in.

'So what exactly did Alla see?'

'A corpse.'

Madame Shishani's voice cracked a little as she forced the memories to return.

'Alla was a nice girl, a sweet girl. I liked her so much. The child was very upset when she returned. Even though everyone had seen so much, it shook her to the core.'

'What did?'

Madame Shishani raised her right hand and stretched out her index finger, pushing it against her larynx.

'Somebody had stuck him with a kind of glass tube. In his throat.'

37

The Union of Composers building was on Bolshaya Morskaya, not far from the Hotel Astoria. Decorated with marble busts and friezes, the mansion had once been the luxurious home of the wealthy Gagarina family. Vronsky had become head of the union in 1950; shortly afterwards he had moved into a grace-and-favour apartment in the building.

It was twilight by the time Rossel's car drew up to the pavement opposite the white stuccoed entrance. A man was waiting for him, leaning against another vehicle. It was Nikitin. Rossel peered through the misted back windows of the major's car, expecting to see more MGB. But Nikitin was unaccompanied.

'I asked at Vosstaniya Street as to your whereabouts. They didn't want to tell me. But I insisted,' said Nikitin.

The major was unshaven and a little dishevelled. There was something about his manner, too, Rossel thought, which was different. He seemed less certain of himself; somewhat subdued.

'If all you are interested in is following orders and just want to pin it on Eliasberg, I can't stop you,' said Rossel, 'but I'm determined to apprehend the real killer.'

Nikitin pushed himself upright. For a moment, Rossel thought the major was about to draw his pistol. Instead, he simply said, 'Lead on, Lieutenant.'

They stamped through the snow down Bolshaya Morskaya.

'A small army to arrest Eliasberg, who is innocent, and just you and me for Vronsky?'

'Eliasberg is a nobody,' said Nikitin, adjusting his blue-topped cap. 'Vronsky is Vronsky.' But Rossel sensed there was some other reason Nikitin had come alone.

They trudged a few yards further. This part of Bolshaya Morskaya reminded Rossel of the siege. He had limped down it once, towards the temporary hospital at the Astoria, with a small piece of shrapnel from a German shell stuck in his right ankle. The spring sunshine, he remembered, had just started to loosen the snow and shrunken hands, withered arms and twisted icy faces had begun to sprout – people had called them 'black snowdrops'. He would soon see a lot more of them at the front.

His left boot slopped into a deep puddle of gritty sleet as they reached their destination. The composers had only moved there in 1948. It was a beautiful building, but then Bolshaya Morskaya had beautiful buildings to spare.

As he rang the big brass bell, he looked down at the kerb, about five feet away from where he was standing. The corpse of a child had once lain there. A boy of perhaps ten years old. Only the greying tip of his nose and a pair of broken wire-frame glasses had been fully visible above the slush. His lifeless eyes had seemed to scan the indifferent white clouds above him.

Rossel pulled his greatcoat tighter at the neck as a young man in a servant's outfit opened the door, saw Nikitin's uniform and cap and swallowed. They were shown in.

*

She was well into her sixties, greying and diminutive. But there was danger to her, a cool, effortless magnetism of someone who had spent a lifetime turning heads. Everything about the way she held herself was an almost balletic calculation, one intended to hold the attention of anyone who gazed upon it.

'You are looking for my son, perhaps?' she said.

Nikitin stared at her. 'That depends, comrade,' he said after a pause. 'Identify yourself. And him.'

'My son. Nikolai Nikolayevich Vronsky. The maestro.'

She tilted her head, almost imperceptibly, towards the servant at the door. As she did so, a flickering light from the jewelled candelabra above her traced a shoal of tiny pink dots across the skin of her neck.

A silver-framed photograph on a dresser in the corner of the room showed the composer's mother in her twenties. The face was thin, the chin round, the lips bow-shaped, the eyebrows arched suggestively upwards, like a Russian Marlene Dietrich. Now, her once lustrous dark hair was cut short and speckled with grey but she remained powerful and alluring. And she knew it.

The servant – a squat, middle-aged man with a bull neck squeezed into a white, gold-trimmed waiter's jacket – stepped forward and refilled her cup. She reached across and spread a little beluga onto a tiny crêpe. Then fed it to the tiny, yapping black dog at her feet – a mutt that wouldn't last five minutes in a Leningrad winter if it had to call the street its home, thought Rossel.

The two visitors hadn't moved.

She sat in one of two large matching chaises longues. The room was oak-panelled and covered, on all four sides, with banks of polished shelving. Every available space was cluttered with gold and silver ornaments – snuff boxes, candlesticks, trays, mirrors – and a collection of Dyatkovo crystal. In pride of place, above the mantelpiece, were two blue Fabergé eggs, tiny and exquisite. Rossel felt as though he had stumbled upon the antechamber to some magnificent palace in which all the riches of the Romanovs were being held in safe keeping.

Madame Vronsky followed Rossel's eye.

'You like my trinkets?'

He gave her what he hoped was a cold look.

'I haven't seen such a display of privilege outside the Hermitage itself,' he said.

It was the kind of blunt accusation that had sent millions to the gulag. Madame Vronsky made no attempt to deflect it. To do that, a Soviet citizen had to be utterly confident of their own status and position.

'As a girl, in the days before our great and noble socialist revolution, I worked in the Elisseyev Emporium on Nevsky. The store is still there, of course, but only a pale shadow, I'm afraid, of the way it was in those far-off days. The silks, the perfumes, the dresses, my goodness. The tsarina herself visited on occasion, with her daughters. I was told by a close friend that the chemise pretty little Maria was wearing when she came face to face with the bullets of revolutionary justice in Sverdlovsk came from Elisseyev's last-ever collection. So shameful to put holes in an item of such unsurpassed quality. This casual cultural vandalism makes me, on occasion, question my own Marxist zealotry, Lieutenant Rossel. And you must be Major Nikitin?'

Madame Vronsky leaned down and fed the dog more caviar. It barked and then demolished the delicacy.

Rossel found his voice.

'Where is the maestro?' he asked.

Madame Vronsky shrugged.

'Rehearsing, I expect.'

'The Kirov Ballet is performing *Swan Lake* this evening. There is no rehearsal of *The Blockade*.'

She looked at her nails. 'Then I do not know.'

Nikitin cleared his throat.

'Forgive the interruption, comrade,' he said. 'We were just . . .'

Rossel took out his pen and notepad.

'Just to clear something up for me,' he said. 'Could I ask you to recall if you issued instructions to all music conservatories and concert halls to collect all copies of your son's work, *Raskolnikov's Feast*, after it was performed for the first and only time? And that the staff of the library of the Leningrad Conservatory of Music were, in turn, instructed to go about the city and pick them up?'

Madame Vronsky patted the dog gently on the head.

'There, there, Zib, good girl, good girl.'

She stared up at Rossel, her right eyebrow arched *à la* Dietrich.

'Zib is a movie star, Lieutenant. Do you recognise her?'

Rossel shook his head.

'Oh, yes. Vladimir Yazdovsky, a Lenfilm director, is a personal friend. He gave Zib to me once she had played her role.'

'Her role?'

'Zib here was just a scruffy mongrel bitch that hung around the Lenfilm studio kitchen feeding on potato peelings. Then one day a dog scheduled to be in a film ran away. They couldn't change the scene, they were on a schedule. And so Zib, being a young lady of prescience, sensed an opportunity. They grabbed her, hoped she would sit still until encouraged to walk across the set, and she behaved perfectly. She practically won the Stalin Prize. And Yazdovsky gave her to me. Now she resides under a chaise longue that once belonged to Princess Gagarina, being fed the finest caviar by the mother of Nikolai Nikolayevich Vronsky, the head of the Leningrad Union of Composers and soon to be lauded, once *The Blockade* has premiered, as the greatest Russian composer that ever lived.'

Madame Vronsky made a swift, twisting movement with her right hand. She grabbed the dog's ear and yanked it roughly. The yap turned into a growl. It lurched forward to snap at her hand. She moved her red silk slipper and kicked it forcibly.

'But I must always be careful because, as you can see, this bitch hasn't forgotten how to bite.'

Whining, the dog scuttled off into the corner of the room.

'Your son's music, Madame Vronsky,' said Rossel. 'Was it you who persuaded Deputy Kommissar Shevchuk to order the collection of all of your son's music that was not already in your personal possession?'

She shrugged.

BEN CREED

'I really have no recollection. Everything about those times, the siege, was unworldly. I like to think of it as something that never really happened at all.'

Rossel matched her stare. Her eyes, he noticed, were a brittle metallic blue.

'You are an investigator, Comrade Rossel. And yet I'm led to understand that, in a somewhat ironic turn of events, you and your militia colleagues are now also under investigation.'

He began to mouth another question. But thought better of it. Madame Vronsky clapped her hands. The liveried flunky stepped towards them.

'Yes, Madame. Shall I show them out?'

He had an accent – southern, Rossel thought. From the Caucasus? He didn't look it.

'Show them out, Razin.'

Rossel picked up his cap and stood. It was a good Cossack name, and though plenty of ordinary Soviet citizens were at liberty to call their children Razin, it would be just like Madame Vronsky to give herself a pet warrior Cossack.

She smiled at him.

'So sorry not to have been more helpful.'

*

Outside the living room was a gold-painted vestibule. Off to one side was an oak door decorated with an armoured hand holding a magnificent scimitar – the ancient coat of arms of the Gagarina family. Beyond that door were the areas of the mansion now used by the Union of Composers for rehearsals, recitals and academic work.

The Cossack escorted them out, with a look on his face suggesting he would have liked them served up for his lunch. Nikitin was in a hurry to leave but Rossel lingered at a large, gilt mirror near the entrance. Under the mirror was a vase filled with fresh flowers. It was pseudo-Grecian in shape, with a golden handle, and looked – just as the ones in the living room did – as if it was made of the most expensive Dyatkovo crystal.

Rossel finished buttoning his coat and headed out after Nikitin into the dark. As he stepped back onto Bolshaya Morskaya, he smacked his gloves together with a retort that made the MGB major turn.

He had seen the vase once before. In Sofia's sketchbook. Perhaps one of her last drawings.

*

The encounter had left Nikitin agitated. He ordered Rossel to get in the car. They drove off, Nikitin silent and brooding, heading back the way they had come until the major glided to a halt not fifty metres away from the House of Composers, in a spot out of the lamp light, a place where they had a good sight of the door but where anyone emerging would have difficulty seeing them.

They did not have long to wait. About ten minutes after they had exited the building, Madame Vronsky, wearing a black sable coat and accompanied by the sullen Razin, emerged. A gleaming red car pulled up to the pavement. Madame Vronsky and her bodyguard got inside.

'Look at that,' said Nikitin. 'A Moskvich 400-420. Brand new. Isn't she a beauty?'

Lit by the dull glimmer of the street lamps, the Moskvich pulled out into the snow and advanced into busier traffic as Bolshaya Morskaya drew parallel with the Moika Canal. Nikitin followed, keeping the car a good hundred metres behind. After only a few minutes, the two vehicles turned left, crossed the bridge and bore right, following the canal but on the other side. Only two minutes more and the Moskvich pulled up in front of an orange and white building fronted with white classical columns, the Yusupov Palace.

Nikitin drove straight past. The major continued for another hundred metres and pulled into an empty space behind a battered Gaz truck and next to an old bicycle, chained to the embankment railings and missing both of its wheels.

He switched off the engine and adjusted the driver's mirror so he could see the front of the Yusupov.

'Watch,' he said. 'Use the side mirror.'

After a minute or two, a woman came out of a dimly lit side street and got straight into the back of the Moskvich.

Rossel recognised her immediately. It was Dr Volkova.

38

'Did I scare you?'

Vassya yawned and wiped some sleep from her eyes. Then opened her door a little wider.

She looked down the passage, left and right, before answering Rossel's question.

'Scared? I simply thought you'd come to do what you failed to do the other evening and show a girl a good time.'

Rossel stepped into her doorway, closed the door behind him and kissed her.

'That is better,' she said.

His voice dropped to a whisper.

'I think this thing involves some important people who are beginning to regret my involvement,' he said.

'Beria?'

'We should go.'

He had hit on the idea as he was driving over, wrestling with the steering wheel as the car skidded and slid from one side of the road to the other. The new metro – nearly complete as an engineering project, not yet open to the public – Vassya would know it better than anyone. The MGB might have the plans but every project of that scale was only truly known to those who had worked on it.

'You could hide down there forever,' he said. 'There must be side tunnels, shelters, storage rooms.'

'And why would I do that?'

'Nikitin has seen us together. Colonel Sarkisov knows that you flew us over the tracks – he was fully debriefed when we went to Moscow. Anyone with a close connection to me is now in danger.'

'And then what?' She raised her voice. 'Roll around like a mole for the rest of my life? Hunt for scraps of potato peelings dropped by my fellow workers? I was a Night Witch. I flew over Stalingrad. On moonlight nights the anti-aircraft gunners hit us as easily as tins at a fairground shooting stall and because of the weight of the bombs and the low altitude of the planes, we never bothered with parachutes. I flew forty-seven missions. What did you do in the Great Patriotic War, Rossel? Catch burglars? Put out fires?'

Rossel let go of her arms and stepped back.

'At the beginning, yes, I put out fires with the civil defence. Have you ever tried putting out a fire caused by an incendiary bomb? I saw one man lose the skin from his entire body. Later, I was in the 2nd Shock Army – at Sinyavino. I was in a detachment of forty-seven men. Two of us survived the first week of fighting. When they sent in reinforcements, I watched from a crater as nearly three hundred men were killed in the first ten minutes. About thirty made it through so we formed a new detachment. This time three of us survived to the following week. When no more reinforcements came, we crawled out through slime and shit and dead bodies and the NKVD soldiers were so stunned they forgot to shoot us.'

Vassya sighed.

'I am sorry. But all that does is make you a survivor, like myself,' she said. 'I won't hide in a tunnel.'

*

They had laid out the fifth body on a trolley in the middle of the morgue.

Rossel pointed to the victim's chest.

'He is still a mystery. Male, black-haired, despite signs of starvation still carrying a little belly fat. Pattern of cuts slightly different from the other corpses, in that the killer had also sliced heavily into the back of his neck on the right-hand side, so the flesh was fully separated from there, as well as on his face. In her report, Dr Volkova estimates the age of the victim as fifty-five to sixty.'

The Night Witch looked again at the corpse.

'Do you know who it is?' she asked.

'I have a good idea.'

Rossel walked across to the heavy door of the morgue and checked, for a second time, that it was properly locked. Then he turned up the radio to full volume before undoing the bottom two buttons of his uniform jacket and pulling out a blue file he had pushed into his belt. He spread it out on a small metal table that Dr Volkova kept her surgical instruments on. Vassya stepped closer to him and stared down at the file. She could see the usual black and white photograph and densely typed columns of information. And the unmistakable stamp at the top of the file.

'You really are on a suicide mission. You've stolen an MGB file.'

'Two, to be precise. When I was last in the Bolshoi Dom I didn't waste my time. I've got the other one somewhere safe.'

'Nikolai Shevchuk.' Vassya read out the name on the file. 'Who is he?'

'Deputy Cultural Kommissar Shevchuk was one of the people who decided what was "good" or "bad" in Soviet culture. Who chose what our great patriotic Soviet state considered to be a work of artistic genius, or a piece of "bourgeois, reactionary recidivism" that might earn its creator a little time sunbathing in the Siberian permafrost. But Shevchuk also had an extra special role. He was given the task of deciding what great work would be the Soviet Union's music for the war. A few months ago, he disappeared from his workplace. To a gulag, people supposed. But I believe it is more likely that he had fallen into the embrace of dear Comrade Vronsky.'

'How can you be certain it is Shevchuk?'

'Four of the victims we found on the railway tracks were in their early thirties – not surprising, since they were all classmates. But one was in his early fifties. According to Dr Volkova, he had access to luxury items like caviar. Thus he was likely to hold a position of privilege. He is the right age, the right rank, and the only other person Vronsky would have wanted to kill, since he chose Shostakovich as the Soviet Union's war composer. And there is one more clue. See that?'

Rossel pointed to a column in the file headed: *Distinguishing marks*. Vassya read from it aloud.

'Three large black moles, one of very distinct triangular shape, each about a centimetre in diameter, found at the base of the neck on the right-hand side,' she said. She looked up. 'So?'

'So that is why we have hoisted him out of the freezer. Roll him over.'

On the count of three, they manhandled the corpse onto its front. The wound was immediately obvious – a deep, crude incision a little below the nape.

'So, the murderer had to slice off the skin on his neck to disguise the moles, otherwise it would have been too easy to identify the body? Is that it?'

Rossel nodded.

'Meet Comrade Shevchuk. Body number five.'

Vassya stared at the corpse. 'Did Dr Volkova not work out who it was?'

He smiled. 'Possibly. But perhaps she was more preoccupied with keeping maestro Vronsky and his good mama abreast of our investigation.'

'How long for?'

'I'm not sure. At least, I suspect, for the last few weeks.'

Vassya's mouth twisted as if she had tasted something unpleasant. 'An informer.'

'Yes. She seemed frightened at times, but never enough,' said Rossel. 'Only two forensic pathologists in the whole of Leningrad have managed to escape arrest in the Doctors' Plot, and she was one of them. When the MGB came to the station, despite their unrivalled revolutionary zeal, urgency and purpose, which saw them kill Taneyev in cold blood, they did not pursue Dr Volkova and arrest her even though her profession is under such scrutiny. And she returned to this station to help us when most sane people would give it a wide berth. Either she is incredibly lucky or extremely dull-witted. Or, she has been protected by someone very well connected. Her mother is a history professor who wound up in a labour camp in the Urals and recently contracted tuberculosis – she might get medical attention or it might be withheld. There are plenty of ways to put pressure on someone in Dr Volkova's position, and plenty of things, on top of protection from the MGB, which Madame Vronsky could offer her in return for her eyes and ears.'

Rossel turned his attention back to the late Deputy Kommissar.

'And now that Comrade Shevchuk and I are at last reacquainted, I think I understand everything. Or almost everything. The madness of it I do not understand.'

'You knew this man, too?' Vassya said, shaking her head. 'As well as the others?'

'No, I didn't know him. Or, more exactly, we were never introduced. I was in the same room with him briefly only once in my entire life, as were, I'm almost certain, Nadya, Felix, Max and Sofia. And a trumpeter named Gusts Landau.'

'When was that?'

Rossel stepped a little closer to the trolley and stared down at Body Number 5.

'March 12, 1942, at the RadioKom headquarters of the Leningrad Radio Orchestra. The day of the greatest all-Soviet composers' competition. The day Shostakovich and Vronsky went head to head to see which of those great men would become famous throughout the world as the eternal symbol of Soviet resistance against the Fascist menace and, eventually, come to represent something even more powerful than that: hope for all of mankind.'

*

Afterwards, Rossel found he could recall very little about the music in the competition. Not the thunderous first movement of Shostakovich's seventh, or the intense adagio of Vronsky's submission. The Shostakovich had involved a drummer, he recalled that much, but otherwise very little had remained with him. Both maestros had protested at the lack of time to prepare their pieces. Both were doubtless aghast at the performances of their music by a motley band of stinking scarecrows rounded up from the city's defenders. And the scarecrows were equally unimpressed by the composers' protestations.

The percussionist who had tackled the side drum part, a pounding, endless ostinato, had collapsed near the end with dystrophy and been taken out. Otherwise Rossel could remember none of it.

But he could remember the onions – the small, glistening onions that floated like tiny gastronomic jewels on top of a battered blue tin bowl of pale soup. They had given a helping to each member of the ensemble. How those tiny onions looked, how they smelt, how they tasted! 'A bowl full of Heaven, served up in the midst of hell,' Felix had said. Vital provisions had been flown in, past the German guns, over Lake Ladoga. They had indeed seemed miraculous. Eliasberg had managed to get extra rations for every skeletal fiddler, percussionist and brass player who turned up. For the most part, that had been the only reason why they played. Not one of them – not Felix, clutching a loaned violin, not Nadya, staring at her clarinet like she had never seen it before, not Gusts Landau, with his red face and apologetically unclassical Sunday-afternoon-band style, not Maxim with his long hair and meditative French horn playing – not one of them would have been able to play a single note in front of Deputy Cultural Kommissar Shevchuk without those onions.

Rossel's own hands had been shaking. Nothing made you feel the cold as keenly as starvation did. They all wanted more food, needed more, demanded more, but Eliasberg the maestro was a hard taskmaster. 'If you want a second bowl, then you must play for it,' he warned them just before he raised his arms to conjure some music out of his scarecrows.

Then, as he sat in the midst of the first violins, eyes flickering between the sheet music and Eliasberg's baton, bow biting string once again, it happened.

The pure joy of playing coursed through him.

How he had missed it.

As they pounded through the opening pages, the violin of the woman sitting beside him slipped off her shoulder and onto her lap – she had no strength left to lift it up and so sat there, resting her fiddle on her knees. Around them, other string players were doing the same, some unable to stop their instruments falling from their fingers. Woodwind solos died in mid-phrase, brass fanfares wheezed into silence.

But he played on.

He did not remember the opening to the Vronsky, only that it was profoundly moving and that his own part was a long, sweeping solo above pulsating strings.

Soon – too soon – his own soaring phrases were over and Eliasberg was cueing the others. But the musicians were seeing nothing but stars and hearing nothing but the *pounding of their own blood, and hoping only that the fiasco would not mean their second bowl of onion soup would be withheld.*

*

They had moved into the station to escape the chill of the morgue but the grate was black and lifeless. Rossel slouched back into his chair and blew out a stream of smoke. Now he knew it was time to sleep. Time to give in.

Vassya would not let him.

'So, the killer is Vronsky? Winner of the Stalin Prize, People's Artist of the Soviet Union, one of the country's leading artistic figures. A murderer. Put dead bodies on the tracks as if they were a composition?'

'Five on the line, arranged like notes on a score. Landau he killed during the war. The trumpeter was a stranger in the city, knew no one, and no one knew him. He was Vronsky's first kill, I think. The others were murdered later. Recently, in fact.'

'How will you ever prove any of this?'

'Prove it? Proof depends on who is willing to listen and what they want to hear. But there is a long, long trail, much of it laid for me to follow. To begin at the beginning, the unexplained death of a young musical genius at a school on Krestovsky Island, a school he and Vronsky attended. An early example of the hatred he has for anyone he sees as a rival.'

Rossel poked the embers.

'Eliasberg also mentioned a nickname, Thanatos, which Vronsky gave himself back then. A name from Greek mythology. A sketch I saw in Sofia's sketchbook had that name written on it: Thanatos & H . . . And I now believe the shadowy figure in the same drawing was Vronsky, because in one corner is a Grecian-shaped vase of crystal – and it is sitting in Madame Vronsky's apartments in the Union of Composers.'

'Coincidences? Hunches.' Vassya's voice rose.

'It's the little things that spark one's suspicions,' said Rossel. 'Speaking of crystal, the librarian at the conservatory told me of a search for some of Vronsky's music that led to our trumpeter friend, except that when he was found he was a mutilated corpse with a glass tube in his throat, identical to those we found inserted into the necks of the bodies on the railway tracks. Proof? No, I don't have absolute proof yet. But I have motive, modus operandi, mute witnesses from beyond the grave.'

'That is not all, though? You said Shevchuk's identity made you understand everything.'

Rossel looked at Vassya through eyes he could barely keep open.

'Back then, after the Germans had invaded and the initial chaos had abated, Stalin had decided there needed to be an anthem for the war. Music that would bear witness to the unconquerable Russian soul. Both Vronsky and Shostakovich were working on compositions that might serve but had written only sketches, themes, half-formed ideas. But Stalin ordered it to be done, and that gave the Party's cultural arbiters a headache. Shostakovich was the obvious choice but Vronsky was the coming man and had the better connections – plus his scheming mother, always making friends in high places.

'So a competition, an audition, was devised, and the composers given two weeks to make progress. And on that day in March 1942 they both presented their pieces – or as much of them as they had written – at the Radio Symphony Orchestra's broadcasting hall, to be performed and assessed by Shevchuk.

'There were two problems. One, the musicians were half dead. Most could not hold their instruments up, let alone blow into them or scrape them. They had found only fifty – fifty-one, to be exact, as I now know from a list that ended up tucked into a score of the Leningrad Symphony. They were shadows. And yet someone was setting out music stands and distributing parts as if they still played every day.'

'The second problem?'

'The competition was fixed. "Everyone knew Shevchuk was in Madame Vronsky's pocket." That's what my old teacher told me. And Felix knew it. She also told me Felix had said "Nadya had the inside track." Which makes sense. Nadya was just the sort of woman to try and get close to Deputy Kommissar Shevchuk.'

'But how could it be?' said Vassya, dragging a chair closer and sinking into it. 'Shostakovich wrote his Leningrad Symphony and that is the music the whole world heard.'

'That was because the performance of Vronsky's composition was a disaster. The clarinettist could hardly produce a sound, the trumpeter had barely learned to read music – he was a big-band man used to improvising his way through tea dances, not sight-reading a score as complex as this one. The singer could manage little more than a thin squeak. And so on. It was ridiculous. The Shostakovich was hardly

335

a triumph of musical performance but you could sense the scale of it, the power, the ambition, even with only half the right number of players.

'Vronsky was furious, screaming at Shevchuk, at the musicians, threatening to send everyone to penal battalions. But he still thought the contest was a done deal. It was the Magnetophon that made him storm out. The very moment he set eyes on that, he really lost control.'

'The Magnetophon?' Vassya looked puzzled.

'The tape recorder. They recorded the whole thing. Shevchuk saw to that. It baffled people at the time but now I know why.'

Rossel took another drag on his cigarette, exhaled and then shrugged.

'When he heard the Vronsky cacophony, Shevchuk got cold feet. He couldn't be the man in charge of a catastrophe – that was the way to the firing squad. So he did what any Soviet underling does: passed the judgement up the chain of command. Vronsky understood Shevchuk had double-crossed them as soon as he saw the tapes being spooled off the Magnetophon and packed into boxes – the decision was being left to the Kremlin. So he blew his top and stormed out.'

Vassya thought for a moment but then shook her head.

'For a maniac like Vronsky, I can see why that might be a reason to kill Shevchuk. But why the others?'

'There is something I haven't told you,' said Rossel. 'Of the six soloists who fouled up Vronsky's composition, four of them were conservatory students and friends of mine: Felix, Nadya, Max and Sofia. Gusts Landau was the fifth.

And the last musician you know well, because he is standing in front of you.'

Vassya shot to her feet.

'You played?'

Rossel nodded. He stood upright, raising his arms as if about to play his violin. 'Despite the cold and the hunger, I think I played well. I hadn't practised for months but as soon as I picked up my instrument it just felt right. As though the music was nourishing me, almost as much as a proper meal. It made me realise that the hope of getting back to playing was a big part of what had got me through the first months of siege. That after the war, there might still be a place for me in a world I felt I belonged in.'

Rossel stubbed out his cigarette.

'But things didn't turn out the way I had hoped.'

*

As for Sofia, the shock of seeing her after six long months, after the worst of the siege, had almost broken him.

Her face was gaunt, the cheekbones switchblade thin.

When she took off her fur hat, her lustrous black hair was now tinged with grey. She looked no worse, he had realised, than he did – than anyone else there in the RadioKom rehearsal rooms. They were all dystrophic. All starving. But it was the image of her he carried in his mind – Sofia as she had been, small, perfect and, to him, impossibly beautiful, his Sofia – which had carried him, this far, through the war. A fragile, internalised, personal icon that he had worshipped every night and believed kept him safe.

He had made himself live only for this moment. Everything he already had suffered during the siege was only possible because he felt he might see her face once again. And now it had arrived in the dusty rehearsal rooms of the RadioKom building on Gogol Street and he could hardly bring himself to look at her.

She walked towards him and, with a faux air of jollity, kissed him three times, lightly, on the cheeks. Then she stared into his eyes. Hers were wide and watery, the lids stretched back making the eyeballs protrude a little. She saw him see her exactly as she was and understood his ridiculously quixotic romantic dissatisfaction. Then she had squeezed his hand.

'I'm still here, Revol. All our friends are, for the most part. Now's let's make music. I need to sing. My voice, at least, will always remain for you, just as it was, just as it always will be.'

*

It was late. They had almost run out of cigarettes.

Rossel stood up and walked towards the mantelpiece above the grate. He stared at the etching of the ship and the seabirds.

'Shostakovich is declared the winner soon after and sets to work completing his symphony. It is performed in Kuibyshev, then Moscow, then New York and London and – when the army and the NKVD and Eliasberg himself had rounded up every musician they can find – in Leningrad. August 9, 1942. An unforgettable day. Vronsky goes away, licks his wounds and plots his revenge. He gets hold of the names of the sextet, the musicians who spoiled everything for him through their rendition of his piece, and devises a new composition. It's a very exclusive one. He allots parts to Maxim, Nadya, Felix and Sofia, and adds Shevchuk to the list for his betrayal. Only this time the thing the great maestro orchestrates is their death, and the score on which he writes is a pair of railway tracks in a forest clearing.'

'Did you play in the actual orchestra for the Leningrad premier of the seventh?'

Rossel closed his eyes.

'No.'

'But they wanted every musician they could find?'

'By then I was no longer what they were looking for. In the May of the same year, I had already been denounced, arrested and tortured.'

Rossel bit the tops of his gloves and tore them off his hands.

'Because our glorious socialist state destroyed my fingers and tore the music out of my life. I remember the concert, everybody does, but that day I was at the front, lying in a crater and looking at a blazing late summer sun. All the while struggling, thanks to my still-bandaged hands, to point my gun in the right direction. The overture was a massive artillery barrage to shut the Germans up, and then they blasted the symphony out of loudspeakers all over the city and even in the direction of the enemy. "We're still here, we're still alive, and this is our anthem that you will never silence."'

Rossel held his left hand up to the bare light bulb, staring at the remnants of Nikitin's butchery.

'Three weeks later we were thrown into a major battle – tanks, artillery, aircraft. We hurled everything at them. Made progress, too, for a while.'

His hands fell to his sides.

'Then they fought back. I hope never to live through anything like that ever again.'

'Did you ever find out who it was that informed on you?' Vassya asked.

'No, but it doesn't matter.'

'How can you say that?'

'At the time, I thought I deserved it. That's what part of me still thinks.'

'But how could anyone deserve something like that?'

'A long time ago, I retold a joke in front of lots of people. A joke about the Party my father had told me. Somebody reported it to the authorities. That's why, I believe, my parents were sent to the camps. It is probably why my sister is missing.'

He stretched out his left hand towards the faded seabird carved into the mantelpiece.

'Their luck ran out. Because of me.'

*

It was nearly six when they made it home. They headed for Vassya's apartment, as if it was somehow a sanctuary.

'What will you do now?' she asked.

Rossel considered this.

'We have already decided we are not going to run. So, we wait. It won't be long. If I am lucky, I will get the chance to explain the case to my interrogator before I am shot.'

She killed the light and stepped close to him.

'Then we don't have much time,' she said.

39

Monday November 5

The knock was not at all loud. Almost polite. Rossel sat up straight in Vassya's bed and checked his watch. Seven thirty. They were late – they usually called on their victims between two and four in the morning to ensure maximum confusion and compliance.

Another knock. This time louder and more demanding. He climbed out of bed and put on his trousers and vest. Vassya's eyes began to blink open.

As he walked down the hall, adrenalin shot through him – he braced for a swarm of clubs and boots. But as he swung the front door of the apartment open, Rossel felt his heart steady. Only one MGB officer stood in front of him.

Nikitin stepped into the hallway and closed the door. His breath stank of cigars and vodka, his eyes were red-rimmed. The MGB uniform, usually crisp and tight, was rumpled and there was an L-shaped yellow stain on his collar. When he spoke, it was a slurred whisper.

'They like to pick out girls, Minister Beria and Vronsky,' Nikitin said, slumping against the wall. 'That's how they amuse themselves together. They go out at night and drive; sometimes, when it's Moscow, in the Packard, other times, when it's here in Leningrad, in an MGB limo. Me and Sarkisov, we've driven them a few times. They point. The car slows down. Then a girl is told to get in. Any girl. Blonde, redhead, brunette. Young, twenties, thirties. Any girl that takes their fancy. That's how it works. It's Beria they are talking to. It's Vronsky who is stretching out a hand to greet them. Both famous men, both terrifying. What choice do these girls have? None, none whatsoever.'

Nikitin stood upright, grunting with the effort.

'They don't like whores, Uncle Lavrentiy and Uncle Nikolai. They don't like sluts. Not for the most part. They like the innocent ones. The girls who look like chaste virgins. The fresh flowers. The Flower Game, is what they actually call it – what they whisper in the back of that limousine. The black door of the car opens. The girl gets in. And that's it. She can no longer be herself ever again. Beria has a soundproof room in the house you visited on Malaya Nikitskaya Street. They take them in there and do things to them. I'm a torturer. I've worked at the Bolshoi Dom for fifteen years. But I'm also a father to a nineteen-year-old girl. And the only thing that keeps me from sleeping at night is thinking about the noises those girls make inside that soundproof room. The shapes their lips make as they mouth cries no one ever gets to hear.'

Nikitin's voice had risen as he told the tale. Now, it dropped back to a whisper.

'In the morning, me and Sarkisov have to give them irises. Can you believe that? That's Beria's test. If they take the flowers, he lets them go, sees it as a sign that they have acquiesced and won't cause trouble. We give them flowers and then take a snap with a little camera in which we command them to watch the birdie. Not all of them do.

The ones that say no to the flowers, they and their entire families end up in the camps.'

Nikitin's left knee buckled. He steadied himself by resting a hand on the small wooden hall table where some of the *kommunalka* residents kept their gloves. He was more than half-cut. Almost at the rambling stage of inebriation. He took out a handkerchief and blew his nose, following that up with a belch.

'I've been dismissed. Sarkisov rang a few hours ago. A lifetime of service then goodbye, comrade. Which basically means I'm a dead man walking. They'll come for me soon.'

The major's voice rose in pitch and he almost sang out the words.

'He was fucking her.'

A torturer's smile spread across his flat-nosed face.

'Have you worked that out yet, gundog? Your beautiful Sofia – Vronsky was fucking her.'

'Yes, I . . .'

'Oh, but not just him. Beria, too. Me and Sarkisov picked her up for them in the Packard one summer, after the war. Sarkisov keeps a list of all the names – a little leverage in case he ever falls out of favour. She had come to Moscow to meet Vronsky, a story he had spun about needing a singer. Usually they loved the random nature of the hunt – they used to snigger when they pointed, out of the car windows, like mischievous gods hurling down thunderbolts. But not her. She was on purpose. Vronsky had been in touch, told us where to collect her – from the station. Vronsky . . . well, I'd never seen him so exultant. He was really salivating at the prospect of him and Beria fucking the little slut's brains out.'

Nikitin's head jerked backwards at a preposterous angle.

Blood splattered from his bottom lip. He had not expected Rossel's blow but did not fall to the floor. The major was a streetfighter and, drunk or not, he swung back, his left fist catching Rossel on the temple. Rossel shuffled, then dropped into a crouch and hit Nikitin fast, two sharp jabs, one with the left fist, the other with the right. The blue-hat crashed downward onto the faded parquet and almost immediately tried to push himself upward. Rossel was too quick for him. He flung himself on top of Nikitin and took only a moment, using his knees – one across each of the major's shoulders – to pin the man down. Rossel's shattered hands clamped down on his torturer's windpipe. His eyes were flickering with a feral rage and he began to squeeze. Nikitin tried to use his own feet to push back, rocking his body back and forth, so he might loosen his attacker's grip. But it was hopeless.

'They're coming for you now,' the MGB officer gasped. 'Sarkisov is coming. I'm only an hour ahead of him. I'm here to help you . . .'

Rossel's fingers loosened.

'And why would you do that?'

'In my pocket, there's a picture of her in my left trouser pocket.'

Rossel's grip began to tighten again.

'Of Sofia?' he shouted.

Nikitin had to spit out the words.

'Of Svetlana. My darling little girl. Sweet, good-hearted Sveta. Last night, I found out those bastards had been fucking her, too.'

ACT 5

40

As they drove across Kamennoostrovsky Bridge, flakes of snow drifted out of a late-morning sky that was as grey as tarnished pewter. Rossel sat behind the wheel of Nikitin's ZIS. The major, sitting in the passenger seat, was nursing a cut lip and a bruised temple. He had sobered up.

'So, we are agreed?' said Rossel.

Nikitin nodded. 'The Party elite are already gathering at their dachas south of Lake Ladoga ahead of the festivities. Malenkov, Molotov, Beria, Khrushchev – all of them. I take the list of musicians and the jeweller's ledgers to Malenkov. You go to Vronsky's island. You're still determined to go alone?'

Rossel nodded.

'If I try and formally arrest Vronsky – go with Lipukhin, or involve militia headquarters – he, or his mother, will just talk their way out of it. Use their contacts in the Party to escape the law. Point the finger back at Eliasberg. Then destroy any evidence. I can only get real justice if I go on my own.'

'And what will that look like?' said Nikitin with a wry smile.

Rossel shrugged.

'He murdered Felix. He murdered Sofia. Tortured them. I want to kill him. But the policeman in me won't let that happen. So, I'm going to need the maestro to give me a written confession.'

The car picked up speed.

'And you? Why take the risk?' said Rossel.

Nikitin grinned.

'Beria doesn't like loose ends. Now I'm dismissed, it's simply a matter of time before he comes for me. This way there's a slim chance I can save myself and pay him back for my daughter.'

The major tapped his breast pocket.

'Otherwise, I'd be far too smart to take evidence against the second most powerful man in the Soviet Union and deliver it into the hands of his greatest political enemy, Malenkov.'

Rossel stared at the road in front of him. Once they got to Vronsky's island, Nikitin would head southwards to Shlisselburg, to where Malenkov's dacha overlooked Ladoga's southern shore as he and his rivals waited for the call to Leningrad for the Party Congress and the days of celebrations to mark the anniversary of the Road of Life.

He gestured to the black and white photograph, lit by the thin morning light, that Nikitin had fixed to the car's dashboard with a piece of tape.

'She has the air of an innocent, your Svetlana. Sofia had that, too.'

Nikitin stared down at the portrait of his daughter. The pretty nineteen-year-old was wearing a simple spotted pinafore and clutched a small bunch of poppies to her breast.

A frozen gargoyle's smile was fixed to her face. As if she had been snapped by a Medusa.

'She *was* that . . . before . . .'

'I'm sorry.'

They rumbled on. That morning's newspapers had promised a new wave of cold weather – minus twenty-five, at least.

'How did you find out about the girls?'

'Like I said, Sarkisov is disgusted. He keeps a list of their conquests. They love lists in the MGB. The whole country is run on lists. But Beria doesn't know.'

'Why should he care?' asked Rossel, steering around some metal fencing that protected an open manhole. 'Beria can do what he likes.'

'Not entirely,' scoffed Nikitin. 'You think people like Malenkov, Molotov, MGB generals, army generals, admirals, party bosses with family and friends in the camps, you think they aren't out to get him? One little vice, sure – but add that to something he said twenty years ago, someone he drank with thirty years ago, add it all up . . . "I heard Beria say you were looking a little ill the other day, Comrade Stalin. And did you know what he gets up to in his special cellar . . .?" That's how it's done. A list like that is an insurance policy.'

He fell silent, watched as the city's outskirts drifted past.

'But Sarkisov doesn't know that I've read that list. We were around his apartment the other night, drinking. Celebrating the arrest of Eliasberg. Singing, of all things.'

He began to bellow out an old army marching song.

'My ears are bleeding, comrade,' said Rossel.

Nikitin stopped singing.

'You know, outside the service, you are the only person in the Soviet Union who would dare talk to me like that,' he said. 'Anyway, we had several bottles lined up to applaud our every note. Sarkisov got smashed and started showing off. He brought out five pieces of paper and waved the top sheet at me. Then he slid off his chair and fell asleep. I was curious, of course, so I took a look. And there, on page six, was her name and my address. I wanted to strangle him right there, and then find Beria and put a bullet straight between his eyes. And then go to Vronsky's pad and do the same. But I have a wife and another child. A simple man does not make life complicated. That's how I got to live this long.'

The car slowed again as a filthy truck pulled out from a side street.

'So, I bit my own lip until I could taste the blood in my mouth like I was gargling with it and decided to come and see you outside the Union of Composers.'

A road sign appeared about fifty metres in front of them. It showed the way to Lake Ladoga.

*

It took three hours of crawling through the growing blizzard to reach the edge of Nizino, on the southeastern shore of the lake. Rossel glanced down at the picture of Svetlana. It could have been just another family snap – but the expression on her face and the flowers in her hand told a different story.

'How did you get your hands on that photograph?' he said.

Nikitin, who had been half asleep and slumped forward, opened his eyes and stretched. Then slapped his gloved hands together.

'When he was still drunk and asleep, I rifled through the drawer Sarkisov had taken his list from. Taped underneath it was an envelope filled to bursting with pictures and negatives of Beria's victims. Some of Vronsky's, too. It was in there.'

Rossel dropped a gear as he overtook a horse-drawn farmer's cart filled with lumber. Then he looked at the photograph again.

'Poppies. Your daughter is holding poppies. You said roses and irises before. Did Beria or Vronsky ever mention a story, a Greek myth, about Thanatos and Hypnos?'

Nikitin nodded.

'That's what they called themselves when they went out in the Packard, Thanatos and Hypnos. Some creepy joke between them which me and Sarkisov never properly understood. The poppies only started when Vronsky arrived on the scene. How the hell did you know about that?'

In the distance, through the swirling snow, Rossel made out a sign: Krestovsky Island. He pressed his foot down on the accelerator.

'Hypnos is Sleep, Thanatos is Death,' said Rossel. 'In the legend, they lived in a cave. Through it ran the River of Forgetfulness and outside it grew poppies. That's where the opiate came in, I think. Extract of the poppy, used to instill a deep sleep from which the victims awoke into an endless nightmare. Vronsky had used the names before, as nicknames for himself and a boy called Andrei Suvorin, when they both attended a school for gifted children. Suvorin went missing in the summer of 1916.'

351

The car slid and skipped over a patch of the road and Rossel performed a complicated dance with brakes, gearstick and steering wheel.

'You know, you're good at this,' said Nikitin. 'How long have you been in the militia?'

'Since '46. After the war, they were kind enough to give me a choice between the fire brigade, the militia and pushing paper in some meaningless department. I chose the militia. I wanted to be a detective.'

'You had good training?'

Rossel laughed. 'We had basic tuition in the criminal code so we could tell drunks, whores and thieves what they were being arrested for. There was a little less training around forming tips and clues and hunches into a real investigation.'

They pulled up onto a slushy bank next to a hedge. Nikitin stared out at Lake Ladoga. About a half a kilometre away was a phalanx of black pine trees that lined the shore of an island. And one hundred metres to their left was a slightly lopsided telephone pole, studded on each side with the metal steps the engineers used to climb it, a tangle of wires leading from it to a pole on the opposite bank.

'As agreed, I will wait until you get to the island, then take the phone lines out,' said Nikitin. 'This school – it was here, on Krestovsky?'

Rossel took his revolver out of its holster and checked the chamber.

'Yes. If I'm right, I'm about to cross not a river but a lake of forgetfulness.'

Nikitin picked up the picture of his daughter and kissed it.

'I can't stop thinking about what those bastards did to her. I can never forget . . . Remember Stalin's slogan from before the war? Life has never been better, life has never been more beautiful?'

'Yes,' replied Rossel. 'To be honest, I was never totally at one with the sentiment.'

Nikitin smiled his tormentor's smile.

'I used to use that all the time in the cells. I'd make the counter-revolutionary scum recite it – sing-song style. Repeat after me, I'd shout: "Life has never been better." Then I'd kick the *mudak* in the balls. Repeat after me: "Life has never been so beautiful." Then I'd break their knee-caps. Louder, I'd bellow. Say it so I believe that *you* believe it. "Life has never been better, never been more beautiful," and thud go their heads against the wall.'

Rossel got out of the car and began to walk through the still deepening snow towards the thin line of dark pines that ringed Vronsky's island. Behind him he could still hear the voice of his former torturer shouting, as Nikitin banged out an accompanying rhythm on the dashboard.

'I want you to sing it to me one more time! And make sure you sing it so convincingly that Comrade Stalin himself believes it. "Life has never been better, life has never been more beautiful." *Sing it to me now . . .*'

*

Wind-whipped flakes whirled around him. Whiteness blurred into whiteness. If only the whole world could wipe itself clean like this, he thought, in preparation for the creation of some other, better version of itself.

Only the thin smudge of the distant horizon and the pines on the shoreline, now about two hundred metres in front of him, punctuated his sense of abandonment – of being lost, even to himself. He had, he felt, now become a mere thought in that other malicious mind, a minor character in the plot it had devised, an inanimate stage prop, as were the bodies on the lines. He, like them, had been arranged upon a page. Orchestrated. Scribbled into the margins of a score, as Vronsky's imagination cast him as, no doubt, a dullard detective.

Although the distance was relatively short, it took him twenty minutes to cross the ice to the middle. He stumbled twice in the drifts but picked himself up and moved forward.

At last, Rossel reached a ridge at the edge of the island and crouched behind it. He caught his breath before making another three bounds forward. Then he stepped between the dark sentries of the shoreline pines and began to make his way toward the rotunda of the old house, of which Eliasberg had had such fond childhood memories. The island was only just a kilometre across; somewhere within were its grand mansion and gardens.

The trees were twenty deep but as soon as he emerged through the last row, the dacha came into view. Its walls were stuccoed white and so, in the snow, barely perceptible, making it appear as if the golden dome of the rotunda roof was hovering high above the ground.

To his left, near the shoreline, about one hundred metres away, a huge tarpaulin. Sagging with the weight of the fresh drift, it was hung between some pines. Beneath it were some rusting petrol pumps and five trucks, three looking in very poor condition, two as if they had been recently repaired and used. Leftovers from the war, he thought. This must have been one of the many temporary filling stations set up around Lagoda to fuel vehicles before they crossed the ice; there would be a fuel pit under there somewhere. They were all ZIS-5s – that old warhorse. One was fitted with a snowplough and caterpillar tracks.

To his right, about fifty metres away and surrounded by black stumps poking through the snow – the remains of thirty or forty trees – was what seemed to be the top half of an entrance.

A door to a cellar?

Rossel reached down and took out his gun.

He walked forward, pulling down his hat to shield his face from the wind that was blowing up the long drive leading towards the rotunda, still some distance away. When he got to the door, he could see it was half submerged and surrounded by the drifting snow. The building it led into was stone and brick, and looked as if a giant had pressed it into the earth. Six steps led down to it – recently gritted. A spade and shovel rested against the door post at the bottom. The wooden door was ajar.

As he shoved the door further open, the pale winter light showed a deep interior – six metres down, he reckoned, which felt deep and very cold.

He looked over his shoulder to make sure no one was behind him and continued down the thin steps until he stood on the bottom. It was hard to make much out in the gloom. The space was obviously for storage of some kind. Forage, perhaps? No, ice – ice for the summer, cut from the lake in winter and packed in straw for insulation. But during the war anything could have been stored here – fuel, weapons, spare parts for the trucks that crossed the Road of Life . . .

The space was about five metres long and the same wide. He looked up to see frost glittering on the ceiling. The walls were for the most part unmarked but here and there he could see traces of faded graffiti. He took out his lighter to read it.

Hitler kaput, Sokolov was here. After Leningrad, onward to Berlin! Masha, I love you.

There were six small alcoves cut into the walls at about waist-height. Rossel thought he could see more clearly into one of them than the rest – the one in the right-hand corner, furthest from the door. He bent down, listening, but there was only silence. He crept forward towards a lump of stone, almost a cube.

The source of light became evident. Two candles on top of the stone. Rossel could see what looked like more graffiti. But it was different: five irregular lines carved into the stone.

And into those lines had been carved musical notes scraped. Five of them.

Rossel leant forward and traced a gloved hand over the carvings. Unbidden, the notes rose in his throat.

Fa, la, mi-bemol, si-bemol, sol . . .
F, A, E-flat, B-flat . . . G

Rossel shot to his feet, intending to race for the steps and the safety of open ground. It must have been then, he thought afterwards, that Madame Vronsky's Cossack bodyguard hit him.

41

The sound seemed to be coming from somewhere distant. Out on the very edge of consciousness. Not from one point. But everywhere.

Now the noise changed in pitch. Became thicker and rounder. A pulsating shadow that stilled back into blackness in the moments between each beat. But then, on the numbing notes themselves, would ripple out into a single vague image. A thing barely discernible but provocatively real. Like a childhood glimpse of something forbidden that instantly disappears behind a closing door. Sofia, the apple brandy on her breath. Her eyes lowered. *No, Revol, because* . . . The scribbled pages of her notebook. Thanatos & H. Galya mute among the drifting snows. A cursing Nazi sergeant whose throat he'd stabbed in a muddy shell hole during the hand-to-hand fighting in Shlisselburg. The blood on his tongue and fear in his pumping heart induced by Nikitin's percussive violence. A black snowdrop – the partly decomposed body of a thawing boy he had once seen outside the Union of Composers.

Rossel's lips were cracked and dry. He blinked his eyes open. A large, shadowy circle of brick and stone, divided into sections. No natural light, so somewhere a lamp or some candles burned.

But the space was not empty. Five empty steel mesh cages, each about a metre and a half square, hung by dirty chains to the beams of the ceiling. Each one hovered about a metre above the ground, inside an empty stall that made the whole place look like it had once been a stable. Suspended from the ceiling by a piece of insulating cable, a microphone hung in front of each one of them. They looked, to Rossel, like the very best – the kind used for professional recordings.

He winced as he felt the pain from the back of his skull. He tried to lift an arm but found he could not. He was seated but his arms and legs were bound. There was the noise again. Insistent. Rippling. Now he felt he could place it. He turned his head left, trying to locate the tapping in the gloom.

His eye caught a sliver of a different spectrum of light. For a moment he was unable to process what he saw but then they came into focus – five glass tubes. Each one a little taller than the next, arranged on a table before him.

He could hear the noise more clearly now, persistent and hypnotic.

Rossel squirmed in his chair. Looked down. His gloves had been removed. His feet were bare and, like his hands, tethered with a thick twine. It was a smart move to remove his boots. Even if he escaped, he wouldn't get very far in these temperatures.

Then the voice spoke in a baritone whisper which seemed – like the beats – to be in front of him, behind him, to his left, to his right.

'Stolypin, the original resident of this house, was the tsar's very own Beria. He used to keep his Lipizzaner here. When we were friends, Suvorin – you will know who he is by now – and I would come and admire them.'

A last beat, then the metallic rhythm stopped. A sudden movement to Rossel's left and Vronsky loomed above him, grey and massive, like the Commendatore in *Don Giovanni*, a stone nemesis conjured to life by the maestro's percussion.

The maestro circled him a couple of times, saying nothing. Tapped his gold-ringed fingers on top of the table as though he were stilling the undisciplined cacophony of tuning in the pit. There was a little dampness on the composer's brow but otherwise he looked no different from the last time Rossel has seen him, at the Kirov. After a minute, Vronsky took a seat at the other end of the table.

The click of a latch. A door set into the farthest alcove of the wall opened slowly. A woman entered carrying two circular silver platters on a tray and some cutlery. Madame Vronsky placed one platter in front of her son. Then put the other one down in front of Rossel.

'I sensed you did not like my little dog, Lieutenant,' she said. 'A pity. I think my little one liked you. Or perhaps she merely pities you. In her world there is no MGB, no gulag, no citizens ready and willing to inform on a next-door neighbour for the price of a Party membership card, and so it must be, just as you are about to discover, a much kinder world than this one.'

Her tone was cordial. That of someone greeting an old friend they had just bumped into after only a day or so's parting.

'Your son is not in any way sane,' said Rossel. 'And yet it does not seem to concern you in the slightest, comrade?'

Rossel heard his own voice as though he were listening to someone else. It was dry and deep. Basso profundo.

And sounding ephemeral. Otherworldly. He assumed he had been injected with the same drug as the others. That would explain the intensity of the images in his head. Dehydration, too, was a common side-effect of an opiate.

Madame Vronsky smiled.

'That is what the doctors said during the siege. After Razin found him standing over the dead body of that useless Latvian bugler Landau, I arranged for my son's psychiatric evaluation. Pulled strings, to ensure an order was issued which meant that any existing manuscripts were immediately recalled from the conservatory library. I did it to calm him after his defeat. My son demanded it. Told me that he had come to despise its imperfections. But that within its "crude phraseology" lay the embryo of a much greater work – *The Blockade*. "And now, at last, after the trumpeter's death, I finally understand what is necessary. The level of ambition a true artist must possess." Those were his words. If he were an ordinary man, I would have agreed with the doctors' assessment of his psychopathology. But my child is not that. Has never been that. He is and has always been *extraordinary*. To those with such special gifts everything must be allowed.'

She turned and looked at her son. Vronsky was staring into one of the empty cages and seemed to be barely registering the conversation. She resumed her address to Rossel.

'Sanity is a question of perspective, Lieutenant. Should a man of prodigious talent squander his destiny simply because our society does not allow him to express it? Is it not, after all, Nikolai's duty, as a great artist of the Soviet Union, to break down such petty ideological barriers? Did

Lenin himself not say, "You cannot make a revolution wearing white gloves?" The same is true of a great symphony.'

Rossel looked again around the room. The cages hanging in the air, the soundproofing that covered the old brickwork of the stable and, in one corner, a long length of green metal shelving that was almost entirely covered with neat stacks of annotated tape spools. In the half-light, the cages looked like giant versions of the incense burners the monks used at Pskov.

Madame Vronsky leaned in and took Rossel's broken left hand. Her perfume was rich, exotic. She squeezed his fingers.

'Thanks to Dr Volkova, we have watched your progress with interest.'

She drifted to the other side of the table and kissed her son on the top of his head before removing the lid from the platter in front of him. She placed it between Rossel and the plate so he could not see its contents. Then, holding the lieutenant's gaze, she took a knife from her red satin clutch bag and began to cut up what was on it. This took a full minute, perhaps more. Then she left the room, the door clanking shut behind her.

Feeling nauseous, Rossel leaned forward as far as his restraints would allow and stared at the thing on Vronsky's plate. A bloody chunk of something. The composer's mocking eyes held Rossel's. His huge hands wrapped themselves around the dark slab. He waited another moment before devouring it. Stomach knotting, Rossel turned his head towards the empty cages.

The composer sat back, patted at his wet beard with a pale blue napkin and swallowed.

He nodded to the nearest cage to Rossel's right.

'When he was here, Maxim, our crazed priest, recounted – after a gentle prompting – a macabre tale. He had a little niece, Anfisa. A charming child by all accounts, liked to play the balalaika and, as they all do, worshipped Grandpa Lenin. But this was in the middle of the siege and so, like everyone else, Anfisa had hardly eaten for weeks. Her tiny ten-year-old stomach was round and swollen, her legs thin and bony. They gave her most of their own rations, Maxim and his sister. Their mother was already dead from malnutrition, their father, too. They tried everything, he and his sister, but eventually, clutching a picture of Lenin, their niece closed her eyes for the last time.

'Why, they were distraught. But then one of them glanced over at an empty plate lying on the kitchen table, and, a little after that, perhaps five minutes, perhaps ten, at an old pot on the stove. They sat there looking, only looking, for hours. In the end, it was Maxim who was the first to pick up the knife. He did it, he said, so his sister would not have to.'

As Vronsky leaned forward in his chair, Rossel could feel his heart pounding.

'You think that milksop Shostakovich ever had the heart to score the real story of the siege? How some human beings lasted for nine hundred days – nine hundred days! – on a few grams of sawdust and chaff. How that *sounded*? The rumbling of empty bellies, parched mouths and loose teeth gnawing down on innocent bones, the whispering, babbled self-exhortations behind the dulled eyes of a creature who was once a man but has now become something utterly other, as he scurries down the street waiting for the spring to give up its harvest of blackened limbs so he might boil them up and partake of a little soup?'

Vronsky's right arm began to stretch out, as if he were preparing to conduct.

'Or the sound of steam,' he continued, 'hissing and bubbling from a pot on a stove that none dare look into?'

Rossel spat onto the cobbled floor of the stable.

'"Something utterly other" is what you have become, maestro.'

Vronsky picked up the largest of the five glass tubes on the table and took a step closer.

'Everything Maxim did after that was in some way an attempt to forget what he had done when he sat down with his sister and partook of that simple plateful of familial salvation. He and Shostakovich are one and the same, Rossel. For what else is the Leningrad Symphony – in all its po-faced pomp, its empty brittle cacophony – but the crudest propaganda? Every time we Soviets celebrate it, what we are really celebrating is our own collective amnesia. I do not forget, Lieutenant, cannot. Great art demands of its creators only one thing: to look truth squarely between the eyes and have enough steel in your soul to never once turn away again. I have that unflinching gaze; an unflinching ear, too. So, I have composed a work like none that has ever been written before, one that will force all who hear it to remember.'

Rossel flexed his wrists but the rope only bit deeper. Buying time by keeping Vronsky talking was the only option open to him.

'I always thought you were better than him, Vronsky. Better than Shostakovich,' he said. 'Better than them all, in fact – Borodin, Rimsky-Korsakov, Rachmaninov, Mussorgsky. Or, at least, I used to.'

Vronsky ran his fingers over the shaft of the piece of glass in his hand and smiled.

'I am what I was born to be, Lieutenant. A great composer. Even when I went to school here, I understood I was supposed to be that. You went straight for the notes carved into the stone so I imagine that fool Eliasberg has been talking. Andrei Suvorin and I were the best of friends. But I came to realise that my talent was destined to outgrow his.'

'I imagine this was what you told yourself just after you realised that he, not you, was most likely to win the tsarina's prize,' said Rossel. 'And probably every other prize, too.'

Vronsky placed the glass tube onto the floor. Rossel couldn't take his eyes off it. The composer put the heel of his black boot over the end and crushed the tip.

'They were lovers, Stolypin and my mother,' Vronsky said. 'After he died, Mama befriended his widow. Then she persuaded her to set up the competition and invite the tsarina. But, one evening, Madame Stolypin told her that our professor considered Andrei the greater prospect. And that he intended to recommend the boy should make the principal recital when the tsarina came to visit. Nonsense, of course. Had Suvorin lived, I would have, in any case, proved the old fool wrong.'

'But your dear mother decided not to take that chance?'

Vronsky nodded.

'At first, she simply tried to persuade them to have the boy excluded from the competition, but they would have none of it.'

'And so, your mother killed Suvorin?'

The composer smiled again.

'Matricide is the word used for someone who kills their mother but, as far as I know, there has been no lexicographer yet farsighted enough to invent a word for someone who kills *with* them. We both did for the boy.'

'You left him in the ice house. Left him in there to freeze to death and while he was dying, he carved the notes I saw into the stone.'

Rossel was trying to mask the anger and loathing in his voice. But failing.

Vronsky put a finger to his lips and began to speak in hushed tones.

'I told Andrei I had forgotten to bring matches for the tobacco we already smoked. Then, as soon as I left, my mother, who was hidden nearby, shut the door and bolted it.'

With his cuff, Vronsky dabbed at a bead of sweat on his brow.

'At first,' he continued, 'Andrei thought I was joking. We could hear him shouting out. Then his cries changed to ones of petulance and frustration. Finally, tears and sobs. After twenty minutes, we walked away just as the evening sun began to fall. My mother had arranged a recital so that everyone was busy and no one could hear.'

Vronsky ambled over to the nearest cage and pushed at it. It swung back and forth like an outsize thurible.

'Andrei was a religious boy. At night, before bed, he would recite the hymn to the Virgin Mary, what the Greeks call the *axion*. The refrain he carved into the rock was an unfinished final prayer of some sort, I imagine.'

365

Vronsky pushed the cage again and it began to rock faster, the chains groaning as it moved to and fro. Then the composer took three quick steps forward so he was standing directly in front of the detective. He struck Rossel once in the face with the outstretched palm of his right hand. Then a second time using his left fist – there was an echoing crack as the cartilage in Rossel's nose broke. Vronsky's arm swung back as if to strike another blow. But then he stopped. The composer glanced at the glass tube on the floor. He bent down and picked it up. He stepped to the side of Rossel and placed its jagged end against the bare flesh of the detective's neck. The lieutenant could feel the scratch of the glass prickle against his carotid artery and hear his own breathing punctuating the silence with sharp staccato bursts.

'This one is exactly the same size as the one I had designed for your friend Felix. When pushed into the windpipe it turns a last breath into something beautiful, Comrade Rossel. Not a perfect E-flat, I grant you that, but at that late stage of his life, I truly believed it helped young Felix express the inexpressible, everything he had failed to get across in his mediocre violin playing. He confessed to everything when I had him inside his cage and began to slowly starve him to death. He was desperate to live. By the end he would tell me everything I asked. All about how much in love you were with sweet little Saint Sofia.'

Rossel felt the tube nick his throat. A sudden wetness there he knew must be blood. He braced himself for the end.

'Initially, he gasped as I pushed the pipe in, greedy for air. Just like they all did. But then, at the very end, he clamped his mouth tight shut; tried to put a stopper in the bottle.

That was when the sound was at its most haunting – as his last essence slipped away.'

Rossel grimaced in fear as the glass pierced his skin again. Then, suddenly, the composer took a step backward.

'No,' Vronsky muttered to himself, looking around as if he had forgotten something. 'Not like this. You, after all, are my listener. I must prepare my performance.'

He lumbered out of the room, shouting for Razin, leaving Rossel to eye the shard of glass – the broken tip of the crystal tube – he had left on the floor. Just out of reach.

42

For the fifth time, Rossel managed to move the seat an inch or so forward. The bindings on his ankles were not quite as tight as those on his wrists and so, now he was this close, he managed to move his left foot towards the sliver of glass, about two centimetres long, which lay half a metre away along the cobbles. He stretched out his bare foot again. This time, he made contact with the glass. Used his toes to scrabble it a little closer. He repeated the action: once, twice. Then a third time. Now the shard was close enough.

Adrenalin coursed through Rossel's body and sat him back – bolt upright – as he heard the doorknob rattle.

Vronsky swept back into the room, bloated and grandiose. Behind him walked his brutal retinue of one: Razin. Rossel got the sole of his left foot over the shard just as the Cossack heaved a Magnetophon tape recorder onto the lacquered table. Vronsky waved his servant away and took two reels out of a box.

'Sofia Fedotova . . . Maxim Avdeyev . . . Nadya Bazhanova . . . Felix Sorokin . . . They played like automatons, like instruments playing instruments, with no heart, no feeling, and no understanding,' the composer said. 'The horrible caterwauling they produced made it even easier for the authorities to deny me. But you were different, Rossel. Your playing stood out.'

Rossel shifted in the chair, his legs numb.

'We were under siege, being bombed every day, half starved,' he said. 'Nobody could feel anything except the emptiness of their bellies.'

'I am Nikolai Nikolayevich Vronsky, Hero of Socialist Labour and People's Artist of the USSR. Where music is concerned, I do not make mistakes. You played well.'

The composer began to connect cables from the Magnetophon to one of the microphones.

'I needed to score my opera in the first person,' he added. 'I needed to *live* it. Because of what had happened to Suvorin and the trumpeter Landau, to a degree I already had. But now, I knew that before I shaped a chord, I needed to again commit the act. For the truly great man is the one who steps across the line others dare not cross. Lenin knew that, Stalin knows it. To write *The Blockade*, I could not put pen to paper without – once again – pressing a blade to the nape of someone's neck.' He tutted as he fumbled with one of the tape reels.

'It took me years to track down the philistines who ruined my work – such is the chaos war leaves behind,' the composer said.

Rossel scraped the glass an inch closer. It grated against the rough ground and he froze, but his captor was too absorbed in the dials on the tape machine to notice.

'I have no expectations of mercy, maestro,' said Rossel. 'Not least since if you released me, I would ensure you spent the rest of your days in the salt mines of Kolyma. But I must ask you nonetheless. You said I played well.

Your revenge upon me is not because I ruined your fledgling score?'

Vronsky extended himself to his full height. He reached into the left-hand pocket of his jacket and took out a folded piece of paper. He opened it out with a flourish and held it in front of the lieutenant. Rossel took in the embossed red *CCCP* header and typed script. It was a single sheet torn from an MGB report.

Fifth Directorate MGB, Report by informant Sofia Fedotova.

There was a small section in the middle of the text underlined in red ink. Vronsky tapped a finger on it. Rossel focused on the page. Tried to understand it. At first, the words doubled up, ran each into the other, but after a few seconds he could read it:

. . . The informant, describing an encounter in the conservatory canteen, said she had asked Rossel what he had thought of Vronsky's latest work, a Revolutionary Cantata to mark Stalin's birthday. R told her: 'Normally I am a great admirer of his work but here I heard nothing other than banality, a mixture of Shostakovich and Strauss, a dash of Rachmaninov, a bit of Stravinsky when he had run out of ideas. It put me in mind of our masters, Sofia. Full of pompous arrogance and precious little to be inspired by.'

The revelation hit him harder than any blow.

Rossel looked at Vronsky. 'I thought it was Nadya who had informed on me,' he mumbled.

The composer was exultant. He folded the page again and slipped it back into his pocket.

'My dear boy, Nadya informed on you and a great many others. But Sofia's betrayal was the one that counted. That makes it all the sweeter, does it not? Her mother was a Menshevik. This leverage was used to recruit the daughter to inform on dissenters at the conservatory. In looking into your background, I skimmed a few of her reports. She always gave just enough information to show she was trying but not enough to condemn anyone. Hoping, I presume, that her dispatches would simply be checked, stamped and filed away. Yours was. Until, in May '42, increased political pressure for more arrests caused some bureaucrat to open a filing cabinet somewhere in the Bolshoi Dom – most likely at random – and retrieve it. All those youthful clever remarks. Just one joke about our Bolshevik masters might be overlooked. But page after page . . . Which led to your original arrest and interrogation. If I were you, I would put it down to bad luck. It might be easier on your mind.'

Vronsky walked to the far corner of the room. He picked up the metal railroad rod and began to trail it over the sides of the cages. Steel struck steel. Vronsky swung to his left again and sent one of the cages spinning on the chains. Then one more. Now another. Five whirling metal dervishes. The jarring noise echoed around the room, cannoned off the walls, found a way inside Rossel. Brought up acid from his stomach into the back of his throat.

More than anything, he wanted to put his hands over his ears to block out the sound.

'Six weeks with only water, not even a smear of Vologda butter or a bacon rind,' Vronsky was shouting as he swung. 'I would have Razin set the table, once a day, only the very

BEN CREED

best china, the best dishes from the Party shops I had laid for them. After a few weeks, they would wail and gibber as soon as they heard the clinking of china in the hall outside the room. It took most only a few days to exhibit all the classic symptoms of hunger: impulsivity, irritability, hyperactivity.'

Vronsky's breath was coming in bursts now. His face and body dripped with sweat; patches appeared like newly forming continents on the loose white shirt that covered the round globe of his belly.

Rossel's head jerked to the left as he felt the rod swish by.

'Felix, a lecherous soldier, Max, a depraved priest, Nadya, an inept spy, and Shevchuk, a hapless politician. It was only once I got them here that I realised I had assembled a cast filled with the moronic archetypes of cheap comic opera. It amused me greatly. So, I had Sofia dressed as the Snow Queen. My little joke, Rossel. And we know you're a connoisseur of them.'

Vronsky struck right. One of the cages began to spin even faster.

'At night, I would thrash the bars. Record their pleas and screaming. Little evidence of any baritone on the Magnetophon. Fear, it seems, makes sopranos of us all. They screamed out the dregs of their beings into the abyss they knew I would soon consign them to. I cut them differently, mutilated them differently, so my imagination might feast upon the differing sounds. Slice, slash, gouge, gash, each extracts its own particular melody. Cut off a hand and in that, I discovered, is little enough inspiration for a cheap tavern tune. But chop off a man's prick and you have the beginnings of an epic symphony. And, even before that, they would growl and scurry and beg and plead, roll over on their backs and abase themselves in any way possible – anything for the smallest morsel.'

Vronsky stilled his hand, let it fall to his side.

'By the end, just stretching out the tips of my fingers and simply listening – it was electric.'

43

Vronsky's hands stretched out towards the unopened silver platter for a third time, letting them hover. His grin was ghoulish and terrifying.

'Sofia was the hardest one to entice up here. She had no interest in my offer of a job in the chorus of the Kirov Opera. No interest in Marina's offer of lessons and patronage. But your name, Lieutenant. That got her on the first train to Leningrad. I promised her a reunion with you at my dacha – and to use my influence so she would never have to inform again. And so, of course, she came.'

Rossel's eyes remained fixed on the platter. There was no way he would let Vronsky know the pain of the wounds he was causing, no way he would grant him that satisfaction . . . but his fastened hands could not wipe away the treacherous tears that were pooling in his eyes.

'How does it feel, Lieutenant Rossel, to not be the person you were supposed to be? To know you will never play your violin again?'

Under those silver bowls there could be . . . For Vronsky it had just been some sort of raw meat, he thought.

But this one was meant for him. This dish could contain anything.

'You know how that feels, maestro,' he said. 'That's what you're trying to say, isn't it? You missed out. I did, too. We are kindred spirits, you and I?'

Vronsky shrugged.

'The thing that has eaten my heart,' the composer said, 'is knowing that if I came back to Leningrad in a hundred years and strolled down Nevsky, I would find Stalin remembered, I would find the siege remembered, but – and this above all I abhor – I would find Shostakovich remembered. A court bard, a modernist parrot, now fixed in the cultural memory of the nation as the keeper of its spirit. The guardian of its eternal flame. But not me, Rossel. No one would remember me.'

Rossel spat a little blood onto the floor.

'I used to feel exactly as you describe,' he said. 'Imagine myself playing at the Kirov instead of opening a cell in the morning and gagging at the stench of shit. But no more, comrade. Militia station 17 is my destiny now. These days if I tried to tap my foot to the national anthem, I'd probably end up a half-step behind but it doesn't really matter anymore. Because I get to hunt down people like you.'

'You didn't hunt me down, Lieutenant. I simply picked up my baton, extended my arms, and here you are.'

Vronsky lifted the lid of the salver.

The package was six inches square, brown with a yellow sticker the size and shape of a rouble stuck to the front. It read: AEG Magnetophon. Vronsky tipped it and out slid a spool of tape.

'Only *five* cages, not six. I assume you noticed that immediately, on waking. So, why is he here, Lieutenant Rossel must have asked himself, if he is not to be part of Maestro Vronsky's chorus? What is his purpose – his melodic function in the second part of this particular aria? Have you worked it out yet?'

Rossel did not even acknowledge the question.

No, Revol, not for you . . .

His eyes were on the salver where the reel lay but all he could see was Sofia's face close to his.

'At the Kirov,' continued Vronsky, 'I *told* you, gave you the answer to the entire riddle, and on our second meeting I also clearly reiterated it. I thought you might have an inkling then. And yet, you still haven't worked it out.'

He stood and walked to the nearest of the three tape recorders squatting on the green metal shelf nearest the door. Pushing the tape onto the empty left-hand spindle, he wound the first strip onto the right-hand one and pressed a button. Then he walked back to the table and took his seat again.

'They had food there. Can you imagine that? At the Leningrad State Mental Hospital, on the very night I was admitted – shortly after what I did to Landau, all of that – I ate a chicken seasoned with rosemary and salt, even some tinned beetroot. Imagine how that tasted? Whilst the city's belly was round and empty, its madmen grew fat on contraband. The brother of the director was prepared to grant favours to those with a certain influence and a wallet full of roubles. So, I dined well. And each evening, once sated, I could stare out of a skylight at the searchlights of St Isaac's as they swept the clouds and watch as the Nazi Dorniers flew by. One million dead, the world on fire. How could I capture that, I asked myself? And then it came to me.'

As the tape whirred, Sofia sang. Her voice seemed no more than a melodic whisper, faltering as she either failed to recall the words or, when they did remember, vocalise them with any conviction. Occasionally, true notes were attempted but the voice cracked and died. At times she muttered only a single word without any connection to what had gone before or to the sounds to come. As though the sound itself had been freed from the body and now journeyed on alone, shorn of all meaning. Had she been drugged, or was it the hallucinations of famine? Or – and here Rossel glanced at the cages again and shuddered – something much worse.

If ghosts could sing, he thought, *and, in doing so, forced themselves to recollect the horrors of the life they had left behind, this is what they would sound like.*

'Listen,' Vronsky said. 'I need you to *listen*. That's why I've brought you here. That's why I needed a musical detective. You have always been my listener. So listen, I implore you.'

He was pacing up and down in front of the Magnetophon. As soon as the spools had begun to whirr, he had become animated.

'I have it here, Rossel. I have it pinned down. A lifetime's work.'

The composer gesticulated at the stacks of spools lying on the shelves that surrounded the walls near the door.

'But I was unable to reveal it to another living soul. Until now.'

Vronsky lowered his voice.

'The Road of Life? I heard the subtle cadence of a different road, one of death – the roll and rattle of the rails as the trains that transport the hundreds, the thousands, the millions out to the gulags. That, comrade, is Lenin's lullaby, Beria's little ditty, Stalin's refrain. The wolves in the taiga can hear it. The stray mongrels in the back alleys can. The people try to drown it out. For what is it now to be Russian if not to clap your hands over your ears and refuse to hear? But my refrain is also a timeless proclamation – all that we humans have ever been – a first sigh, a last breath. The low rasping moan . . .'

Vronsky tapped on a suspended microphone and smiled as the dials on the Magnetophon danced. He kneeled in front of Rossel and placed one of his huge hands around the detective's throat.

'. . . . made by a slowly compressing trachea, as one man presses his boot down upon the throat of another, a sound which always contains within it that other noise, its *twin* – triumph. Is that not what Dostoevsky means when he asks us: "Am I a monster, or a victim myself?"'

Vronsky exerted more pressure on Rossel's neck with his left hand as his right picked up one of the remaining glass tubes on the table.

'Finger placement, Rossel. As a violinist, you know it's everything.'

Rossel began to gulp in an effort to take in extra air. The end was near if he didn't talk, fast. It was time for some revelations of his own.

'A photograph,' he mumbled.

Vronsky's left hand pressed down even more firmly.

'In my pocket . . . a photograph.'

The composer hesitated. With the left hand still on the detective's throat, he dropped the tube from his right and began to delve inside Rossel's jacket. It took him only moments to find the wallet. As soon as he did so, he relaxed his grip. Then stood up and began to leaf through it. After a few seconds, he found and drew out the black and white image.

Rossel swallowed hard. Then took in three more big lungfuls of air before he spoke.

'Her name is Svetlana. She is the daughter of an MGB major by the name of Nikitin. She is carrying poppies, too. So, the major knows it was you who raped her. Probably after Beria, maybe before, but definitely also. Poppies are your flower. Nikitin knows as much as I do about everything – the girls you abducted, the people you murdered. So does his fellow officer, Sarkisov. They have lists with all the names on it.'

Vronsky stared at the photograph. His grip loosened. Air wheezed through Rossel's windpipe.

'That list is on its way to the finest dachas about fifty kilometres south of here, where Malenkov and all those other Party high-ups are. Let's just say Beria has never been their favourite person.'

The composer still couldn't take his eyes off Svetlana. Did he remember her? Did he recall her small, doleful eyes? Her delicate body?

'We also know about the jewellery too,' said Rossel.

He nodded to the tapes on the shelves.

'I don't need to listen anymore, Vronsky. Just look at how much you have laboured. Shostakovich understands the concept of brevity – would have instinctively known two notes were all that were necessary. An MGB car, a black raven, parks in the street outside, boot-steps echo in a stairwell at midnight, and then two notes ring out.'

Rossel suddenly slumped back in the chair and began to laugh. After a moment, his body was shaking.

'Perhaps the great composer might call it his Doorbell Symphony?'

Vronsky looked back up into Rossel's eyes. Then he released his grip, picked up the photograph and tore it into pieces. Dropping them, he picked up the steel rod from the table.

When the blow came it was delivered with such force that the chair to which Rossel was tied toppled over.

44

Vronsky had left the dacha in a hurry, presumably after finding the phone line dead. Rossel still took five minutes before he felt able to stretch out his fingers and move both the chair and his torso, inch by inch, close enough to pick up the shard of glass he had been concealing under his foot. And then a further ten to cut through the loosened twine and free himself. Two more to locate a small porthole window at the back of one of the box-stalls, break the glass and wriggle free into the freezing night.

His right arm was in bad shape. His throat was bruised and swollen. Blood flowed from the palm of his left hand where he had cut himself with the glass shard. But Vronsky had done him the favour of toppling the chair. And left him alive, or for the Cossack to slay at his leisure, in his haste to get to Beria and warn him of the deadly threat to their partnership. And to their lives.

The composer had at least twenty minutes on him. But Beria's dacha at Sinyavino was more than fifty kilometres away, and driving at night, following the edge of the lake in this snow, would take at least an hour, possibly more. There was still a way he could intercept Vronsky. It was not an enviable option and no one would take it unless desperate. But ten years ago, such desperation had given birth to a miracle.

The lieutenant looked towards the distant ice house and, with two heavy tape spools under one arm, began to stagger through the snow.

*

At night, in this kind of temperature – about twenty below – it was his feet that worried him the most. Without boots he might last only five minutes, ten at the most, before frostbite set in.

Rossel left the main building and stables behind him and ran towards the ice house, his breath coming in staccato exclamations each time the soles of his bare feet touched the frozen ground. Before he got there, he found what he was looking for – through the shadows where the moon broke the dark, where the pine trees ringed the edge of the island. Now he saw them. To his right, the line of old ZIS-5 trucks that he had come upon earlier. One of them was already missing – Vronsky must have taken it.

There were still four trucks left. But it wasn't them the detective was interested in. He had to head Vronsky off before the composer could get to Beria. It was his only chance of defeating the maestro and it was probably a suicide mission, but, at this juncture, pretty much every road led to his end anyway.

After hearing Sofia's voice, after reading her words, he would be glad of it.

The snowplough was about three metres long, scooped, V-shaped and attached to a truck, the back wheels of which had been replaced by caterpillar tracks, its front ones under-pinned by two wide metal skis. It was a bizarre-looking vehicle but Rossel had seen plenty like this one during his army service. Every soldier worth his salt knew how to drive one of these in case the poor bastard who had last driven it was killed.

But there was no need – the key was in the ignition and a metal hip flask and an entrenching shovel lay on an old copy of *Sovietsky Sport* on the driver's seat. Someone had just parked it? Rossel swung round but it was too late – Razin was already pointing a pistol at him.

Rossel grimaced with the pain from his right arm as he put his hands in the air.

'I shoot you now, not think twice, militia man. But it might be more fun to just stand here and watch your toes begin to swell. Frostbite is not a pretty sight. I saw plenty of it during the war.'

The Cossack was wearing an *ushanka* fur hat, an ex-army greatcoat and Kirza boots.

Rossel stared down at them. Then back up at Razin.

'I need your shoes,' he said.

Razin smiled.

'Yes, you do.'

Rossel sprang forward into a deafening retort as the Tokarev discharged. A zinging vibrating sound near his left ear as the bullet passed by. Razin stopped him with an arm like a steel bar and thrust him back. He pushed the pistol into Rossel's face and squeezed the trigger. But he was too slow – the second shot disappeared into the night as Razin's body buckled and he fell to his knees. Before he had touched the snow, Rossel hit him again with the shovel he had grasped on the floor of the ZIS. This time in the face. Razin keeled backwards and his body lay in the snow, an eddy of blood leaking from his left temple and pooling on the white ground. His shoulders and neck jerked and trembled, contorting his features.

Rossel knelt down and started untying the Cossack's laces.

'As I say,' he said, 'I need your shoes.'

*

Everything inside the ZIS snowplough rattled. It would only take another mile or two to shake the fillings out of his back teeth. The rasping of the engine was matched only by the squealing of the caterpillar tracks as they protested about being forced to grip the icy surface of Lake Ladoga.

'Please God, let there be ice.'

At least a metre of it. Two, if possible. About fifty centimetres would support a small car but the ZIS weighed over three thousand kilos. He needed fifty solid centimetres at a bare minimum. And as little current as possible, because the motion of the current thinned the ice. 'That other road, not one of life but of death' – the composer was right about that. Many had never made it. Only a fool would risk it at this time of year, and especially at night. Even in a snowplough. Which is why Vronsky had opted for the road.

He was wearing Razin's bloodied greatcoat over his own jacket, his life-saving Kirza boots and the dead Cossack's socks. Beside him were the newspaper and two round metal cases that contained the tape spools he'd taken from

Vronsky's macabre collection. They were all the evidence he could carry and still slither out of the tiny stable window. The hip flask in his pocket, he had been pleased to find out, was full of something alcoholic. Rossel had already drunk about half.

His headlights, on full beam, stretched a few dozen metres ahead. Everything to the left and the right was pitch black; thick cloud covered the moon and stars. The only things that seemed to be twinkling anywhere on the vast surface of Lake Ladoga were the tiny, slightly cockeyed headlamps of his vehicle.

'White good,' he thought, 'dark bad.' The whiter the ice appeared, the thicker it probably was. Darker ice meant water close to the surface. At this season of the year, the lake waters often ran with strong currents.

And, given enough time, a strong current could mean no ice.

*

White good, dark bad.

It had taken Rossel about thirty minutes to reach the southwestern corner of Ladoga, between Vronsky's island and the shore road that led to Sinyavino and the complex of dachas reserved for the higher echelons of Soviet politics. He had finished all the alcohol but his feet were still ice.

'*White good, dark ba . . . To hell with it . . .*'

In the distance, beyond the headlamps' beams, he saw a single light flickering. And, moments after that, the outline of a building.

A shore cabin, he thought. Or a banya. Shelter for ice fishermen to warm up and get drunk.

Rossel rammed his left boot down on the accelerator. As he did so, the wail of the engine-and-track chorus rose and the ZIS lurched towards the snow-covered beach. Beyond the wooden cabin and another column of pines would be the road to Shlisselburg and then Sinyavino. And somewhere in the countryside around it was Beria's dacha.

Vronsky, he was betting – only using the road and having to travel around Lagoda's southwestern shoreline – would not have reached this point yet.

The sound of the tracks changed as they crossed onto deeper snow; a softer, muffled creaking. Rossel turned the snowplough hard right and headed further up the shoreline.

The headlamps ran along the dense rows of trees and he noticed a break in the shadow, a little up ahead, near what looked like a stone post. As he got closer, he realised his luck was in. It was set at the side of a small path that was being used to haul boats down from the main road to the water's edge. A rowing boat on a two-wheeled trolley, mostly covered by snow, was parked in the middle of it.

Rossel maintained the pressure on the accelerator and the boat popped about a metre in the air just as the snowplough swept it aside. Another twenty metres of path and then he hit a huge bank of snow that looked like a frozen wave racing towards him. For a second the rubber wipers strained left and right and the snowplough faltered. Yet he emerged onto the other side and realised he had reached the road.

*

Rossel positioned the snowplough in the middle of the single track, its headlights still on and facing the way he expected Vronsky to come. Few people would be mad enough to be out at this time of night in this kind of weather. The next vehicle that turned up, if any did, would almost certainly be the composer.

On the other side of the road, beyond a rough stone wall, was a small farmer's byre, about three metres square and almost completely submerged under snow. Rossel could just see the top of a line of hay bales peeping out from beneath its corrugated iron roof.

As the minutes went by, a thought struck him. He searched behind the driver's seat and, after a couple of minutes, found a battered green metal tool box. He tipped out the spanners, bolts and screwdrivers and replaced them with the two tape spools he'd taken from Vronsky's dacha. Then he crossed the road and pushed the tool box down inside the byre, making sure it was completely hidden and, as much as was possible, protected from the weather by the bales of hay.

He checked his watch again – almost midnight.

Maybe he had missed him?

Rossel shivered as he waited behind what remained of the large snow bank. His revolver, which he had reclaimed from Razin, was drawn.

No, it wasn't possible. It had only taken him thirty minutes to cross the ice. And, on the shore road, it would take at least an hour from Krestovsky Island to Sinyavino.

Another five minutes went by.

Then, in the distance, he heard the low rumble of an engine. He dropped down behind the drift and trained the pistol on the road in front of him. As Vronsky's truck rounded a sharp bend about twenty metres ahead of Rossel's hiding place, the detective saw the composer's silhouette as the full beam picked him out. His hair wild and unkempt, his eyes now wide and staring, and his huge frame dwarfing the cab and wheel. There was no space to pass on either side of the snowplough – that, at least, had been Rossel's assumption. He'd hoped to bring Vronsky's truck to a hard-braking standstill.

Vronsky whipped the wheel to the left and his truck headed straight for what remained of the drift. Rossel fired once and then threw himself to his right as the other vehicle shot past, destroying the rest of the snow bank, taking out three pine saplings and knocking splinters out of a telegraph pole before re-centring on the other side of his rudimentary blockade in the middle of the road.

Rossel rolled over and began patting the deep snow all around him.

He swore under his breath – he had just constructed the world's worst roadblock and now the Tokarev was buried somewhere deep in the drift.

He climbed back into the cabin of the snowplough, yanked on the rusty gearstick and started reversing.

*

Sparks leapt up in front of the snowplough's wipers as the metal skis on its front and, sometimes, the base of the plough, hit rocks and potholes hidden beneath the snow.

About a kilometre before Sinyavino, with the frozen lake visible to his left and a squat, half-built barn to his right, he slowed to take a blind corner. As he rounded it the boxy frame of Vronsky's ZIS suddenly came into sight. It was lurching from side to side. The left-back wheel was flat and it was limping along as Vronsky tried to control it.

I got lucky with my shot. The thought had only just crossed his mind when Vronsky and the ZIS disappeared into an unlit tunnel. Seconds later, Rossel followed, hoping to get close enough to do some damage with the snowplough.

Now he was no more than a metre behind, but Vronsky had accelerated. Sparks burned orange and blue as he hit first one wall of the tunnel, and then the other, in an effort to escape.

Rossel matched him, got to touching distance, close enough to see the back of Vronsky's head through the glass panel of the cabin.

Then a searing light made Rossel throw up an arm to shield his eyes.

Another truck, another car? Something right in front of them. Blinded, he stamped on the brake. The snowplough rocked from side to side and made a screeching sound as it began to slide. He heard a crash up ahead, just as the light vanished, and as he thundered on he saw the astounded face of a uniformed MGB soldier manning a searchlight and realised Vronsky had turned sharply and smashed through the outer security gate of Beria's dacha.

Rossel stamped on the accelerator again and barged into the back of Vronsky's truck but his own vehicle was starting to protest. Bolts popped – spat into the trees that lined the driveway, as the caterpillar tracks sheared away. Glass shattered as a chunk of metal took out the wind-screen. Rossel's forehead smashed into the driver's mirror.

Blood began to flow. Vronsky's truck shuddered to a stop just before the snowplough lurched sideways and ended its journey in the back of the composer's ZIS.

Rossel scrabbled for the passenger door handle and leapt down into knee-deep snow. As he did so, Vronsky fell out of his vehicle. Rossel launched himself at the maestro, put both hands around his throat, used the full weight of his body to drag him down onto the ground. One punch – one single blow – was all he was allowed. Then he heard the safety catches come off the PPSh submachine guns and the familiar shouted command:

'*Ruki vyerkh! Ruki vyerkh!* Hands up!'

Rossel staggered to his feet and obeyed.

45

Vronsky's huge arms stretched skyward. Rossel stood no more than a metre behind. The maestro looked as though he were ready to conduct the final act of one of his own operas, and was pausing to build tension and anticipation among an admiring Kirov audience instead of six MGB officers holding PPShs. They were fanned out, three to each side of the drive, and aiming directly at Vronsky and Rossel.

About twenty metres behind them was a set of stone steps that rose into the elegant private residence, shining in the blaze of lights that the security guards had trained on the scene. Off to one side stood the birch trees that shielded the elite dacha from view. On the other, its icy surface glittering in the moonlight, was Lake Ladoga. At the top of the steps, Kalashnikov slung over one shoulder, was Colonel Sarkisov.

Half a minute later, Beria appeared and stood next to him. The minister glanced to his left and right, taking a moment to familiarise himself with the unexpected turn of events. He looked unperturbed, as if he were about to inspect a troop of particularly unpromising young recruits lined up in some provincial town square. Then he took off his glasses and used a small cloth to polish them. Satisfied, he slipped them back on again and, followed by Sarkisov, began to walk down the steps towards Vronsky and Rossel.

Vronsky was standing just in front of Rossel. Something about Beria's unruffled composure had unnerved the maestro. He turned his head a little so he could talk out of the side of his mouth.

'Arrest me.'

The composer's normal deep baritone had become a tremulous whisper. 'Arrest me, Lieutenant. Murder is a militia matter. Not something that should be of any interest to the ministry of state security. I still have friends in the highest echelons. I will arrange for you to be promoted. What do you want to be? A captain? A major? Arrest me, for God's sake, Rossel. The militia have jurisdiction here . . .'

The composer's voice trailed away. Beria was standing directly in front of them. 'You wish to see me, Comrade Vronsky?'

'To warn you, Lavrentiy. I was coming to warn you.'

'Really, am I in some kind of trouble?'

Rossel, his arms in the air, snorted. Beria's gaze settled on the lieutenant.

'Ah, yes. The man who likes jokes. What is it this time, Lieutenant?'

Blood still trickling down his forehead from the collision with the driver's mirror, Rossel looked back.

'I don't think the maestro can be feeling well, Comrade Minister. He just asked me to arrest him and then claimed, if I did, he would get me promoted to the rank of major.

Of course, his assessment of my current situation and job prospects does not fully align with my own.'

Beria's expression was a study in stony-faced restraint. Then a grin began to spread from one side of the minister's sallow face to the other, and – shoulders shaking – he began to laugh. No one else dared join in.

After a minute or so, the chortling subsided into silence. Beria took out the cloth again but this time gave his glasses only a cursory wipe before nodding at Sarkisov who – taking a club from a deep pocket in his greatcoat – stepped behind Vronsky and swung it. The composer dropped to his knees.

Beria popped his spectacles back on and stared at Vronsky.

'I never used to like it,' he said.

Vronsky reached back to the crown of his head and then gazed uncomprehendingly at the blood on his palm.

'Like what, Lavrentiy? Like what?'

'That stupid name you gave me: Thanatos – Death. There was always a certain intellectual bourgeois conde-scension in the way you used to pronounce it. As if you didn't expect some Mingrelian shitkicker, like me, to ever have heard of the Greek myths.'

Another nod to Sarkisov.

Another swing of the club.

A sickening sound: wood playing the simplest of scales on bone.

Vronsky's huge frame toppled forward into the snow and lay prone. Beria leaned over him and spat onto the side of his face.

'Thanatos, Death, yes, back then, I never used to like it, Nikolai Nikolayevich,' he said. 'But, tonight, I find, I do.'

Vronsky began to wail. 'Please, comrade, I told no one, I don't know . . .'

Beria clamped a gloved hand over the maestro's mouth.

'Girls, Nikolai. Mere musical extravagances. I can make the Party look the other way at even the most depraved escapades. But the jewels. *The jewels*. To festoon your slut in our smuggled baubles and then allow them to be traced to the ledgers of Djilas the jeweller – and from there to me. That I do not forgive.'

Beria let Vronsky go. 'Take the maestro to the lake,' he said to Sarkisov, 'make a hole in the ice, and drop him in it.'

Then, with a stiff bow, he turned and began to walk back towards the house. Sarkisov raised his club. All around Rossel, MGB men cocked their weapons and aimed them at him.

Just as he reached the foot of the stone steps, alerted by the sound of approaching vehicles, Beria stopped and turned.

A sleek Packard limousine, followed by two snub-nosed military trucks, rolled into view and came to a halt on the drive. A dozen Red Army special forces clambered out of the trucks and, almost nonchalantly, trained their weapons on Beria's MGB.

The driver of the limousine opened his door and slid out. He adjusted his cap and sauntered round to the passenger door, which he opened as if its occupants were arriving at a state function. Out stepped a tall middle-aged man, dressed head to toe in black, who wore the concerned air of a punctilious funeral director. This was Georgy Malenkov, Second Secretary of the Communist Party of the Soviet Union, member of the Politburo. And presumptive heir to Stalin.

Another man got out from the opposite side of the limousine and stood next to him. Major Nikitin.

'Cordial greetings, Lavrentiy,' said Malenkov to Beria. 'And here is our maestro too. Why this is a stroke of luck. I was on my way to his hideaway on Krestovsky Island when we noticed your gate security had been compromised. I do hope there's nothing amiss?'

Beria's face gave nothing away. But it took him a moment to answer. When he did so, however, his voice sounded calm, gentle – solicitous.

'What I always ask myself at times like this, Georgy, is the same thing you – with all your practical experience of the world – undoubtedly do too.'

'Which is?' said Malenkov.

Beria took a moment to adjust his glasses and then grinned broadly.

'Why simply this – what would Comrade Stalin do?'

Malenkov considered the question. Finally, after a moment or two, he nodded at Nikitin.

'Comrade,' he said to the major. 'Do your patriotic duty.'

Rossel, his arms still in the air, watched as Nikitin walked forward and took the club from Sarkisov. The MGB major placed a boot on Vronsky's cheek. Then he began to beat a rhythm on the maestro's body, singing as he did so.

'Life has never been better,' the torturer sang, 'Life has never been more beautiful. Sing it to me, bourgeois. Sing it to me now!'

The lieutenant turned his eyes away and stared out toward the vast, mute, frozen lake upon which Captain Mikhail Murov had once built a miraculous road.

CODA

PRAVDA 12 November 1951

Obituary

Nikolai Nikolayevich Vronsky

A Hero of Hero City

I weep as I write this – just as every true socialist and member of the People's Party of the Soviet Union must, surely, shed a patriotic tear as they, in turn, read it.

'Nikolai Nikolayevich Vronsky is dead.' When I first heard those terrible words, and learnt of his accidental death in the fire which burnt down his dacha, I felt almost exactly as I did on 21 January 1924, when news reached me of the death of Lenin himself, at Gorki Leninskiye.

And if Lenin was still with us, I have little doubt he would lead the outpourings of socialist grief that must now surely stretch all across our great Soviet Union; from Minsk and Baku to Donetsk and Rostov, and, of course, in Moscow, and here in the maestro's home city of Leningrad.

It is a bitter but nevertheless true honour to be, even in such tragic circumstances, chosen to write the official obituary for my esteemed colleague, cherished friend and fellow member of the Union of Composers.

399

No Russian composer, in modern times, not Stravinsky, nor Scriabin, or Boradin or Korsakov, Rubenstein or Medtner, has come close to matching the breadth of Vronsky's creative range and vision. No one understood more of what it means to be a citizen and comrade of this great revolution than he did.

The widest masses of the toilers of the whole world will lament his passing. As the farmer puts his shoulder to the plough and the factory worker his heart into his vital production targets, in the exact same way Nikolai Nikolayevich applied his prodigious intellect and profound musical sensibilities to examining and penetrating the suffering of the workers in their unceasing struggle against the bourgeois.

In this way, he became a hero to us all, most certainly to me. For no one has expressed the soul of socialism – captured its joyous cadences, melodies and undertones – with more clarity and precision than he did.

Nikolai Nikolayevich Vronsky 12.04.1904 – 06.11.1951

D. D. Shostakovich

46

Monday November 19

'Citizens! In case of artillery fire, this side of the street is extremely dangerous.'

It was because the shelling had come in from the south and west. As the German shells arced in, they had made the northern side of Nevsky Prospect more vulnerable, so if caught outside you cowered on the south pavement and got the hell out of there as soon as possible. The warning signs, stencilled into buildings, had been left as a cheap memorial to the blockade.

As he and Vassya hurried past one now, Rossel tried to remember the sound of sirens and whistle of incoming fire. But a shrill voice emanating from dozens of loudspeakers along the broad boulevard and exhorting all Leningraders to welcome visitors to the city's commemorations of the Road of Life drowned out every thought. Except the ones to do with their current quest.

Rossel drew his greatcoat a little closer to him. The wind picked up, stirring the snowflakes into a gently dizzying dance, and he drummed nervously on a round metal container hidden in his greatcoat pocket. When they got

401

to the corner of Mikhailovskaya Street, close to the grand entrance of the Grand Hotel Europe, he saw – exactly as Vassya had said he would – the scaffolding and tarpaulin that hid one of the many entrances to the half-built Gostiny Dvor station of the underground railway system. Since she had helped to design it, Vassya knew her way around.

As it was early evening, no construction workers were about. They looked left and right before crossing to the same side of the road where the Philharmonic Hall was and stepped behind a green tarpaulin. Vassya felt in her great-coat pocket for a key. Then turned it in the rusty padlock attached to a wood and chicken-wire door and opened it.

*

The service tunnels running under the hotel, the concert hall and various other buildings would be blocked off when the metro station finally opened, Vassya said, but while open they had served several purposes. 'Storage. Shelter during the blockade.' And for Rossel, a place to stash the record-ings he had returned to recover from the tool box he had hidden in a hay byre at the shore of the lake, as well as a way into the Philharmonic Hall without being seen.

The tunnel ran straight to another makeshift door that led to a basement room, then to stairs behind the stage that ran all the way to the top of the Philharmonic Hall, from where they could observe everything. The hut was small, only about two metres square, and perched alongside a sad troupe of three ageing stage lights, at the very back of the auditorium.

The lieutenant checked his watch: 6:45pm. The performance was due to start at quarter past seven. There were already plenty of concertgoers sitting on the red velvet seats with the gold trims in the circle and stalls. The Philharmonic Hall had been built in a classical style, with huge white ionic columns, five large chandeliers – similar in shape to the ones Sofia had loved so much in her 'ocean room' at the Kirov – and could seat over fifteen hundred people.

It would be full tonight.

The Blockade was a hugely anticipated Soviet cultural event. Vronsky's death could not derail it. As *Pravda* had declared, the Leningrad City Committee of the Communist Party of the Soviet Union had unanimously decided it should go ahead to 'write forever into history the name of this august hero of Hero City'. Everyone who was anyone was going to be there. And, like the first Leningrad performance of Shostakovich's Symphony No. 7, Vronsky's work would be broadcast far and wide on loudspeakers to thousands of people in the city centre who had eagerly complied with requests to stand in the cold in Arts Square, next to the concert hall, and listen to this masterpiece.

As well as a small control panel, sometimes used to help with the lighting, the gantry also contained two Magnetophon tape decks which were, on occasion, used for public announcements and to play recorded music. They were hardly used but serviceable. Rossel had done his homework well.

The lieutenant took the round tin from his pocket. He opened it and placed the spool it contained inside the second, and seemingly newer, Magnetophon.

Then he took out two cigarettes, gave one to Vassya, who seemed more comfortable than him at their elevated position, lit them up – checked his watch again – sat back in his chair and waited.

*

Shostakovich looked, Rossel thought – even from this distance – more than a little self-conscious. As if he were hoping that no one could possibly believe the *Pravda* puff-piece about Vronsky – one which some Moscow hack had so obviously knocked off under orders from the Kremlin and attached the composer's name to – was anything to do with him.

The composer stood in the middle of the stage, next to a large microphone. He had neat hair and brown-framed glasses, radiated anxiety, and was worryingly thin. It was Shostakovich's task to deliver a faltering eulogy to Vronsky which, in its clichéd verbosity, had clearly been authored by the same hack who'd churned out the obituary.

Now, dressed all in black, and wearing a veiled pill-box hat, Madame Vronsky appeared. A young woman dressed in a Komsomol outfit handed the composer a large bunch of blood-red poppies. He, in turn, handed them to Vronsky's mother. This morning's All-Union First Radio programme had talked of how the deceased maestro's grieving mother had requested this specific flower and colour as her son had always said it made him think of the 'many children of our nation who gave up their lives for socialism in the Great Patriotic War'. As she accepted the flowers, the audience rose as one and applauded. After a minute, Shostakovich and Madame Vronsky left the stage and took their seats in the side section reserved for the most important members of the audience. The audience sat and the large orchestra – almost a hundred strong – began to wend their way on stage and tune up.

Rossel waited for the babble to die down. Finally, all that could be heard were the occasional parping of a tuba or the low griping of a violin – the last-minute checks that all was well with the instruments.

Nikitin had a new master now. The list detailing the extent of Beria's depravity was safely in Malenkov's hands. Of even greater interest, however, and far more incriminating, were the ledgers. According to Nikitin, Malenkov had perused them with delight before placing them under lock and key.

On the drive of Beria's dacha, neither of Stalin's seasoned henchmen had been brave enough to make their move, each man refusing to play a hand they could not be certain of winning. Even victory could be deadly: if either man succeeded in eliminating the other, the Great Leader was likely to interpret this as a move on his own position. No – the list and the ledgers were weapons for another battle at another time. For now, Beria and Malenkov would appear at the Party Congress, at speeches, dinners and concerts, smile and shake hands. And, by unspoken agreement, happily blame Vronsky for the unfortunate distraction of five dead bodies being found on the tracks and anything else that suited them both.

Rossel knew that he himself was unfinished business. A line in Beria's own meticulous records under a column marked 'pending'. Unless Major Nikitin could be persuaded to use some of his new-found influence . . .

The fortunes of the Vosstaniya Street station had been mixed. Gerashvili was still unwell. But he'd sensed the last time he had visited her that her keen investigatory instincts were starting to revive. Lipukhin had sworn never to touch another drop. Half the junior ranks had been released and some had already returned to their former duties. A few would need more time. Grachev, along with a dozen others, had been given ten years in the camps. Rossel doubted he would ever see the sergeant again.

In the days since Vronsky's death, Rossel had pieced together the details of how the composer had ensnared his victims. As with Sofia, the maestro had matched his invitation to Krestovsky Island to each person's different desires. For Maxim, he had proffered sanctuary from the labour camps and the chance of musical redemption – to collaborate on the creation of a new choral work. For Felix, a letter from Marina – written under duress, she had claimed between sobs – had hinted at the possibility of rekindling their old dalliance.

As for Shevchuk, ambition was the bait – the promise that Vronsky would use his influence to secure him a promotion. And Nadya had been the easiest of all. Money, jewels, Vronsky's patronage at the Kirov. Each must have been in optimistic mood when they arrived on Vronsky's island, buoyed by the promise of better days ahead.

Only one question remained.

'Not for you, because . . .'

Rossel now knew how to complete the sentence. He understood, and so had already forgiven, her betrayal.

Rossel gazed down at Madame Vronsky, a tiny figure almost lost among the party bosses, military leaders and other dignitaries around her. The applause rose again as the saturnine figure of Mravinsky, the principal conductor of the Leningrad Symphony Orchestra, padded on stage. He bowed, and silence rolled over the hall once more.

Leningrad was listening.

High on the gantry, the lieutenant shrugged and leaned forward. Vassya pressed a red play button on the Magnetophon. They both watched as the spools began to whirr and, once satisfied all was working as it should, exited the hut and began the winding journey back to the service tunnel, catching snatches, as they descended, of the terrible recordings and the swelling uproar.

*

Leningrad, every inch of it, seemed to have been colonised by a mute army of giant black crows. As Rossel and Vassya stepped back out from behind the tarpaulin onto Mikhailovskaya Street, he felt, momentarily, as though the entire population of the city had assembled to greet him – not just on the square, but crammed onto every pavement for streets around. They were all dressed funereally to honour the maestro, just as *Pravda* had said they should, and standing, as one, under the light snow. A workers' brigade of dark scarves, gloves, sables, greatcoats and fur hats. Each head raised and staring upwards at the microphones attached to the poles.

In places, people were packed fifteen-deep across the road. Unable to turn right off Nevsky, a queue of traffic had stopped. Now drivers and passengers were clambering out to hear better the noises coming from the loudspeakers.

Most of them were unfathomable unless you knew, as Rossel did, what the sounds really were. The light jangling of the railway switch on the bars, the ape-like hollering of the creatures inside the gently undulating cages, the screeches and moans of the tormented – it all played on and on.

Rossel loosened his greatcoat so his uniform became partially visible, took out his militia ID and raised it so he could clear a path. He had locked the gantry hut using the padlock he'd opened to access the metro tunnel. What could be heard inside the Philharmonic could also be heard all over Leningrad.

Intent on listening, the crowd hardly seemed to see them – every pale shocked face a study in concentration, every mouth pursed and closed. Rossel grabbed Vassya's gloved hand in his, pushed his way past the main entrance to the Philharmonic Hall and headed towards the huge crowd on Arts Square.

They had got almost to the middle, hiding among the befuddled, upturned faces, when the voice on the tape became clearly audible for the first time. A collective gasp went up. It was so loud, Rossel thought, the combined exhalation of warm breath might rise up, as one cloud, and blot from view the dome of St Basil's.

'God is dead, Maxim,' said Vronsky, 'that's what Dostoevsky tells us. God is dead. So, everything is permitted!'

In reply, Maxim bawled out his own hypnotic incantation. 'My appetite was sin and of that sin I made a feast. And through that feast I came to know you . . .'

The tape played on for another thirty seconds. The beat of vicious blows clearly audible. The sound of men and women begging for mercy. Begging for death. The sound of

Vronsky's contempt. Caterwauls, clangs, roars and, finally, whispers.

Then, suddenly, Rossel heard another sound – a single pair of hands clapping. At first, they clapped on alone. Then, after a little while, others inside the hall began to applaud too.

It's her, Madame Vronsky, Rossel thought. *It has to be her.*

And, once she'd fully realised what was on the tape, he assumed, it had only taken her a minute or so to formulate her plan of action.

The story of this moment, Ekaterina Vronsky had instinctively understood, would not be written by the audience or the crowd in the street but by the same hacks from All-Union First Radio, *Pravda* and *Izvestia* who had obediently typed out all those fawning obituaries.

As Rossel and Vassya listened, the applause in the Philharmonic got louder. They would all be standing now. Once she'd made the generals and apparatchiks get to their feet with one of her looks – *You think I'm finished, but I'm still close enough to Minister Beria, how close to him are you?* – everyone else would have followed.

As they walked on, the noise grew thunderous and drowned out Vronsky's tape. Now it was not just coming from the microphones on the poles. The applause had rippled out from the theatre and spread amongst the people standing in the square and on the streets. No one knew what, or why, they were applauding. Only that it was safer to applaud.

The noise followed the lieutenant and the Night Witch as they pushed their way down Inzhenernaya Street. It outpaced them all the way to the Griboyedov Canal.

Madame Vronsky had given *Pravda* exactly what they needed – a citywide standing ovation for her dead child. She had written tomorrow's headlines for them – *Leningrad stands as one and applauds Vronsky, Hero City's most heroic son!*

As they turned right, heading towards the massive gaudy green and gold baubles that topped the towers of the Church of the Saviour of the Spilled Blood, the sound of the clapping rose up from the opposite bank and the square beyond that. It now seemed so loud it would shake the foundations of every building in the city. The bovine masses, perplexed but always obedient.

'It doesn't matter what *Pravda* writes,' he said to Vassya. 'That's not what these people will remember in ten or twenty years. Nobody can speak in public of what they listened to today. But everyone heard it.'

The clapping began to subside as they turned left onto a little metal bridge behind the church and kept on walking in the general direction of Station 17. Rossel thought he might like, for possibly the last time, to admire the carved seabird on the mantelpiece and offer up a final hopeful exhortation.

About the Author

Ben Creed is the pseudonym for Chris Rickaby and Barney Thompson, two writers who met on the Curtis Brown creative writing course.

Chris, from Newcastle upon Tyne, found his way into advertising as a copywriter and, after working for different agencies, started his own. He has written and produced various TV programmes for ITV and Five, and some award-winning experimental fiction.

Before deciding to pursue a career as a journalist, Barney spent two years studying under the legendary conducting professor Ilya Musin at the St Petersburg Conservatory. He has worked at *The Times* and the *Financial Times*, where he was legal correspondent, and is now an editor, writer and speechwriter at UNHCR, the UN Refugee Agency.

WELBECK

PUBLISHING GROUP

Love books? Join the club.

Sign-up and choose your preferred genres to receive
tailored news, deals, extracts, author interviews and
more about your next favourite read.

From heart-racing thrillers to award-winning historical
fiction, through to must-read music tomes, beautiful
picture books and delightful gift ideas, Welbeck is
proud to publish titles that suit every taste.

bit.ly/welbeckpublishing